THE CAVES OF MARS

PART ONE: THE HOUSE OF JOR-TAQ

GREGORY KH BRYANT

ROGUE PLANET PRESS

THE GREAT NORTHERN SEA

The Ochre Plains

Battle of the
Ochre Plains

Marghots

Qum Q

D'ar

AZORA,
JAMARRA
AND
GRAG-DON
MADE
LANDFALL
HERE

The Silken Sea

U'myr Chasma

Contents

FOREWORD

My dreams are tedious. They are monotonous, interminable.

I should say 'my dream'; singular, not plural. My only dream, because for years it has never changed. It has been but a single dream. The same dream, over and over.

Each time I sleep, I dream that I waken into a body that is sick and wasted, motionless, leaden, and dead. My legs are useless. My arms are futile, puny, pale and gray. Bedsores are huge upon my back. They torture me. I cannot even raise myself up on my elbow.

Over and over, I dream the same dream. I dream that I wake in this bed, in some strange hospice, unable to raise my head, unable to feed myself, to wash, or even breathe without the aid of a machine, hoses run into my nose forcing air into my lungs. My soul is bound to a deadened mass of wasted flesh.

The air is oppressive and heavy. It weighs upon my chest. It crushes me.

The walls of this place are painted a sterile white, and the patch of light that comes through the window from the day outside travels tediously, painfully, across them. The sky is never the same color twice—sometimes it is gray with horrendous downpours of rain, sometimes black with night, sometimes orange and golden with the rising sun, but, too often, a strange and idiot blue. Blue skies? What insane world is this, where the sky should be blue?

And when I dream thus, it seems to me then that the dream is more real than my waking life—that all my waking is but illusion, and this dead body I am chained to is what is real. It is all that is real. That is what makes these dreams so hellish, that they seem more real to me than life itself.

So I avoid sleep. I sleep as little as I can, only but a few brief hours at a time, and then, only when my body can no longer avoid the demands of total exhaustion.

She is there. She comes to me in that tiny room, with expansive solicitude writ large and huge upon her face. She wears a white hat upon her head, and looks to the sheets that bind my legs. She prods me, adjusts the tubes that plumb my throat and my veins. She speaks to me in a strange language. More strange, still, that in that tedious dream, I understand her and the words that she speaks. I hear myself reply, in a voice thin and weak, my throat choked with fluid.

She touches my forehead with her hand, and her touch is cool, soothing.

She sits beside the bed in which I lay, long, long and tedious hours, with a notepad on her knee. She listens as I tell her of the world where I live, that place where I am truly awake, truly alive, and I carry my tales of that place into the tedious world of this interminable dream. She writes down my words in her strange language.

The Great Northern Sea

I do not know when I was born, nor where. If I was born of a mother, of a father, I never knew them. What I have are deeps of memory, fluid and undifferentiated. What I remember is a wordless time, a time before language came to me, before I knew the names of things.

What I remember is the sea, a boundless transparent sea, where I drifted, time beyond reckoning. It was a shallow sea, water tepid and buoyant, and I floated as a piece of flotsam, neither happy nor unhappy, only being. I saw nothing but this sea, stretching away on all sides into the distance, until it met the boundary of the sky. The surface was still, and I drifted in slow and gentle currents.

How I came to be in this place, it did not occur to me to wonder. I recalled, dimly, a shock, moments of terrible scalding coldness through infinite black. I sensed I was blasted through it with an explosive force, one beyond description, and an awful, wordless swiftness. And then the water, the gently slowing sea that warmed me with its sensuous touch.

The sky that met my eyes was a tender peach set above this transparent sea of amber and gold. Tiny, high clouds of salmon and pink, remote and delicate, hung almost unmoving in the far distance.

As my eyes searched higher in the sky, I saw that it grew darker. Midway between horizon and zenith, the tender peach deepened to burnt orange and sienna, and then, directly overhead, the sky plunged to purple and black. Tiny points of light gleamed through the blackness above, and I wondered at them.

The air was thin, and it delighted me. A cool breeze soothed my face, even as the sun, tiny like a burning jewel, burned my brow and warmed my flesh.

The water in which I drifted, careless and uncaring, was absolutely transparent. The sands of the bottom were rusted yellow, orange and gold, and the water was so shallow that at times I could find the sand bars with my feet, touching them with my toes and with my chin just breaking the surface of the tepid sea.

No hunger touched me, nor cold, nor heat, but only a slow and languid motion. And so I was borne by the lazy currents. How long I drifted thus, I cannot say.

A time without time, and gradually the sky dimmed. A lavender tint began to pervade upward from the horizon as the sun, a bright point of orange, dropped slowly toward the sea. The soft peach of the sky deepened to scarlet—a sudden purpling, and then, abruptly, the sky plunged into the cold blackness of night.

My eyes were met then with an astonishing sight. Now the pinpoints of light that gleamed meekly through the dark crown of the sky during the day burst suddenly forth into a breath-taking blaze that cascaded across the firmament—shining diamonds and tiny ruby beacons, sapphire, indigo, crimson and vermillion.

Though the sea was enveloped in darkness, the burning lights above rendered it luminous. The beacons of the sky shone upon the transparent waters, and were reflected upon them, their shining manifestations radiating back and up into the sky again with a brilliance that dazzled my eyes.

I wondered at the beauty of these wondrous sights, but I had no words to form so much as a single question, nor even a solitary expostulation of delight.

All that night I watched the skies and the radiant seas in silent awe. All these points of light traveled together, it seemed, in a vast array that moved slowly across the firmament, except for two bright beacons that moved, by themselves, first one, and then the other, and they rushed through the darkness, hurtling overhead and shining down upon the waters, casting brilliant umbrae of silvery light.

Finally, timelessly, after time, the dark sky began slowly to quicken. It brightened, and a lavender tint crept upward from the horizon, and day returned with the sun, tiny and distant.

How many days passed in this manner, how many nights, I cannot say. I took no reckoning of time, but only languished in the water, carried with the languorous currents.

I came, in time, upon a place in the sea where strange things drift (I have since learned that they are called `wahe-el`). Vast and transparent, they are circular in shape, and they lie upon the surface of the tepid water, floating with the currents. The smallest of them was larger in diameter than I am tall. The largest spread out across the sea as far as my eyes could reach.

Transparent though they were, they had color. The smallest were the brightest, crimson and burnt orange, the color of bright rust in the summer sun. The larger of the *wahe-el* were yellow and gold, and some of them sparkled with silver.

Later I was to learn much about these things. They are living creatures, but neither animal nor plant. A little of both, perhaps, and much of neither. Most of them, vegetative in nature, draw their energy from the sun, and the water in which they dwell. Some of them consume their neighbors, assimilating them, as microbes might. First they drift close, and then they entangle their prey with long tendrils that grow from their center and float outward, like sinuous vines.

Some others, I was to learn, have organs very similar to eyes, sensitive to light and motion, that grow in multitudes along these long and sinuous tendrils. The tendrils drift outward, dragging along the sandy dunes of the sea bottom, and even, among the largest, beyond the horizon.

Some others, I learned, were quite carnivorous—fortunate for me that I did not happen upon these fellows in these my first days in this world. The carnivorous varieties of the *wahe-el* do not live so far to the north, where the waters were tepid, and sea-life scarce. The carnivorous *wahe-el* thrive in the torrid regions, far to the south, where the currents are strong and the sea-life plentiful. These, the carnivorous *wahe-el,* are huge creatures with eyes that are monstrous in size and shape (longer across than I am tall), and with muscular tendrils that are as big around as two men's bodies bound together.

All this I was to learn much later. For now, in these, my first days here, I knew nothing, but lived wordlessly among the *wahe-el*, as an infant lives among adults.

I came upon a vast group of these *wahe-el*, in numbers beyond reckoning, as I lay upon the water, sometimes floating on my back, sometimes wading through the shallows. They bumped against me, unconscious things, and then they floated away, carried by the sluggish current. Their tendrils were thin and translucent things, entangling my arms and legs, but as easily broken as a stream of water from a fountain.

On an impulse, I strove to climb up on one of them, but even as I put the weight of my elbows upon its rim, it tore under me, and I spilled back into the shallow sea.

Another one drifted close, and this one was made of hardier stuff. After considerable trouble—it folded where I placed my weight, and sank into the water—I managed, at last, to clamber on its broad and flat back and crawl toward the center to explore this strange thing.

I scrambled on my belly, forcing myself instinctively forward by pushing with my elbows, knees and feet. The *wahe-el* was elastic, and it gave under my weight, but it was buoyant and it supported me.

Now, for the first time, my head was raised above the surface of the clear and tepid water, and I could see further into the expanse of the sea. Now my eyes made out tiny bumps upon the horizon, burnt red in the distance. What they could be I did not know.

But for the first time since I awoke, drifting in these sluggish currents, curiosity arose in my heart.

There were things out there—things other than the changeless, ceaseless sea, and the cyclical sky overhead, all of which it had never once occurred to me to question, until my eyes made out those tiny protrusions.

Those tiny bumps upon the horizon broke the unending sameness, the slow rhythm of day followed by night, which had been my world since my quickening from unconsciousness.

What were those mysterious things my eyes made out upon the line of the horizon? I watched them through the long morning, and slowly, they seemed to grow larger. I now, having learned the ways of this world, understand that the currents were then carrying the *wahe-el* slowly toward these things. But to my eyes, then yet immature, it seemed to me that these strange bumps were growing larger as the day grew long.

Instinctively, and not understanding what I was doing, nor why, I struggled to my feet. A tricky business, as the skin of the *wahe-el* gave way as I rose. It sank beneath me. Several times I fell, landing upon my face, but, at last, I managed to stand precariously upright upon the gently swaying surface, and there, I raised my head several feet further above the water.

Slowly we drifted, my *wahe-el* and I, and slowly the strange bumps on the horizon grew larger, taking on shape and definition. They were solid things, the first solid things my uncomprehending eyes made out in this world, and their colors ranged from rusted orange and burning gold to sepia and umber.

A dozen of them spread out in a long string along the horizon, and they were wreathed with clouds at their summits.

These were islands, I later learned, and the only archipelago that pierced the surface of this great northern sea for many thousands of *yurlma*[1] .

Long into the afternoon I drifted slowly toward these islands upon the broad back of my *wahe-el*. When evening came at last, first purple, then black, the islands disappeared into the yawning darkness. All but one of them, that is, the largest of the group. Unlike the others, this island burst forth with dazzling light that outshined even the lights of the multitudes of tiny beacons that shone down from the sky.

Now I became aware of the cravings of my body. For the first time since I came into any awareness, I felt the pangs of hunger, and of thirst. But I did not know what these sensations were—I felt only the pit that gnawed from within my belly and the painful, urgent craving in my throat.

---

1. Editor's note: Yurlma: Untranslatable. Plural form of yurlmat. A yurlmat is a measure of distance traveled through a period of time. The actual distance so traveled is variable, depending on who is doing the traveling, and how. Someone young and energetic, for example, may travel further by foot in an hour than one who is convalescent. Yet, whether it is what we would call ten miles, or ten feet, both are considered ten yurlma. Another example would be a mountain slope, which may be twenty yurlma in climbing, but only two yurlma in descending. This odd and rather fluid form of measurement is one of the many idiosyncrasies of the world in which the author of these pages (my patient, whom I will identify by the pseudonym, Paul Morgan) most inexplicably, found himself—one is almost tempted to say 'born into'. I shall seek to intrude upon the narrative as seldom as I possibly can, preferring to let the author, who dictated the pages to me in his rare moments of lucidity, to speak for himself. However, certain terms and concepts are simply untranslatable, and do require some explication. A.G.

It was as if I were an infant, albeit an infant in the body of a man, unconscious and unknowing, driven by no awareness—with no memory in my mind, and no sense of anticipation, I was unaware of either future or past. I knew only the present, and had been content within it.

But now, as I watched the ever-growing spectacle of light unfolding before me, mounting larger upon the horizon and illuminating the night, my body wakened to its needs, and the hunger that grew gnawing within me. I was overcome with impatience, annoyance and irritation—all, which my then immature mind did not understand.

That night was the longest I endured, sleepless and with an unaccustomed anxiousness coursing through me. I suddenly became aware of the passing of time, and found I could not bear the weight of it.

When dawn finally touched the sky with her timid pink hue, the strange island had come quite close, now only but a part of a *yurlmat* before me.

Wafting across the thin breezes there came sounds across the water—the first sounds, aside from the insistent lapping of the waves, I had heard—and odors that cut directly to my belly and caused me no end of anguish. I did not understand the cause of my anguish then, but now know it was the faint aroma of food that touched my virgin nostrils, carried by the breezes from the island, and causing me to be aware of the hunger of my body.

I crawled to the very edge of my *wahe-el*, scarcely understanding what called me, only knowing the instant and insistent craving that impelled me. I leaped into the water to make my way toward the delicious odors and seductive sounds that called to me from the island.

Here, the transparent water of the sluggish sea was very shallow. It came only to my waist, and I waded with long strides over the barely submerged sand bars to the isle. The water was warm, and cool, against my naked flesh, and I marveled at the strange sights unfolding before my eyes.

Long things jutted outward from the island—these presented to my wondering eyes the first straight lines, borne of artifice, they had seen. The artifice of the straight lines left me in wonder, and caused me to sense many things. I sensed an awareness of other awarenesses, an awareness of the things that must have made these things, though then I had no words to describe what I was intuiting.

How to describe my sudden awareness? Nature works in curves. Consciousness, in straight lines. A straight line implies a consciousness, a knowing, a system of knowing—and even in my infant state of bare awareness, these straight lines told me that, of minds other than mine.

The long, straight things that jutted into the water, as I later came to learn, were jetties, quays and piers. Just beyond them, lining the entire shore of this island, so mysterious to me then, was a high wall. It ran the entire length of the island, blocking all egress from the water, except by way to the jetties and piers that led into dark and narrow portals through the walls.

Above the walls and beyond them, sprawling upward upon the slopes of the island was a vast and magnificent city (though I did not know then what this strange thing was). Upward, climbing higher upon the slopes of the small mountain peak that jutted its head above the sand bars of the sluggish northern sea, came wall after wall, and structure after structure. Tall poles carried thousands of pennants, all in silhouette, and fluttering, flapping and slapping against the background; crimson and ruby, scarlet and vermilion, Ocher, pumice, viridian, green, emerald, jade, olive and lime.

Impatience grew within me. I waded urgently forward against the water, all unaware of the terrible hazards over which I strode.

The sands that make up the bottom of this shallow sea—I was to learn, but only much later—are treacherously porous. Only in rare spots can they support the weight of a man, and these spots are themselves ephemeral things. They come and go with the endless shifting of the tides. No one ever wades in these dangerous waters. A man may set his foot down, only to find it caught and sinking quickly into the sand—and he be sucked into it inexorably, pulled down by his own weight and the suction created as the porous sand gave away from beneath him.

By miracle, or chance, I happened to thread my way across solid-packed bars of sand, avoiding any footfall upon the treacherous sinking sands.

Now, when my mind returns to that moment, my stomach tightens with the thought of how narrow my escape was. I have since had the chance to see what these terrible, treacherous sands can do. It is a horror.

Perhaps it is best that I had no inkling of the peril I so unthinkingly trod. Had I known the awful death that lay at my very feet, I'd certainly have been too overcome with terror to move even a single step.

But—miracle, or chance, I cannot say—I did somehow make my way to the rock-strewn shore of this island, past a fleet of huge things floating, all of them tied up to the jetties and the quays. They towered over me as I made my way past them, casting deep and transparent shadows that plunged deep into the water with profound gold and ruby hues. These huge things, I was to learn, were ships, but I knew that not at this moment, looking upon everything I saw with the unknowing eyes of an infant.

1

THE HOUSE OF JOR-TAQ

T HE SHIPS AND THE quays were crowded with multitudes, their eyes all turned upon me. I felt the immense attention, not understanding what it may be. A huge clamor arose upon my approach, but I did not know what the clamor was, nor what it was about, nor that it had anything at all to do with me.

It was all but a hubbub of sound and colors. My attention was without focus, but only a blur of bewilderment impelled by the cravings within my belly. Thirst and hunger drove me, and I clambered heavily upon the rocks that lined the steep shore, my body dripping and sodden.

The boulders were huge things, tumbled high in ramparts, and I made my clumsy, unknowing way over them with great difficulty, slipping often and scuffing my knees, feet, knuckles and elbows till the blood flowed freely from them.

But at last I made my way over them to find myself standing, for the first time, on solid land. The solid land was a path of red gravel, the stones rounded and smooth.

I was unaccustomed to standing on solid ground—this was the first time I essayed it without the buoyancy of the sea or the *wahe-el* to assist me, and my first experiment was met with catastrophe. My feet slipped out from under me, and as I sought, instinctively, to keep my balance, my arms made huge circles in the air. I overcompensated for the forward slipping of my feet, and began to fall backwardly.

Again, my arms, acting, it seemed, on their own, made huge circles in the air as I strove to regain my balance, but all my efforts only perturbed my balance even more. At last I fell backwards, landing on my rump in a confused sitting position.

Dazed, I looked about helplessly for a moment, and took in my surroundings with uncomprehending eyes.

Now, those who had observed me wading ashore came forward in huge crowds, babbling at me in sounds I did not understand.

"Bar-bar-bar," they seemed to say to me.

"Bar-bar-bar-baroi, bar baroi, bar, bar!"

Once again I attempted to rise to my feet, and again I stumbled, falling forward this time, almost landing on my face. Still the heavy odors wafting from somewhere ahead called me forward, and so I raised myself and crawled on hands and knees.

This elicited a round of strange noises from the folk who crowded close, a concert my innocent ears did not comprehend, but which I now know was laughter. The sight of this strange naked man who came walking out from the sea, where none had come before, crawling on all fours as a baby would, proved a most ludicrous sight to them.

My baby-crawling also relieved them, for the moment, as I later learned. Upon first glimpsing me striding through the sea, where none of them had ever dared to set foot, because of the deadly sinking sands, the populace of this strange island city was overcome with a profound and superstitious terror.

What was this manlike creature that strode from the sea? Was it man? Was it monster? They hurried down along the rocky shore where I made landfall, all filled with dread and curiosity, all of them ready—as

I later learned—to stone me to death on the spot, had I proved dangerous to them. Ready, as well, to welcome me as a herald, or an omen incarnate, should I have proven to be such a one.

As it was, I was neither monster nor messenger, but only an ignorant infant of a man who knew nothing, not even how to walk.

Observing my struggles with locomotion, several of the many people who surrounded me stepped out from the crowd, and made gestures to me I did not understand. They were offering me assistance, as it turns out. Comforted by my clumsiness, they gently took my hands, and then hoisted me up by my armpits and my elbows. These three people then undertook to teach me how to walk, two of them holding me up, one on each side, while the third strode back and forth in front of me in an elaborate pantomime of walking, offering me an example of it to practice by.

"*Sak! Sak!*" she said, smiling sweetly and laughing tenderly—as a mother would—at my awkwardness.

"*Sak!*' Out of the babble of sounds I heard, that was the first one I heard as a single word.

"*Sak?*" I repeated, not understanding the meaning.

And that provoked another round of laughter from the crowd. What I heard was 'bababarbaroi... '*Sak!*' bababa, ba, ba, babaroi, *Sak!*'

Delighted to have isolated a single sound from the babble of noises, I repeated it again, "*Sak!*" And I heard the word echoed endlessly though the crowd, ever outward like ringlets upon the surface of a lake.

All this was accompanied by melodious laughter, and I was soothed by the sound of it. I smiled, and laughed, as well. And that seemed to have broken down the last barrier of distrust between this multitude of strange people and myself. They all laughed loudly, in great relief, and the three women who had undertaken to teach me how to walk returned to the endeavor with redoubled effort and greater enthusiasm.

Soon I was stumbling about, awkwardly balanced upon my legs, as the crowds gathered about and applauded my every effort. I was able to take several steps at a time now, unaided, and without falling flat upon my face. But still my balance sometimes rushed ahead of me, and I raced to catch up with it, only to stumble into the arms of one or other of my smiling teachers who kept me from falling.

As we were so occupied, a man strode forward out of the crowd, one with a very officious manner. He barked at me with sounds I did not comprehend, and I must have returned a blank expression as my answer.

Seeing my silent reply, he repeated his peremptory bark, more loudly this time, and with an authoritarian tone that even I, in my ignorance, sensed demanded reply.

But I knew not how to reply. I looked from one face to the other, in the many that were gathered in the crowd, seeking some clue, but found none.

Then one of my teachers, the one who taught me my first word, `*Sak*' (though I still did not know what it meant), spoke to the officious one in lilting tones.

"*Abbaabba-habla'abba*," is what it sounded like to me.

"*Damarap-nop! Sopna wak!*' is what the officious man said in reply (or so it sounded).

Whatever the exchange between them may have meant, it was clear from their gestures that I was to follow this man, wherever it was he meant to lead me.

I hesitated, having grown fond of my teachers in the brief time that I had come to know them, but they indicated by gestures to me that from here I was to go on alone, and they sadly (so it seemed to me, but perhaps I flatter myself) made their leave.

The authoritarian man made a barking sound at me, and then turned decisively on his heel. I followed him as he led me across the gravel pathway, past the ships that lay tied up at the quays on my left, and the high red wall that surrounded this strange city, on my right.

We passed many people as we walked, he marching, almost, while I still moved forward awkwardly and inexpertly. Men and women—and children, too, running about unclothed and playing boisterously—all with shining eyes and golden skin, their hair, straight and long and black and gleaming (I was to learn that my yellow hair and pale skin were both extremely unusual, and they made of me something of a spectacle to these people).

My eyes were not practiced at taking in details, and all was a blur of color and pageantry. Ornaments and elaborate headdresses with plumes and gems that sparkled. All the men carried weapons, long thin swords that they wore strapped to leather harnesses fixed to their hips.

The women wore daggers, and many carried two or three or four. All adorned themselves with ostentatious jewelry, huge pendants and rings that hung from their ears and dangled against their shoulders, chains of precious metals studded with translucent stones strung in wide circles about their necks, elaborate breastplates of bone, bracelets and anklets that shone in the morning light, and all creating a symphony of sounds when they walked; *chi-ching, chi-ching, chi-ching, chi-ching, tch-tchut, tch-tchut, tch-tchut.*

The officious man who led me on paid no attention to any of those we passed, though they all scrutinized us most particularly. He never turned his head either to the right or the left, and ignored those who called to him with questions.

Presently, we came to a great portal in the wall, an archway inlaid with bright gold metal richly carved with cunning niches and symbols inlaid in silver and blue stones.

My guide strode through the archway without pausing, and I followed him into the city beyond. The spectacle of it left me stunned.

We entered into a wide street that curved upward in both directions. High walls confined it, and from sluices set in the walls, tall waterfalls cascaded down, splashing into narrow canals that threaded here and there through the broad avenue, spilling into pools and grottoes. This complicated waterway of canals and grottoes was lined with polished stonework, elaborately crafted with subtle patterns that shone turquoise in the shadows of the great wall. Footbridges crossed the narrow canals in many places, and people swam, splashed and played in the cool waters, while those on the avenue passed by.

Tall plants grew there, arching upwards and leaning against the high red walls of the avenue. Heliotrope and lavender, mauve and pale purple, their trunks were soft, so soft, in fact, that you could pull out large swaths with your fingers. I found that there are several varieties of these plants, one that grows only a few leaves—four or six—at their very top, but these leaves are huge. Amethyst in color, some of them span the entire avenue, in places creating a sort of ceiling high above the street.

Another variety grows no leaves at all, but shoots straight upward, and then, at its peak, it coils into a huge violet spiral. It is in the endless uncoiling of this spiral that this plant's growth occurs. Yet another towers high above the others, its stalk straight, with yellow layers of fleshy foliage that peel off in great sheets. At its summit it swells into a knob, with a complex pattern of whorls and knobs that are its seedpods. Periodically they swell and burst, showering the avenue below with smatterings of damp, golden seedlets. They are edible, and sweet. Children chase the moist seedlets as they drift down onto the street, and make a great game of catching them in their upturned and opened mouths. The stalk of this one, too, is soft and flexible, though it grows to be so large that three men with arms outstretched cannot reach around it, and it can be torn apart with the fingers.

And these plants move. Responsive to touch, and temperature, and light, and sound, and the breezes that come down through this avenue, they sway constantly, turning and leaning, bending and slowly twisting their trunks and leaves, tendrils and coils. Later I learned that with the setting of the sun, they fold into themselves, shrinking against the night. Leaves close and trunks bow, many fall back against the walls, or whatever support they may find, and they hibernate, as it were, awaiting the coming of the new dawn.

As my officious guide led me through the crowded streets, I looked upon all this, bewildered and confused, wishing to pause and to linger over the sights that dazzled my eye. But he did not loiter, and I hurried to keep up with him as well as my unpracticed legs would allow.

Temporary stalls were set up against the walls, between the many falls of water that cascaded from the ramparts into the many waterways we passed over. I did not know what they were, but later I found that this was the marketplace of this city, where traders from the other islands in this isolated archipelago came to buy and sell the many things they carried here on their ships.

The odors from the stalls were rich and alluring, and the cravings in my belly became more pointed as we stalked through the city. Food was being traded there, robust smells of tangy baked fruits and roasted spiced meats. My hunger grew more insistent, and I was drawn to the stalls by the powerful aromas. But the officious man who led me would not be delayed. Turning back once to see that I was following, he saw where it was my attention wandered, and he grasped me rudely by the wrist to pull me away, and toward wherever it was he was taking me.

This was the first time a will other than my own attempted to direct me with physical restraint, and I must say I did not respond to it well. The moment he grabbed my wrist, I heard myself let loose with a huge scream. Though I had no words in my head to describe, even to myself, my outrage, I knew that I was shocked that anyone, ever, would seek to impose his own will upon me in this brutal manner.

Those in the multitudes that rushed by us—stately women wearing naught but strings of jewels, muscular men with swords and brawny chests, naked children splashing in the pools at our feet—turned away from what they were doing to see what the cause of this commotion might be.

And the officious man who demanded that I follow him slapped me. Once! Twice! He slapped my face, left and right, and then he snarled at me in that incomprehensible tongue.

The wrath I felt at that moment went beyond speaking. Never had I felt pain, not that I could recall, and that first instance of it filled me with such fury that it silenced me on the spot. I blinked at the officious man in shock and astonishment, choking on my rage, and once again he clasped me by the wrist, dragging me forward, I knew not where.

Though I did not have the words at the time, his rude treatment was vivid, and I knew then, even without the words, exactly what I felt.

"Someday," I would have said to him, did I but have words to say it, "I will kill you for that."

Now he led me through the streets impatiently, and I had no mind to take in the sights, so confused with rage was I. A blood red mist flowed before my eyes, and I saw everything far away and distant, as if through a tunnel. Noises crowded hard upon my ears, but I paid them no attention. My mind was in a blinded fury.

We marched through numerous streets, all of them curving upward and tending toward the peak of the island. As we marched, the streets grew narrower, the walls that bordered them, smaller. Now we moved past huts and houses that cluttered the byways, built all haphazardly. Those who live in this city build where they like, with whatever they can purchase, so long as they do not block the streets, and so houses are built with no overarching plan.

Here, too, there were no crowds, and the people we passed were not so finely dressed. Here were people engaged in many kinds of work, stonemasons and carpenters, grocers and cooks. Women, wearing only short skirts of pounded leather, with daggers strapped to them, suckled babies at their breasts, or worked under tents, dying fabrics in large steaming vats. Some of them kneeled over flat stones, pounding grain or working at stone ovens that stood outside the houses.

But I had no mind to notice all this now. I was still filled with rage at this officious stranger who dragged me, now most unwilling, to I knew not where. Higher and higher we mounted the city through narrowing and ever-steeper streets. At last we came to a place where the street ended in a series of stairways that spiraled even higher, above the greater part of the city that lay below us on the slopes of this peak.

We were now above the walls of the city, and I could see that the streets and avenues below were a series of circles. Beyond was the golden sea I had drifted upon for so many days. Placid, still and unhurried, it seemed distant now and faraway, and a place I could never return to.

Now we came at last to a huge block of a building, one that would have overlooked the entire city, had but a single window or balcony pierced its wall. But none did. It was a massive block of anonymous stone, red and ocher, as all the buildings in this city were, but completely without the elaborate decorations of paint and gilding and inlaid stones that were integral to even the poorest structures.

This building was plain and unadorned, surrounded on all sides by a high, narrow wall. The man who led me here walked up to a portal in the wall, and tapped on it rapidly with his knuckles. From within came a muffled response. My guide, as I suppose I may call him, leaned forward and brought his mouth close to the door. He spoke into a hole there, and an instant later the door was flung open.

Two men stood inside, glaring at us with elaborate suspicion. My guide nodded his head once, and spoke to them, and they nodded curtly in return, stepping aside to allow us to enter.

We came into a yard that was bare. Nothing but a flat stone pavement between the walls and the structure within. Later I was to learn that this was most unusual, for those who can afford these patios usually maintain them with gardens and porticos, fountains and pools for their own comfort and delight.

But not the owner of this building. He was a most unusual man in this city, as I was to come to discover.

Now my guide drew me ahead, and he pushed me with the flat of his hand to indicate to me that I should go before him. Again the rage that smoldered within me flared up, but I did nothing except follow his directions, for I knew not what else to do.

We came to a tiny black door, and after the officious man made himself known to those within, by rapping upon it, and then speaking into a hole cut into it, the door opened and we stepped inside.

We came into a darkened anteroom, and in it were a number of men, dressed similarly to the one who led me here. They all wore short leathern aprons studded with metal, and each with a cape that depended from the shoulders by means of a metal chain that looped around the neck and chest, in an elongated V-shape, the point of which was affixed to the belt of the leathern apron, in the front. On their feet they wore sandals with leather straps that crisscrossed up their legs to their knees. Each one carried a sword at his hip.

Upon seeing me, the men in this anteroom questioned my guide for several moments, and then, apparently satisfied of something—I did not, of course, know what—one of them turned away to a far wall and opened another door I had not noticed before.

My guide gave me a push, and I stumbled forward. With him pushing me from behind, we entered through this dark door, and then walked through a long series of corridors and stone stairs, all leading downward into the pits beneath this strange and oppressive structure.

At last we came to a lighted room that was filled with tables and cabinets, counters, stands and slabs on metal legs. Numerous bottles filled many shelves, and in them were liquids of various sorts. Some of them bubbled and some of them steamed. Everything was agitated, nervous and busy.

Huddled over one of the slabs was a very old man, busily engaged in something—I did not know what, for my view of him was blocked by a tall rack of glass tubes and jars. I caught only a glimpse of his furrowed face, his bald head, and occasionally his hand, as he raised it above a row of decanters.

He muttered to himself as he worked, deeply engrossed in whatever it was he was doing. We stood there, my officious guide and I, for many long moments. Finally, my guide announced himself with a slight clearing of his throat.

Even then, the old man at the slab ignored us for many more long moments, before he finally turned away from his work and vouchsafed us his attention.

Now my officious guide spoke to the old man, in tones humble and almost wheedling, while the old man examined me closely.

I returned the favor, observing him in great detail, though I could not, of course, understand the significance of the details I was observing. He seemed very old, though in my infant mind, I could not comprehend what 'old' was. I only sensed that his visage was not pleasing, his expression was one of petulance and irritation, his eyes clouded with near-blindness. He stooped as he stood, upon narrow legs that bowed outward, his knees grotesque and exaggerated knobs. His elbows, too, were huge, and his hands were cracked and spotted. The nails of his fingers were long and stained, and uneven, some of them broken, while others curled obscenely.

His skin was golden, as it was with all the others I had met so far on this, my first day upon land. But his was a flatter gold, closer, perhaps, to an ocher, his complexion uneven, in places it was brownish and red, with patches of pale blue that looked as if an intractable disease had found its way into his flesh.

The old man's chest was narrow and sunken, his ribs protuberant, while his belly was gross and misshapen, a bloated mass that stuck out like an overripe melon about to burst, it distended downward over the leather apron he wore about his narrow waist.

His nose was huge upon his face, his eyes narrow, and his ears were large flaps of flesh that hung upon the sides of his head, the edges ragged and torn. Long white strands of hair grew out from the flaps of his ears, and bounced in the air when he nodded his head, and they trailed behind him when he hobbled about.

He poked at my body and prodded it with his gnarled, yellowed fingernails, all the while muttering to himself, occasionally looking at my face as he barked some sounds at me in tones that seemed to demand something from me.

But I could only stare at him helplessly. I had no knowledge of anything, least of all the language he was barking at me, and as this interview progressed, he grew more and more impatient with my unresponsiveness.

At last he was stamping his feet on the floor and nearly screaming in my face with absurd frustration, when the officious guide who brought me here stepped in and spoke to the old man.

I had no idea of what he said, but whatever it was, it seemed to placate the old man, somewhat. Pausing in his little tantrum, he stepped back and studied me again for a moment. Then he snapped an order at my guide, who responded by grabbing me rudely by the upper arm and dragging me out of the crowded, cluttered room and away from the presence of the old man. The old man, apparently putting me out of his mind, returned instantly to his work upon the slab.

Now my guide led me, almost forcibly, through another long series of corridors, all dimly lit with yellow light by luminous rectangles that protruded from the walls above our heads. The yellow light against the dark red stone gave the corridors a lurid, menacing cast.

We came to yet another door, which my guide opened for me, and within it were two women, who looked up at us when we entered. My guide pushed me forward and spoke to the women for some moments in commanding tones. They looked from him to me, then back to him again, and wordlessly, they nodded to him.

"*Yut!*" I remember the sound he uttered. "*Yut!*"

And then he turned and left me with the women.

One was tall, with full curves, generous breasts, and black hair that she grew long, hanging even to her waist, behind. The other was slightly shorter in stature, and slimmer. Her hair, too, was long and black, and it shimmered in the yellow light. Her legs were muscular and her hips taut—both women looked at me with eyes that were large, round and astonishing in their beauty.

They both wore the short leather skirt that was the custom among these people. Both sported daggers, as all women did, but these two did not wear the gems or the finery of the women I had seen in the avenues of the city. Their skirts were plain and unadorned, wholly functional dress.

Their skin, too, was of a golden sheen, which was exaggerated by the lurid light of the room. Their eyes were green, a deep and penetrating viridian.

While my officious guide was present, they spoke not a word, but made a huge display of silent obeisance.

But, the instant he left, they both straightened themselves and laughed lightly and merrily. Somehow, I sensed, they were laughing at the expense of my officious guide. Now they both took me in hand, each taking one of my hands in her own, and leading me to a small low table. They sat me down at the table, upon the floor, then sat down on either side of me, peppering me with a chorus of sounds.

As before, I could only stare helplessly at them, while they chattered at me—apparently quizzing me. Their voices were somehow soothing, with a soft musical lilt that was deeply pleasing to my ears and which gave me great comfort.

But I could not listen to them long, for my attention was drawn to the many colorful things that lay upon the table we shared, and which gave forth the most pungent and compelling aromas.

Impulsively, I picked one up and brought it to my face to smell it more closely. And with that gesture, the two women seemed to come to a sudden understanding.

"*H'aph!*" they said, lightly laughing, "*H'aph!*"

I gave them a look of puzzlement, and then the taller woman with the full curves and rich breasts plucked another object from the table and brought it to her own mouth. She took a bite of it, breaking the skin, and then sucked upon it, demonstrating to me, I suppose, that it was safe to eat.

These colorful objects, I later learned, are a kind of fruit, filled with juice, and which the people of this city bake with syrup and *ga'la*[1].

Following her example, I brought the fruit to my own mouth and bit down on it. Rich, sticky juice shot out and spilled down my throat and chest, but I was too hungry to notice. With that first bite, my appetite was unleashed, and I essayed another bite, when both women, laughing lightly at my clumsy attempt, restrained me.

The slimmer, and apparently younger, woman, laid a hand upon my forearm, saying, "*Hai-la! Hai-la mo!*" She gestured to herself, indicating that I was to watch her.

Now she plucked another of these fruits from the table and brought it to her mouth, biting down lightly upon the skin to break it. And then she began to suck on the fruit, quickly draining it of its juice, until the rind was flat and flaccid.

"*Haloi*?' she said. "*Haloi*?"

Getting the idea, I brought the leaking fruit that I still held in my dripping hand up to my mouth, and sucked upon it. It was nearly drained, already, most of its fluid damp and sticky on my chest. But I now understood and reached for another.

---

1. Ga'la; A substance similar to honey. It is produced by an arachnoid creature called the Tumat, a very dangerous animal that lives in huge colonies in some of the northernmost islands of this archipelago. Untamable. Ga'la gathering is one of the most dangerous professions among these island people. A.G.

I gorged myself upon the sweet and sticky juices of those fruits for a very long time. As I sucked upon the fruit, first one, then the other of the two women took turns in speaking to me.

Holding up one of the fruits before me, a lavender thing with an obloid shape, the older women with the ample curves and the smiling eyes of viridian said, "*Fuma*."

When I reached for it, she pulled it away from me, and repeated the word, "*Fuma!*"

"*F-f-fuma*," I repeated.

She laughed happily, handing the fruit to me (which I made quick work of) and the younger woman clapped her hands with pleasure. Grabbing up another fruit, and displaying it to me in delicate and tapered fingers, she said, "*Lama*."

"*Lama*," I repeated, and now she handed it to me with a smile brightening her face.

And so began my instruction in the language of these people. With my instructresses making a game of it, offering me rich, sweet-tasting, and frequent rewards, I became an avid student, and before that—my first meal—was finished, I had mastered nearly two-dozen words. I had also made quite a mess of things, having spilt more of the juices upon myself, than getting them into my mouth.

The younger woman rose from the table and quickly returned with a dampened cloth that she laughingly tossed to me. But I, all unaware of the customs in this place, simply looked at it with what must have been a puzzled expression. Seeing my befuddlement, the older woman took the cloth from my hand, and wiped it over my face and chest, speaking to me all the while, in tones she could have used in reprimanding a messy child.

Afterwards, the two women continued their instruction, pointing to, or holding up various articles in the well-furnished suite, and speaking their names, as I repeated them.

We did this for some time, and again, I felt the cravings in my belly. The two women laid the table again, this time not with fruits, but with *stala* and *h'rafa* and a bottle filled with golden *ellihi*[2].

The *ellihi* was thick and syrupy and sweet. It sparkled with a tanginess that was not at all unpleasant, but which proved rather strong for my inexperienced palate. The drink went straight to my head, and with my belly full, at last, I found myself becoming very drowsy.

Seeing my eyes and shoulders beginning to droop with sleep, the two women led me into another room, which had furs and blankets strewn upon the floor. This was to be my sleeping quarters in this suite, which the two women shared.

I laid myself out upon the blankets and furs, and was soon sound asleep. How long I slept, I do not know. What I do recall, though, are my dreams, and they were a torment. I dreamed that I woke into a body that was useless and dead, unable to move—and all the while, consciousness, tedious consciousness, weighed down upon me like a heavy penance.

Finally, unable to bear the tedium of that interminable consciousness any longer, I forced myself awake, and found myself alone in the room where the two women had left me. For long moments I lay there,

---

2. Stala, h'rafa and ellihi; Foodstuffs, somewhat corresponding to bread, cheese and wine, respectively.

terrified to test my body, fearful that I would find that here, too, it was a dead and useless thing.

But at last I roused myself, rising up on an elbow, and floods of relief washed instantly through me. It had all been only a miserable dream. I could sit up, I could walk!

Thrilled to be able to move on my own, I wasted not a moment. No, I would not squander this glorious mobility!

Now I was filled with enthusiasm to learn as much and to do as much as I could. Somehow, with that waking from the tedious sleep, I sensed that the time I had would not be long, that every moment I lived was precious. So I must, somehow, cram as much learning and living into every instant as I possibly could.

Upon finding me awake, my two lovely tutors returned almost immediately to teaching me the words of their language, and they found me a most keen and passionate student.

They took to the task of teaching me with great delight. Every meal was another opportunity to add to my growing vocabulary, and they applauded my every success, giving me treats of food and drink to further encourage me.

Sometimes one or the other left, to go off and do various tasks in this vast house, and occasionally they both were gone, leaving me to myself in that suite of rooms. I used these times to continue practicing my new-found faculty of speech, reciting aloud to myself the names of everything I saw.

Eventually, it came time to put me in clothing. The two women brought me a harness to wear, which was a leather thong, with the short apron-like thing I saw the men wearing. I did not like it at all, and my body chafed at the tightness of it. It was painful and constricting, especially the sandals they put upon my feet, and tied tightly to my ankles with long leather straps.

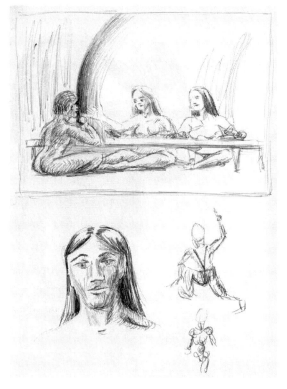

And many times I pulled the things off, preferring my comfortable nakedness to the tyranny of clothing, but the women insisted.

"Only the children run about naked," they explained. "And though you are much a child in your heart, yet yours is the body of a man."

So each time they caught me undressed, they forced me back into the scanty costume. Finally my tender flesh became accustomed to the abrading of the leather, and I reconciled myself to it.

Occasionally the overbearing man who had brought me here stopped by to learn of my progress in language. I was puzzled that my instructresses always answered him by saying, "Oh, he learns very slowly, Horath (which was the man's name). Very, very slowly. He has a few words, but still, he cannot make a sentence."

Horath grunted each time he heard this. As time progressed, he grunted at us with increasing impatience. But each time after his inquiry, he left us, and we returned to our lessons, as before.

"Shala, why do you tell him that I cannot speak?" I once asked the older woman (Shala was her name, one of the first things she taught me. Haia was the name of the younger woman, who was Shala's daughter.)

"Oh," she answered, deep concern growing in her eyes. "There is much you must learn, much you must know, before Jor-Taq takes you away from us. If he knew that you understood, he would take you from us now, and then..." She shuddered at some fear that she did not wish to make known to me, not at that moment.

"You are not ready. You are still but a child in these things. There are many very bad people, people who would delight in hurting you. Here, you are safe," she said. "As safe as you can be in the house of Jor-Taq. But once Jor-Taq has taken you..." and she let her voice drift into silence.

"What?" I asked. "What then?"

"When you are ready, Grae-don," she answered, her voice heavy. "When you are ready, Haia and I will tell you things." ('Grae-don'[3] was the name she came to call me by.)

How long my lessons with these two women took, I cannot say. Now that I had language, I took keen notice of time, something I had not done before I learned to string words into sentences—but though

---

3. Editor's Note: Grae-don: 'Orphan', literally 'without parents'. A.G.

I took notice of it, the time I spent in this suite was not unpleasant. My lessons occupied my mind greatly, and the three of us often passed the time with games they taught me to play.

One is played upon a wooden board that is marked with a series of lines with holes punched into them. Pegs of different colors are placed into the holes and moved along the lines, in competition with the other players.

Another game is played with a series of notched straws, tossed upon a piece of brightly marked cloth. The cloth is folded upon the straws, and then flung into the air, and the game is in the patterns that the straws make when they land upon the floor. Straws of a player that land athwart those of the other players cancel out the other players' straws, and the winner gets to keep both. When several straws land atop each other in a confused pile, the game gets extremely interesting. We start with one straw each, and by the end of the game, we may have dozens piled into the cloth.

Between games and meals, Shala told Haia and me stories of the world we lived in, stories that she, Shala, had learned from her mother, and who, in turn, had learned from hers. Some of these tales were ancient, some of a recent vintage, but through them all, my knowledge of this strange world broadened and deepened.

I learned that the name of the island upon which we lived was Pella'mir, that many thousands lived upon this island, and had done, time beyond all reckoning. Pella'mir was but one of several islands of an archipelago in the great sea. It was the largest of all these islands, the richest, and the most ancient.

The people of Pella'mir lived largely in peace among themselves, and had but few enemies in the wider world beyond. Among these were the Brigands of Boramok, who sailed the shallow sea in large, flat-bottomed ships. Of a season, they stormed Pella'mir, stealing goods, and capturing her citizens to barter as slaves. But they never sought to destroy Pella'mir.

"No, they simply return, to harvest us," Shala told me. "They never take so much that we might starve, or collapse. They want us to thrive, that they may plunder all the more."

Shala also took it upon herself to teach me how to write, as well as how to read the language that we spoke, but she insisted that this be kept an utmost secret.

"Jor-Taq is most adamant on this. He does not want you to read. Not a word."

"But why not?" I asked.

"He seeks to make you his servant. He has many enemies, and trusts no one. In you, he sees one who may be his loyal slave forever. You have no family, no city, no tribe, no memory, even, of anything but what you've seen here. That you appear to be so slow in learning also works well to your favor, in his eyes. He wants you to be not too intelligent, nor too inquisitive. Promise me that whatever you do, when you leave us and enter into his service, that you will not show him too much intelligence. Who knows what he might do to you, then?"

"And if I don't want to be his servant?" I demanded.

"What you may want, or what anyone else may want, could hardly concern Jor-Taq. It is only what Jor-Taq wants that is of any importance. All else is merely a nuisance. Pray, do not make yourself a nuisance to Jor-Taq."

Now Horath became more impatient with us, and more insistent. Jor-Taq himself was demanding to see me, and Shala and Haia both went to great pretenses to prolong my lessons, that I may be as well armed with knowledge as I may be, before embarking out into this very dangerous world.

I learned that they were not here willingly as paid household servants. Theirs was one of indentured servitude.

Shala's husband, a man named Torq-aa, had fallen into debt. It was a minor debt which he was already well on the way to paying off. Shala told me that Torq-aa had only two, perhaps three more payments to make on it.

But Jor-Taq, ever seeking ways to increase his wealth, purchased that debt from the man to whom Torq-aa owed it. And once he'd purchased the debt, he immediately raised the interest on it, beyond that which Torq-aa could ever pay off, and increasing it with every season. In time, he came to raise the rate of interest to something that was several times greater than the original debt.

So Torq-aa finally found himself in a situation where no matter how much he paid, the debt to Jor-Taq only grew larger and larger.

At last, Jor-Taq demanded Torq-aa's wife and daughter to come live in his house as his servants. They would clean, cook and do other menial tasks that Jor-Taq's staff found too demeaning or tiresome to do.

Jor-Taq could do this, Shala explained to me when I questioned her, because he kept a small army of bodyguards in this house. They were well-armed and notorious for their brutality. Torq-aa, who had only his honor and his livelihood, could do nothing against Jor-Taq's army of thugs, except die. And that, of course, would have left Shala a widow, and Haia an orphan, both of them most unutterably and inescapably ensnared within the clutches of Jor-Taq. Alive, at least, Torq-aa may hope one day to affect their freedom from this loathsome man, but dead...

So, most unwillingly, he permitted his wife and his daughter to go into what Jor-Taq insisted was but 'temporary bondage', against the day that Torq-aa could finally pay off the debt and have his family returned to him.

Anger grew within my heart as Shala told me her story. She and Haia had both been kind to me, and I had come to feel toward them as I might a mother and a sister. They were both beautiful, in spirit as well as in form, gentle and patient, generous and nurturing. That they—that any human creature—should be treated so shamefully, as if merely pieces of furniture to be bartered, filled me with rage against this Jor-Taq.

Now I was keen to meet the man again, that I may exact punishment upon him for his effrontery upon these two gentle creatures I had grown to love.

And when Shala saw the fury burning in my eyes, she immediately sought to calm my anger.

"It is not so bad," she said. "One day, we will be free. We have only to be patient. Please, do not bring his wrath down upon yourself. He is terrible in his rages."

And so I allowed her to placate me, for the moment. I had no desire to cause her any further anxiety, so kept my counsel to myself. One day, though, Jor-Taq would suffer for the insult he put upon my friends.

Events began moving more quickly after that. When Horath came again, to query into my education, I studied him keenly, as he did me. Perhaps I allowed the distaste I felt for him to show upon my face. I had not forgotten his rude treatment of me, when he slapped my face that first day of my coming to this city.

Now I understood that I was merely hungry, and that the aromas from the marketplace through which we passed beckoned to me, and I simply responded, as a hungry man would. It was outrageous of him to have treated me so.

That slap he gave me burned yet upon my face, and he saw the smoldering anger in my eyes.

"Now, Shala, is he ready or not? He looks upon me with intelligence, and I cannot believe that he has not yet learned to speak. Jor-Taq grows impatient, and would put this one through his paces immediately."

"Only but a bit more time, Horath. He is only a child in his mind, and comprehends but little. I am afraid that Jor-Taq expects much."

Haia stood beside her mother.

"Please, he has so much to learn..." she began.

Horath turned on her, with a look in his eyes that repelled me.

"I would not be so quick to speak, child," Horath said. "Jor-Taq is unsatisfied with your efforts. He has promised you to me, for discipline, should you not improve, directly."

Haia recoiled from him and huddled next to me. Instinctively, I threw a protective arm around her shoulder.

"Ah!" Horath exulted. "He understood that! Tell me, *koraph*[4]," he spat, "Do you understand what I say?"

"I don't know what a *koraph* is," I answered, trying hard to appear as if I were having difficulty with the words. "But I know some words."

"Ha!" Horath replied. "Good enough! Jor-Taq demands to see you. I will tell him you are ready for your audience."

With that, he spun on his heel and left us.

"Oh, whatever you do," Shala said, when we were alone, "do not antagonize Horath. He is cruel, so cruel. They call him `Horath the

---

4. Editor's Note: Koraph, an omnivorous creature with six legs, and a poisonous dart-like tongue. About the size of a pig, apparently, its flesh is inedible, it consumes its own filth, and is considered a pest. To call a person a koraph is to offer an insult. A.G.

Bloody One' and he has killed many men. He would gut you as soon as look at you."

Haia and Shala both spent the few moments we had left to hastily explain to me what this audience with Jor-Taq would mean.

"They will test you, and quiz you," they warned me. "To see if they can use you. If they can't use you... if they can't use you alive, well, they can use you dead. Jor-Taq wastes nothing."

"But do not show them too much intelligence," Shala said. "They will not like that. Horath is an ignorant brute, and Jor-Taq is jealous of his genius. There can only be room in his world for one mind, and that is his.

"Whatever you do," she added with great urgency, even as we heard Horath's footsteps returning down the long red hallway, "Do not let either of them know that we have taught you how to read."

"Why not?" I quickly whispered.

"Reading is forbidden among the common people. It is a skill reserved only for the privileged. If Jor-Taq knew we had taught you, he would kill us all."

And at that moment, the door opened, and I saw Horath's grinning face. Behind him were six other men, who kept their hands upon the pommels of their swords.

"Jor-Taq will see you now," Horath said.

2

My Education Continues

HORATH LED ME THROUGH a series of long and narrow corridors illumined by the yellow rectangles of the light of lamps set into the red stone walls. He strode arrogantly before me, while his escort, my guard, followed behind.

We marched in silence. Horath uttered not a word, and I took these moments to examine him most closely. He stood perhaps a head taller than me, and his body was heavy with muscles. His chest was broad and his waist was narrow. He let his arms swing freely at his sides, and I saw that his hands were huge and callused. Horath swaggered when he walked, and every fiber of his body bespoke arrogance and cruelty.

I'd noticed the smirk of smug self-satisfaction on his face before. I had already learned to hate the man. Now, I compared his visage with his body and carriage, and in those moments walking behind him, I came to despise him completely.

Seeking to annoy him, I asked, "What is a *koraph*?" I already knew, of course. Shala and Haia had given me a very thorough education, but I sensed it would irritate him to answer the question, impertinently asked, but disguised as naïve. And it did.

"Shut up!" he said, without turning. One of the guards behind gave me a cuff at the back of the head with the pommel of his sword.

The blow was hard, but not sufficient to harm me. But I saw that Horath was indeed annoyed, and that gave me some satisfaction.

We climbed several steep stairways, passing a number of chambers, all of them dark, and then down a winding passage to a black door that was securely bolted. Horath rapped on the door with his knuckles, and a small portal opened, revealing the face of another guard.

He looked past Horath to scrutinize my face. After several moments, he demanded, "Is this the one?"

"It is he," Horath said.

"Then bring him inside. You and this one. The others wait without."

We stepped into a small anteroom and waited while the guard securely bolted the door. Then, once that was locked, he stepped to a door on the opposite wall and opened it.

"Wait here," he said, and he disappeared behind the door.

Now Horath turned to glower at me. "You are about to enter the presence of Jor-Taq. Keep a respectful tongue, *koraph*, or I'll cut it out and feed it to you."

"As you say," I replied.

Without a word, Horath punched me in the head.

"Speak when you're told to, slave!" he spat, by way of explanation.

I glared at him in silence, and he read the expression on my face. He laughed.

"If you think you can, then do it now, *koraph*!" He raised his fist and held it before my nose.

"Ha! I thought so," he said, when I made no move. "You're not the first man to look at me like that. Many men have thought to kill me. Some have even tried. Ha, ha, ha!"

Obviously Horath gave himself much amusement.

The door opened suddenly, and the guard stepped in with a quick gesture.

"Do not keep Jor-Taq waiting," he said. "Nor seek to impose upon him, or it will go not well for you." That last comment was directed at me.

Horath ushered me forward, where we found Jor-Taq at table, having just finished his supper. A girl was removing the crockery, and she caught my eye, for she was different from all others I had seen here.

She was petite, almost tiny, you might say. Her head came no higher than my shoulder. But what struck me first about her was her golden hair, which she wore loosely and cut rather short and curled about her ears. All the others I had seen to this moment had hair that was black, straight and glossy.

And then I noticed her complexion. Her skin was light, like mine, rather pinkish in tone, and not at all of the golden sheen of all the others I had met here. That surprised me, and because we shared a strange complexion, I felt a sudden affinity toward her, and a sense of a strange familiarity.

Were we kindred, in this place? Were there other places, other worlds, other lives where our paths may have crossed before this moment? I do not know. To this day I do not know. All I can say is that at that moment when I first laid eyes on her, it with was with a sense of strange recognition, all unexplainable.

And then I saw her eyes, and they were an astonishment, for they were blue, an unheard of blue. In a world where everyone's eyes were green, or black, or—in my case, brown—blue eyes were undreamed of. And I saw that they were eyes that were meant to be happy, always smiling, often laughing, eyes of good-humor and gentle friendship. She should not be in a dismal place, such as this. She should not be subjected to serving these cold and heartless creatures, treated with endless discourtesies. Whoever she was, she had a place in the world, and this was not it.

She wore only a tiny cloth wrapped about her loins. It was not of leather, but of white fabric, stained with the soil and discoloration of the menial tasks she served. About her neck was a collar, and this studded with a ring in the back. Later, I learned that collar was for the convenience of her keepers, that they may use it to chain her securely when her guards were not present.

She never looked up from her tasks, but moved silently through the room, removing the cutlery and crockery from the table of Jor-Taq, and then swiftly removing herself from his presence.

But I caught fleeting glimpses of her eyes, glances that bespoke a quick mind and an intelligence that was attentive to her environment. This girl, I sensed, was more intelligent than those who presumed to be her keepers. She was—I realized, of a sudden—more dangerous to them than they were to her.

But Jor-Taq was oblivious. He glared at me over the table as Horath ushered me forward, ignoring the girl completely.

She finished her task, and then she was gone, leaving me alone in the room with Jor-Taq and Horath.

Jor-Taq glared at me for several long moments saying nothing. Then he rose from his table and walked up to me, hunched with age, and peering up at my face.

"Pale skin," he remarked, more to himself than to me. "Yellow hair. Brown eyes."

He hobbled a full circle around me, poking at me with his gnarled fingers and muttering. Then he came to face me once again, squinting with ill-temper.

"Who are you?" he demanded.

"I don't know. Shala and Haia call me Grae-don."

"You don't know?" he demanded.

"No."

"They tell me you walked in from the sea. Is that true?"

"Yes," I answered, shrugging my shoulders, helplessly.

"And where do you come from?"

"The sea, I suppose. I remember nothing, but drifting for days and days, and then I saw the islands."

"We have seen some few like you before," Jor-Taq mused. "They claim to come from the southern seas. Do you know of these?"

"No. I only know what Shala and Haia have taught me."

Turning abruptly to Horath, Jor-Taq demanded, "What do you think? Is this man lying?"

"I think he does not have the intelligence to lie," Horath answered with a sneer. "He is very stupid."

"Is that right? Jor-Taq asked me, a supercilious smile touching his lips. "Are you stupid?"

"It took him long to learn to speak," Horath put in. "Longer than even a child."

"If you say I am stupid, then I must be," I answered. "I know almost nothing."

"Good. Good," Jor-Taq replied. "No, I do not believe you are lying to me, stupid one. I can tell a liar. Don't ever try. I will have you put to death, if ever you lie to me."

"I will not lie to you," I lied.

"Good. See to it you don't. Don't even think a lie when I am about."

Jor-Taq led Horath away to the other side of the room and they huddled together in close and whispered conversation for several moments. At last they came to an agreement between them, and returned to me.

"You will go with Horath now. He will see to your training."

"What of Shala and Haia? Will they not teach me anymore?"

Horath reached out and slapped me hard, so hard that I fell sprawling upon the floor. Jor-Taq simply smirked.

"Do not question Jor-Taq, slave! Do what you are told, and be grateful for it!" And then he stepped forward to kick me, while I was still down, but I was too quick for him. Instantly I was on my feet again.

His foot came within an inch of my nose. Without thinking, I grabbed it by the heel tightly in both of my hands, and raised it suddenly to the level of my shoulder. Instantly, Horath's face was ridiculous with dismay.

With his right foot gripped firmly in my hands, and raised high, he was suddenly helpless. He could not strike me with his fists, which flailed uselessly in the air, and his attention was otherwise wholly engaged with bouncing madly on his left foot, as he strove to keep his balance.

Jor-Taq laughed out loud, delighted at the fearsome Horath's suddenly silly figure. Horath's face was contorted with anger and he burned orange with livid, impotent, rage.

For an instant, I was as surprised at the result of my impulsive act as he was, but only for an instant. Goaded on by Jor-Taq's merriment, I dragged Horath in circles about the room by his upraised foot, while he shouted, sputtered and cursed, hopping absurdly to keep from falling.

A stream of obscenities spewed from his mouth, words too foul for me to countenance, but the threats were most clear.

"I'll cut your filthy throat!" he bellowed. "I'll gut you, I'll slice your manhood from you and shove it down your neck until you choke, you stinking *kra*-gorging[1] *koraph*!"

Jor-Taq, laughing uproariously, interjected, "You'll do nothing of the sort. This Grae-don amuses me. You will leave him unharmed, Horath, unless..." he said with a sudden and severe look pointed directly at Horath, "... you seek to incur my wrath."

The overbearing Horath was instantly cowed.

---

1. Editor's Note: Kra; excrement. A.G.

"Please, no, Jor-Taq," he wheedled. "You know I am loyal to you. Have I not proven myself a hundred times over?"

"That is better," Jor-Taq replied with a casual imperiousness.

"Now, Grae-don, you may release my servant," he said.

And so I did. I gave his heel a push with my hands, and Horath fell flat upon his back.

"I have uses for you, you who call yourself Grae-don," Jor-Taq said. "Those uses shall become manifest, in time. For now, you shall submit yourself to the gentle teachings of my most loyal servant, Horath. Do you understand?"

I understood that Horath's instructions would be anything but 'gentle', but I kept my silence on that point. All I said to Jor-Taq was, "I understand."

"Now, Horath," Jor-Taq continued. "You shall take this Grae-don under your tutelage, and teach him well. Enough of the soft teachings of women for this one. Make of him a man."

"Yes, Jor-Taq. I shall do as you say…"

"'Shall'?" Jor-Taq instantly challenged. "'Shall'? Is it not your *will* to do as I command you?"

"I have no will but yours, Jor-Taq," Horath humbly replied. But I could see, by the sidelong glance he threw at me as he said those words that he said what he needed to say, to Jor-Taq's face. When Jor-Taq was not present, Horath did indeed have a will of his own. And it was his will to ensure that my days ahead were not to be pleasant, not at all.

After our audience with Jor-Taq, Horath brought me to another part of the old man's huge and fortress-like residence. This was a room where Jor-Taq's guards dwelt. All of them slept together in a single cavernous hall of bare walls and hard stone floor. The room offered no comforts to the eye or the body—all slept on the floor, with naught but a single sleeping blanket that was issued to each of them.

Every wealthy man in Pella'mir has his own private guard, for who will offer him protection, if he does not protect himself? Every wealthy man fears all others, for he has that which others seek—and it is this fear that keeps many men poor, that they may not attract the attention of burglars and murderers.

All of them fear assassination, some of them obsessively so, and all of them have, among their guards, those who they specially train in the art of assassination.

But some men crave wealth more than they fear death, and so these men provide for themselves guards who they pay to protect them from those who would do them harm.

These guards also keep order generally through the city of Pella'mir, for the wealthy men of the city know that they could not thrive if their world was unsound. So it is left up to them to mete out whatever justice was needed among the citizens of Pella'mir. Since the justice of the guards is usually short and brutal, and dealt without any regard to the well-being of those who receive it, the citizens of Pella'mir seek to avoid any contact with this justice, and so they are generally very well-behaved.

Any minor problems that arise between them, they keep minor. It profits no one to make a small problem great, and so Pella'mir is a generally happy city.

There are a number of wealthy men in Pella'mir, such as Jor-Taq, some who have joined together to form partnerships, the better to protect themselves, not only from the dissatisfaction of the poor, who outnumber them by orders of magnitude, but also from each other, who they each fear more than the poor.

Jor-Taq did not join any of these partnerships. He lived in isolation from all others, almost never leaving his great house, and spending all his days in his study, pursuing his researches with a fanaticism, I would learn, that drove all other thoughts from his mind—save alone for his fear of assassination. He was also the wealthiest man in Pella'mir, and the most hated. And so his obsessive fear of assassination was not without foundation. Even his own guards despised him. Though they took their payment from him, none of them, not one, felt any true loyalty to the old man.

Jor-Taq's guards were hard men, cold men. They had no need for comfort, held it in contempt, and lived with a cult of pain. For pastimes, when they were not on duty, they played games with their knives upon their bodies, to build their endurance.

In one such game, one guard laid his hand upon the floor, fingers splayed, while another thrust the point of his knife between the splayed fingers, one after another, in rapid succession. Sometimes the guard with the knife missed and sliced off a fingertip. Each time a fingertip happened to get sliced off, all those in the room watching burst out into roars of laughter, including he who lost the digit. Losing a finger in this exercise was considered a point of honor among these guards. I saw this game played almost constantly.

In another such game, one guard laid his hand upon the wall, fingers once again splayed, while others threw knives at his outstretched hand, to see who could hit the wall closest to the fingers. Wagers were placed upon these tournaments, and many days' pay was often lost in an instant.

These were hard men, as I say. Brutal men, but, unlike Horath, they were, for the most part, honest men, and honorable.

They practiced a form of scarification that was ritualistic among them, decorating their bodies with welts and scars that described complicated circles and spirals. In some cases, they opened the flesh of their bodies and placed metal beads under their skin, creating rows of bumps in patterns that indicated their rank and accomplishments.

Each part of the body, I learned, had a special significance among them. Arms and hands were devoted to recording feats of the individual. On their chests, they stitched patterns that gave display to their rank and to whose house it was they served. Their backs and legs were given over to symbols that indicated their family and genealogy. By means of these symbols, one could literally read a man, learn from his body who he was, who he served, and what he had done.

These symbols were matters of great honor among them. No man could scar his body alone. It had to always be done with great ceremony, even the least scar, with many witnesses to attest that the scar was deserved, and had been either earned or rightly inherited.

When Horath ushered me into the hall, a dozen of the off-duty guards surrounded us. Horath, the leader of the guard, barked out his orders.

"Take this one in hand, and teach him well. Jor-Taq demands it."

And then he spun on his heel and left me to the kind mercies of the brutal guard. Now my education took a different, harsher, turn. Gone were those happy moments with Shala and Haia, when learning to speak and to read was accompanied with games and treats.

Punishment became the impetus. When I did poorly, my teachers punished me harshly. When I did well, they rewarded me with light punishments.

Every morning, Horath himself awoke me with a kick in the ribs, which provoked great rounds of laughter from the guards. And all through the day, they took turns cuffing and punching me, as they set me to my various tasks.

In addition to my regular duties, they put me to a regimen of exercises to toughen me up; running in place, and climbing ropes, pulling myself up on a bar set into a frame, and squatting and thrusting and pushing and climbing.

I took to it, as I had set it in my heart to kill Horath, and knew that my slight frame would be nothing against his. I must make myself bulky, and hard, like stone, to challenge him. So I endured the cuffing and the punching with as good a spirit as I could muster, knowing that every punch, every slap only made me tougher and stronger than before.

"Half of the fight, boy," one of the guards explained to me, "is stamina. If you can take more pain than your opponent can give, then you've won." And then he banged the back of my head with his fist to emphasize his point.

Those words have stayed with me, for I have seen it often, since, that a man will provoke a fight, expecting no resistance, but instantly falls to crying like a baby girl, when once he gets the fight he was looking for.

Only but endure—you need not even be able to throw a punch, to make a coward cringe, to recoil in fear. And most men, I have learned, are cowards.

I took the punches, as I say, with as good a spirit as I could muster, but after a time, I had had enough. One evening after I'd been at chores all day, and was sore, and tired, one of the guards shouted at me to clean his muddy sandals for him. I called him a stinking *koraph*, and told him to do it himself.

He came at me in a rush and a rage, with his fists upraised, bellowing that he was about to give me the beating of my life.

Without thinking, I swung my fist at him, just as he came within striking distance, and hit him fairly on the chin. His head snapped back, with a look of astonishment on his face that I will never forget, and then I quickly followed that punch with two more to the belly.

The wind went out of him and his face went white. He dropped to his knees, hunched over and clutching his stomach. I brought my own knee forward quickly, and kicked him twice in the face, and he fell sprawling backward.

Such a commotion! The instant my antagonist fell on the floor, the guards who saw the short-lived fight between us filled the hall with their laughter and loud applause.

"It's about time you showed us some spunk!" I heard several say.

"Good job!"

"Well done. You did him right and good!"

The guard I felled to the floor picked himself up, and I was astonished to see him laughing, through bloodied lips and broken nose.

"Haw! Haw! Haw!" he said. "Did you see that? I'm the one who taught him that trick!"

And they all crowded around me, slapping me on the back and generally congratulating me.

Now their attitude toward me changed. They still cuffed and punched me, as before, but now they ducked quickly away as I swung back at them.

From this point on, they included boxing and wrestling in my education—I found that I preferred the boxing, but realized that wrestling was a needful skill, so I strove to excel in that, as well.

After I had gained some mastery in these two skills, two of them, one called Brekkex, and the other, Koax, took it upon themselves to teach me the use of the knife and of the sword. Brekkex taught me how to use the knife. Koax, the sword.

The knives are various. Some are short and straight, some are long and curved. Some come to a point at the tip, some have tips that are curved upward from the cutting edge, some have serrated edges, and some have two, rather than one cutting edge. Some have handles with finger grips, some with holes in the handles for the fingers to fit into. Some have guards between the handle and the blade, and some do not. Each has its own use, I learned, and I was to become proficient in all of them, before my education was to be considered complete.

The swords they use are rather short, with thick, slightly curved blades. They do not come to a point, as I have since seen in other swords, but are cut straight at the end, with a blunt tip. These are brutal weapons that can sometimes be used as clubs. They have only one cutting edge, the opposite edge being thick enough to crack a skull, if necessary.

The two men who undertook to teach me the use of these tools were both excellent teachers, who were patient, when needed, but not too patient. As I first bumbled with the use of these things, they warned me to take care, lest I cut my own head off.

"And you'd be no good then," they said.

But, as I gained in skill, as practiced against them, in sword and knife fighting, they were quick and merciless in taking advantage of any opening, however small, I gave them. So in short time, my body was covered with innumerable scratches, cuts and scars from our practices.

And in the end, we three became rather close friends, especially when I managed to slip in a point of my dagger, and gouge a bit of flesh from them, myself.

"They called you a slow learner, boy," Koax laughed in his loud way. "But I'll be damned if you're not picking it up 'most as fast as I did."

There was a rigid hierarchy among Jor-Taq's guards. Those who I was quartered with here were among the lowest ranks. They guarded the house and its walls, and were never permitted to the higher floors where Jor-Taq lived. Most of them had never even laid eyes on the old man, but had been recruited into his service by low-ranking guards, themselves.

Somewhat higher in rank were those guards who were permitted to go outside and into the streets of Pella'mir, especially in the neighborhoods surrounding Jor-Taq's house. Higher in rank than these were Jor-Taq's spies, who infiltrated the guards and houses of the other men of wealth in Pella'mir. Highest in rank and fewest in number were Jor-Taq's assassins, of whom Horath was the chief.

I learned from Brekkex and Koax, and the others among the guards with whom I had established a rough kind of friendship, that Horath was heartily despised by all who knew him. Even Jor-Taq himself, it was rumored, had grown sick of the man and his overbearing ways.

"I am Jor-Taq's assassin," he proclaimed loudly, to all who would hear, "And I can do whatever I want!"

Whatever he wanted to do was usually to bring misery and suffering to anyone he could. He strode through the streets of Pella'mir, bullying and fighting, and taking what he wanted without paying, daring anyone to challenge him. None did, and the discontent he caused was coming to be so large that even the great Jor-Taq, isolated in his studies away from all humanity, could not ignore it.

So it was that one morning, as Brekkex and Koax were teaching me how to hurl a sword—a nice piece of work that requires strong muscles in the forearm, great coordination of hand and eye, and a delicate feel for the weight of the blade, to give it the proper rotation in the air, so that it hits its target fairly—Horath came into the hall with his usual strident bellowing.

"Where is that *koraph*, called Grae-don?"

"Right here!" I answered, loudly, and with a touch of brashness I knew would annoy the man.

"Jor-Taq demands to see you, now!" he shouted at me. The man always looked upon the world with a smoldering anger in his eyes, but this day, I sensed, he glared at me with something more than his usual, generalized rage. Now, for some reason, it was me, in particular, that he hated.

"Yes, Horath," I answered. It was terribly impudent of me to address the man by name. Properly, a lower-ranking guard should address a higher-ranking guard only by his title. It was impudent of me to address him at all, for I was the lowest-ranking of all, and properly, should not have uttered even a sound in the presence of the great assassin, but only silently obey his every whim.

He lashed out to give me a clout upon the head for my impudence but I was too quick for him. Before his fist came near me, I raised my sword so that it was in the path of his blow, and he smacked the flat of it dead on with his hand. Knuckles bruised and skin torn, he let loose a howl of pain and rage.

"You will die for that!" he bawled, as the guards in the hall laughed at his discomfiture.

"And you will keep the mighty Jor-Taq waiting, upon your own pleasure?" I taunted him, and loudly enough so that all could hear.

The bullying Horath looked quickly about, seeing that all eyes were upon him. Outnumbered by those who hated him, the assassin was quickly cowed.

"Come with me," he blustered. "Jor-Taq will deal with your insubordination."

"Yes, Horath," I twitted him, again.

"Fare-thee-well, Horath," heckled another guard.

"Good-bye-e-e, *Horath*," called out another, affecting a high-pitched, mincing tone.

"Toodle-oooo, *Horath*."

And so Horath ushered me out of the hall to a chorus of ridicule and laughter, his face burning with stifled rage. He would have killed me on the spot, I knew, had not Jor-Taq demanded to see me. I would live that long, at least, but I knew that Horath would not let me live longer than Jor-Taq required me.

And so ended my education among the guards of Jor-Taq. I would see my friends of the guards only once again, in the days to come, under extremely altered circumstances, and many would be the times that I am grateful to Brekkex and Koax for their brief, but very timely, friendship.

3

THE GREAT JOR-TAQ

ORATH, WITH A GUARD of his assassins surrounding me, all of them wearing the capes that identified them as such, marshaled me to Jor-Taq's presence. It had been many weeks since I had last seen the old man, and I had begun to believe that he had forgotten me.

But luck was not with me. Rather than forgetting me, the old man had, I learned, spent much time thinking about me, and paid close attention to my progress.

The old man had set aside this time for a particular interview with me. Horath and his assassins led me into an expansive room that had almost no furnishings in it whatsoever. There were no chairs, nor benches, no place at all for any but Jor-Taq to sit.

The walls were entirely without decoration, with the exception of a single gold and black stripe painted horizontally along the walls at eye-level. For illumination, a large glass lamp hung from the ceiling in the center of this hall, leaving the corners in shadow. I wondered, briefly, what kind of secret observers the old man might have hidden in those shadows. Aside from that, two other lamps, burning oil, stood on high metal stands on either side of Jor-Taq, where he sat.

Jor-Taq sat upon a chair of stone set in a deep niche cut directly into the red stone of the wall. The stone chair was expansive enough to seat three people in it, and it was strewn with cushions and blankets to give comfort to the old man's bent and spindly spine.

Three broad semi-circular steps led up to the stone chair from the level of the floor, and before them was a low table of highly polished stone, upon which lay any number of papers, scrolls and codices.

"Do you see those things upon the table?" Jor-Taq demanded of me, abruptly.

"Yes," I replied.

"What do you make of them?"

I glanced at them, and then shrugged my shoulders.

"Do you see the markings upon those reams?"

"Yes," I answered.

"Do you know why those markings are there?"

"No," I lied.

"Do you know what 'writing' is?"

"I have heard of it," I answered, carefully, and remembering Shala's urgent warning never to reveal to anyone that she had taught me to read.

"Do you know how to read?" he demanded, peering at me intently. "Tell me the truth, or it will go badly for you. I can tell when anyone lies to me."

And I, among the guard, and playing their many games of chance, had learned how to lie convincingly. At least, convincingly to the untutored guards. Whether my gaming face would work on Jor-Taq or not, I could not be sure. But I decided to take the chance. Had I told the truth, the next question out of Jor-Taq's mouth would surely be, 'And who taught you to read?' Nor would I do anything to bring harm to Shala, whom I loved as a mother, nor Haia, whom I loved as a sister.

"No," I said. "I do not know how to read."

Jor-Taq responded by staring at me hard for many long moments. I sensed that the hard stare was intended to make me quail, to make me hedge my answer and try to change it. That blunder, of changing one's story under questioning, I learned among the guards, is the hallmark of a liar. Once you have told your lie, stick to it. Never change it, by even so much as a word.

Horath and the other assassins felt the intensity of Jor-Taq's stare themselves, and they fidgeted uncomfortably in its harsh and probing light.

But I did not. I simply stood before Jor-Taq, unmoving, presenting to him the sight of a man who did not know what this was all about, and who was waiting to see what would come next.

At last Jor-Taq eased his serpent-like gaze and he let a small smile of satisfaction touch his lips.

"Good. Good," he said. "I have many secrets written upon these papers, and do not wish to share them. Now tell me this," he went on. "Do you think you can best Horath is a fair fight?"

Horath visibly started at that, and almost gave voice to a protest, which he quickly stifled.

"I don't know," I replied. "I have never seen Horath fight fairly."

Jor-Taq laughed loud at that, greatly enjoying Horath's discomfort.

"I have need of a personal bodyguard, Grae-don," Jor-Taq said with a pointed glance toward Horath. "I have many enemies, and it has come recently to my ears that my enemies have placed spies here, in my house, even... *among my own guard*!"

Jor-Taq's voice rose to a high-pitched scream with those last words, and he glared directly at Horath.

"Oh, Jor-Taq!" Horath interrupted. "I have always been loyal to you, the most loyal of all who serve you."

It was most amusing to me to see the bully cowering before the old man.

"It is not your loyalty that I doubt, Horath, but your *intelligence*! Fool! Idiot! How do you dare to allow spies to come into my house! While you have been drinking and wenching and thieving in the streets of Pella'mir, you have allowed my enemies to find a foothold, here! In my own *house*!"

"You," he spat, now turning fully upon the assassin, and standing on his bent and knobby legs, "You will find these creatures out and you will destroy them! Do you hear me? Destroy them, even if it means you must kill every man who lives within these walls, yourself included!"

Horath, chastened, hung his chin upon his breast.

"Your will is mine," said he.

"Now be gone with you! All of you! I will speak with this Grae-don alone!"

"Most noble Jor-Taq..." Horath began.

"Shut up! Did I give you leave to speak? Shut up and get out!"

And, casting dubious glances filled with smoldering hatred at me, Horath obeyed. His guard of assassins filed out of the mighty Jor-Taq's chambers, leaving us alone.

The old man stared at me in silence for many long moments, as if he were striving to read my mind. When he spoke, at last, it was to pepper me with questions about my origins. Doubtless he had heard everything there was to hear about me before this moment. I sensed, though, that the purpose of this intense interrogation was to hear my story again from my own lips.

The questions came rapidly. Often he shot two or three questions at me in quick succession, even as I was answering the first. Many times he asked me the same question over and over, only slightly changing the wording of it, and on occasion, he threw questions at me that made no sense whatever.

He was at times hostile, then friendly, antagonistic and ingratiating, pleading, wheedling, and whining, and I sensed in all of it that he was seeking to trip me up, to tease out any lie I, or any others might have told him. He sometimes responded to my answers with surprise, sometimes with a knowing smirk, sometimes with a cunning leer, but I could not know whether his responses were sincerely felt, or merely show, in order to confuse me.

Repeatedly he demanded to know whether I could read, whether I could interpret the marks written on the papers that were strewn upon the table at his feet. I sensed that his pestering me on that point reflected his own concern, his own almost pathological need for secrecy, rather than any suspicion that Shala and Haia may have taught me that forbidden knowledge.

For he never once asked me about them by name. Only did he ask me about what I had learned from them.

"How to talk," I answered. "How to dress myself. How to eat."

"Very good," he replied, with a strange satisfaction spreading over his face. "You were long enough about it, though. Which gave us all concern about your intelligence."

"I am very slow to learn, it seems," I said.

"Good. Good," Jor-Taq said. "All the brains I need in this room are right here," he remarked, tapping himself on the head. "All I need from you is a set of eyes and a pair of hands. I have many enemies, Grae-don. Many seek to harm me. Some would seek to murder me. You, by virtue of your singular birth, have no particular loyalties, either here in Pella'mir, or elsewhere. Is that not so?"

"That is so."

"Good. Good. You are a stranger to all. Thus, all are strangers to you. So you shall be loyal to me. I will treat you well. You'll want for nothing. Nothing at all. And you shall watch over me, night and day, and ready, always ready to answer my call."

"Yes, Jor-Taq," I replied.

And so I became Jor-Taq's bodyguard. I quickly found the job to be one of endless tedium. All my waking hours were spent in attendance upon him, following him wherever he went and watching over him closely as he moved about his house.

He placed me in a tiny anteroom outside his own private apartments within the building. Within this room were four walls, a tiny closet, and a few furs piled into a corner where I spent a few short hours in sleep each night.

Jor-Taq spent most his days deep in his researches. When he was closeted away alone in his studies, in the chambers above his private apartments, it was my task to stand outside his door, without moving from the spot, neither engaging in conversation with any who may come near, nor distracting my attention in any other manner from my sole purpose of guarding the old man.

Sometimes he took his meals while closeted away in his studies, and I was then to take the trays from the girl who brought them, and signal through the door to Jor-Taq that his supper had arrived.

Other times, he took his meals in the same chamber where I had my first interview with him after my period of education with Shala and Haia. There, I stood in the doorway, watching as the old man ate, and listening patiently to his endless monologues.

It was the girl with the golden hair, who I had seen before, who silently brought in his meals. Each time she passed me it was without a word or glance. Moving efficiently, she placed the platters holding Jor-Taq's meal upon the table before him, and then she swiftly vanished away through a door. She only returned, sometimes several hours later, after the man had signaled that he was done with his meal.

It was only after he had finished his usually lavish meal that I was permitted mine, which consisted solely of a few poor dried cakes of *fuma*, and a paste made of *h'rafa*, and which I ate while standing outside the door of his study.

Every waking minute I spent in attendance on the old man, and I chafed greatly at the onerous duty. It gave the old egotist great gratification to cause me to spend uncountable hours in boredom and monotony, waiting upon every whim, and I have no doubt that he was hugely amused at watching me endure his ceaseless impositions.

In addition to this tedious duty of standing guard, I learned that Jor-Taq also expected me to be his listener. He was an extremely egotistical man, given to long and tedious monologues of profound self-absorption. I came to understand, over time, that much of his self-imposed isolation came from a powerful distaste for normal habits of conversation, where those involved insist on replying to what is said, and making their own points heard.

This was not for Jor-Taq. He had no interest in any opinions but his own, which he could expound on for long and tedious hours, without pause. I was most in awe at the inexhaustible energy he displayed, for the man could begin talking—usually about himself—early in the afternoon, and show no signs of letting up, even after all others had wearied from the day's tasks and had already been long abed.

So it was that my primary task, other than providing protection for his precious self against his many enemies (whom, I'd already concluded, were all self-inflicted), was simply to listen to the old man's self-absorbed musings, offering no reply, but only to nod my head in agreement to whatever came out of his mouth.

"They say you are a slow fellow, Grae-don," Jor-Taq once remarked. "But I don't know about that. I begin to think you're one of the brightest fellows I've met. You haven't once interrupted me with any irrelevant observations of your own, and I must say that I always find those intrusions into my own thoughts most disruptive."

In time, Jor-Taq slowly began to take me into his confidence. Perhaps it was my willingness to listen passively as he droned on, perhaps it was a creature need for company that even this grotesquely egotistical man could not ignore. Perhaps it was simply a pathological need for attention, from a stunted creature who could not bear to be alone.

I don't know. I don't care. Over time I came to despise Jor-Taq, but kept my feelings about him carefully hidden away behind a mask of imperturbable neutrality.

"They're jealous of me," he complained, time without number. "Jealous of my genius, for they know that I am bounds ahead of them all in everything I do! Jealous, do you hear me? They are jealous!"

"Of course, Jor-Taq," I always made my reply.

"That is right! I am now delving into things so profoundly metaphysical, so impenetrable... why it would take a man of normal intelligence a thousand years of constant study to even begin to comprehend the nature of the problems I am on the verge of breaking through. But these fools all waste their days in idle pleasure, seeking nothing more from the moment than to fill their faces with food and make themselves drunk on *Ga'la*."

(This was said toward the end of a four-hour meal the old man treated himself to as a reward for solving some particularly difficult problem. He poured himself out yet another tall goblet of *ellihi*, remarking to me, as he spilled it down his throat, "To my health!")

Now he was allowing me into his study, where he kept a huge accumulation of scrolls and papers, all of them covered with writing. The old man spent hours poring over these scrolls, as I stood nearby. Now he compelled me to hold a lamp behind his shoulder that the light should be just right for him to read by.

Jor-Taq enjoyed taunting me with what he thought was my illiteracy, and I quickly understood that this was the primary reason for his ordering me to stand with him in his study as he read.

"You don't know what these marks are, do you, Grae-don?" he teased, when he tired of reading. "All of them simply brown marks on paper that make patterns too complicated for your untutored eyes to decipher, eh? Ha, ha!"

"I am unschooled in these things, Jor-Taq," I said.

"Of course you are, you poor ignoramus. All you poor dolts are illiterate, and that is as it should be. We don't want you getting yourselves confused with all these ideas, do we?"

"Your will is mine, in all these matters, Jor-Taq," I answered.

"Of course it is, you uneducated boor. But how would it be if I were to teach you to read these marks? Would you like that?" he taunted.

"Whatever is your will, Jor-Taq."

"I don't think I will put myself to the trouble," Jor-Taq replied, in a manner that indicated that he expected me to feel disappointment. "I just don't think you have the intelligence to comprehend. Why, it takes great discipline of the eye to make it follow a line of script, did you know that, Grae-don? Do you think you could learn that discipline?"

"I do not know, Jor-Taq."

And then, each time, after amusing himself by so taunting me, the old man returned to his deep studies with a shrug.

"Enough diversion for now," he'd say. "I must return to my work. Hold that lamp steady and do not let it shake."

And the old man was completely unaware that as he studied over his scrolls, I was carefully and quietly reading over his shoulder. Most of what I read made no sense to me, for my skills in reading were at that time very rudimentary, and the texts were filled with many complicated and difficult marks, seeming to discuss matters of which I had no comprehension whatever.

I was able, however, to sound out the symbols in my head, and was greatly aided by the fact that when he was deep into reading, Jor-Taq fell into the unconscious habit of reading aloud.

So it was that, over time, I greatly increased my vocabulary, while at the same time deepened my understanding of this strange, strange world. Eventually, I think, I came to understand the subjects Jor-Taq studied as deeply as he claimed to understand them himself.

Of greatest interest to me were the geographies, with drawings in them he called `maps', purporting to be pictures of the world, all flattened out and rendered with lines to mark the places where land and sea met, depicting the islands of Pella'mir all in relation to each other. These maps were marked with words that gave the names of the various features shown upon them, and I was keen to learn as much as I could about the wider world beyond the walls of Jor-Taq's house.

But these geographies he only very rarely pulled from their stacks, and then usually only to confirm a point in his mind, before he rolled them up again and returned them to their shelves—so tantalizing! Only glimpses of world, so brief, yet so heavy with potential. What was beyond these walls? What lay out there, beyond Pella'mir? Beyond the shallow, golden sea, where I first awoke into this world?

The maps themselves depicted only the islands of Pella'mir, all surrounded by a vast ocean. To the south were hints of other islands, but these were marked out only roughly, without the detail of the Pella'mir islands, where every cove and outcropping of land was plainly delineated.

These other islands were only vaguely sketched in, with faint broad lines and legends that told me that nothing was known of these islands, aside from their name, *Boramok*, but that they must exist, for this is where the Brigands of Boramok launched from to make their periodic assaults against Pella'mir.

Once, when Jor-Taq was in one of his rare expansive moods, and my curiosity piqued by what I had seen on the maps, I asked him about the wider world. (He did not mind being asked questions, as long as they were not too pointed, or challenging, and related, in some way to his endless self-absorption. Instead, he seemed to enjoy what he perceived as flattery, that I would seek my wisdom from his great intellect.)

"What lies beyond the Great Sea?" I asked him, when his usual self-centered monologue had touched briefly upon the sea surrounding Pella'mir.

"Eh? What's that? Beyond the sea?" he replied, and it seemed to me, for an instant, that he was at a loss for an answer.

He seemed to stake his pride on his ability to answer any question put to him—whether the answer was true or not was irrelevant, so long as he was able to fill in the silence that followed a query with a volley of sounds that asserted his own superior knowledge.

Quickly recovering himself, he replied to my question with the kind of laughter we give to children when they reveal their ignorance with a guileless query.

"Ha, ha, ha! Beyond the Great Sea? Why, nothing, boy. Nothing at all. It is but the sea, rolling on, forever, in every direction. What a silly question. How could you not know something as very fundamental as that?"

"Nothing beyond the Great Sea?" I asked.

"How could there be anything else?" Jor-Taq demanded.

"No islands, like Pella'mir?"

"Oh, there may be other islands, far beyond our maps, but they are of poor account, small, insignificant things we need not countenance. Were they of any importance, we'd have heard of them, of course."

And, never one to miss an opportunity to put in a jab, Jor-Taq finished up by saying,

"It's just as well I've decided not to teach you how to read, or to write, Grae-don. I was just thinking, this morning, of trying the experiment, to see what you could possibly learn, but what if I should succeed? What then? I can't have you spreading your hopeless ignorance among the educated. Best that you keep your foolishness to yourself. A pity, really. I was thinking, at least, of teaching you how to write your name. Wouldn't that have been something for you to be proud of? But no, I think not. It's best you stick with what you do so well, and leave the difficult matters to better heads."

Jor-Taq's jibes meant nothing to me. I had come to doubt his intelligence, and was more and more convinced, especially in what I had learned by studying over his shoulder, that he was neither so educated nor so worldly-wise as he pleased himself to believe.

Now, how I knew it that he was wrong about the sea surrounding Pella'mir, I do not know. But however I did, I knew with certainty that Jor-Taq was wrong, dead wrong. It was not an endless sea surrounding the islands of Pella'mir, which the people who lived there were pleased to consider the entirety of the world. There were lands beyond the sea, and beyond those lands, other places, other worlds, even, that the people of Pella'mir were ignorant of.

And I craved to see those worlds, to walk through them, to touch them and to experience them with my own eyes, my own hands.

More than ever, I chafed at the close restrictions that Jor-Taq placed upon me. And though his endless jabs at me, his ceaseless, petty denigrations meant nothing to me, still they annoyed for their pettiness, and at last they came to irritate me. For as he grew more comfortable with me, so his selfish and egotistic monologues came to be more liberally peppered with the trifling jabs, meant to puncture and to deflate any self-assurance that may have grown within my breast, before it had a chance to come to full flowering.

I grew weary of his swollen pettiness. I decided that I would stay but long enough to make the most of my furtive opportunities to learn as much as I could from the library of Jor-Taq, and then, the first chance that came, I would quit this post and roam free in the wider world.

"Do you have any idea, the depth of my studies, Grae-don?" Jor-Taq demanded of me, one evening, after his protracted dinner, and he had sated his thirst with several goblets of *ellihi*. It had gone to his head, I could see, and he was in an expansive, chatty mood.

"I cannot, Jor-Taq," was my answer.

"Of course you cannot, Grae-don, for you are a fool. Oh, do not take my comment too deeply to heart, for all men are fools, and you are but one among them. You are somewhat less a fool than most, however—though your education is extremely rudimentary—for have you not stood at the shoulder of the great Jor-Taq himself, and had the benefit of his many wide-ranging ruminations upon life, the world, even the infinite cosmos itself?

"That is so, Jor-Taq," I answered.

"Yes, yes, it is so," he agreed with himself, wearing a smile of supreme and half-drunk self-satisfaction. "Most generous... most generous of me to share so much. Yet you have served me well, for a man cannot speak to the walls. Even one such as I, the great Jor-Taq, needs a human ear to hear, needs a fellow such as yourself, who will listen willingly, even if most of what I say is beyond your feeble comprehension."

"As it must be, Jor-Taq," I said.

"Yes, yes. And so it must be. Perhaps, Grae-don, if you prove yourself sufficiently... ah... discreet, I might allow you into my laboratory, where I carry out my most serious investigations. I could make use of an assistant, and that Horath has proven too bungling. Oh, he is good enough to carry a load, and to help me strap down a few of the more recalcitrant specimens, especially when they flail about. But for the more, let me call them 'delicate' tasks, he has proven particularly clumsy."

And here, Jor-Taq pierced me with a half-drunken glare.

"Do you think you could be such a man, Grae-don? Do you think you could assist me with the delicacy my difficult experiments require?"

"Only you can judge that, Jor-Taq," I answered.

"Ah! A most cunning reply, Grae-don! Most cunning! Ha! Admit it! You are burning with curiosity, aren't you? You are dying to know what I am up to in my laboratory! But you dare not admit your burning craving, lest you provoke me with your enthusiasm, and I send you away to starve, alone and unwanted, on the streets of Pella'mir. Isn't that the truth?"

Jor-Taq had made his yearnings clear with his questions. It was important to his egotism that I be consumed with curiosity about everything to do with him, and so I answered him, "You know me all too well, Jor-Taq."

"Yes! I do! And don't you ever forget that, Grae-don! I know your innermost heart! I know what you are thinking, even before you know it yourself. So never, ever seek to betray me, Grae-don, and I might, perhaps, let you into my inner-sanctum at last, and allow you to see for yourself the things that I have permitted no other, save Horath, to see. And that poor, stupid brute, is simply too witless to comprehend what I have been about."

"And what is it, Jor-Taq, if my curiosity is not an imposition, what is it that so exercises the mind of the great Jor-Taq?"

The old man replied to my flattery with a self-satisfied and gloating smile, while pouring himself yet another goblet of *ellihi*. The golden liquor spilled freely down the sides of his goblet, and onto the table itself.

He took a long swig, and then wiped his sloppy face with the back of his thin and bloodless hand.

"Beauty, my boy. Beauty!" he declared with a triumphant leer. "Beauty! All men crave it, all women desire it. All seek it, even the meanest and most brutish. Beauty arouses the deepest passions in all of us. From the poorest to the richest, the rudest among us, and the most noble—we all have a sense of it. We all seek to surround ourselves with it in beautiful women, beautiful men, beautiful flavors and dress, beautiful homes, beautiful experience. Why even you, I know, and those drunken sots who are my guards, you, too have a sense of the beautiful, and wish to make of your small existence something of beauty, in your own small and brutish ways.

"And yet there's not a man alive who can say what beauty is. What is this 'beauty'? What do we mean when we say a thing has it? Or does not? Nobody can say, because nobody knows. What do we mean when we call a thing beautiful? Is it the difference of single millimeter that makes a woman beautiful, or ugly? Is it the touch of a shade in the complexion? A subtlety in the manner that eludes definition?

"Yet all who crave this beauty do so blindly, stupidly, without intel-ligence! You do not care, do you, why she is beautiful? All that matters to you is that she is, and that is sufficient! Poor, stupid, craven crea-tures, driven by your blind impulses, never once questioning them, never once asking of yourselves, 'why?'.

"Ah!" he suddenly shouted, raising a finger to the air to make his point. "But I have! And I do! Every moment of my existence is devoted to this quest, to decide and to determine, once and forever, what we mean when we call a thing beautiful! I have not pondered this question weakly, like a poet, nor pandered to it, like a painter, who is satisfied to daub his pretty colors upon a wall, mindlessly selling his confections for the eye, oh, no!

"I have put the question to the most rigorous challenges. None of that silly sentimentality for me! I have stared hard upon this question, Grae-don. I have studied it cold-bloodedly, dispassionately, and have put it to experiment, yes! For no one has ever put the question as I have, as a scientist[1]. No one has put it to experiment. No one has ever thought to actually measure beauty, as I have done, and do.

---

1. Editor's note: I have used the word 'scientist' here, though there is no corresponding word in the world that that Paul Morgan (here called Grae-don) describes. Science, as we understand it, is quite unknown in this world, though clearly Jor-Taq is engaged in something very similar to it, if we understand science as an organized approach to knowledge based on structured observa-tion. However, also quite clearly, though Jor-Taq and others like him understand the use of some of the principles of observation, experiment, quantification and falsification, it seems, from Paul Morgan's descriptions, that other principles, mainly replication and verification, are considered by Jor-Taq and his fellows to be completely meaningless in their pursuits. A.G.

"Ah, Grae-don, my investigations have carried me far. I have had to do many things, things that the common run of man might think horrible. Repulsive, even."

Jor-Taq made that last remark with a cold glint in his eye. He grinned, and then downed another huge mouthful of *ellihi*.

"Yes," the old man said. "Yes. Many among my fellows would be repulsed at what I have done. Even I have, at times, trembled as my hand carried out my will. But it is needed, and all must make sacrifices for knowledge. Even my own sensitivities I have sacrificed at that altar.

"And it has all been well worth it, do you hear me?" Jor-Taq demanded. I saw that the old man was getting himself quite drunk now. I acknowledged him with a nod.

"Eh? What's that?" Jor-Taq insisted. "What's that, you say?"

"I hear you, Jor-Taq."

"Quite right, quite right," the old man muttered. He let his head drop, and he mumbled into his chest.

"I have done it," he rambled on. "Where others have been content merely to lust after it, I have taken its measure. I have defined it, pinned down its ineffable essence, and can calculate, gauge and compute it. Yes, I have!"

The old man's drunken ramblings began to irritate me. I did not know how I knew it, but again I knew that he was wrong. I knew that he was speaking like a fool, an old, obsessive fool who had devoted himself to a meaningless quest. Again, I did not know how I knew this. Even to this day, I don't know—but many times I find that I have an intuitive knowledge on matters I have never studied. From whence this knowledge comes, I cannot say. But on this occasion, used as I was to Jor-Taq's self-absorbed and self-deluded ramblings, I felt a deep resentment welling up from within me. I *knew* he was wrong. He was as wrong as a man could possibly be, and when he spoke of beauty, he was an ignoramus.

"It seems to me, Jor-Taq," I said to him, "That beauty is not the kind of thing you can measure. It seems to me that beauty is a quality, rather than a quantity. One cannot say, rightly, that beauty is a thing, that one can have more of, or less of. For beauty is an essence, not a thing. It is perhaps something you can describe. But I do not think Beauty is the kind of thing that you can define, or measure, or even give number to."

"*What?* What did you say to me?" Jor-Taq nearly screamed, rousing himself from his sodden half-stupor. "What did you say? Do you question me? The great Jor-Taq? I, who have studied things you can't even name?"

The man grew positively orange in a livid rage. He staggered to his feet, flailed his thin and bony arms into the air, and hurled his goblet filled with *ellihi* against the wall. It shattered.

"You, who can't even read, who does not even know how to sign his own name? You illiterate fool! Scum! *Koraph!* You moldering mound of *kra*! How dare you! How dare you speak to me like that!"

The old man ranted at me in this manner for several minutes, until he had exhausted his rage.

"Idiot," he finally said, wearying, his voice hoarse from shouting. "Idiot. What do I care for what you say, anyway? You are but a slave."

Then, waving me away, he said. "Leave me now. It is time for me to sleep, and I don't need you about."

And so I left him there in his apartment, now swigging his *ellihi* directly from the bottle, sucking at it greedily as a baby sucking at his mother's breast. Disgusted with the sight, I returned to my own quarters, and there, I turned over in my mind what Jor-Taq had said.

I felt a dread queasiness come over me, as I considered the implications of his words, the hints he had dropped, and the suggestions he had made. I did not think I wanted to assist him in his researches, and knew that I did not care to be made privy to the investigations he carried out in his laboratory.

Finally, drowsiness overcame me, and I slept unhappily for a few hours. Again, as it is every time I sleep, I dreamed myself trapped in a dead and wasted body, lying in a bed and wallowing in monotony. Wakefulness came to me not soon enough.

That following morning, Jor-Taq seemed to have forgotten his drunken rage of the night before. He said nothing to me of my impudence in questioning him, but I sensed a change in his manner, a sudden brusqueness that suggested to me that his monologue of the previous night had been more calculated than I had at first perceived. He'd been testing me, I sensed, probing my willingness to go along with him in some forbidden thing—his suggestion that I might make a better assistant to him in his laboratory than Horath came to my mind—and that I had failed his test.

If that was the case, then I was pleased, for I had no desire to assist Jor-Taq in his mad and meaningless quests, especially if his researches caused him to do things that—as he had put it himself—the common run of man might think horrible.

One other consequence of my failing Jor-Taq's test was that his demands upon me diminished. He suddenly seemed less interested in cultivating me as an intimate. He called me into his presence less frequently, and now he did not subject me to his endless, rambling monologues. This was, as you can imagine, a huge relief to me, but I suspect that, in his own mind, Jor-Taq was showing me that I had fallen out of favor, as I was no longer privileged to hear the deep ruminations of the great mind.

Nor did he allow me to hold the torch over his shoulder, as he read through his manuscripts in the evenings. This troubled me, as it meant that I was no longer able to continue my surreptitious learning, but that loss was quickly made up for by what I soon gained.

Now I had leisure to explore my own tiny quarters, and to venture into the hallways of Jor-Taq's great house, and to learn more of my immediate environment. My own quarters were but a single small room, with a tiny closet. I had never used the closet before this time, as I had only the two harnesses to wear that Jor-Taq had issued me, and no possessions of any kind whatever.

So, I had never really looked into the closet, except to give it a glance when I first made my quarters here. Now that Jor-Taq was alienating himself from me, I had more time to look about, and now I paid some attention to this closet. It was tiny, so small, in fact, that I could barely squeeze into it.

But near the floor, I noticed that a bit of molding seemed to have pulled away from the wall. Running my fingers along it, I quickly realized that the molding was flexible, and would pull away from the wall completely. I gripped it in my hands, and pulled, and saw that I had revealed a pocket behind the wall. Pulling further, I created an opening large enough to permit me to thrust my head and shoulders into it entirely. Now I saw that this opening led into a wide empty space beneath the floor of my quarters.

Pushing the molding back into the wall, I was elated. I had a space to secrete things into, if the need should ever arise—my own little hidden sanctum.

Privacy! At last! A place no one knew about, something about me that was not known to others. Before this instant, I had had no privacy at all, and did not even know that I had been craving it so intensely. But now that I had found a place where I could have it, suddenly the huge relief of it washed over me, and I found myself overcome with an astonishing sense of selfhood that I did not recall feeling ever before. My step was buoyant, and I felt my chin elevating as I walked.

And again, now that I could venture into the halls of the house of Jor-Taq, I quickly learned to find my way around. Inwardly and outwardly, I was growing.

Jor-Taq dwelt in the highest levels of his house, relegating his guards and servants to the lower floors. As my own quarters were an anteroom immediately outside the sumptuous apartments of Jor-Taq, I too, was housed within the upper floors.

Here there were few to take note of my comings and goings. Those servants who waited upon the person of Jor-Taq were not of sufficient position to challenge me. And the few guards and assassins who passed me in the halls saw that, as his personal guard, I still wore the crest of Jor-Taq on my harness, and so, in point of fact, I outranked them. Each, when they saw me, saluted me, and then hurried on—though in reality, my standing in the house of Jor-Taq was tentative, even more tentative than theirs, and I could find myself with my throat slit by any one of Jor-Taq's assassins whenever the whim struck the old man.

But, however tentative my position was or may have been, I took ample advantage of my new-found liberties to learn as much as I could, and quickly, too. Exploring widely, and walking boldly into empty apartments, I found many codices and parchments that the old man had left lying about. Some of these I carried back into my quarters, secreting them into my hiding place in the closet, perusing them late at night when I was sure that all had gone to sleep.

And so I lived—for how long, I cannot say, because I never saw the outdoors. Not even a single window permitted the world outside to intrude into Jor-Taq's private world, where he ruled supreme. But I learned much in that time, from the purloined parchments, and the stolen hours of study. Jor-Taq had accumulated a huge library. He did not notice that the manuscripts I had spirited away to my hiding-place were missing—at least, I never heard word from him or his servants that he was at all aware that they were gone. And I forged for myself a solid education from the far-ranging collection of written materials.

At odd moments, Jor-Taq sometimes called for me to escort him when he moved from his apartments to the lower levels of his house. At other times, he ordered me to stand guard outside his private laboratory, next to his own apartments, where none but he alone, and his most trusted servants, were ever permitted. There, he and Horath were closeted away, sometimes for hours at a time.

The walls were thick, and the doors were heavy, and I heard almost nothing through them. But occasionally a muffled sound came through the door, sometimes a clashing, as of things falling from a table. Sometimes it was a sound that could have been the wailing of some animal that Jor-Taq was submitting to his experiments—brief, and quickly stifled. I did not know what they meant, but the sounds sent chills through me, and I was always glad when that duty was over and I could get away from that laboratory.

4

AZORA OF TAAKBAR

O NE TIME, LATE OF an evening, as I was readying myself for the sleep I could not avoid, when the house was darkened and silent, and I was sure that Jor-Taq was asleep in his own apartments, I was roused by the sounds of a shuffling in the hallway outside my quarters.

Normally the house was silent at this late hour. Never before had I heard a noise at this time, when all were sleeping and the house was swathed in dead silence.

So I was suddenly alert to the strange shuffling outside my door. Mindful of my responsibilities as Jor-Taq's personal guard, even though I had fallen from his favor, I quickly roused myself from my sleeping blankets and dressed myself in my harness. Plucking my sword from its sheath, which I hung on a hook near my door, I leaned against the door, listening intently to the sounds without.

They grew closer, and I knew that someone was moving, probably in haste, and quickly testing the doors as he or she moved down the hall. Even through the heavy panel of my own door, I sensed the stifled panic of the person beyond.

Footsteps padded closer, scuffling against the hard floor, and then I felt the handle of my door turning in my hand. Whoever it was in the hallway had come to the entrance to my quarters.

I jerked the door open suddenly, my sword ready in my right hand, and found myself staring into the beautiful face of the girl I'd seen before, she who attended to Jor-Taq's dinner.

She stumbled backward upon seeing me, her blue eyes widened in terror. Her hand shot to her mouth.

"Huh!" she cried, in a stifled gasp of fear.

I saw that she was naked, a blood-stained bandage wrapped tightly about her forehead, and a leather strap dangling from her neck.

Backing against the further wall, she stared at me in silence for several long instants, then, seeing that I did her no harm, she stepped forward and whispered urgently, "Will you hide me? They are coming for me!"

"Who?" I demanded.

"Them! Jor-Taq and that horrid Horath."

Hearing that, I cast aside all doubt, and told her, "Come with me." I ushered her quickly into my own tiny quarters, and then hurried her toward the closet where I had found my secret hiding-place.

"One moment," I said, as I reached down to pull away the molding from the wall.

"Hurry," she urged me on in a voice husky with fear. "They are coming. I can hear them in the hallway."

"Down you go!" I answered. "In there."

Wasting not an instant with questions, she dropped down to her hands and knees and crawled quickly into the tiny crawlway. Hastily I closed up the wall behind her, checking to make sure that no seam or crack would give evidence of it having just been opened.

Then I removed my harness and returned to my sleeping blankets, lying down upon them so that, should either Jor-Taq or Horath appear, as the girl intimated they would, I could make the pretense that I had been asleep.

And well it was that I did, for no sooner had I lain down and pulled the blanket over me than did both of them come storming into my quarters. The first notice I had of their presence was Horath himself, who kicked in my door with his huge foot. Jor-Taq came squealing in rage behind him, frothing—literally frothing—with anger.

"Where is she?" he screamed. "Where?"

"What? What?" I answered, protecting my eyes from the lamps that they shined in my eyes.

"She came this way!" Jor-Taq frothed. "We saw her turn into this hallway! She cannot have gone anywhere but here!"

"Who?" I asked. "What are you talking about?"

"She... she..." Jor-Taq sputtered.

"One of our specimens has escaped," Horath explained, sneering at me with undisguised contempt. "She came this way. Where did you put her?"

"Your... specimens...?" I asked.

"Don't question me!" Jor-Taq screamed. "Turn her over to us, now! Or die! Do you hear me! Turn her over now, or die!"

"I don't know what you are talking about," I answered. "I have been sound asleep these many hours."

"Don't lie to me!" Jor-Taq shouted. "She cannot have gone anywhere else! Horath, go look in the closet! That is where she must be."

Horath strode quickly across the bare floor of my quarters, and opened the door to my closet with a jerk that nearly ripped it from its hinges.

It was empty.

Both Jor-Taq and Horath were crestfallen to find it so, except for my single spare harness, which hung from a hook on the wall.

"She... she's not there..." Horath stuttered.

"Look under his sleeping blankets," Jor-Taq sputtered. "She must be here. There is nowhere else she could have gone!"

I climbed out of my sleeping blankets quickly, as Horath jerked them out from under me.

"Nothing," he said, utterly defeated.

He had been sure I was hiding the girl, and was certain that Jor-Taq would order him to kill me on the spot. Carefully, I maintained a look of complete incomprehension as I stepped into my harness and tightened the belt around my waist.

"Do you always leave your sword on the floor next to you, as you sleep?' Jor-Taq asked me, suspicion growing in his voice, as he pointed to the weapon.

"Of course," I answered, perhaps rather acidly. "I never know when someone is going to come charging into my quarters with foul accusations, and threats of death."

Jor-Taq glared at me for a moment, but there was nothing he could say. My quarters were but a single room. They had no furnishings, except for the sleeping blankets, no desks or chairs or cubbyholes to hide anything. Jor-Taq himself had seen to that. There was, as far as Jor-Taq and Horath could tell, absolutely no place in my quarters where I could have hidden anything, not even a coin, and certainly nothing as obvious as a naked girl.

"One of my specimens has escaped," Jor-Taq explained, with tiresome redundancy. "Now that you are awake, Grae-don, you will assist us in our search for her. Come!" he snapped.

So I followed the two out into the hallway, and with them, I made a pretense of searching for this escaped 'specimen'. We tried all the doors along the hall, and every one was locked.

"Perhaps she locked the door behind her," I suggested at one point. Both Jor-Taq and Horath answered me with a rude grunt.

"These doors are always locked," Jor-Taq spat.

But after saying that, the old man sent Horath to his private apartments to fetch his keys, and we opened each door methodically, searching the rooms within.

We were many hours in this search, and I could tell by their remarks, and the occasional question thrown at me, that the two of them were still quite suspicious of me. Even so, a façade of ignorance is not difficult to maintain. One simply replies to every query with a blank look and a helpless shrug, and avoids the needless vanity of giving out hints of having some secret knowledge.

Jor-Taq and Horath were both, if not fooled by my façade, at least put off by it. Though they suspected me, I gave them nothing tangible upon which to hang their suspicions. And so it was, at last, many hours later, the girl not yet found, and both Horath and Jor-Taq stumbling with sleeplessness and exhaustion, they gave up the search and sent me back to my quarters.

I returned through darkened empty hallways, listening intently at my back, for I was sure that Horath, upon the whispered instructions of Jor-Taq, was following me. And indeed, the faint scuff of a sandal against the stone floor of a hall, far in the distance behind, came to my ear. Yes, Horath was following me. Yes, suspicion was still strong against me.

I made my way back to my own quarters, and stepped inside, making a huge pretense of complete guilelessness as I did. Then, closing the door, I waited, my ear pressed hard up against it. A moment later, my own suspicions were confirmed again, when I heard Horath's heavy breathing outside, and I felt the pressure of his own head pressed hard up against my door.

Quietly as I could, I removed my sandals and walked barefoot across the room, removed my harness, and lay down upon my sleeping blankets. My mind worried over the developments of this night. Horath at my door. A girl, hiding, naked, in the crawlspace below my quarters. What was I to do?

I waited silently in my quarters, listening for the soft pads of his feet that would tell me that Horath had given up his watch. It seemed forever. His heavy breath and the shadow of his form in the crack between the door and the floor gave him away—he was a very stupid brute, after all.

But at last he did give it up. I saw his shadow move away from the crack beneath the door, and the sound of his breathing diminish as he returned to his own sleeping quarters for what was left of the night.

Yet still I did not move for many long minutes, waiting, listening, for any clue that might prove I was yet under surveillance.

Nothing. Not a sound.

Finally, and carefully, I made my way to my tiny closet through the darkened room; not daring to light a lamp for fear the light would bring attention to me. With great and painstaking care, I slowly prized away the molding from the wall and whispered into the tiny cubbyhole, "Ssst!"

A shuffling in the dark, and presently I heard the girl make her way to the tiny portal, and felt her breath against my face. Like a blind man in the darkness, I groped with my hand until I felt her hair brushing against my fingers. I drew her close, and by feel, placed my lips to her ear.

"I think you are safe for now," I whispered to her. "Though Jor-Taq and Horath suspect I have hidden you away."

I felt her hair brushing against my cheek as she nodded in the darkness to indicate that she understood.

"But we must remain quiet," I explained. "For Horath stood outside my door for an hour after I returned, and he may come back, or Jor-Taq may send another to spy upon me."

Again her hair brushed against my cheek as she nodded her understanding.

I felt her hands searching for my face, and then finding it, she turned my ear toward her mouth.

"Horath is a beast," she whispered.

Now it was my turn to nod my understanding, and I smiled as I did so. This girl shared my opinion of the man.

"And Jor-Taq is a heap of *kra*," she added.

Again I nodded and smiled. Whoever this girl was, we agreed on that much.

"Are you hungry?" I asked her.

"Yes. I have not eaten since yesterday morning."

"Wait a moment," I said. I returned to my sleeping blankets and retrieved from there some rations that I had stored in my pouch; a bit of dried *fuma*, a few crusts of *stala*, and a flask filled with *ellihi* to wash it down with.

"It's not much," I told her, handing it off to her in the darkness. "But it is something."

"You are so kind," she said. "I am sure that this is plenty. But you are not going hungry yourself to provide this?"

"No. Not at all. I always keep something handy to eat. Jor-Taq feeds us all so little, I have learned to set some aside. Now eat this. There will be more when I can get it to you."

"Thank you," she replied.

"Can you sleep in there?" I asked. "Do you have enough space?"

"There's just enough space for me to turn around in and curl up. I can even sit up a bit. It is a trifle stuffy, though, but I can manage."

"I daren't leave an opening for the air to circulate. Jor-Taq would surely find your hiding place. But I will bring you a blanket, at least, to lie upon."

I brought her the blanket, which she pulled through the tiny opening, and she padded it against the floor of her cubby hole.

"We must both sleep now," I said. "The night is nearly done, and I have duty in the morning."

"Yes," she agreed. "Again, thank you. You are so very kind. I hope that I may repay your kindness someday."

"Think not upon it,' I answered. "I am only happy to be helpful."

And then I closed up the wall, returned to my sleeping blankets and threw myself upon them. In an instant I was asleep.

I took my breakfast, as usual, in the eating room that Jor-Taq had assigned to his assassins, and to me, his personal guard. We ate separately from the house guard who lived and ate on the first floors of the building.

This morning, I noted, several of the assassins eyed me with great suspicion, and the cooks who served out our morning food carefully avoided my eyes.

Horath, on the other hand, was in a great good mood, and if the others had not put me on my guard by their behavior, Horath most certainly would have by his loud joviality.

"Ah! Grae-don!" he shouted as I entered the dining hall. "You arrive! Come! Fill your plate and join us here!"

Never before had Horath invited me to share his table. Instantly I was filled with suspicion. I did, however, as he bade, and carried my platter with me to the table he shared with three assassins.

"Sit! Sit!" he demanded, in unnaturally high spirits. "We have been too long at each other's throats," he said. "Perhaps we should put our animosity away and be friends."

I hid my distrust of the man behind a façade of affability.

"Certainly," I replied. "A man needs all the friends he may find."

"Well said! Well said, Grae-don!" Horath answered, with a laugh. "We did have a night of it last night... or this morning, as I should say. I was telling my friends here of our search."

"For the girl, you said," I answered.

"Yes... she vanished as rightly as anyone ever did, and I'll be damned if I know how she did it."

"So you haven't found her yet?" I asked.

"Jor-Taq thinks you are hiding her," Horath said, chuckling.

He elbowed me and gave me a wink. "Couldn't say I would blame you if you were, though I don't know how you managed it. She's a ripe one, all right. Would have liked her for myself, but Jor-Taq insisted. He would have her for his researches."

"Um," I grunted, noncommittally.

"Well, I'll say, if you have hidden her away, and kept her for yourself, I wouldn't be the one to blame you for it," Horath said, with a laughing leer. "Would have been a damned shame to squander a girl like that for Jor-Taq's research. So if you have put her away somewhere, you can be sure, Jor-Taq won't be finding it out from us."

So that was it.

That was the reason behind Horath's sudden pretense of camaraderie. He was clumsy and obvious.

"I don't even know which girl it was," I said. "There seem to be a number of them here. But if you say she was pretty, I'll take your word for it."

"Pretty isn't the word for a girl like her. She's a rare one, all right, with yellow hair, like yours." Horath replied. "And her eyes are blue. Something I've never seen before, blue eyes. She served Jor-Taq his meals, you must have seen her, then."

"Ah!" I answered, pretending a sudden recollection. "The little one, with her hair cut short about her head, and curly."

"So you did notice," Horath said.

"Who could not?" I asked. "And she is the one we were searching for this morning?"

"No less. If you haven't got her holed up somewhere," he winked at me, "We'll find her."

"Perhaps she has found a way out of the house of Jor-Taq," I suggested.

"No," Horath said, shaking his head with certainty. "There is but the single entrance into the house, and but the single portal through the wall. She is still within, but where, we do not yet know. It is only a matter of time, though. We shall find her. And when we do..." Horath laughed loudly.

"Yes?" I asked.

"Jor-Taq has promised her to the man who finds her. And then, when he is done with her, she will become Jor-Taq's specimen again. I must say, though," Horath went on in a more serious tone, "That

Jor-Taq is most agitated over her disappearance. He is most jealous of his investigations."

I was finished with my meal. With Jor-Taq and his assassins watching me keenly, I did not dare to secrete any food in my pouch that morning. Rising, I said, "It has been good chatting, but I must be off."

"So soon?" Horath demanded.

"I have my duties," I answered.

"Remember, Grae-don, Jor-Taq has promised the girl to whoever finds her. That means you, too, you know."

"Then I shall keep my eyes open, you may be sure," I answered.

I returned to my quarters, with an ear open, to hear if I were being followed. No one did follow me, but I knew from Horath's clumsy interrogation that Jor-Taq's suspicions centered wholly upon me. He would keep a keen eye upon my comings and goings.

Quickly I went to my tiny closet and once again opened the molding near the floor.

I saw her expectant face at the portal.

"I think it is safe for you to come out for a moment," I said to her. "It must be very cramped for you in there."

"Yes, it is," she replied. She crawled gratefully out of the cubbyhole and stretched her sore limbs.

"I have little for you to eat this morning," I said. "Horath and his thugs were in the dining hall. They were watching me closely. They suspect I had something to do with your disappearance."

"That is no matter," the girl replied. "I am not hungry now. And I will not be here long."

"Who are you?" I asked her.

"I am Azora, of Taakbar," she said.

Taakbar. I knew that place from the maps and parchments I had surreptitiously studied. It was an island, far to the west, one of the few outside the archipelago of Pella'mir to be marked on the maps I had found in the house of Jor-Taq.

"They call me Grae-don," I replied.

"Yes," she answered. "I know. You are Jor-Taq's personal body-guard."

"And you trust me to hide you from him?"

"I had nowhere else to go. All the doors were locked. Besides, everyone knows you have no love for Jor-Taq."

"Have I been that obvious?"

"No, but Jor-Taq has. He speaks poorly of you, when you are not about. Of course, he speaks poorly of everyone. We have all heard his drunken harangues."

"Hum!" I replied. "So I am not the only one he has treated to his long-winded dissertations."

"Oh, do not think you are special, by any means," Azora laughed. "He will talk the ear off anybody who cannot escape him."

"But how do you plan to leave the house of Jor-Taq?" I asked. "There is but a single doorway out of here, which is constantly guarded."

"I don't know," Azora answered.

"You haven't even any clothing to wear," I said.

"I left Jor-Taq's laboratory rather in a hurry, and did not have time to grab up my harness," she answered.

"What happened there? What are these researches that he is so proud of?"

"Horrible," Azora answered. "They are horrible. He is horrible. He... he and that loathsome Horath... I think they hate beautiful things... he keeps going on..."

And then she stopped speaking.

"What?" I prodded.

"There were three of us there. I was but one. He called me away after I cleaned up his dinner this evening past. The man was quite drunk, and had been staring at me all the time I cleaned up his dinner plates."

"'I think it is time,' he said to me, "'That I take you into my laboratory.'"

Azora shuddered.

"'I'll have another girl attend to my dinner,' he said."

And then Azora shuddered again.

"He told me that he had been making quite a study of me, and had finally decided which way his investigation upon my person should go."

"This is all…" I began.

Without a word, Azora unwrapped the bloodstained bandage from her head.

I started with horror when I saw the long thin wound that had been cut about her forehead, just below the hairline.

"Jor-Taq did that?" I asked.

"Yes, he did," Azora said, simply.

I had long since learned to dislike Jor-Taq, and Horath, as well. But at that moment there was born in my heart a hatred that raged against them both. Beauty is a sacred thing. That they should seek to foul it with their impure hands… I saw a mist of blood-red anger welling before my eyes.

I looked at the wound closely, touching it gingerly with my fingertips. Azora winced, but she made no complaint.

"It will heal, I think," I said. "Nor will it leave much of a scar."

"No?"

"No, it is not deep. You were but lightly cut."

"He thinks himself an *artist*," Azora said, with a sneer upon her lips. "And uses his scalpel, he says, as an artist does his pen."

"'Just lightly, just lightly,'" Azora said, pursing her lips and imitating the old man's nasal voice. "'Just a light, preliminary sketch, before we begin our final work.'"

"'How soon can we make this one ugly?' he remarked to Horath, as he cut into my skin. Oh, it was horrible. Horrible. The pain was searing, and they both leaned over me as Jor-Taq cut. I kicked and I flailed, and at last I broke the strap that they bound my arms with. Horath quickly grabbed my arms and pinned them down, because Jor-Taq, once he got started, could not be interrupted.

"But I managed to break free. I fought and kicked, and don't know how I did it, but somehow in my frantic flailing I managed to put my foot squarely in Horath's loathsome face. He broke away and let loose of my arms. I punched Jor-Taq, and he fell back, squealing like a scared *koraph*, then I grabbed his scalpel from his hand, jumped from the table, and slashed him in the thigh with it.

"While they were both staggering about, I rushed out of their filthy laboratory, and slammed the doors behind me.

"Jor-Taq had a bundle of swaths on a cart next to the table where he and Horath had tied me down. I grabbed one up quickly before I fled, and outside, in the hall, I tied it around my head so the blood would not drip on the floor and give me away.

"Then they came after me and I ran and ran through the halls, silently as I could. I hid once behind a wall hanging, unmoving, as they rushed by, just inches away.

"Then I came down this way, testing every door I passed, looking for any place where I might hide. I heard them coming back for me, and was ready to give it all up when you suddenly pulled your door open.

"Oh! I was scared. I thought I was caught, and that you would turn me over to Jor-Taq, but when you did not call out, I was heartened."

"No," I answered. "I would not turn you over to Jor-Taq. Neither before, when I did not know the depths of his depravity, and certainly not now, that I do."

And on that instant, I made a sudden decision.

"However we shall do it, we shall leave this place together. Jor-Taq sickens me. Horath appalls me. This whole house disgusts me."

"And how shall we do it? Escape?" Azora asked.

"I don't know," I replied. "But we shall! First we must find you some clothing. I have a spare harness, but do not think it would fit you."

"Perhaps I can make it fit," she said. "I am good with a knife and stitching."

"There are the sleeping blankets, as well," I added. "Perhaps with the leather from my harness and a bit of fabric from the blankets, you can make something that will suit you well.

"Here," I said, handing over one of my knives to her, along with my spare harness. "See what you can do with these."

At that moment, there came a loud pounding at my door.

Azora and I cast each other a quick look. No time for her to hide her in the cubbyhole. With a speed that astonished me, Azora dashed into the pile of my sleeping blankets, and pulled them over her in such a manner that no one could have guessed that they hid anything, or anyone, beneath. It certainly helped that Azora was of such a petite stature. I could not have hidden myself so cunningly, or quickly, in that pile.

The door to my quarters burst suddenly open, and there was Horath, grinning broadly.

"Come, Grae-don!" he bellowed. "The search for the girl continues, and Jor-Taq says we are not to rest until she is found."

"Yes," I answered, heart pounding. Behind him were three of his thugs. Had he, or they, seen Azora dart under the blankets? Not one of them gave my blankets a second glance. No. They had not seen. They lacked the intelligence to be duplicitous. If they had seen her, they would have taken her at that moment.

So I left my quarters with Horath and his thugs, the assassins, making a huge pretense of searching the house of Jor-Taq, room by room. We were at it all that morning, and late into the afternoon, forgoing lunch, and taking no rest breaks. Still, though we had minutely searched dozens of rooms, and all four of the top floors of Jor-Taq's house, upturning furniture, flinging open closets, cutting open chairs and divans, yet we found no clue of the girl's whereabouts.

Horath was becoming angry at the failure, and his thugs, quite sullen. They'd missed their lunch, and were well on their way to missing their dinner, as well. Yet Jor-Taq had demanded that we should search until we found her, and put aside all else.

It looked to be a long night. We still had a hundred or more rooms to search, and five more floors, not including the basements and sub-basements.

"Damn that girl!" Horath bellowed.

At that very moment, the house of Jor-Taq shook with huge explosions.

Loud concussions and blasts of angry detonations came from beyond the walls. The floor shook under me, and an enormous crack ran suddenly up the wall.

"What...?" I gasped, astonished.

"Brigands!" Horath shouted. "The brigands are come!"

"Bri...?" I began to ask, but none were near to answer me. All had rushed off with Horath, down the hallways and the stairs, to what purpose, I did not know.

Left alone, I hurried back to my own quarters, even as the house of Jor-Taq quaked under my feet. Blocks fell from the ceiling before me, and I scrambled over them, even as the walls trembled.

One time the force of the concussions knocked me off my feet, and another time, I slid down a stone stairway, even as it rolled and rumbled under me. But finally, I made my way to the uppermost floor of Jor-Taq's house, to where my quarters were.

The door was broken, hanging from its bolts, and the ceiling overhead weaved and bobbed wildly. I was filled with dread that Azora may already have fled, or worse, have been recaptured by Jor-Taq.

My fears were instantly put to rest though, when I saw Azora sit up instantly to greet me. She wore a thong about her waist that she had fabricated from my spare harness, and a bit of fur from my sleeping blanket. She'd slipped the knife I had loaned her for the purpose into a sheath that she stitched into the leather thong, and had also managed to make a pair of flat sandals for her feet.

Of course, I did not have time to take in all those details at that instant, but only noted that she now was clothed and ready to take on the next challenge.

Azora ran quickly across the room and threw her arms around my neck. I felt her breasts against my naked chest, as she whispered, "I was so afraid."

"Let us go, now," I said to her.

"Yes. We must. The brigands are attacking, and we must take advantage of the confusion."

Saying no more, I took her by the hand, and led her down through several floors. We met no one along the way, as all Jor-Taq's retinue of servants had fled the building out into the yard, while his guards and assassins had moved to the roof of the building, from where they launched their counterattack against these brigands.

In a brief moment of lull, in both our escape and the attacks, I asked Azora, "The brigands? Who are they?"

"Of Boramok..." she answered, catching her breath. "They come for loot and slaves..."

Instantly I understood. Shala had first told me of them, and I had read more of the brigands of Boramok in the parchments of Jor-Taq. They come to Pella'mir, like farmers who harvest their fields, once or twice a year, shimming the islands of fabric and gems and slaves, then allowing Pella'mir to heal and regrow for a period, before they come again.

The brigands attacked by bringing their flat-bottomed ships close to shore. They launched missiles from huge catapults in the bows of their ships at the walls of Pella'mir, missiles that exploded in flame when they landed. When they'd brought sufficient chaos to the city, they deployed from their ships on long planks, rushed into the city and grabbed up all they could get, before the various guards of the great houses of Pella'mir charged upon them and drove them back into the sea.

These sorties were always very short and opportunistic, and for us, this one had come at a very good moment.

The brigands' missiles were landing very close to the house of Jor-Taq, causing huge confusion within. Azora and I made our way downward, with a hazy notion of reaching the ground floor, to see what we could do from there. As we were fleeing, one of these missiles struck the side of the building itself, blowing a hole into the wall just before us, and leaving it a heap of rubble spilling out into the yard.

We were three stories from the ground, and smoking wreckage was piled to a point ten feet below us. It would be a drop, but without a word, Azora and I both made our way through the dust and ruin. She shimmied over the side of the gaping hole in the wall, hanging by her hands. And then, lying myself upon the floor, and reaching over, I took her hands and let her slip further down. With the extra three feet my arms gave her, she found a bit of footing.

"I can do it from here," she said, and she slipped from my grasp.

Then I swung my legs over the edge of the broken floor, and hung from the wall, my feet slipping, searching for the toehold that Azora had found.

I felt her grasp my ankle with her hands, and direct my foot until my toe came into contact with a deep gouge in the stone wall. And from there it was but an instant before we both stood side by side, examining the ruin before us.

The rubble upon which we stood had fallen against the wall that surrounded the house of Jor-Taq, and had broken through it, revealing a wide gap.

Again, without wasting a moment in unneeded talk or explanation, we both made our way straight to the broken gap, even as the fireballs from the brigands' ships were landing about us.

We fled the house of Jor-Taq, giving no heed to where we were going, thinking only that we should put as much distance between ourselves and that loathsome house as we could.

We ran far into the descending streets, losing ourselves well. Turn after turn we took, fleeing blindly into the darkness, and making as circuitous a retreat as we could. All the while the city shook with constant explosions and blasts all around us.

We came at last upon a closed and narrow alleyway, when suddenly the assault from the brigands ceased.

The silence that abruptly followed was as shocking to us as the chaos that reigned as the bombardment was happening. We both stopped in our tracks, panting heavily from our exertion, and looked at each other. Azora's breasts heaved as she took in huge breaths of air and her eyes shined with excitement.

She smiled at me.

"We did it!" she exclaimed. "I can't believe it! We did it! We're free!"

"Yes," I agreed, rather dazed, and savoring the realization as it sank in. "We're free."

Freedom! It intoxicated us. After so many months trapped within the suffocating confines of Jor-Taq's house, the free air, crisp and cold, exhilarated us. It cut through our throats as we filled our lungs with it. A scent of sweet cinnamon, and dizzying delight.

"We were lucky," Azora declared, still breathing heavily, and leaning against me with her hand upon my arm. "Never before have the missiles of the brigands reached so high. Never have they struck the house of Jor-Taq. He must be quite upset. Ha, ha!"

"I certainly hope so," I replied. "Hopefully he will be too busy cleaning up the mess to concern himself with us."

"Don't count on that," Azora replied. "He's a mean and vindictive person, and he has his spies in Pella'mir. He'll have them looking out for us, you can be sure of that. But it may be a few days before he can find them. With luck, they've been killed in the bombardment. They'll certainly be licking their own wounds for a while."

"In any case, we must avoid them, if we can," I replied. "I don't think Jor-Taq will be kind to us, if he should get us in his clutches once again."

"Oh, no, he won't. But he won't catch us. Come," she said, grasping me by the hand. "Pella'mir is big. And we're small enough. If we're smart, we'll find someplace to hide out until we've made some plans."

"Perhaps we can return you to Taakbar," I suggested.

"No," Azora resolutely shook her head. "I can't go back there, and I don't want to."

"Isn't Taakbar your home?"

"No more than Pella'mir is yours," she answered curtly.

And then, to change the subject, she pulled me down the darkening street. Azora, I noted, was very muscular, and very strong for her elfin frame.

The sun was just setting, and the glorious night sprang forth. Brilliant stars lit up the sky, and the beacons of Pella'mir began to shine.

This had been a particularly vicious assault by the brigands, Azora informed me as we moved past numerous heaps of rubble, and the crowds emerging from their shelters. Well used to these assaults, the people of Pella'mir were already industriously going about the business of cleaning up and rebuilding.

"They'll have it all back to normal in just a few days," Azora explained. "The brigands never want to do *too* much damage. They always want to leave something left over for their next attack."

"Most prudent of them," I remarked.

Azora laughed. I noticed this of her, that she laughed often and easily, and her laughter was bright and pleasing. It made me smile to hear her laugh, and heartened me.

"I must say, you are very cheerful, for all you've been through," I remarked.

She shrugged her shoulders and gave her hair a toss.

"The bad times are over now, and that makes me happy," she answered.

I took notice of the streets around me, lit by the lights of the city, and the brilliantly luminous leaves of the plants that grew in wild profusion here. Lavender and viridian, gold dancing upon the pavements and silvery shadows that shimmered as the tall luscious plants weaved and bobbed in the brisk night air.

All the people engaged in cleaning up after the bombardment seemed to me most incongruously cheerful—they simply set themselves about their tasks, without complaint, without, even, remarking that there might be anything particularly onerous about these repeated assaults.

I mentioned as much to Azora as we moved further down into the heart of the city.

"Oh, it's never so bad up here, higher away from the shore," she answered. "The brigands never get too far into the city, but only take their capture from the streets closest to their ships, so that they may make a quick getaway. It's down at the bottom of the city where they get it the worst. Up here, it's usually only a few missiles lobbed at them, taking out a few walls and starting a few fires here and there. As I said, this was a very unusual bombardment. I've never seen them hit so high or so hard before."

"Still, it seems to be a most oppressive way to live," I remarked.

"But this is as it always has been," Azora answered. The people of Pella'mir don't know any differently. And I have no love for them or their precious city, so I can't say that I grieve for them. Serves them right, that's what I say."

"And how did you come to be here?" I asked. "This is far from Taakbar."

Azora gave her shapely shoulders an exaggerated shrug.

"Oh, it's a tiresome story."

"Tiresome?" I asked.

"Taakbar is not my home. I was sold there to a farmer in Taakbar when I was too young to remember. I don't remember my mother or my father, only the farmer, and he was a *koraph*. So were his sons," she said. "The farmer kept me on for a few years, working in the house and the sheds, cleaning, and such. Then his sons started pestering me. One of them got too familiar," she said, her face turning furiously red at the memory. "So I slipped a blade into his belly. He lived, but he has a nice scar to remember me by," Azora declared, her eyes flashing.

"Good for you," I said.

She looked at me with surprise.

"You don't blame me?"

"Why would I?" I asked.

"I belonged to that farmer. He owned me, and by rights, he could do with me whatever he wanted. And his sons, too."

"That's repulsive," I said, with disgust showing on my face.

Azora smiled into my eyes.

"I like you," she said.

"I like you, too," I replied, feeling a strange thrilling warmth in my belly. I liked the sensation, and continued looking into Azora's happy blue eyes to prolong it as long as I could.

Finally recalling myself to our circumstances, I looked away, down the street, and said, "We should move on. We are still much too close to the house of Jor-Taq."

"Yes," Azora agreed. "We should."

We moved on down through the darkened, winding streets lined with luminous plants. Pella'mir is a large and sprawling city, with many tiny byways and alleys leading through countless boroughs. Some are rich, and the houses are lavish and sumptuous, with many lights and balconies.

Here, in these wealthy neighborhoods, the people dress in sumptuous garb and ostentatious jewels, wearing their hair in ornate headdresses that sparkle with ornaments and tiaras. The women are always accompanied by a retinue of servants, and the men wear swords of precious metals encrusted with gems.

In the poorer districts, the houses are more modest, built, sometimes, one atop another, with long stairways wrapping about the buildings and leading down into the street. The people here dress more functionally, with harnesses of plain leather showing much use, though even here, the people take great pride in their appearance. They are all quite muscular, with strong chests and bodies well-adapted to work, and they bathe every day in the open-air canals that wind through every street.

Azora and I trudged on for many hours through the winding streets. Lavender light from the luminous plants that swayed overhead, brilliant lemon beams that shoot through the windows, dancing upon the pavement at our feet.

We did not feel the exertion, and even when the night was long-drawn, we were still exhilarated to be free. We moved quickly through the crowds and the hubbub of the markets we passed through, musicians filling the air with the melodies of their instruments.

But as the night progressed, we grew hungry, and we knew that we must eat, somehow.

"There was that, at least," I remarked. "We did have food at the house of Jor-Taq."

"Oh, we can do much better, fending for our own selves," Azora said.

"But how?" I asked. "Jor-Taq did not pay me. I have no coin to make purchase with."

"I can dance!" Azora said. And instantly she took up a spot next to the table of a seller of fruit, across the avenue from where a trio of musicians made their music. Without a word, she began to move to the music, which was a very lively tune, and her body moved in perfect harmony with it. She kicked and spun, and leaped, throwing her arms and elbows into the music with an abandon that was most contagious.

I was astonished to see this new talent from Azora, and must confess that her almost liquid movement was very pleasing to the eye. As I watched her dance, I felt the impulse to join her, even though I knew nothing about it.

The musicians across the avenue, playing on their instruments of string and wind, saw Azora dancing to their tune. They nodded to her, and picked up the pace, playing faster now than before, and louder.

Soon a crowd had gathered round to watch Azora dancing, and several of them began moving in motion with the music themselves, clapping their hands and goading Azora to even more elaborate moves. She kicked high and higher, leaping and spinning in the air, and now her body began to burn in the lights with warm perspiration. She glowed. She was absolutely radiant, and she moved now so quickly that I found it almost impossible to follow her with my eye.

The music and her dance built to a wild crescendo, and then, at last, it suddenly ceased, with a wild explosion of applause from the crowd that had gathered. All who watched cheered, and I heard many compliments shouted from the throng. Many of them opened their purses and tossed handfuls of coins upon Azora, which, she explained to me a little later, was the custom in Pella'mir. Flushed with her exertion, and looking more beautiful now than I had ever seen her before, Azora smiled her thanks as she was showered with coins that sparkled and gleamed as they fell upon her.

Then she bent down to begin picking them up, gesturing to me to come and assist her, which I did. And as we went about our business of gathering up our new wealth, the crowd that had gathered moved elsewhere into the night, seeking out new entertainment.

"We did very well," Azora said, gathering the coins into a pile on the street with wide sweeps of her arms.

"You did," I replied. "You did all the work."

"We did," she insisted. "If not for you, I'd be lying on Jor-Taq's table right now, with the flesh of my face tacked on the wall."

A shadow must have crossed my own face as I recalled the horrible experiments of Jor-Taq, for Azora quickly said, "Forget it. We're free. And now we're rich, too!"

"The people of Pella'mir are most generous," I remarked, eyeing the pile of coins between us. "But how shall we carry all this?"

"You wait here, and I shall go over to that stall and buy a purse," she answered, pointing to one with a wide awning and golden lamps that shined. "I see a particularly nice one hanging from a pole."

And she hurried across the way, purchasing the purse, which was a leather pouch that she could fix to her harness, and then she quickly returned. We filled the pouch until it was nearly bursting, and still we had coins that we could not carry.

"What shall we do with these?" I asked.

Azora shrugged. "Leave them," she said. "If they don't want to come with us, they can stay right there."

"We may need them, someday."

"Coins are easy to get," Azora replied. "Didn't you see that? The people of Pella'mir are foolish with their money, and spill it like a drunken man spilling his drink. When we run out of these, we'll get more in the same way. Besides, we're not going to be in Pella'mir long enough to spend all this anyway."

"But where shall we go?" I asked.

"I don't know," Azora confessed. "Just away. There must be some place in the world where two orphans can find a place to live in peace. But it is surely not here in Pella'mir.

"But for now," she added. "We must eat!"

She led me away to a place where food was cooked and served. Everything was new to me. I felt myself still a stranger in this city, and I peppered Azora with questions, for none of these customs had I learned at the house of Jor-Taq. All of my meals, save for those I took with Shala and Haia during my first days here, I took alone, standing guard outside Jor-Taq's apartments, or in the vast eating hall where Jor-Taq's guards and slaves ate.

There, we took our trays to the cooks, who ladled out our portions of food from their cooking pots with huge spoons. The surly cooks made a game of splattering the food upon our trays so that it splashed and spilled on us.

But here, in this eating place, instead of going to surly cooks at the kitchen, we sat at a table, and servers came to us, pushing large carts up to us where we lounged, half-reclining on cushioned divans. The carts the servers brought to us were laden with many foods on small plates and Azora explained to me—once she saw I did not know what to do—that I was to take what I pleased.

These servers made the rounds of this eating place continually, and every few moments another server came up to us with a cart laden with different kinds of foods. One server brought us plates filled with what was to me an astonishing variety of *stala*—coarse and fine, brown and yellow, some with seeds, and some toasted lightly. Another server brought us a cart filled with bowls, all brimming with soups and broths.

Yet another brought us many kinds of meats, most of which I had never seen before. Some were spiced, some were baked in *ga'la*, some were roasted, and some were charred. One bit of flesh meat I found particularly tasty was completely uncooked, and after it was dipped in a sour broth, which the server provided, it was to be eaten raw. The broth was very tangy and burned my tongue, but I found the sensation most appealing.

Other servers brought us drinks, and others, many kinds of marinated fruits served up in glass goblets, and yet others brought us pastries of many kinds, as well as nuts and a certain kind of treat made with ice and *ellihi*.

It was all a most delightful experience for me. The food was exotic to my eye and palate, a welcome change from the drab fare I endured at the house of Jor-Taq. The eating house itself was sumptuous, with many splendorous things and colors to appeal to the eye.

And Azora was, I found, most delightful company. She delighted in talking, which suited me well, for I had little, myself, to say, and was content simply to listen to the sparkling babble of her voice.

I asked her, at one point, "How was it that you made it here, to Pella'mir, from Taakbar?"

"Oh," she answered breezily, with a pretty wave of her hand. "There's not much to the story. After I stabbed the farmer's son, I hid in the hills of Taakbar for a time. It is a small island, but with many wild places in it, where a fugitive can stay hidden away, if she knows how to take care of herself.

"But at last, I missed sleeping indoors, where the wild beasts may not find me. And since I had stabbed the farmer's son, Taakbar was not a safe place for me, outside the wild hillsides. So, on a night, I snuck aboard on a trading ship that harbored there, secreting myself, and not knowing where it would take me.

"It took me here, to Pella'mir, and I easily slipped away when it was docked, and tried for some time to make my way in this city. It was hard. I danced in the streets for my daily food, but making a home here was another, and more difficult, matter. One must have a sponsor to purchase property here. Though the people of Pella'mir are friendly enough, superficially, they do not warm to strangers, and for those who come from without, who are not born of Pella'mir, life can be very hard, indeed.

"At last, one of Jor-Taq's agents spoke to me on the street, and he offered me employment, and, if I accepted that, the sponsorship of Jor-Taq. And, with that lie, told me through his agent, Jor-Taq captured another slave for himself. I served Jor-Taq's table for, I don't know how long.

"That moment I saw you there, when Horath brought you to Jor-Taq's table," she said, with a sudden heartfelt look that pierced my heart through the dim light of the dining room, "That very moment, when my eye first fell upon you, I felt as if I found through you a path to my own freedom. And then..."

She paused. Her voice fell silent, and she blushed at me through lowered eyelids.

"We are free now," I said, filling the silence that had fallen between us.

"Yes," she replied, a sudden smile lighting her face. "We are free!"

We tumbled the coins from Azora's purse and played with them upon the table while we spoke. I was most interested in them, for they came in a wide assortment of shapes and colors and sizes. Some were round and flat, others, shaped like ovals, yet other were square, or had six edges, or eight, or nine. Some were spheres and pearly, others, were lozenges, or cubes. Some were golden, some were silvery, turquoise, onyx, green and opalescent. Some were transparent, all were brightly colored, metal, stone, even gilded wood.

At last I asked Azora about these coins.

"There are so many, and of so many kinds. How can one possibly keep track of the value of them all?"

"Each house makes its own coin," Azora explained to me. "There are twelve or maybe eighteen great houses in Pella'mir, depending on how you count them, each house ruled by a family. Jor-Taq rules over one of them. He is the last of his family, and he has squandered his inheritance, choosing to live alone in selfishness than to produce an heir. So he has none who are vested in his survival. We are done with him now, and when he dies there will be a fight among the families to take over what is left of his ruined empire.

"Each house, each family," Azora explained, waxing to her subject, "controls one or several neighborhoods, or boroughs, within Pella'mir. All of Pella'mir is ruled by these competing families. They are ancient. They fight continuously among themselves, sometimes enlisting the people to serve them in their internecine wars.

"For those who are not born into the great families, security is bought by seeking their sponsorship.

"And the great families, as I say, each one issues its own currency to those they sponsor. In exchange for the currency, the citizens of Pella'mir offer their service, either in providing goods—food and clothing, and the like—or open service, as Horath has done with Jor-Taq, in labor, or as guards, or assassins, or spies, against the competing families.

"It all works out well enough, I suppose," Azora said at last. "Though the people of Pella'mir bicker often, and often fight amongst themselves, neither the bickering, nor the fighting, grows to such a

magnitude as to threaten the overall tranquility of the city, and most
live in peace."

We stayed there at that eating place for many hours, tasting many
foods, the names of most I have forgotten, and drinking a variety of
fermented drinks that made us both quite tipsy. And we chattered and
talked, and enjoyed ourselves through the night.

When we left that place, I don't really recall—everything came to
be something of a blur of color and sounds. But at last we did leave,
late in the night, unsteady on our feet, and, with no place in particular
to go, we simply wandered through the streets of Pella'mir, each of us
leaning upon the other, until we were both footsore and weary.

Azora and I finally found a place to rest, upon a stone bench that
was tucked in a niche under the faint luminous viridian light of the
languorous leaves of a *fuma* tree.

Our feet were sore, and our bodies ached. My head was fuzzy with
fermented drink and night air, and I sat upon the bench, grateful it was
there, letting my legs sprawl on the stone pavement before me. Azora
crawled onto the bench and laid her head upon my lap. Encircling my
waist with her arms, she promptly fell to sleep.

I looked down upon the head of the sleeping girl, who was so quick
to put her trust in me, so quick to let herself feel comfortable in my
company. Her hair was the color of pale gold, a rare thing in Pella'mir.
All throughout the evening, we had drawn stares, and only once or

twice had I seen another head of yellow hair in the multitudes that crowded through the streets of the city.

I touched her hair with my fingertips, and found it soothing. Letting my fingers play, I stroked her short tresses, softly so as not to wake her, and found myself drifting into a sweet half-waking reverie.

Perhaps giddy with our freedom, we were careless. We ought, instead of spending the evening in idleness and pleasure, to have found some shelter, a place to stay where we could have put a bolt upon a door, with a roof over our heads. But our freedom was such a novelty, and the night so resplendent, that we did not think, that evening, of providing for our welfare. We played, instead, and that was almost our undoing.

I had dozed off to sleep myself, with Azora's head upon my lap. How long we slept thus together, I cannot say. But I was not alert to my surroundings. The first indication I had that I should have been on my guard was a rude kick to my foot.

I awoke with a start, half-rising from the bench. Azora awoke at the same instant, and we both stood to find ourselves facing a gang of half a dozen thugs. They smirked at us, and one of them—I suppose he was the leader of this gang—announced, in sneering tones, "This is a pretty one. She's mine. You can have what's left when I'm done."

Then he jerked his head toward me and simply said, "Kill him."

Azora's knife was out in an instant, and my sword flashed alongside. The thugs rushed us in a group, and in my heart I gave thanks to Brekkex and Koax for the hard training they had given me.

Azora was quick with her knife. As two of the thugs rushed her to grab her from either side, she slashed at them, once to the left, then to right. The first one jumped back with a deep cut to his wrist, blood spurting like a fountain, and his face instantly ashen. The second fellow took her blade directly into his belly, well below his navel. And as he doubled over, clasping his bleeding abdomen in pain, Azora's knee came up to meet his face. I heard a loud crack, and down he went, unconscious on the pavement with a broken nose.

In the meantime, I was busy with the other four fellows who rushed me with their swords. They were well practiced at this tactic, I instantly saw, for though they pressed me close, they did not get in each other's way. Swords flashed quickly, cutting at my throat, and only barely grazing me.

I focused all my attacks upon the ringleader, only sidestepping the other three, and avoiding their blades as well as I could. I knew that individually, these were clumsy fighters—if any had attacked us alone, we'd have made short work of the fellow. They were slow with their blades, and projected their moves loudly. I always knew precisely where they would thrust, and where they would slash by the way they slung their arms before each move.

But four of them at once, however clumsy they were, were most dangerous. Pressed too close by one fellow, I lashed suddenly at his face with a backhanded slash of my sword, slicing right through his cheek. He fell backwards, stumbling over his own feet, and Azora was upon him in a flash, neatly slicing his throat where he lay, before he could find his feet again.

Now I had but three to trouble me, and these fellows seemed to have lost their heart for the battle, seeing their numbers cut in half in only a dozen seconds. I pressed the advantage hard, and in a fortunate move, lopped off the left ear of the ringleader. He clapped his hand upon his bloody wound, and began a huge bellowing, his shouts echoing loudly through the empty streets.

Twice more I lunged, piercing him through the armpit, under his shoulder—and now his sword arm was useless. Bleeding profusely, his bellowing turned to screams, and even as I applied the thrust that ended his life, I saw from the corner of my eye a dozen more thugs rushing up, in answer to the ringleader's dying screams.

These were too many, and I was just at the point of telling Azora to flee while I did my best to hold them off, when suddenly I felt a huge concussion at the back of my head. It seemed the world exploded in white light, and then all went black.

I fell headlong into unconsciousness.

5

THE HOUSE OF TORQ-AA

AWARENESS CAME WITH A shock of pain. My head ached. I felt a severe throbbing at the back of my eyes. Then, a moistness at the back of my head, and my vision slowly recovered. All was a painful blur, except for a gentle touch, cool, soothing and warm, upon my forehead.

"He's waking," I heard a familiar voice say. Azora?

"Yes, Grae-don," she answered. "It is me."

I felt her lips upon my face as she nuzzled me close. Her breath was sweet and warm.

"So he is not dead," another voice said. This voice I did not know. A man's voice. "That is good. All is well."

My head was swathed in bandages. My eyes swollen shut.

"Where is this place?" I heard myself ask. "What has happened?"

"Oh, Grae-don, we are safe," Azora answered. I felt her fingers glide gently upon my chest, lingering first here and then there, and then at last she laid the palm of her hand flat upon my abdomen. Her touch was healing, and I felt myself gathering strength.

"You gave a good account of yourselves, I should say," the unfamiliar man's voice said. "Two dead, and two others crippled from their wounds."

"These men came out from their house," Azora explained.

"Hearing all the commotion," the unfamiliar voice interjected.

"And just as one of the thugs laid you low with the butt of his sword..."

"A most cowardly attack," the unfamiliar voice put in, "Coming from behind..."

"This man here cut him down, and his friends routed all the others..."

"These ruffians are a problem," I heard the unfamiliar voice say. "They prowl our streets, looking for easy prey. We've taught them to be wary of our own little neighborhood, my boys and I. But still, they come back on occasion, testing and teasing to see what they can get away with."

"I am thankful to you," I said. "Were it not for you, I would now be dead, and Azora..." I left off, shuddering to think what would have happened to her.

"You two did us a great favor yourselves," the unfamiliar voice replied. "You have dispatched that filthy *koraph*, the one called Kopros, and his lieutenant, the stinking piece of *kra* they called Phago. Those two had been a sore misery upon us, but with them dead, their gang will never trouble us again. Cowards, all of them!"

"But I do not know who you are," I said. Now struggling to sit up, I found that I was lying upon a couch, with Azora sitting upon the floor, near my head. My vision returning, I could see that I was in a room, the walls of which were of red stone, the stone floors matted with carpets made of straw. A fire burned in a hearth in the center of this room. I was facing an amber-skinned man of middle-age, who sat cross-legged on the floor near to the fire. His hair was black, and it fell straight to his waist. His eyes were gray, and they were filled with both sadness and wisdom. He wore but a leather harness strapped tightly about his waist, and a single string of small gilded shells draped about his neck. Upon his harness was a long knife, and lying next to him was a sword, similar to the one I carried away from the house of Jor-Taq, but more curved, with a crescent cut at the tip, rather than the straight point of mine.

"I am called Torq-aa," he said. "And you are in my house. I hope that you shall remain as my guest until your wounds are healed."

"Except for a head that aches, I feel I am well," I replied, now sitting up fully, and allowing the sudden dizziness to pass.

"I am called Grae-don," I said, after my head had cleared. "And this, my friend, is Azora."

"She has told me that," Torq-aa replied.

"But the name Torq-aa is familiar to me," I added. "Have you a wife, called Shala? And a daughter, called Haia?"

Torq-aa's face clouded.

"Yes, I do," he answered me, suspicion now growing in his voice. "How do you know this?"

"I met them in the house of Jor-Taq. They were my teachers."

"You did? They were?" Torq-aa demanded, with sudden animation. "Are they well?"

"They were when I last saw them," I answered. "But I fear that no one can do well in the house of Jor-Taq for long."

Torq-aa spat. Rage gathered upon his face, and he unburdened himself of a long string of invective against Jor-Taq. I learned many new words from him in those few short moments.

"... I would sell my house and all my belongings, even down to my last harness, my sword, pull the very teeth from my head and sell them in the market, did I think it would finally pay off this onerous debt. But no! No! Were I indeed to pay Jor-Taq even the last spillage of blood from my opened wrists, he'd but raise the interest on the debt, yet again, as he has every time I came near to paying it off, at last.

"Were it in my power," Torq-aa finished, "Jor-Taq would already be dead, his entrails lying in the streets, and his head decorating a post outside my house!"

"We share your hatred of the man," Azora said. "And would gladly assist you in any way we can to bring your wishes for Jor-Taq's future to fruition."

"Yes," I added. "I have no love for him, nor that heap of *kra*, who is Jor-Taq's chief assassin, the one called Horath.

"I know that creature, Horath," Torq-aa said. "As stupid and brutal a man as they come. But how is it that you are so well-acquainted with Jor-Taq and his foul creatures?"

"We have only yesterday escaped from his house," Azora said. "The brigands breached his walls with their missiles, and we took advantage of the confusion to flee." And then Azora and I both told Torq-aa the story of our imprisonment within the house of Jor-Taq.

We spent the better part of that morning describing what we had seen while we were there, answering Torq-aa's many very detailed questions. At one point, Torq-aa stopped us, and left us alone for a few moments. When he returned, he brought with his several other men, a friend, who was called Bendar, a brother, called Turuk, and another young man, called Jotar, who, we learned, was affianced to Haia.

With them gathered, Torq-aa asked us to repeat our tale, and as we spoke, these three men peppered us with questions, as well.

"As I have already told you, I have more than fulfilled my debt, and long ago," Torq-aa explained. "But Jor-Taq continues to add further conditions upon it. Already I have paid him more than a hundred-fold upon that debt, which I never owed to him to begin with, but to another. He bought the debt from that man, when I was near to paying it back completely, and now Jor-Taq claims I owe him a thousand-fold upon the original claim.

"Not a season goes by, but that he levies even more onerous duties upon the debt. He has no intention ever of releasing my wife and my daughter. But what can I do? To whom do I appeal? Jor-Taq enforces his obscene claims upon me with the swords of his assassins, the poisons of his spies.

"Your presence here, and the intelligence you bring us, is most fortuitous, my friend. We," and here he indicated the other three men in the room with a gesture, "Have long planned to make an assault upon the house of Jor-Taq, and to take our women from him, since he will not treat with us honestly."

"His security is strong," I answered. "I do not think that four of you can make much of an assault against him. There is but the single gate in his outer wall, and but the single doorway into his house itself. Both are guarded, day and night."

"But his walls are breached, and he cannot have repaired them so soon," Torq-aa said. "Indeed, it will take him many days to repair them, and should we move quickly, stealthily, in the night, we may make our way into his house…"

"And then what?" I asked. "You do not know where Shala and Haia are kept. The halls are so bewildering, and I was taken through them only once, that you cannot hope that I should be able to direct you to them. And that is even assuming that they are still in the same apartments that they lived in when I saw them—that was months ago."

"Assuming, also," Azora interjected, "That Jor-Taq has not decided to use them in his experiments."

The stifled rage that overcame all four men upon hearing Azora's comment, was palpable, even though they struggled mightily to main-

tain their outward composure. Long minutes passed before Torq-aa
was able to bring himself to speak again, and when he did, it was with
a voice choked and husky with passion.

"You do, however, know where to find Jor-Taq himself, and his
creature, Horath," he said.

I nodded my head slowly, watching Torq-aa's face keenly.

"Jor-Taq has encouraged no great loyalty among his people,"
Torq-aa said. "When I show them his head upon the point of my
sword, they will not think to avenge Jor-Taq. No. Their first thoughts
shall be only of their own welfare. The smart ones will be too busy
ransacking the house of Jor-Taq to trouble us. The stupid ones... well,"
and Torq-aa gave his shoulders an elaborate shrug.

"When do you plan to do this?" I asked.

"At the first opportunity, of course," Torq-aa replied.

"Then I shall show you the way," I said.

"Me, too," Azora put in.

"Thank you, friends. Thank you," Torq-aa answered. "You must
stay here today, in my house, as doubtlessly, Jor-Taq will have his spies
combing the streets for any sign of you."

And so Azora and I spent that day indoors, and the next three following, resting and recovering from our wounds, which, though slight,
had taxed us.

While we rested, Torq-aa's neighbor and friend, Bendar, made his
way to the house of Jor-Taq to see for himself the extent of the damage
to the walls. He was gone for several hours, and did not return until
the afternoon.

"The news is not so propitious," he said, as he came in through the door. "Jor-Taq has been busy. The outer wall is in repair already, with a large number of workmen busy on it. It is still scalable, as they have left their scaffolding in place, but it looks as if they shall have the wall completely closed up again by this time tomorrow."

"And the walls to his house?" Torq-aa asked.

"Much patchwork has been done there, as well, but large holes still pierce the house in several spots. Jor-Taq has placed many guards about, and crossing the open yard between the outer wall and the house itself without being seen will be a very tricky business."

"Then tonight is indeed the night," Torq-aa said. "We shall leave this evening, when darkness has come, and watch at the house of Jor-Taq for our opportunity. And when that opportunity comes, we shall strike."

It is in the way of things, however, that our plans fail, even though through no fault of our own. Chance (which, I've heard it said, is the mask of the Absolute), intrudes with her own plans, and we can never prepare for all the absurdities that may overtake us.

Jor-Taq's spies in Pella'mir were legion. These spies knew many people who made it their business to know what happened in the streets of the city. Word of the two golden-haired warriors, armed each with deadly knife and blade, and who had laid low the notorious thugs of Pella'mir, Kopros and Phago, went widely through the city.

That one of these golden-haired warriors was a man, and the other, a woman of petite stature, was a point that had not been lost upon Jor-Taq's spies.

Turuk rushed hard into Torq-aa's house early the afternoon of our fourth day there to warn us. A contingent of Jor-Taq's men were scouring the neighborhood in search of us, going from house to house and searching every room they found. Turuk had seen them himself. They were but two streets away, and coming this way.

"Horath is with them," he said.

"By what right do they do this?" I asked, astonished at the audacity of Jor-Taq's men.

"By right of force," Torq-aa answered grimly.

"They cannot find us here, Torq-aa," I said. "Or all is lost."

"You have no place to go," Torq-aa answered. "That hair of yours will mark you, and even honest men will give you away to Jor-Taq's thugs to save their own homes."

My mind was in a rush, and thinking quickly, I said, "Azora, do you stay here, with Torq-aa. With your small stature, he may be able to hide you, as you hid under my sleeping blankets."

"What are you going to do?" she asked.

"I don't have time to explain. I must go. I will meet Horath, and guide him away from here, if I can."

Azora's eyes widened with anxiety.

"I can't..." she began.

"No time!" I interrupted. Then, to forestall any more protestations from her, I threw my arms around her, forced her face to mine, and kissed her.

She responded with huge surprise, her face blushing furiously, and very prettily, I might say. And then, before another word was uttered by anyone, I hurried out the door, only remarking to Torq-aa as I left, "Be sure to be there at Jor-Taq's house this night, as we planned. I will meet you there!"

—◦✠◦—

Hurrying away from Torq-aa's doorstep, that no one may witness me leaving from there, I rushed through the streets, seeking out Horath and his men who were searching for us.

I spotted them only moments later, before they had turned into the street where Torq-aa's house was. Thirty men moved in a force from house to house, kicking in doors and shouting loud demands upon the inhabitants.

Horath was with them. I recognized him instantly. And with Horath, among the contingent of men were two who took his orders with a sullen mien—my old burly friends, Brekkex and Koax! I was overjoyed to see them again, their brawny bodies stitched with scars. They cast many surreptitious glances of contempt in Horath's direction, as he bawled and barked at them. Only grudgingly did they follow his orders to accost people on the street and grill them as to word of the whereabouts of Azora and me.

So engrossed was Horath in bullying and making displays of his brutal and overbearing power, that he did not even see me until I was nearly upon him. Boldly, I hailed him, shouting above the din he made, "Horath, my friend! We are well met!"

Hearing my voice, he instantly stopped bellowing, and seeing me, his jaw dropped in surprise.

He was confused, I saw, that I did not run from him, nor seek to elude him in any way, and hearing me call him out as 'friend' only left him in a state of complete stupefaction, which is precisely what I expected from the stupid fellow.

"Have you found her yet?" I asked, coming up to Horath.

"Found her?" he replied, stupidly. And then, recovering himself, he said with a snarl, "I found you, at least..."

"And I, you," I answered, smiling brightly. "And as I say, we are well met. But you have not found the girl, yet, I am supposing?"

"What are you talking about?"

"Why, the girl, the one who escaped us. I happened to see her taking advantage of the bombardment to slip out. I did not have time to call you then, so I followed her out into the street to capture her and bring her back."

This was a completely unexpected development for Horath, I saw, and I knew that his stupid brain would not pierce through the web of lies I spun before his eyes, so brazen was my telling of them.

"Oh, she gave me a good chase, I must say," I went on, speaking quickly so as not to give Horath time to consider.

"She must have known I was pursuing her, for she fled quickly, without stopping, and I followed her long into the night. But I finally caught up with her a few streets away from here, and had her in hand to bring back to Jor-Taq, when a gang of thugs set upon us.

"I did my best, and managed to slay two of the fellows, wounding two more, but they were too many for me. Finally one of the rude brutes attacked me from behind and laid me low."

I showed Horath the huge knot on the back of my head, as evidence of the encounter.

"And the last I saw, two of the thugs were carrying Azora away. I don't know how long I was unconscious. It must have been a day or two. I woke up on the pavement in an alley, and managed to patch myself up a bit. When I made it out onto the street again, I heard from the people that you were searching the city. I hurried over to meet you and assist you, and now here I am."

Horath stared at me stupidly for several moments, completely at a loss for words. Brekkex and Koax both stood nearby, and they heard my story as well, but I could see by the furtive smiles they strove to hide that they were not nearly so gullible as Horath, or stupid, and they were mightily amused at the ease with which I confounded the hulking bully.

"Huh!" Horath finally grunted. "Huh! So the thugs have her, do they?"

"The last I saw..."

"Where did this happen?" Horath demanded.

"This way," I said, pointing away from the house of Torq-aa. "Several streets down. I'm sure I can find the place again, though I did get a pretty bad knock at the back of the head, and it left me rather dazed. But I am certain, at least, that the alley was behind us, and several turns to the right."

"Show me," Horath said. "Take us to the spot."

And so I made an elaborate pretense of leading Horath toward the place of our encounter with the thugs, while taking him and his guards further and further away from the house of Torq-aa. As we marched away through the streets, I acted as if I were becoming more uncertain of where the spot was, exactly, that I had had the encounter with the thugs Kopros and Phagos.

Finally, I had completely confounded Horath, and he, weary with walking, gave it up, and said, "I will take you back to Jor-Taq. You can tell him your story yourself. If that girl has been taken by the thugs, then she's probably dead now, or pretty close to it."

And so I found myself being led away, once again, to the house of Jor-Taq.

Though I was pleased to have affected Azora's escape from Horath, my heart was heavy with the prospect of returning to Jor-Taq's evil control.

I walked slowly, weighed down with my thoughts and falling behind Horath by several paces. As I did so, Koax sidled up to me and whispered.

"It's very good to see you again, old friend," he said.

"I am happy to see you, as well."

"You may have fooled Horath with your story. I doubt Jor-Taq will be so easily convinced, though."

"I did not think that you would fall for my tale," I replied. "But no matter. I have accomplished my purpose."

"It does not look well for you, friend. Jor-Taq was in a froth, when he discovered that you and the slave-girl were both gone. He will be most pleased to have you back in his power, nor do I think he will go kindly with you."

"I do not doubt it," I remarked.

"Whatever may happen, Grae-don, you may count on my sword. Brekkex, too, is a friend. We have never had a better student than you. It would be a pity to see all our efforts gutted by Jor-Taq's scalpels."

"What are you chattering about back there?" Horath suddenly shouted, turning quickly on his heel to confront us.

"I was merely speaking to my old student," Koax quickly retorted. "I am pleased that he is no traitor to Jor-Taq, and have only been telling him what has passed since he was gone off in search of the slave-girl."

Horath grunted. "No more speaking, till we get back to the house of Jor-Taq!" he barked. "Then, Grae-don, you may explain yourself to the old man in person!"

6

— · —

JOR-TAQ'S VENGEANCE

HORATH USHERED ME THROUGH the gate—I had but a glimpse of the work that was being done to repair the outer wall, as well as the walls of the main building, before we were deep inside, hurrying through many long and darkened halls.

My guard—for that is what I concluded Horath and his assassins must be—took me directly to Jor-Taq, who waited in his apartments.

Jor-Taq glared at me without speaking, as Horath recounted to him the circumstances of my return. When Horath finished speaking, I told the same story to Jor-Taq I had to Horath earlier that day, and the old man listened in silence, the only indication of his response a sneer that grew slowly as I spoke.

When I had done, the old man glared at me for a long moment, rapping his fingers on the table before him.

Suddenly rising, he thrust an accusing finger at me.

"Liar!" he fairly screamed. "Liar! Oh, you can fool an idiot like Horath, but you can't fool me!"

Turning to the assassins who surrounded me, he shouted, "Take that sword away from him and lock him up! We'll lay him out on my table!"

One of the burly fellows swiftly plucked the sword from my scabbard, while three others pinned my arms behind me, and then they hustled me out of Jor-Taq's apartments. They took me down many flights of stairs to the dark basements beneath his house.

They threw me into a tiny room with stone walls and a metal door, which they instantly slammed shut. I heard the bolts sliding outside. I sat on the floor, consoling myself that, bleak as things seemed for me at the moment, at least Azora had eluded recapture.

And, too, there was the hope that Torq-aa would make good on his plans, and come in that night to kill Jor-Taq. But would that happen before Jor-Taq had splayed me and flayed me? I had no doubt but that was what he intended. Azora had already told me in some detail what it was that went on in Jor-Taq's laboratory. I was not sanguine about my immediate prospects.

The time weighed heavily upon me in that dark room. It was so dark I could not even see my hand in front of my face. All was silent and the room was quite stuffy. To pass the time, I explored the room, feeling about with my hands. One, two, three paces in depth, and then I bumped up against a wall. Feeling along that wall, I made three more paces, and then bumped up against a third wall. Another three paces, and I found myself touching the fourth wall, this one with the door bolted shut.

So that marked the extent of my freedom, three paces by three square. I reached upward and my knuckles came into instant contact with the stone ceiling, but a foot above my head. That was it. There was no hope of escape from those remorseless walls.

How long after that it was that Jor-Taq's guard came for me I do not know. It seemed ages, yet it could not have been more than a few hours. There were six of the fellows, in addition to Horath himself. Though Horath made no effort to disguise himself the others all wore black hoods over their heads, with narrow slits cut through for the eyes. The hoods covered not just their heads, but their chests and backs as well.

Horath stood outside the door of my cell, while one of the hooded men opened the door and gestured to me to come outside. Horath kept the point of his sword directed at my belly. Once I was in the hallway, two of the hooded men bound my arms tightly behind my back with leather cords, cinching the cords painfully tight, so that my wrists were at a level with my shoulder blades.

And then, once I had been securely bound, Horath led us all down the long and darkened hall. Three men walked before me, the other three behind me, while Horath himself walked alongside me, the point of his sword now touching the small of my back all the way.

Not a word was uttered. We moved on in silence. I smelled the rank sweat of the men in that narrow corridor, and heard only the soft pads of their sandals against the stone floor.

They ushered me up many stairs to the laboratory where Jor-Taq carried out his sadistic inquiries. There, the six hooded men stepped aside, taking their places on either side of the door, while Horath knocked on the door to the laboratory. A moment later, Jor-Taq, who had been awaiting us, opened the door, and nodded in silence to Horath.

With the point of his sword, Horath pushed me into Jor-Taq's laboratory, and then he turned and shut the door, locking it.

The sight that met my eyes devastated me. There, upon a table, was the naked form of Shala, hands and ankles bound tightly to the corners.

Nearby, Haia was bound by her wrists to a chain hung from the ceiling. She, too, had been stripped of all garments.

They both seemed unconscious—their eyes closed, and their faces stained with the streams of dried tears. I could see that Jor-Taq had not yet paid them his attentions, but how long it would be before he did, I could not guess.

It was clear that the cruel old man intended this night to be an orgy of sadism. His eyes shined with evil anticipation of the horrors he was soon to inflict. Horath's face, too, was illumined with malevolent glee.

Jor-Taq nodded at Horath—an obviously pre-arranged signal between them, for without a word, Horath muscled me into an iron chair and chained me into it with metal cuffs around my wrists, my ankles and my throat.

And now Jor-Taq spoke.

"We have given you the best seat in the house, Grae-don, that you may savor the spectacle of your friends' slow demise. Your precious Shala will go under my scalpel first. Then Haia, after I have allowed Horath his little pleasure with her. And then you shall be the last. Perhaps I ought to remove your eyelids for you, that you might not blink and miss even an instant of tonight's little show."

Turning to Horath, Jor-Taq asked, "Do your guards stand yet outside?"

"Yes, Jor-Taq," he answered.

"I do not trust them. Send them away," Jor-Taq said. "We need no witnesses this night."

Horath did as Jor-Taq instructed, and a moment later he returned.

"Now wake the two ladies," Jor-Taq said with a smirk. "We shall permit a little reunion between these old friends. It should be most instructive to see how these silly sentimental creatures will respond to their situation."

Horath strode across the room and picked up a metal pail from near the table where Shala was strapped down. It was filled with cold water, and he splashed it upon her naked body. The shock of the cold water roused her instantly, and she jerked awake.

Then Horath threw the remainder of the water upon the insensible form of Haia, and she, too, wrenched into consciousness.

"Ah! Ah!" she cried, her voice cracking in her wretchedness.

Jor-Taq chuckled, gloating at the tableau of misery he had made.

"Awake, my dears, awake," he said. "I have brought you a friend, and now our party can begin."

Shala turned her head, and spying me, she cried out, "Oh, Grae-don! I am so sorry he has caught you. Now we must all die."

"Not so quickly, dearie," Jor-Taq said. "You are so hasty, you women. Everything in its turn."

Haia, now fully roused, saw me as well, and though her eyes were heavy with sadness, she said nothing.

"Horath," Jor-Taq snapped. "Loosen the girl's chains a bit, so she may say her goodbyes to her friend. Perhaps I shall change my plans. I think we shall start this evening's experiments with her, instead, so I may study the mother's response to the slow demise of her daughter before her living eyes."

The chains from which Haia was hanging were strung through a metal loop in the ceiling, and tied down to a bolt in the wall. By loosening the chain at the bolt, Horath gave it sufficient length that Haia was able to stumble across the chamber to the metal chair where I was bound.

She crawled up into my lap, nuzzling her face against mine, as the tears flowed freely down her face. She wept silently, and did not cry out, for she knew that the old sadist would take great pleasure in her misery, and she would not give him the satisfaction. Images of happier times ran through my mind, moments when we, Shala, Haia, and I lived in peace and they taught me how to speak, how to read, how to write. Vividly I recalled the happy hours we passed playing board games, and puzzles.

"A pretty picture," Jor-Taq intruded. "A pretty picture, indeed. He, he, he," he cackled.

"Come, child," the old man said, grabbing Haia by the arm and seeking to pull her off my lap.

"Let us begin. I have such plans for you, such delights to show you, and I have promised Horath his bit of fun before I spoil that pretty face of yours. Now, come to Horath."

With her wrists bound by the chain that held them, Haia looped her arms around my neck and stubbornly buried her face in my chest.

I spat at the old man, and said, "I pity you, Jor-Taq. A pitiable creature you surely are."

"*You* pity *me*?" Jor-Taq screeched in mocking tones. "If there is anyone here in need of pity, I should think it would be you!"

I laughed in the man's face. "Whatever my sufferings may be, they will be over shortly, and I will be free of you. So will Haia. So will Shala. We will all be free of you. But you, you are condemned to be Jor-Taq forever, and there is nothing you can do about that."

"Ha!" Jor-Taq laughed. "'Condemned to be Jor-Taq'," he mocked. "I can think of worse things."

"I can't," I retorted. "What a miserable, unhappy thing you are, never to know what it is to have a friend. Never to know what it is to have the trust or the honor of another. I have not been long in this world, Jor-Taq, but already I have made many friends, and there are many who will grieve my passing from this world.

"You, though, you have lived long, and never once in all these years have you ever once felt the touch of friendship, never once have you known what it is to be loved.

"Oh, you have accumulated your cold wealth, and you sit on your pile, surrounded by those who loathe and despise you. There is not one who would but slit your throat if he thought he had the chance.

"You could have had many friends, old fool. You could have had the honor, and the love that I have known. Shala here could have been a friend to you, and Haia, too. And Azora—for they are all people with great friendship in their hearts. But you, cold and cowardly creature, you've thrown that all away. Fearful of friendship, jealous of beauty, you spend all your crapulent days hiding out here, afraid of your enemies, and doing what you can to avoid all contact with your kind. You coward!"

"Coward? Coward, you call me?" Jor-Taq sputtered. "You... you..." his face grew purple with rage.

"Why you insignificant... you petty...

"Of course, of course..." he said, recovering himself somewhat. "Of course you call me a coward, for you cannot understand the intellect before you! You are no different than all the rest, confounded by a mind so far beyond yours, you reach into your packet of common epithets."

Jor-Taq whipped himself into a fine rant. At that moment, he had everything his craven heart wanted or could understand. A captive audience, all within his power, all who had no choice but to listen patiently as he expounded at great length upon his favorite subject, himself.

"You do not know... you cannot know the thoughts that have passed through this mighty mind of mine, you little creature, you, who can think of nothing but your own appetites, your own cravings and desires!

"What do I care for this 'friendship' you speak of? What do I care for this 'honor'? Both are sham conceits, existing only to keep you petty creatures down, and to curb your petty appetites. 'Oh, I do not dare to do this thing, or that,'" he said in mocking tones, "'Or my *friends* shall cease to *honor* me!' Ptah!" he spat. "That is what I think of your honor! That is what I think of your friendship! Ptah! I say! Ptah!"

The old man fumed and cursed. And he launched himself into a long monologue, haranguing Shala, Haia and me at huge length for our ignorance, our pettiness, and the smallness of our souls, in comparison with him, who braved all kinds of moral horrors for the sake of expanding human knowledge.

"But that is courage that you cannot comprehend, isn't it? That is a virtue that is beyond your selfish, sentimental imaginings. What is a bit of pain, especially inflicted upon small and insignificant creatures such as yourselves? You should feel pride, pride that I, the great Jor-Taq, have deigned to include you as subjects of my researches.

"But instead you insult me, you chide me, as a spoiled child may chide an adult. You..."

At that instant, the door to Jor-Taq's laboratory was rent with a huge pounding.

"*Boom! Boom! Boom!*"

Jor-Taq spun and looked at the door, ready to call Horath, when the door suddenly burst from its hinges and fell to the floor.

"What?" Jor-Taq screamed. "What? What is this?"

Koax and Brekkex came bounding through the shattered door, their swords drawn and ready.

Before Jor-Taq could utter another word, Torq-aa leaped through the door, his eyes blazing.

Jor-Taq must have seen his own death in the blazing eyes of Torq-aa, for he let loose with a high-pitched scream, stumbling backward and away until he bumbled into Horath.

"Kill him! Kill him!" Jor-Taq howled.

Horath, shocked, fumbled his sword from its scabbard, but he had no sooner grasped it, poised to swing, than three quick darts flew through the air, puncturing his wrist. He jerked his hand away with a cry of pain.

I craned my neck in my chair to see where the darts had come from, and was surprised to see that it was Azora who had hurled them. Even as I looked, she was reaching into a pouch slung from her harness and withdrawing another handful to throw.

Horath swept the darts from his forearm, just as another four struck him. They pierced his arm and his chest, and he grunted in pain. Azora's tactic worked well, for she kept Horath busy, giving Bendar, Turuk and Jotar time to rush in and surround Horath.

Seeing that Horath was fully occupied with three swordsmen at his throat, Azora ceased hurtling her darts at him, and rushed over to me, where I was locked in Jor-Taq's metal chair of torture, with Haia still upon my lap. Wasting no time with words, Azora put her full attention directly to the task of loosening the bolts that held me down.

Haia clambered down from my lap and ran the length of the chain that held her to the table where her mother was bound. She instantly set about seeking to unloose Shala from her straps.

Horath, I must say, gave a good account for himself. Bellowing loudly to call for reinforcements, he swung his sword in vast circles about himself, narrowly missing Bendar and Turuk time after time. They lunged in at him repeatedly, seeking to cut through his defense, but Horath's arms were long, and he managed to hold the two at bay.

Jor-Taq, on his side, proved himself the coward he was. With Torq-aa bearing down hard upon him, the old man fell back, and barricaded himself behind the table where Shala was tied down. Pushing Haia away with one hand, Jor-Taq whipped a knife from his harness and laid it upon Shala's throat, declaring in a high-pitched voice of panic, "Stop! Stop! Or she dies!"

Torq-aa stood upon the opposite side of the table, his sword pointed directly at Jor-Taq's head. With a single swift motion, he could have cut the man's head in twain, but no matter how swiftly he plunged his sword into the face of Jor-Taq, the old man would surely cut Shala's throat quite through before he died.

Haia lay upon the floor at Jor-Taq's feet, not daring to move, lest she cause her mother's death.

And just at that instant, twelve of Horath's assassins came bursting through the broken door. They instantly set upon Bendar, Turuk and Jotar. Torq-aa spun on his heels to meet the three swordsmen who broke off from the group to attack him.

All, it seemed was suddenly lost.

But things happened then with a swiftness that was appalling. Even now I can scarce recollect all that transpired in those instants, so rapidly did so many things take place.

At that precise instant, Azora completed unlocking my bonds. With a single smooth motion, she turned and plucked a half dozen darts from her pouch, hurling them in swift succession directly at the faces of the men who attacked Brekkex, Koax, Bendar, Turuk and Jotar. Two of them went down instantly, Azora's darts having pierced them through the eye. A third caught a dart in the ear, and his head jerked to the side with the sudden shock.

Quickly taking advantage of the opening, Bendar leaped in and ran his sword through the man's chest. Now the five men were facing only seven opponents, including Horath, who still filled the room with his huge bellowing and curses.

Torq-aa, in the meanwhile, was proving to be a most dangerous swordsman. Already he had accounted for one of the three who attacked him, with a slash to the head that sent him stumbling backward, and another jab at the man's groin that laid him open to his waist. Now Torq-aa faced two.

Instantly Azora freed me from my bonds, I leapt up from the chair to lend my assistance to my friends. As Azora threw the last of her darts at the two men who faced off with Torq-aa, then swiftly pulling her knife from its scabbard at her hip, I looked about helplessly for anything I might use as a weapon.

My eye fell upon the long chain that still bound Haia. It dragged along the floor, along the path from where it dangled by the hook in the ceiling. I saw that Haia had carried it partly along with her as she ran back to her mother, Shala, strapped to the table. And that the chain was most inconveniently underfoot—inconvenient for our enemies, that is.

As Azora hurried forward to plunge her knife into the side of one of the men who confronted Torq-aa, I grasped the long chain in both hands and gave it a huge jerk upward. Torq-aa's opponent fell to Azora's swift blade, with a huge gash in his side hemorrhaging shocking quantities of blood, and the chain caught two of the men who opposed Brekkex, Koax, Bendar and the others. I yanked upon the chain again, swinging it to the left, and then, again, to the right, and the assassins found themselves slipping, trying to keep from getting tripped up by the chain.

With the floor slick with blood, this was no easy feat, and I was ecstatic to see my efforts rewarded, at last, when two of the assassins fell to the floor. Bendar ran one through with his sword, and Jotar easily dispatched the second.

Now, seeing that the odds were beginning to fall in our favor, Jor-Taq commenced squealing in high-pitched terror.

"Stop! Stop, I say! Stop, or she dies!"

But Haia had seen the confusion I had wrought with the chain that bound her, and instantly picking up on the example, she swung the chain about so that it caught Jor-Taq by the ankles. He fell backward, still screaming, and Haia quickly looped the chain that bound her hands together about Jor-Taq's neck.

Standing suddenly, she pulled on the chain, giving it several hard yanks, striving to choke Jor-Taq, or to break his neck. Her arms were too young, and too frail, for the task, but she did keep Jor-Taq occupied, skipping about the room with his neck looped in the chain, as he swung his knife in futile circles, striving to cut her.

With Azora's ready knife assisting, Torq-aa found little trouble in finishing off the last of the three assassins who faced off with him. Leaving the remainder to Brekkex, Koax, Bendar, Turuk and Jotar, Torq-aa ran to Shala's side, and with three swift strokes, he cut her loose from the table where she had been bound. She stumbled from the table, and allowed Torq-aa to wrap her in his arms.

"Ah! Torq-aa!" she wept, tears running freely down her face.

"Shala. My wife. At last," he said, looking down into her eyes.

Now it was but Horath, Jor-Taq, and three of the assassins opposing us.

Jotar pulled away from the fray and turned to assist Haia. The struggle between she and Jor-Taq had come to be almost comical now, so grotesque had Jor-Taq's useless flailing become. Constantly slipping on the floor, slick with the blood of his assassins, while trying at once to loosen the chain Haia kept secure and tight about his neck, and to slash at her with the knife he gripped in his panicked hand, he made sure only that all his efforts were useless.

Now Jotar stepped up, and placed the point of his bloodied sword at Jor-Taq's throat.

"Cease your babbling, old fool," he demanded.

Jor-Taq fell to his knees.

"Have mercy on an old man," he squealed.

We looked about his laboratory, and were revolted by what we saw. Everywhere we looked, the evidences of Jor-Taq's many victims assaulted our eyes. Parts of bodies lay in a heap in a moldering corner—hands, feet, legs and arms, all sundered from their bodies. Flesh flayed from the faces of sufferers innumerable, his 'subjects', hung from the walls like so many trophies, their blind, lidless eyes staring hopelessly in death.

With horror growing, we saw that the beast had made fetishes of the bodies of his subjects, chains strung with human ears, pendants and necklaces of human fingers. Indeed, the wretched man wore several of these about his scrawny neck, even as he begged us for mercy. We saw now, with horror, that the apron he wore strung about his bloated belly was fashioned of human flesh. Dried twisted fingerlike projections dangled upon his bowed legs.

We were all repulsed at what we saw. Indeed, now that the battle was done, and she had the time to appreciate what her eyes were taking in, Azora was overtaken with a fit of retching. Jotar and Turuk, too, doubled over with nausea, vomiting copiously upon the bloodied floor.

"You foul, soulless thing!" Torq-aa declared, his voice rising in rage.

He raised his sword above his head, and with Shala hanging upon him, he brought the sword down upon the gibbering form of Jor-Taq.

Once! Twice! Three times! Torq-aa's sword flashed in the dim light, and Jor-Taq, the self-proclaimed genius of Pella'mir, was dead.

Azora ran to my side, and buried her face against my chest. I felt the warmth of her breasts, and the heat of her breath. I encircled her with my arms and held her close.

We had only Horath and his two remaining assassins to deal with now. They kneeled on the floor, disarmed, with Brekkex, Koax and Bendar watching over them, their swords aimed directly at the men's chests.

"Shall we kill them now?" Koax asked of us all.

"No! Not I!" one of the assassins screamed.

"Nor I! Nor I!" quailed his fellows.

"We did not know," the first one said. "We did not know what horror Jor-Taq wrought!"

"No!" said his fellow. "Had I known what Jor-Taq did, I would never have set foot in this foul place. I am glad he is dead. Give me but a moment, after learning this horror, I would have killed him myself."

"Gladly!" the others agreed. "We'd have killed him gladly!"

"You have heard your assassins, Horath," I said to him. "You do not have their excuse. You were not ignorant of Jor-Taq's abominations. You assisted him."

"What else could I do?" Horath pleaded. "The man was a monster, and I was but his servant, as you were, yourself, Grae-don. You stood guard outside, yourself, as Jor-Taq inflicted his torment upon these creatures. Did you not fear him, as I did? As we all did? He would have killed you in your sleep, Grae-don. And me. No one was safe."

7

SACK OF THE HOUSE OF JOR-TAQ

"T HIS EVIL HOUSE AND everything within it must come down," Torq-aa commanded. "You," he said to the assassins. "You may go this moment. Tell everyone you meet within these walls that Jor-Taq is dead, and that his house is to be razed. Take everything that belongs to you, but be gone!"

The three assassins hustled out of the room, but we did not allow Horath to move. He watched them longingly as they departed, and asked of us all, "What will you do with me?"

"That depends on you, Horath," Torq-aa replied. "You are a liar, nor do we trust you. But we are not murderers."

Turning his face to Shala's, Torq-aa asked her, with grim purpose, "Has this man offered you any insult?"

Smiling faintly, she answered, "Jor-Taq did not grant him the leisure."

"And you, my daughter?' Torq-aa asked. Jotar had released her from her chains, and held her tenderly in his arms. She looked to her father, and replied, "Oh no, my father. He wished it, and Jor-Taq promised him the pleasure of my body, but no, the old man never permitted him the time to carry out his impulse against me."

"Fortunate for you, Horath," Torq-aa said, "That Jor-Taq was so demanding a taskmaster. Otherwise you would already be dead. As it is, I should kill you for what you had in your heart against my family, but, as I say, I am no murderer. You may go."

Horath was astonished, and he blinked stupidly at Torq-aa. "What?" he asked. "I may... you are releasing me?"

"I am no murderer, Horath, though I doubt I have ever met a man less deserving of mercy than you. Go!"

Horath stumbled back to his feet.

"Leave your sword," Torq-aa said.

Horath dropped it to the floor, and began to make his way to the door.

But as he passed close by to me, I happened to catch the sudden gleam that came into his eye. Mischief was afoot.

The man made his way past us, to the door, and just as he was about to step through the portal, he spun on his foot, and hurled a dagger at my head.

"Die!" he shouted, and then he bounded out the door.

I bent backward, avoiding the blade, just as it cut the air past my face. Passing just over Azora's head, it flew through the room and embedded itself in the wall.

Instantly my heart flared with rage, not for Horath's treachery against me, which I expected, but for the fact he came so near to murdering Azora, even as I held her in my arms.

Her head jerked upward, and I saw her startled eyes staring into mine, but for only an instant. Without knowing what I was doing, I pushed myself away from her, and ran out of the room, without a weapon, following Horath down the long and darkened halls.

Death was in my heart, death and murder. The man would die. I followed the sound of his footsteps, hurrying down the halls as the sounds of my fellows calling after me dwindled in the distance.

Turning a corner, I saw his cowardly form ahead, just before he ducked into another hallway. Running hard to catch up, I ran into the hallway Horath had ducked into to find the man waiting there for me.

Listening for the sound of my running footsteps, he threw a punch at me just as I ran into him. Compounded by the momentum of my own body as I ran toward him, his huge fist lifted me completely off the ground, and I went sailing backwards for several feet.

It must have knocked me cold, for the next thing I remember is waking to find myself prone upon the floor, with Horath swinging his heavy foot directly at my head. Fortunate that I roused myself when I did, for had that kick connected, it surely would have smashed my skull.

As it was, I had only sufficient time to grab Horath's foot as it came close. I twisted it in my hands, causing Horath to lose his balance. He fell heavily on his back, on the stone floor beside me. The fall knocked the wind out of him, and I saw him open his mouth wide as he strove to take in air.

Leaping to my feet, I took advantage of his breathlessness, and dropped my entire body on his chest, landing hard with my knee on his sternum.

My ears were rewarded with a cracking sound that told me his sternum was crushed. His face turned purple, and now I knelt over him, staring into his eyes.

"Look hard upon me, Horath. My face is the last thing you shall see."

The man's mouth gaped, his eyes nearly bulged out of his head. I brought my elbow down upon his throat, delivering a punch with the point of my elbow, rather than my fist, as Koax himself had taught me to do. With the full force of my shoulder and my back behind the punch, I crushed Horath's larynx. Then I stepped back to watch with growing satisfaction as the putrid creature slowly suffocated, his legs and arms jerking convulsively. And then he died.

Now the haze that had fogged my vision since Horath's cowardly attack on both Azora and me began to lift, and I heard, as if from a distance, the sounds of voices drawing near.

I rose to my feet and looked about. Torq-aa, Azora, Koax, Brekkex, and the others had all followed closely as I pursued the cowardly Horath through the darkened halls of the house of Jor-Taq.

Azora swung her foot with contempt at his head, and struck it with her heel.

"Ptah!" she spat.

"Let us go," Torq-aa said. "Do you hear the uproar?"

Now he mentioned it, yes I did. The muted sounds of a distant tumult reached our ears from the floors below.

As we stood, listening, the noises grew louder.

"It is the people of the house of Jor-Taq," Torq-aa said. "His slaves, his servants. His guard. Now he is dead, and they riot. They did not love the man, and even now they are looting his house. We had best be away from this place."

"Which way?" Jotar asked.

"The best way is the shortest way," Brekkex said. "I can take you there, but we should first go to Jor-Taq's apartments."

"Why?" Jotar demanded.

"To get ahead of the looters. Jor-Taq kept his most precious things in his private apartments, and as I am now without employment, I would seek to provide for my own well-being in the days ahead."

"As well as would I," Koax agreed.

Making an instant decision, Torq-aa answered, "We shall not keep you then, my friends. Go, and provide for yourselves, but I would quit this foul place, and will not detain Shala nor Haia for a moment longer. We can make our way past the looters. When you have taken what you can, then do make your way to the house of Torq-aa, friends. You shall always find a home with me."

"Luck be with you then, friend," Brekkex replied. He slapped Torq-aa on the back, and then, to me, he said, "You have been a good student, Grae-don. I am glad to call you friend!"

"And I, you," I answered, heartily.

"You come in good stead," Azora said. "I thank you, too."

"She's a ripe one, that!" Brekkex said to me. And then, to her, "You fight well, girl! It gives me honor to have fought alongside you."

"I hope we can go fighting and killing again, someday," Koax added.

And then they turned, and quickly retraced their steps. My eyes followed their burly bodies, stitched with scars and tattoos, as they hurried up the long hallway to do their plundering. Rude and brutal, they were good men.

Torq-aa hustled the rest of us down the hallway, and then down a flight of stairs that led us to a balcony that overlooked a large hall. The hall was bursting with an agitated crowd, looters who carried chairs and tables away, ripping fabric from the walls, and smashing everything they could not take.

"These cannot all be Jor-Taq's people," I said, wondering at the size of the crowd.

"Word has gone out quickly," Torq-aa remarked. "I recognize some of them. These are Jor-Taq's neighbors. They have come to take their part of the plunder."

Fights had already broken out among many of the people in the hall, and the fights quickly became murderous, as passions were enflamed.

"This is not a good place for us to be," Shala said, her voice heavy with strain.

"We cannot make our way through that confusion," Jotar said.

"Come! This way!" Azora put in. "We can make our way through the back rooms."

She hurried ahead, leading us along the balcony. Coming to a hallway at the end of it, she turned quickly to the right, and down the hall. This we followed until we came to an elaborate doorway that was securely bolted. Try as she could, Azora could not get the door to come open.

"With me!" Bendar said, and he threw his weight against it. The door shook, but it stood resolute.

Then Jotar and I threw our weight against the door with Bendar. This time the door quaked on its hinges, but still it stood closed against us. A third time, and the door broke loose. It was securely bolted on the opposite side, so did not come down, and we were several minutes in prying the door down, bending the heavy wood until it snapped.

That gave us sufficient clearance to worm our way past the door, and only just in time for us, as the rioters had made their way up to the hall where we were seeking to make our way to freedom. They were not searching for us, but for whatever wealth they could get their hands on, but maddened by looting and fighting, it was a dangerous crowd.

I saw the glint of knives and swords flashing, as the looters fought over their prizes, and in the instant before I managed to squeeze past the door, behind Azora, I saw two men cut down. Blood was flowing, and we did not wish to be caught up in that tide.

We'd made our way into an anteroom. Jotar, Bendar, Torq-aa and I blocked the door with heavy pieces of lumber we tore from the shelves that lined the wall, then hurried into the next room which proved to be a storage room.

Azora pushed upon a wall behind a rack, triggering a mechanism that opened a passageway before us.

"It leads to the pantries," Azora explained. "I used this passageway every day."

We followed the passageway, unlit and dark as pitch, by feeling our way along with our hands upon the walls. Finally we came to the end of it, and Azora quickly unlatched the portal, and we spilled out into the pantries she mentioned.

"Now up these stairs," Azora said, showing us the way. "And we shall come out to where the wall of the house was broken in."

We followed the stairway without incident, and came, as she said we would, to the same suite that she and I found when we first made our escape from the house of Jor-Taq.

We had a view of the courtyard from here. Now the crowds were massed heavily, and we saw them carrying out everything that they could.

"There's no help for it," Torq-aa observed. "We must make our way through the crowds."

And so we did. We dropped from the breach in the wall, each in turn, and each helping the others, as Azora and I had done five nights before.

The night sky was vivid. A burning velvet black, scattered with brilliant stars and lit up by the lurid orange and yellow glow of the fires that had broken out during the plunder of the house of Jor-Taq.

———※———

We made our way across the courtyard, ignored, by and large, by the rioters, who were more interested in plunder than murder. The few who hazarded to give us trouble quickly changed their minds, when they saw our swords flashing.

Already, the narrow gate that led into the courtyard from without was destroyed, its heavy doors lying in splinters upon the ground, and a constant stream of looters came and went through it.

The walls of Jor-Taq's house, too, were coming down, as many people clambered over the breach that had been blown into them by the brigands only the night before, and wore the gap even further with their ceaseless comings and goings.

At last we made our way through the breach and into the streets of Pella'mir. There, we paused and turned to watch the sack of Jor-Taq's house for a few moments. A tableau that haunts me still—angry, towering flames burned high into the night, shadows, sable and black, danced in long frantic shapes upon the ground. And the frenzied multitudes churned as a single mass. The roaring of the fires, the shouting of the crowds, the death-cries of the dying, all as riches spilled out among them, lavish furnishings, gold and silver, coins, tapestries, silks, jewels, rare things of every kind, all as blood flowed like angry rivers through the smoke.

At last, both horror and awe welling up in us to a pitch we could no longer endure, we turned and left that place.

We found our way through the winding streets of Pella'mir back to the house of Torq-aa, and there, we made as happy a homecoming as had been seen in many, many long months. Shala and Haia, reunited with their family, were in rapture. Tears and smiles, and the house resounded with joyous laughter.

Much time passed with happy reunions before Torq-aa and the others could tell me their story, but at last the kisses, the embraces and the handshakes were exhausted, and I asked, of all, generally,

"How was it you made your way into the house of Jor-Taq? And how did you find my old friends, Koax and Brekkex?"

"Ha! A lucky chance, that!" Torq-aa exclaimed as he settled in to tell me the story. I was half-sitting, half-lying upon the divan close to the hearth, with Azora lying upon my lap. Torq-aa sat cross-legged in front of the warming fire, with Shala, who seemed unable to let him go, even for an instant, draping her arms tightly about his shoulders. Next to them were Jotar and Haia, Jotar lying upon the floor, leaning his head upon the palm of his hand, with Haia wrapped about his body, teasing his black locks with her fingertips. Bendar and Turuk both leaned back in heavy wooden chairs, their wives having come to join us. In all, it was a comfortable and joyous moment.

"We had made our way through the breach in the wall," Torq-aa said, "Bendar, Jotar, Turuk, your Azora, and me. And we were making our way across the courtyard, when we were caught by Jor-Taq's guard. They were twelve in all, and we were outnumbered. We knew we could not fight them without causing a clamor, and thereby alerting the remainder of the guard. So we knew our cause was lost. They surrounded us quickly, and challenged us.

"'What do you here?'" one of them fairly screamed.

"'We come for our women!'" I answered. Though I was without hope, I brandished my sword, ready to make my death costly to these men.

"'What of this one?'" one of these men demanded, laughing at us. Pointing at Azora. "'Is she here for her woman, too?'"

"'Wait a moment,'" said another. "'I recognize this one. It is she who escaped Jor-Taq, only these few nights past. What do you, here? Why do you return? Did you miss waiting upon the mighty Jor-Taq?'"

"'I come for Grae-don!' I said," Azora interjected. "'And I will kill anyone who tries to stop me!'"

"Yes, she did!" Torq-aa said. "A girl of fine spirit!"

Azora blushed and smiled at the compliment.

"'Grae-don?'" this fellow asked. "'Are you a friend of Grae-don?'"

"'We all are!' Azora declared to these fellows. 'We are all his friends.'

"'As well as are we!'" several of the guards announced to us. "You come to free him?'

"'Yes!'" we all declared.

"'Then we shall join with you!' one of these robust men shouted, and then another agreed. These, we learned, were your friends Brekkex and Koax. Well it was for us that they had found us, for we had some fighting to do to make our way to the summit of Jor-Taq's house, and even with Azora to guide us, we were hard pressed to find his laboratory. But with Azora, Brekkex and Koax to show us all the way, and with the extra swords they provided, we did at last make it to the laboratory, and the rest you know."

"Just in time, Torq-aa," I replied. "Jor-Taq was most keen to begin his work upon Shala. I did what I could to provoke him, knowing what a braggart he was. An audience, especially one as captive as we, was something that intoxicated him. I knew that given half a chance, he would waste much time with words, and I prayed that you would come while I stalled him."

"You did well, Grae-don," Shala remarked, hugging tightly to Torq-aa. "I wondered what you were doing, provoking his wrath as you were. But you seemed to know him well."

"He gave me plenty opportunity to study him," I replied. "But another matter provokes my curiosity," I said, leaning my face into Azora's. "Those things you threw…"

"My darts," she answered, smiling proudly. "We use those darts on Taakbar to hunt. They are quick and silent, and you can carry dozens of them in a pouch. I learned the use and the making of them when I was a little girl. I am deadly with them!"

"I see," I said.

"So I spent all afternoon making my darts. These were only lacking the mixture we use on Taakbar to poison the tips. On Taakbar, we use a secretion from the joyu bush which causes paralysis in animal muscle. If I could only have tipped my darts with that, then we'd have made quick work of Jor-Taq and Horath, and the guards, too, without all that messiness."

"And you would have denied me the joy of killing of Horath," I remarked, "And Torq-aa, his vengeance against Jor-Taq."

Azora responded by thrusting out her pretty tongue, and then, on an impulse, she jerked her head upward into mine, and licked my face.

"Ha, ha!" she laughed, as I wiped my face with the back of my hand. And everyone in the room laughed with her.

Torq-aa was most generous with Azora and me, plying us with food and drink until we were almost bursting. We both fell asleep, late in the night, our arms and legs entwined, oblivious to all.

Our celebration at Torq-aa's house lasted many days. We woke to food and drink, music and joy each day, and did not cease our pleasures until we each collapsed, exhausted with rejoicing, only to begin again the following day.

That time is now but a happy haze in my memory, with a few brief images standing out, like gems sparkling in a lavender twilight.

Azora, leaping from the divan to dance, laughing and happy, the smile on her face flashing in the golden light of the fire that illumined the crowded room. Bendar and Jotar joyously playing a game which involved a complicated slapping of each other's hands. They dragged me forcibly into it, and we all laughed loudly at my clumsiness in this new diversion. Shala throwing her arms about me and covering my face with kisses, and then Haia, too, until Azora herself leaped into the fray, and all three were hugging, kissing and squeezing me. Torq-aa, his usually severe face beaming with joy for the return of his wife and his daughters, rising ponderously from the floor where it was his custom to sit, and taking Shala's hand in a stately dance both formal and exotic.

Those were happy times for us, glorious times. It seemed the food would never cease, the liquor, never stop flowing, nor the music, ever to end.

Torq-aa's house was three stories high. The first floor, was, as I have described it, given over almost entirely to this single large room, with stone walls and the hearth in the center, where Torq-aa and Shala received their guests. Off to one side was the pantry, where the utensils and the foods were stored. All the cooking was done on the hearth. The second floor, at the top of a short stone stairway, was given over entirely to Torq-aa's and Shala's apartments. This stairway was the only entrance to these apartments, and it was secured at the top by a large wooden door.

The third floor belonged mostly to Haia, and to enter her suite, one climbed a stone stair built on the outside of the house. This stair wound upward along three walls. At the base of the stair, near the doorway that led into the first floor, was a stone archway with a metal gate. The stair then wound around the house, until one entered the third floor at the back.

Each of the upper floors had a balcony that stretched all the way around the house, with numerous windows, but only one doorway. The lowest floor was the smallest in area. The second floor was wider in all directions, and the third floor was the widest of all, giving the house the appearance of an inverted stepped pyramid.

All houses in Pella'mir were built to this design, and when I asked him about it, Torq-aa explained to me that the purpose is born of tradition, from a time when the defenses provided by such architecture were necessary.

"There were many old rivalries in Pella'mir," he said. "Ancient grudges between families, and it was not unheard of, in days long past, for one family to lay siege to another. These houses, so built, with overlooks upon the street, provided very good vantages from which to launch missiles upon those who laid siege upon us.

"That custom has since died away. Now blood feuds are rare, and when they do arise, they are settled by single combat between representatives of each family. But the houses still stand. They were built well, strong and heavy to withstand many assaults.

Torq-aa generously put Azora and me up in his house, sharing the third story of the house with Haia, who had her own suite of apartments that took up half the floor. Azora and I shared the other half, a spacious suite with several large rooms, and access to the balcony that circled the house. It gave us quite a wondrous view of Pella'mir, for Torq'aa's house stood in a neighborhood nearly halfway up the slope of the mountain island where the city of Pella'mir was built.

In all, the sack of Jor-Taq's house unfolded over many days. He was indeed a man of great wealth and property, and it seemed the street before us was constantly swelled with a stream of people moving back and forth from Jor-Taq's house, carrying huge amounts of plunder. Thousands came to take what they could, and the air was festive and buoyant. Jor-Taq had inspired much fear and hatred in Pella'mir, nor was Torq-aa by any means the only man Jor-Taq had wronged.

We watched the spectacle unfold before us, Azora and I, from the balcony of Torq-aa's house, as the people of Pella'mir celebrated the end of Jor-Taq's horror. From the roof, we could see the pile that had been Jor-Taq's house, standing at the summit of the steep city. Now it was but a shell, gutted and emptied of all within, but even there, the vengeance of the many people Jor-Taq had done harm to did not cease.

They attacked the pile with hammers, smashing in the walls, and at last it came down with a thunderous crash that shook the city, amid a huge cheering that deafened us. Jor-Taq was dead, his house destroyed

Nothing was left but a heap of rubble. The dust from the collapse lingered over Pella'mir for several days before it finally cleared.

8

BRIEF HAPPINESS

W E STAYED WITH TORQ-AA for many days. The man even invited us to stay on with him as his family.

"You shall be my son, Grae-don," he said. "And you, Azora, my daughter."

"You honor us, Torq-aa," I replied.

"Yes," Azora agreed. "You honor us."

"As you have honored me," Torq-aa answered us.

And so we lived, content and happy, for days beyond counting.

That first morning we awoke, after our long celebration of freedom, Azora said to me, "I am grimy. Let us go bathe."

She roused me and took me by the hand, flitting down the stone stairs wrapping around Torq-aa's house, into the street. And there, as the morning passers-by made their way on their daily errands, Azora stripped herself of her harness and leapt directly into the canal.

In the house of Jor-Taq, I had bathed, always in private, scrubbing myself down with water I poured from a pitcher, which I carried to my room from the pumps. Here, in the streets of Pella'mir, it seemed, bathing was quite a public matter.

Following Azora's example, I removed my own harness, and climbed into the canal with her. The morning water was cool, and deep, and it flowed rapidly. Glancing about, I saw perhaps a dozen others bathing in the canal with us, Shala and Torq-aa among them.

"Come," Azora said, encircling her arms around my neck. "It is considered bad form to notice anyone when they bathe. This way." The water was chest deep to me, and Azora's head bobbed just above the surface. She threw herself upon her back, and swam several strokes, under a shaded bridge above the canal, allowing foot traffic on the street above our heads to pass overhead.

There we found a tiny shaded grotto, with a ledge just below the surface of the water. We could sit upon the ledge most comfortably, with our waists and chests above the current. The walls were lined with blue and white porcelain, and decorated with various mosaic patterns of precious metal and semi-precious stones.

"This is nice," Azora purred, and I had to agree.

We remained there through the morning, washing, swimming, and splashing, and exploring the many nooks and small tunnels that wound beneath the street. Sometimes we came out in surprising places, our heads breaking above the water, just at the feet of a group of pedestrians, or at the tent of a trader. In some public pools, near the eating places, we could even sit near the edge of the pool, and women came to us, offering us drinks, if we wished, or even food, for which we could pay later.

Thievery is unknown here, and the people of Pella'mir are, by and large, honest people, who always make good on their debts (and so it was that Jor-Taq, and others of his ilk, who are fortunately rare, found it so easy to prey upon Torq-aa), and so it was that, as we wore no clothing, and obviously could not pay for our refreshments on the spot, the women who served us made no trouble over it. They knew we would come back at a later time to settle up our accounts.

Each one kept these accounts in her head, and it is a wondrous thing that they can keep such very detailed accountings and for many days. But, as I say, the people of Pella'mir are generally honest folk, and seek to pay their debts quickly, nor to incur greater debt than they can easily pay off.

In the days that followed, Azora and I found many opportunities to explore these canals that wind all throughout the city of Pella'mir, and even under it to considerable depths. Luminous subterranean waterfalls spill into underground pools and grottoes, walls of cool turquoise and lavender. Spillways with water rapidly sluicing through sinuous, winding channels, and still ponds, intimate in purple twilight.

The city of Pella'mir is ancient, many thousands of years old, I learned from Shala, who kept a large collection of codices in her apartments in the house of Torq-aa. She is a learned woman, a teacher by nature, who delights in imparting knowledge to others. And in me, she found an enthusiastic student. During the days that we dwelt there, in the house of Torq-aa, Shala loaned me many of her codices, which I studied avidly and we spent many happy hours discussing the many things I learned from them.

Among those things I learned was the history of the city of Pella'mir. The canals, that Azora and I spent so many happy days exploring, were begun early in the history of this city, to provide daily water to the inhabitants, for bathing, cooking, and drinking.

As the centuries rolled by, the canals were continuously added to, built up, and excavated even deeper into the island. Now, no single person knew the extent of them, no map was ever drawn up that included them all within its boundaries. Some were quite expert in this or that particular reach of a canal, and many made a living directing people through them. Some lived within the canals all their lives, never coming to the surface, and never once donning clothing of any sort, it being considered ill-mannered among the people of Pella'mir to wear clothing while swimming in the canals.

Beneath Pella'mir is another city, of many thousand inhabitants, all living within the luminous grottoes, the underground pools, and the subterranean channels. Most of these people have never been experienced dryness, not once in their lives, but live forever in the water, wetness being the condition of their being.

The canals, I learned from Shala, were a necessity to the city. There is a thing called rainfall, which is rare, very rare. Only once or twice in a lifetime, Shala told me, does it ever happen. She had never seen a fall of rain, nor had Haia, nor Azora. Torq-aa, who was somewhat older than Shala, had seen one fall of rain, when he was a very young boy.

When the rain does fall, he told me, as Shala and I pored over our studies of an evening, it comes with huge force, flooding the streets and rushing downward in great rapids into the sea. Houses fall, swept into the raging currents, and whole neighborhoods are washed away into oblivion.

This had happened many hundreds of times in the long history of Pella'mir, and the long and complicated systems of canals was built by the inhabitants to help control the force of these deluges, by sending the floods of water in many directions through the city, and, as well, to store it against the long dry periods.

Fresh, potable water, drinkable water, is rare. The water of the shallow seas that surround these islands is brackish and undrinkable. It is oily, and nearly stagnant. The water that flows through the canals is that which was saved from the infrequent floods, stored in huge reservoirs at the peak of the mountain upon which Pella'mir was built, and distributed through the complicated series of canals and grottoes throughout the city.

The water in which Azora and I bathed each day had been saved from the last flooding, of which Torq-aa spoke, that fell upon Pella'mir in his own childhood. It flows downhill through the city, and then is pumped upward again through a series of cisterns and vats, where it is boiled, the resultant steam rising through pipes and corridors again to the summit of the city, where it condenses, cleansed by the steaming process, into the vast reservoirs that are the crown of the city.

These steam pipes, feeding engines that are built into many subterranean vaults of the city, provide Pella'mir with much of its power.

The sea surrounding Pella'mir was receding, and had been for thousands of years. Day by day, year after year, the tides went out further by several inches than they returned. When Pella'mir was first built, it was but a tiny island city, one of only three small islands that peeked above a deep sea. Now, the island upon which Pella'mir was built was a mountain, one of many dozens of islands revealed by the ever-receding sea.

"Eventually," Shala told me, one evening, as we pored over her collection of scrolls and codices that detailed the history of her city, "We expect the sea to be gone, completely, leaving behind, perhaps, a vast desert of sinking sands. It may spell the end of our world, but again, it may mean only that our landscape will change.'

"The people of Pella'mir live in the moment," I remarked. "Or so it seems to me. Has anyone not made some provision against that day, when our descendants will inherit a desert world?"

"It is not something that will happen soon," Shala replied. "It will not be for many thousands of years to come, not by our present projections, and, of course, it is most impractical to plan for an eventuality that may be tens of thousands of years unfolding. But some of our scholars have made some suggestions, ranging, in my mind, from the outlandish to the absurd."

"Oh?" I prompted.

"One plan is to have us all remove to caverns beneath the surface. This fellow speculates that the seas are not receding, but spilling into a vast network of caverns he postulates must exist. He claims that these caverns must be huge to accommodate all the water that has flowed into them.

"Another fellow proposes that we begin work on a system of canals, dwarfing anything that we have here in Pella'mir, canals to take the place of the sea that surrounds us, to allow water to flow through the extent of the deserts that shall be revealed by the receding of the seas. He is a most optimistic fellow, who foresees a day when the people of Pella'mir will dwell, not merely upon the confines of our island, but spread out across all the worlds that will come to be, far beyond the horizon, for many millions of *yurlma*, beyond all reckoning."

"Most fanciful, that seems to me," I replied.

"I cannot even conceive it," Azora, who often sat in on our conversations, agreed. "A boundless world, stretching away forever in every direction? No, it gives me a most unpleasant feeling. I like the boundaries of our islands. They make the world we live in nicely graspable. I can think about our islands. But a world beyond all measure…"

"However it may all be," Shala concluded, "So long as the rainfalls come, once or twice in a generation, and replenishing our stores, we will have plenty upon which to live, and we see no reason to expect that to stop, for many, many thousands of years to come."

Pella'mir is a city of festivals, frequent and often spontaneous. Indeed, rarely a day passes without a festival or a fête of some sort unfolding somewhere in this city. Music is almost always playing—we awoke each morning to the strains of celebration. Everything, it seems, is a moment to commemorate with festivities, from the rising of the sun to the breezes that blow in from the sea.

Azora and I were strangers to this world—our blonde and yellow hair still drew stares each time we went out in public. Nowhere did we see others who had locks such as ours, and our pale, pinkish skin made us curiosities among the golden-hued inhabitants of this city.

But people of our coloration and hair were not entirely unknown in Pella'mir. Such were sometimes found among the slaves who were bartered and sold in the public squares, captured from unknown and unheard of islands beyond the horizon. Once, or twice, as well, sea traders from these distant shores, or explorers, stumbled upon Pella'mir, and they told stories of other islands, where other civilizations held sway, places with strange customs and stranger peoples.

These traders and slaves were infrequent visitors, though, and while their presence and their tales sometimes spurred intense speculation among the people of Pella'mir, never did they inspire a sustained curiosity about these strange lands. As days and weeks went by, and these traders fell out of memory, or the slaves who were bought were worn down by the drudgery of their existence, so did the interest in their origins.

Azora and I, however, never did lose interest of the tales of faraway lands. When we were by ourselves, we spoke of these strange pink and yellow-haired people with a ceaseless yearning to know more. Even Shala and Haia, my teachers in so many matters, were most incurious about these yellow-haired people. It was only to us, Azora and I, that any interest in them was to be found throughout the length or breadth of Pella'mir.

———※———

So we lived, Azora and I, for days without number. And so we could have lived all our lives, contented, comfortable and happy. We had some few small adventures while we dwelled in the house of Torq-aa, but none of them so dangerous as our flight from Jor-Taq, or our last battle with him, which only served to make these small adventures that much more agreeable.

And in those days, we both had many opportunities to explore the city of Pella'mir. Once, we took passage upon one of the boats that traded among the islands, that Azora might return briefly to Taakbar to acquire some of the secretion of the *Joyu* bush for her darts. On that same trip, we spent a day with the *ga'la* gatherers, a day when Azora and I both were very nearly killed by the *tumat* whose *ga'la* we sought.[1]

Again, we had a number of run-ins with the thugs of Pella'mir, and once broke a minor gang that sought to establish itself as an organized syndicate, seeking to establish control over the neighborhood where Torq-aa and his family lived. That gave us, Torq-aa, Jotar, Bendar, Turuk and even Azora and me yet another opportunity to fight together, while at the same time teaching us much about the sometimes complicated intrigues that unfold—all too frequently—among a people who live in almost continuous peace.

Then there were the games—the people of Pella'mir take huge interest in various blood sports. They have built a number of arenas in the city, where they exact their justice in the form of sport. In the case of the occasional feud between families, each family selects from its own a

---

1. See 'Journey to Taakbar,' in the appendix.

representative to meet the other in combat in the arena. These combats are usually fought to first blood, but it does happen, at least once or twice a year, that the enmity between families is so deep, that only a personal combat to the death will satisfy the hatred between them.

Also, those rare individuals who are guilty of crime are often forced by popular will to expiate their crimes in the arena, fighting those they have committed their crimes against.

Aside from these causes, there lives in Pella'mir a class of men who make their living solely by fighting in the arena, and it is in these combats, held every afternoon, that the people of Pella'mir find their daily entertainment. These fights are normally staged events, and everyone knows it, but that does not detract at all from their enjoyment. It is in the blood battles between families, or in the justice meted out to the rare criminal, that the real blood sport occurs.

And the enthusiasm of the people for these blood sports is a most frightening thing to watch. They crowd into the arenas where such sports are staged, clamoring loudly for blood, dismemberment and death. Often, the enthusiasm becomes so heated that fights break out among the audiences. Swordplay and knife work is frequent in these fights. In several famous occasions, wholesale riots broke out in the stands, wherein many dozens of people fell.

I took Azora to one of these spectacles, only once, and then only out of curiosity, having heard so much about them. Huge sums of money were wagered upon the combatants—a rare instance of a battle to the death. At Azora's suggestion, I wagered a small amount of coin myself, and came out quite well from the bet. Indeed, I made as much coin in that one wager as Azora had accumulated through many nights of dancing for the crowds. After that, she did not have to dance for our coin anymore, and she was happy to leave off.

One time, I too, was called to fight in the arena, to settle a feud that had grown between Bendar and another fellow. This was not a fight to the death, but only for first wound, and I came out of it victorious.

But, though the cheering of the crowd was a most intoxicating moment, I found I did not have the heart for this kind of thing. Battle, it seemed to me then, and still does, I must say, is too serious a business to pass off as entertainment. One may just as well offer up surgery, I thought, or childbirth, or even the butchery of animals for food, as a form of public spectacle. Necessary things, all, and since needful, we must have those among us who are skillful in the doing of them. And among those it is right that they should put their whole minds into study of them. But to offer these things up as amusement for the untutored, it struck me then, and always has, as a disgraceful thing. Jor-Taq, and his obscene inquiries, I reflected, as the crowds of the stadium cheered my victory over the bleeding man who lay at my feet, was not the aberration I would like to have believed. Perhaps he was merely less the hypocrite.

And when I saw the look of sick worry on Azora's face—Shala's, Haia's, Torq-aa's, and Bendar's, too—when they rushed the field after I vanquished Bendar's opponent (he had knocked my sword from my grip, and it looked as if he would violate the terms of our combat by running me through with his sword. I settled him by rushing past his point, and crushing his nose with a punch of my elbow, as Koax had taught me to do) that settled me there—I would never do this thing again. (But I did make out very well from the battle—that one combat made me a wealthy man. Not so wealthy as Jor-Taq had been before he died, but certainly wealthier than I had ever been in all my short life.)

But, other than these, and several other small adventures, Azora and I lived largely in peace and happiness. The food was plentiful and nourishing, the drink sustaining, and often intoxicating. The days were bright, and the nights were beautiful. And we could have lived thus, as I say, all our lives. How long it was that we lived thus, I do not know[2]. I made no notice of the passage of time. All experience flowed seamlessly from night to morning to day to evening, to night again, over and over, like countless waves rolling over each other.

But fortune has her own plans, and finally we were dragged away from these all-too short, but happy times.

---

2. Note: I have imposed the terms 'hours', 'weeks', 'months' and 'years' upon this narrative, solely to give some sense of coherency, overall. No such terms appear in the tales told to me by my patient, Paul Morgan. He speaks as if innocent of the flow of time. As far as I have been able to determine, the people of Pella'mir have no sense of time that in any way corresponds to ours. Rather than seeing time, as we do, a dimension that has a 'flow' or a movement from past to future, it appears, from Paul Morgan's tales, that the people of Pella'mir see time as a static thing, one through which they move. In their understanding, there is but a single day, and a single night, both of which exist independently and eternally. They pass through these things cyclically, revisiting them over and over throughout their lives. Thus, they often speak of past events as if they are present. As far as I have been able to determine, they have absolutely no notion of what we call the 'future'. To them, it seems, what we understand as the 'future' is simply a region of the present which they do not happen to populate. To explain it, I might hazard that their word 'here' refers not only to geographical location, but also location in time, and their words for 'there' are used not only as we use them, but also to indicate past and future. Paul Morgan himself often slides seamlessly from past and present to future, in a flow of narrative that at first caused me great bewilderment. I have been at great pains to translate his tales into a chronological narrative that would make sense within the sequential pages of a book A.G.

9

—◆—

THE BRIGANDS OF BORAMOK

I T HAPPENED OF A morning. Azora and I had gone out that day to pass the time, amuse ourselves and to see some of the sights of the city. Pella'mir is large, very large, and though we had been there, living free for years by this time, we had seen only but a small part of the city.

So many days we spent, simply wandering through the pleasant streets and byways, looking for nothing in particular, but finding many things to delight our eyes. This morning, just before the rise of the sun, started as so many others had.

It had been so long since the Brigands of Boramok had assaulted the city, and our lives had been so full since last they attacked, that our memory of them had receded into a distant and nearly irrelevant past. When we did give them thought, Azora and I, it was usually with a thankful feeling, that their last assault upon the city had been so fortuitously timed for us. Their menace was small in our minds, and we gave them no notice.

Were we not wealthy? Did we not have the friendship of many prominent people within Pella'mir? Did we not have property, prestige, a place among the inhabitants of this, the richest city of all the world?

And yet, though we were strangers to this world, we had done well for ourselves. Wealth, prominence, prestige. We had all we desired, and could have asked for nothing more.

This morning, I was overcome with an odd nostalgia to see the shore and the walls where I had first come to Pella'mir, as I strode through the water and the very dangerous sinking sands. Many things had happened, since I had come to shore, and I wished to see again those streets and byways my eyes had first fallen upon at that moment of my arrival.

So Azora and I set out early that morning, after taking breakfast, as was our custom, with Torq-aa, Shala, Haia and Jotar. Telling them where it was we intended to go, and that we might not be back for several days, we left.

And that was to be the last time we ever saw our friends Shala, Haia, Torq-aa and Jotar. They rose from their places on the floor, where they sat in a squat-legged circle around the hearth, to wish us well on our little journey.

We had no foreboding that this was to be our last leave-taking of each other. Our 'goodbyes' were easy and light-hearted. The kisses we gave each other were breezy and cheerful, yet those last glimpses I had of my good friends have remained vivid and strong in my memory in the long years since.

Had we known that this was to be our last leave-taking, would we have been so light and careless about it? Would we not instead have gripped each other strongly, long and lingering, to prolong the moment when we must part?

Perhaps so, and that parting would have been a most painful thing. Perhaps, I have reflected many times since, and sharing these thoughts with Azora, too, it was best that we had no premonition, no foretelling of what was to come. Perhaps it was best that we did not know then, that that morning we were laying eyes upon each other for the very last time.

For now my memory of that last leave-taking is not weighed down by heaviness and grieving. My last images of Shala and Haia are as I had come to know them, happy and cheerful, with light and melodious personalities, and generous smiles they were always happy to share.

Those are the last, vivid impressions I have of my friends, those are what I have carried in my heart with me, all these long years since. Perhaps it is better that way, but I cannot but agree with Azora, when she replied, "And it were a better thing, still, had we never been parted at all."

We strolled carelessly through the early morning streets of Pella'mir that day, watching as the black sky of night filled with purpling dawn. Each morning was a wondrous display of transmuting color, and I never tired of the spectacle. Deep purple raced swiftly across the horizon, heralding the soft pinks and saffron tones that became the daytime sky. The purple, then lavender, then saffron hues raced across the horizon from the eastern limb, encircling the world until they met again in the west.

Oh! How I love the dawning day! Oh! How I love the mornings in Pella'mir, with the beautiful Azora almost constantly at my side, playful and often teasing. Her infinite touches, her boundless caresses, her happy smile, her dancing blue eyes!

We'd made it down to the very entry to the city, where I had stumbled through, so long before, following awkwardly on legs unaccustomed to walking, as Horath led me brutally to slavery at the house of Jor-Taq.

How little I expected in those days, now long gone by. How little I knew then. How only very little more did I know on this day. A stranger I was then, an infant in the world, who knew nothing of walking, of speaking, nor writing, nor fighting. Swiftly the images from that day came back to me, and I felt myself overcome with a sweet and burning nostalgia for those days when I was so completely ignorant of the world, unhampered, unfettered, and free in my ignorance.

Knowledge is bondage. As we learn, as we come to know, so we come into the responsibility of knowing. We come to understand consequences. We come to understand costs. And as we have knowledge, we cannot ignore the consequences or the costs of our actions. We learn that we are liable, not only for what we do, but also for what comes from our doings.

I had fallen silent with these and other like ruminations, with Azora at my side, her warm arm encircling my waist, with her fingertips looped into the belt of my harness, which was her way when we walked together. She, too, profoundly sympathetic with my varying moods, had also fallen silent, allowing me to wander the corridors of my mind.

I was on the point of stopping, and turning to her, to make an observation of some sort, the point of which I cannot now recall, when the streets were suddenly filled with the loud clangor of a hundred warning bells.

The brigands of Boramok were attacking. They'd come in their swift and silent ships, under cover of darkness, and now the bells of the watchtowers lining the walls of Pella'mir gave warning of their advance.

Until now, the streets had been almost deserted in the early morning, before the light of the sun had completely illuminated the sky. But now, with the insistent clamor of the bells, people ran out from their houses, here, near the entrance of the city, and fled up the winding streets, away from the invading forces.

Azora and I did not waste any words. We knew what the alarm bells meant, and we knew, too, that we must flee upon the instant, lest we be killed in the bombardment, or, worse yet, captured, when they made their sortie into the breaches they would soon make upon the walls.

We turned away, and began to move with the many refugees when a huge explosion blasted a stone building into ashes, not thirty paces from us. We were both knocked to the ground.

We scrambled to our feet, covered with ash and dust, dazed, disoriented and looking about helplessly.

"The brigands!" came the call through the shocked morning crowds. "The brigands have come!"

Instantly, another explosion blasted the city, knocking down a wall that came crumbling to our very feet. And then another blast rocked the ground, sending stones flying high into the air, and broken bits of pavement came falling about our heads.

"Come!" I cried, grabbing Azora by the hand and dragging her away, up the winding street and toward the center of the city.

She followed instantly, even as a rooftop came spilling from above, crashing to the ground all around us.

And then a huge, deafening blast blew a vast gap into the wall that surrounded the city of Pella'mir. The concussion of it sent both Azora and I through the air for many feet, and we landed hard upon a pile of rubble. I think it must have knocked us both insensible for several minutes, for the next thing I recall is both of us rising, groggy, and surrounded by a host of strange men, the likes of which I had not seen before.

They were rude characters, with heavy beards upon their faces—all the more remarkable, as the men of Pella'mir are beardless. They grow no hair upon their faces whatever, and the stubble that persisted—insisted, I might say—in growing upon my own was a source of much speculation, and humor on the part of my friends.

But these brigands all wore long and heavy beards, and their bodies were otherwise thick with hair. Arms, chests, legs and even their burly backs were covered with thick forests of wiry hair.

They came at us with swords that were of different lines than the swords of Pella'mir. These swords were curved, from the haft to the tip, some of them so curved that they described near crescent shapes, almost circles.

They wore tight breeches that covered their legs—another thing that set them apart, for the people of Pella'mir made little effort to hide the contours of their bodies. I had never before this moment seen legs hidden under swaths of fabric, as was the custom of the Brigands of Boramok.

Some wore vests over their naked chests, vests embroidered with gold and silver thread. Most, however, did not, and I learned, in time, that the vests were marks of rank among the brigands.

These brigands were also much different from the people of Pella'mir in their complexions. Where the people of Pella'mir have a skin color of yellow, even golden hues, the flesh of the brigands is red. The range of hues is wide, from a muddy red, the color of bricks, through scarlet and ruby, and, among the darkest of them, a deep blood-blue crimson.

Their visages are terrifying in the extreme, because of the violent coloring of their bodies, their long, wild beards, which they knotted and tied in grotesque loops and bonds, with string and leather cords.

They came at us, Azora and me, all in a mass as we struggled to our feet. Azora was quick. She managed to hurl a dozen darts at the brigands who rushed us, and I saw, for the first time, the deadly effect of the poison with which she had tipped them. Three of them caught her darts, barely scratching their skin, and instantly their arms began to swell and boil, as if with a huge infection. In moments, the afflicted limbs were paralyzed, and useless. The brigands fell to the ground, their faces swollen, now blue and purple. They panted convulsively, their chests quaked spasmodically, and then they were dead.

The brigands were apparently quite familiar with the toxin, and the deadly darts that Azora hurled at them, for seeing how their companions were felled, they stepped back momentarily, pulling small shields from their backs, and strapping them on to their forearms.

Azora threw another half dozen darts at them as they circled us warily, but, armed with their shields, they managed to deflect her missiles. She did manage to catch two more of the brutes, feinting toward their heads, and then suddenly hurling her darts at their ankles, and they fell to the ground, as the others had, their legs swelling almost obscenely, turning first blue, then purple, and dying with spasms wracking their bodies.

But those two were the last she brought down with her darts. Now the others rushed us in a mass, and Azora only barely had time to pull her dagger swiftly from its scabbard as I, by her side, hauled out my sword and swung it over my head to meet their attack.

The fight was swift and brutal, and we managed to kill three more of the fellows—Azora with a pretty little knife thrust aimed at the inner thigh, which neatly sliced the artery of her opponent, and I brought down two others, one, with an overhead thrust, bringing the point of my sword directly into his face and catching him in the mouth, splitting his jaw asunder, following that with a quick lateral slash that caught the brigand standing next to him at the base of his neck.

But my sword got jammed in the bones of his shoulder, and as I put my foot on his chest to push him away and to release my sword, three other brigands rushed me hard. Two of them thrust the points of their curved swords at my throat—each from a different angle of attack, while the third came at me from the side and, grabbing my hair and pulling my head backward, he jabbed my abdomen with a very wicked looking knife, drawing blood, and hissing at me, "Live or die. You choose."

At the same time, four other brigands crowded hard upon Azora. While she whirled about and jabbed at them, sometimes drawing blood, two of them leaped on her from behind and knocked her to the ground. They landed on her heavily, ripping the knife out of her tightly clenched fist, and then they forced her back to her feet, quickly binding her wrists behind her back.

I was devastated, my heart filling with despair. Only moments before, we had been happy and careless in a world of infinite joy. Now we'd been blasted out of that happy world, into another—now, were fortune to smile on us, we could look forward to a lifetime of slavery. And, were fortune not so kind, we would endure things infinitely worse than that.

It was hopeless. I could gain nothing by resisting, except instant death. And dead, I would be of no help to Azora. Whatever may happen, as long as I lived, as long as she lived, we had some hope, however dim. But, either of us dead, the world then would have no meaning for the other. I released my grip on the pommel of my sword, and let my arms drop limply at my side.

Two burly men with elaborately tied beards grabbed my wrists and forced them behind my back, and then they bound my elbows together in a tight knot that was painful and awkward.

And then one of the fellows, with a dark crimson complexion and a well-worn but lavishly embroidered vest, which was stained in places with what I assume to be blood, barked out orders at several of the others, who immediately surrounded Azora and me. They disarmed us, taking from Azora her remaining darts and her small throwing dagger.

With the points of their curved swords poking into the smalls of our backs to guide us, they herded us toward the wall of Pella'mir, and through the smoking gap, toward the sea.

We stepped gingerly, if clumsily, over the bodies of many dead, people of Pella'mir and brigands of Boramok, alike. Once we had been forced, by sword point, through the breach in the wall, my eyes fell upon a fleet of ships clustered hard upon the rocky shore.

This was my first glimpse of the fabled armada of the brigands of Boramok, and I must say the sight took me aback. Hundreds of these ships were lined upon the rocky shore, their prows dragged up from the water.

They were low and flat, with wide berth, each equipped with a single sail dyed a deep crimson. All of them had at least one bank of long oars, and several had two, each bank staggered upon the bank below.

In the prow of each ship was a low-lying contrivance, which I later learned was the ship's catapult. It was from these catapults that the brigands launched their heavy missiles against the walls of Pella'mir. Later, as I became more familiar with the customs of these people, I learned that they begin each expedition by loading their ship down with as many heavy stones as she can bear, emptying them all upon the walls of Pella'mir, and the other cities they preyed upon, and then in the resulting confusion, they make their sorties into the city, quickly capturing prisoners, or looting what is closest at hand. When the ships have disgorged their heavy missiles and the bombardment ceases, the brigands immediately halt their assault and retreat back to sea.

The bow of each ship rose high above the water line, and was carved to resemble the face of a grotesque, grinning monster—and many of these were quite dreadful, indeed, some with multiple eyes, and opened mouths lined with grinning teeth. Seen at sea level from a distance, especially when the sail and the mast were lowered, these ships appeared to be monsters swimming swiftly across the water, and the effect upon those who saw them coming was profound.

My eyes took all this in, but my heart was filled with dread, especially for Azora's sake. I faced only death, myself, or slavery. What she was facing was infinitely worse.

The brigands are brutes. They stink. Their manners are brutal. They wasted no opportunity to cuff me about the head, and as they drove us forward, they kicked both Azora and me repeatedly. It was everything we could do to keep to our feet.

When they had forced us down the stony shore, to the prow of one of their more ornately decorated ships, I thought fleetingly that they must untie us now, so that we may climb over the bulwark. Perhaps, even against such odds, that moment may provide a chance at escape.

But my fleeting thoughts were quickly dashed, for as they shoved us up against the hull of the ship, many hands reached over and grabbed Azora and me up by our shoulders, hauling us up bodily, then tossing us down upon the deck.

And there we lay for what seemed an interminable time, but which was, in fact, only a very few moments. Their bombardment of Pella'mir was done shortly after they dragged Azora and me into their ship. After that, but a few moments passed before the brigands had all returned to their ships, and pushed them back into the sea.

Azora and I lay upon our bellies, side by side, and we could see nothing but the naked feet of the brigands as they moved past us. We heard the shouted orders of the commanders and felt the swaying of the ship, and knew that we had seen the last of Pella'mir.

10

AT SEA

RUDE HANDS GRABBED US both up by the cords that bound us by our elbows. We were forced to our feet. The ship swayed considerably, and we both found it dizzying, especially with our arms bound behind us in such a painful and awkward fashion.

"Courage," I said to Azora, when her eyes fell upon me. One of the brigands who had hoisted us up punched me hard in the face, knocking me backwards.

"Shut up!" he said.

"Careful with those two," I heard a voice from behind me caution. "Salamir will want to see them."

"What would Salamir want with these?" the man who punched me demanded.

"You should have seen them fighting today," the voice behind me whispered. "They killed eight of our men, just the two of them."

The man who punched me looked at me with eyes filled with astonishment. "Eight? You?" he demanded of Azora and me.

"I just killed two," I answered. "She killed the other six," indicating Azora by pointing at her with my chin.

Now the brigand turned to stare at Azora. "*Six* men? You?"

Azora smiled.

"I don't believe it," the brigand scoffed. "The people of Pella'mir are soft. They're no fighters."

Then he looked harder at Azora.

"But you're not from Pella'mir, are you, girl?"

Azora said nothing.

"She's deadly with those darts," the voice behind us remarked. I didn't like that voice. It was oily and unctuous, with a smilingly sinister undertone that made me want to whirl on my heel and slap the face that spoke it hard. Which I probably would have done, were I not bound.

"I saw her," the oily voice went on. "Quick as a viper. She's got them poisoned. Killed five men in a flash, then the sixth one she opened up with her knife. Gutted him proper good."

"That's a Taakbar trick," the man who punched me said. "Are you from Taakbar?"

"Not with that yellow hair, or that pink skin, she's not," the unctuous voice said.

Azora shrugged her shoulders and gave the man who punched me a sullen stare.

He laughed, and then he demanded, "You like to fight, girl?"

"I like to kill brigands," Azora answered.

"She's a spicy one, this!" he laughed. "Right spicy. What about you?" he asked, turning on me. "You let this girl do all the heavy work? She got six to your two?"

"The day's just started," I replied.

With that, all the brigands who crowded round us laughed uproariously.

I was most surprised to see these men take the killing of their fellows so lightly. That we had killed eight of them seemed to have inspired no great feelings among their compatriots.

"So, who'd they polish off?" I heard the question raised.

"Umir, for one…" the unctuous voice behind me began.

"Good riddance to a right ass!" several in the crowd declared.

"And Tuma for another…"

"Ha!" I heard one fellow laugh. He had a huge tangled beard that sprawled across his ample belly.

"Then Rozso. The girl got him in the thigh with her knife. Laid him wide open."

"Ah! I'd have paid good coin to see that!"

"His leg gushed, it did. The girl turned him into a fountain. His face went white and then he died."

"Ha! Ha! Ha!" several of the burly men laughed.

"Glad to get rid of them all! All the more for us!"

"You did us good, girl," the brigand who had punched me decided. "Rid us of some stinking ballast, you did."

"Which is why Salamir will want to see these two," the oily voice behind me put in. "We've never seen such fighters from Pella'mir."

I had grown increasingly irritated with the voice coming from behind my back. As the conversation grew prolonged, the voice grew louder in my ear, as the author of it drew closer to me. At last my patience snapped, and I half turned on my heel to direct my words at this unseen person.

"Why do you stand behind me? Why don't you stand where a man can see you?" I demanded.

For a moment I heard nothing but a hushed silence among the crew of this ship. Apparently my words and my tone were most audacious.

Then, after a dread-filled pause, I felt the blade of a knife come sliding silently from behind my neck, until the edge of it lay sharp against my throat. I heard the unctuous voice whisper with sinister sibilance, "You speak most insolently, for a man with his elbows bound behind his back."

And then, after another long and potent pause, I felt the knife sliding back across my throat, grazing the skin and drawing a thin stream of blood that trickled down my chest.

And then this man filled my ear with his laughter. It was a soft laughter, a subtle chuckle from the throat, an insinuating laugh, almost feminine, and one that chilled my blood. I felt him step away from me, and then he moved in front of me, facing me.

I was astonished to see that this man was no brigand. Here before me was one of the golden-hued people of Pella'mir. His face was narrow and cruel, his body slender and wan, almost womanly, his shoulders were narrow, his throat, sinuous and delicate. His lips were thin, painted blue, and fringed with long black whiskers that trailed from the corners of his mouth. His eyes were gray and flat and lusterless, and they were opaque to the world, looking out upon everything, but allowing nothing to look in.

Observing the surprise on my face, he chuckled. The smile that overspread his features was tinged with sadism and treachery which he made no effort to disguise.

"He, he, he," he laughed, quietly and deliberately.

"You are from Pella'mir," I said, speaking with disgust.

"I gave you no leave to speak to me," he retorted smartly, giving his head but the subtlest turn. And then, cocking an eyebrow at me and tracing a fingertip across my chest, through the tricklet of blood that ran down from my throat he said, "You are bleeding."

I had no idea what was to come next, but from the hush of the brigands who crowded about us, watching, I sensed that something particularly sadistic was about to befall.

He daubed his fingertip in the blood that ran down my chest, then followed the trickle upward, to the shallow cut on my throat where I bled. His noxious familiarity repulsed me and I turned my face away, but he grabbed me by the chin with his free hand and forced my face back to look at his.

Then he thrust his fingertip deep into the cut, scraping it with his dirty nail. I winced with pain, but would not give him the satisfaction of hearing any complaint. When he pulled his fingertip away at last, I saw that it was fairly coated with my blood. And then he brought his fingertip slowly toward his mouth, his purplish tongue darting quickly from his lips, and he leered into my eyes as he did it. Seeing that he was preparing to lick my blood with his oily tongue, I felt myself overtaken by a huge and sudden revulsion.

Though my elbows were bound behind my back, my legs were not. Before he touched his tongue with his fingertip, I threw my knee upward, catching the man fairly in the groin. The kick lifted him from the deck, and he fell down in a heap, clutching himself and gasping for air. His eyes went wide, and he looked for all the world like a beached fish flapping uselessly on the deck.

I fully expected to be cut down by the brigands that very moment, and was astonished that they left me completely alone.

So I wasted not an instant, but fell to hailing the prostrated man with a flurry of kicks aimed at his belly and face. Now the brigands began to laugh, and I saw from that that this man from Pella'mir was no favorite of theirs.

Azora watched in horror as I rained kicks upon the man, and I knew that her concern was not for him, but for the punishment I would surely incur. I dropped myself upon his prostrate body, landing my knee squarely upon his face. The crunching sound I heard, that of the bones of his nose shattering, was most satisfying. I grunted with delight.

Suddenly I heard a shout from the after-deck, "Stop! Stop!" And, seeing that the repulsive man from Pella'mir was sufficiently bloodied by my kicks, I ceased.

"What is all this?" a very beefy and bearded brigand bellowed, as he forced his way through the others who had crowded round to watch.

"Tuso was getting himself kicked," one of the brigands answered.

"Good and kicked," another added, to general laughter.

"Not on my ship he don't!" the beefy bearded brigand shouted. "I'll have discipline, or I'll feed every last one of you to the sinking sands!"

That threat shut every man on board up. Silence reigned among the rude crew as this beefy brigand, who I concluded must be the captain, launched into a long tirade of invective and curses against all who would dare bring confusion to his deck.

He grabbed the golden-hued man up from the deck, and brought him to his feet.

"What's this? Are you starting riots on my ship now?" he demanded, as the oily, sinister man—the one they called Tuso—caught his breath, with many lurching and blood-sputtering gasps. He was bleeding profusely from his nose and mouth and he cast me an evil glance that was filled with fiery hatred.

"Thith prith-oner tried to kill me," he said at last, his voice thick with blood.

The brigand grabbed me by my shoulder and spun me around. I felt his heavy fists grasp the cord that bound my elbows. He jerked it and yanked hard on it, testing the knots that bound me.

"His elbows are tied behind his back!" the beefy brigand yelled. "Do you mean to tell me that you let this man get the better of you, with his arms bound behind his back?"

Tuso wiped the blood from his mouth with the back of his hand, smearing his cheek.

"Theeth two are deadly fighterth," he said. "They killed eight brigandth thith morning. Thalamir will want to thee them."

"Eight?" the bearded brigand howled in loud and shocked unbelief. "These two?"

"I only killed two," I said. "She," indicating Azora by pointing with my chin, "killed six. I'm just trying to catch up."

The beefy captain spun on me, staring hard with his eyes opened wide. I thought certain that he was about to knock me to the deck for my insolence, and he glared at me in silence for several very long seconds.

And then he threw his head back and laughed out loud.

"Haw! Haw! Haw!" he bawled. "Haw! Haw! Haw! Haw, haw!

"Lucky for you, Tuso," he said, tears of laughter rolling from his eyes and disappearing beneath his thick whiskers, "That it was only he who kicked you, and not she! You'd be dead and gutted and served up on my table already, if it'd been her, what kicked you. Well, no matter," he went on, turning to me and slapping me on the back of my shoulder. "Even just bagging two brigands is a good morning's work. I wouldn't let it bring me down, that the girl did better than you."

"You seem careless of your own people," I remarked. "We've killed eight between us, and given the chance, we'll kill eight more."

"You'll have a long way to go to match my bag," this brawny man replied, laughing. "I've killed eighty, myself."

He must have seen the astonishment on my face, for he said, "Treacherous heaps of *kra*, every last one of them! Not one of them sailed under me! All of them Salamir's people, come here, thinking to take my vessel from me. Oh, they try, they try, and they'll keep on trying, I don't doubt it."

I was confused, and made no attempt to hide it.

"Tuso here is one of Salamir's creatures," the brawny brigand said, giving Tuso a cuff on the back of the head to emphasize the point.

"Sent here to keep watch on us, he is. He's Salamir's spy, 'at's whut he is. He knows it, I know it, we all know it. If he gits himself killed, I won't grieve it. So long as he minds his business, I'll let 'im live."

"You are the captain of this ship?" I asked.

"Of course, whadja think?"

"And this Salamir, does he command the fleet?"

"Command nothing! We sail together, but we answer to no one. There's strength in numbers. But this is my ship, and I'm my own man!"

"You are...?"

"The man who can cut you down where you stand for your nosy, inquiring ways," the brawny man replied, laughing loudly. "But we took good bounty this day, and I'm in a fine mood, so I'll let you live and tell you my name, too, though you're a prisoner and bound to be a slave. But if we're trading names, I'll have yours first."

"I am called Grae-don," I said. "And this is Azora."

"A ripe purty one, this," the beefy man said, by way of courtesy, I suppose. "I am Burkov. They call me Burkov the Bloody. Now, Tuso says Salamir will want to see you. It's up to Salamir, whut happens with ya, now, so off ya go!"

Burkov the Bloody turned on his heel and barked a dozen orders to his crew. And then he strode away.

So Azora and I were bundled up and manhandled over the side of the ship into a skiff tied alongside. Tuso, his broken nose crudely bandaged, sat at the helm with a sailor who plied a tiny sail, while four other rude fellows manned the oars.

Tuso hated me already, I knew it. Which was fine with me because I hated him, too. But Azora and I were both in his power, and I would not have been surprised if he had tossed me over the side, into the depths of the yellow, golden sea, my arms still bound behind my back.

But he sat sullen and silent at the helm, glowering over the shallow waters ahead, nor did he offer us so much as a single word or glance.

We rowed for an immeasurable time, further and further into the sea, rounding the horizon, and putting the main part of the brigand's fleet far behind us. As we saw the ships dropping below the horizon, we turned to see where it was we were being taken, and, far ahead, we saw a number of sails dotting the sea in the distance before us.

Our approach to them revealed these ships to be huge, of heavy draft, and deep in the hull. These ships were several times larger than any of the low and flat ships that sailed into the shallow waters to attack Pella'mir.

Though built roughly along the same sleek lines, these ships carried far more sails, and were built up at the stern with high towers that overhung the bulwarks. And where the ships that attacked Pella'mir were trim and fast, and largely undecorated, these ships were vast and ornate, with heavy gilt and gilding upon the rails. Ornamental figures lined the hull and the galleries, figures of nude and naked women, and children of both sexes, cavorting in grotesque lewdness with strange creatures of the sea most predominating. These figures were all painted brightly, in many colors, and as we drew close, I could see that their eyes, nipples, navels and genitals were adorned with many rare and precious jewels.

Bright and gaudy, these ships may have projected a festive air, but many skulls were set into the hulls in long lines, and skulls were hung from the masts in great bundles, belying the festivity of the sight. We saw, also hanging from the yardarms, the bodies of dozens of men, some bound in chains, some confined in tight cages.

As we drew even closer, into the shadows cast by the hulls of the gaudy ships, we realized with horror that some of the bodies hanging from chains and bound into cages were of men yet living. The thin moans of agony from these tortured men, left to die slowly by exposure to the elements, reached our ears as whispers above the gentle surges of the waves against the ships.

In all, the juxtaposition of gaudy color and ornamentation with torture and objects of horror was monstrous, and provoked in both Azora and me a profound revulsion. I was overcome with dread, and in a quick undertone, I said to her, "I'd rather have put you out of your misery with my own hand, than that you should endure the horrors we are now bound to suffer."

Azora gave me a long look and then she said, "We're still alive, at least."

"... at least," I echoed.

And then we came alongside the largest of the many ships. The hull was tall, and, where it was not ornamented, the wood was dark, almost black. Crewmen crowded the railings upon our approach, and shouted down to the men on our boat, who answered back with crude jokes and rough curses.

"Watcha got there?" they demanded.

"Prithonerth for Thalamir," Tuso answered through his broken nose. "Tho keep your handth off. Throw uth down a line. They're bound, and I'll not unbind them."

Several ropes came snaking down from the deck high above us, and Tuso tied them unceremoniously to the lines that coiled around our elbows. Once he had securely tied me to the rope, he called up to the crewmen on the deck, "Haul `im up!" and instantly, I felt the rope jerk me upward.

Dangling in the air just above the skiff, my body scraped against the hull of the tall, dark vessel. Tuso called up to the men hoisting me, "Hold! Hold!" And they stopped hauling me. Then Tuso came close, and grasped my ankles in his hands. He swung me hard and bashed my head against the hull of the ship, once, twice, three times.

I felt an explosion of pain behind my eyes, and fell into unconsciousness. The last thing I saw was Tuso's laughing face twisted with sadistic glee.

The crew hauled me up to the deck of the ship after that, and they threw me upon the boards where I lay until they hoisted Azora up, tossing her in a heap beside me. Barely had I returned to consciousness when I heard a gruff voice bellow out, "Clean `em up!"

Warm salty water splashed down upon Azora and me. The brackish water stung my eyes and roused me completely. Hair damp and plastered on my forehead, I turned where I lay, and saw Azora struggling to a sitting position.

Seeing me move, she said, "Ah! I thought he had killed you!"

Still groggy from the blows, I was not able to answer her. Azora leaned close and gently rubbed her cheek against mine.

But we had no time to commiserate.

"Get them on their feet!" we heard a voice bark loudly. A dozen burly hands manhandled us and pulled us up by the cords that bound our elbows behind our backs.

"Thalamir wanth to thee theeth two!"

It was Tuso speaking. We saw him climbing over the railing with six other men. They all clustered around us and hustled us quickly from the mid-deck toward the aft of the ship.

We had no time to take stock of the ship, so quickly did they force us along. But I caught a hurried glance at the narrowing after-decks that towered high above the mid-deck, all casting deep shadows. Ladders stretched from deck to deck, and I arched my neck to see upward. Overhead, corpses of many men swung from the rigging, their legs swaying with the currents and the breezes.

And then we were rushed bodily under an overhanging deck, into the darkness below.

For many long moments I could see nothing, for the day outside was bright, and the shadows below were deep, and my eyes did not adjust quickly. Lines and lanyards lay upon the deck, and casks were stacked along the bulkheads. Footing was tricky, but I had no chance to stumble, as our guards forced Azora and me forward in great haste, and dragged us when we faltered.

We passed through several portals, and were forced up a number of narrow stairs until, at last, we came to an ornate and gilded doorway that was most steadfastly shut. Two guards stood outside the door, one on either side, and they both carried swords in their harnesses which they unsheathed at our approach.

One of the guards stepped forward as we came near.

"Are these the ones?" he asked.

"Yeth," Tuso answered.

"Not much to look at, are they?"

The guard was hardly one to speak, missing, as he was, an eye, an ear, part of his nose and several teeth—all in all, he made a grim visage. But I kept my remarks to myself. I was still groggy from the beating Tuso had given me a few moments before, and needed to give myself wind before I started picking another fight.

"No, not much," Tuso agreed, "But they are both vipers. Thith one here," he went on, indicating Azora with a jerk of his thumb, "Killed thix of our fellows."

With that, the guard's eyebrows shot upward in surprise. "Six?"

"Yeth," Tuso said. "The man killed only two."

"Ha!" laughed the guard. "Only two?"

"I like to savor my work," I answered. "I will enjoy killing you, and Tuso, too."

Tuso slapped the back of my head, hard, nearly knocking me down.

"Shut up!" he fairly screamed. "Shut up! You are about to enter into the presence of Thalamir. You will keep thilent, unless he bidth you to thpeak, and then you will keep a rethpectful tongue..."

And he bashed the back of my head to emphasize his point.

"... or I will take great pleathure in removing your tongue from your head, mythelf."

The guard grinned openly.

"And then, if he is Tuso, he'll cook it up himself and make you watch as he eats it."

The disgust on Azora's face and mine must have been plain, for both Tuso and the guards laughed loudly at our discomfiture.

"You are repulsive," Azora spat.

"Thut up," Tuso replied.

The guards opened the ornate door and stepped aside as Tuso and his company forced us through and into the presence of Salamir.

Our eyes were confronted by a spectacle of sheer debauchery and opulent decadence. The cabin was low and dark and crowded, the air thick with the stench of incense and sweat and other rank odors I do not care to think of. Many heavy layers of carpet covered the deck and a low table that stretched from bulkhead to bulkhead in a long semi-circle was laden with golden platters, ceramic bowls and bottles,

goblets and decanters. Everything we saw bespoke wealth and extravagant self-indulgence. The cabin was heavy with incense and spices.
Naked courtiers, effeminate men and mannish women, children, too,
boy and girl, they all lounged about the table, on pillows and cushions.
Their eyes were crafty, their manner haughty, and they looked upon us
with expansive self-importance and lavish disdain.

I saw a dozen women, behind the table, all lounging upon a veritable
mountain of cushions that rose steeply toward the ceiling. Most of
them wore naught but jewels strung upon thin golden chains that
depended about their waists or from their throats—I supposed them
to be Salamir's concubines. They turned to look upon us with lazy
curiosity as we entered, their tinted eyes heavy-lidded and their faces
painted.

Salamir himself lounged among them, lazing upon the only piece of
furniture within the cabin, an opulent golden divan behind the low
table. Everyone else lay about on pillows and cushions.

The man was repugnant. My first glimpse of him filled me with
disgust. Everything about him bespoke treachery, laziness, self-indulgence and corruption. His belly was distended, giving evidence of
many feasts, but little work. His arms were thick and flabby, his fingers,
pudgy and grabby.

His eyes were sinister, cynical and cruel. He wore rouge upon his
cheeks, and he painted his eyelids, and the nails of his long and tapered
fingers, as women do. Jewels dangled from the lobes of his ears, and
his nipples were pierced with golden rings. Gross and corpulent as
he was, he radiated a grotesque femininity that only exaggerated the
repugnance of his person.

He gave off a pungent odor of heavy perspiration soaked with perfume—in fact, the entire cabin reeked of sweat and scent. It gathered
in my throat and sickened me.

I did not like Salamir, and made no effort to disguise the revulsion he inspired in me. Casting a quick glance at Azora, who stood by my side, I saw that she, too, did not bother to hide her disgust.

Salamir only grinned at us, but said nothing.

Closely did he examine Azora, from foot to head, the grin upon his face unchanging. And then he turned his attention to me, his eyes lingering long, and salaciously, upon my person. I felt nausea clutching in my throat, but choked it down.

Then Salamir turned his eyes toward Tuso, who stood beside me, and without uttering a sound, he merely raised his eyebrows in question.

Tuso bowed his head, and said, "Theeth are the captives, oh Greatetht one. Theeth are they who killed eight before they were captured. The girl killed thix, the man, only two.

"But, even tho," Tuso continued, "He ith deadly, for you thee the woundth he inflicted upon me, though he wath bound by hith armth."

We heard a gasp from the effeminate courtiers and the women. Several of them looked upon us now, and Azora especially, with great horror showing in their eyes. They cringed toward the protective bulk of the decadent man.

"Now, now," Salamir said. "They shall do us no harm, ladies. You see, they are quite tightly bound."

Those were the first words that we heard from Salamir, and the sound of his voice was oily, sodden with unspoken insinuations.

"But they are not from Pella'mir," Salamir observed. "Not with that yellow hair."

"She," Tuso said, indicating Azora with a gesture, "Comes from Taakbar. There, she wath a thlave."

"Ah!" Salamir replied, opening his mouth and his eyes wide. "Taakbar. It has been too long since we have paid Taakbar a visit. If they produce specimens such as this one..." and he paused, cocking his eyebrows toward Tuso in silent query.

"She is called Athora," Tuso replied, understanding and answering Salamir's unspoken question.

"Azora... Azora..." Salamir said, rolling the name over his tongue as if he were savoring the sound of it. Rage flared in my heart at his gross familiarity, but I kept my features stony and silent.

"A lovely name," Salamir said, with a smile upon his wet and sloppy lips. "Lovely... lovely. Yes, if Taakbar has produced many such creatures as this lovely Azora, then we positively must pay the people of those islands a visit, and very soon. Perhaps this girl, Azora, would offer to guide us to any particularly, um... abundant grounds in need of harvest?"

Though he spoke obliquely, he looked directly at Azora when he raised the question, and it was clear that he expected her to answer.

"I don't know what you mean," Azora said.

"Ah! She is blunt. Quite frank." Salamir laughed.

Tuso turned to her.

"The great Thalamir offerth you a gloriouth privilege," he explained.

"What privilege is that?" Azora demanded, her proud chin high.

"We are always in need of servants," Salamir said, smiling. "Ours do die off so quickly, so very inconveniently. Why, not a day goes by that we don't lose two of them, at least, and sometimes more. So thoughtless of them. So careless. Such a pity," he said, though the sadistic smile upon his lips as he said proved that he did not think it anything of the sort.

"If you can assist us in finding servants to replace those who die so easily, new servants, strong and beautiful as you, well, then..." And Salamir smiled broadly, opening his arms in an expansive gesture.

"You want me to be your slave-catcher?" Azora replied tartly. "Like this repulsive Tuso here? Is that the bargain you gave him?"

Tuso scowled at Azora, but Salamir laughed loudly. His naked, gelatinous belly shook as he laughed, and ripples of flesh ran from his nipples to his navel.

"So astute! Such an intelligent girl. Intelligent as she is lovely," Salamir retorted. I noted a cruel glint in his eye, though, when he said that, and I knew that, though decadent, he was deadly.

Then, quickly, he fended off his own question. He changed the subject. (I sensed that he did so in order to avoid an outright refusal from Azora, which would have provoked a confrontation—none dare refuse Salamir, refusal I was to learn, was punishable by a painful death, and, for whatever his reasons were, Salamir did not wish to kill us just then.)

"Perhaps..." he said out loud, making an ostentatious display of pondering the question. "Perhaps we might find a better purpose for this girl, this Azora. She is quick with her wits as well as with her weapons. Let us give the matter some deliberation. Now," he finished, and turning his attention fully upon me, "This man? The one who killed only two of my men. Tell us of him."

"He claims no land," Tuso answered. "Though we captured him at Pella'mir, with the girl. He calls himself Grae-don."

"Grae-don?" Salamir wondered. "What an odd name. How does one come to have a name such as that?"

"I served in the house of Jor-Taq," I answered. "It was his servants who gave me that name."

"I do not know this Jor-Taq," Salamir replied. "Is he a man of wealth?"

"He was. Now he is dead," I answered.

"A pity," Salamir said. "I might have asked you to introduce us, that we might do some business, if he was wealthy."

"His wealth is now shared among his neighbors."

"In what capacity did you serve this Jor-Taq?"

"I was his bodyguard."

"His slave?" Salamir asked with a smirk.

"His bodyguard," I insisted.

"And yet you let him be killed?" Salamir's face was a caricature of mocking astonishment.

"Jor-Taq was a *koraph*," I answered. "If any man deserved to die, it was he. Did not my friend, Torq-aa kill him, I would have done it myself."

"I am considering now whether to let you serve my person, or to serve as an example to some of my more troublesome crew. Tuso is a very imaginative disciplinarian. Do you wish to tell me that you are so insubordinate a servant as to stand by and let his master be murdered?"

"Jor-Taq was not murdered," I answered. "Only a man can be murdered. Jor-Taq was no man. He was a fiend. He tortured Azora, and he tortured my friends, Shala and Haia. Shala was wife of Torq-aa, so Torq-aa's right to kill Jor-Taq had precedence over mine. As I say, did Torq-aa not kill Jor-Taq, I would have killed him myself. As it was, I had to content myself with killing Jor-Taq's personal guard."

Salamir pursed his lips in a smile. His eyes twinkled.

"How very chivalrous," Salamir chuckled. "How very chivalrous of you, that you should allow this Torq-aa to avenge his wife's honor. And was it chivalry again, that you permitted your Azora here to kill six of my men, while you killed only two?"

"It was her turn to play," I replied.

"Enough of that!" Tuso barked. "No more of your intholenthe!"

Tuso reached out to slap me, but Salamir stopped him with a gesture.

"Let him speak," Salamir said. "This one amuses. I shall take this man's measure."

And Salamir stared at me for many long moments without speaking.

At last, speaking to Tuso, he said, "This man, this Grae-don—he is quite bruised."

"He hit hith head," Tuso explained, without expression.

"How careless of him," Salamir replied, smiling. "Tell me, Grae-don, what do you think of my man, this Tuso?"

"Were my arms unbound, he would be dead," I said, simply.

"Ha, ha, ha!" Salamir laughed. "It seems, Tuso, that you have found no friend in this Grae-don. And what would you have me do with him?

"Give me his heart and I will eat it," Tuso answered.

The great and ponderous Salamir leaned back in his divan to contemplate our answers to his questions.

"We may yet unbind you, he who calls himself Grae-don, that you might amuse us with a performance upon the person of this Tuso, who does not entertain us quite as much as he once did. Then, as well, we might also give to Tuso that which he requested."

Perhaps it was his intent to torture me with uncertainty about my fate. He let his words hang heavy in the air as he poured himself a goblet of *ellihi* from a golden beaker, gesturing, in the meanwhile, to one of the women who attended him, that she should massage his massive shoulders.

But, if it was his intent to torture me, I resolved to give him no satisfaction. I held my chin high, stared at the ceiling above his head, and scowled.

Tuso, on the other hand, turned positively purple in the face upon hearing Salamir's jab at him. Salamir studied us both over the rim of his goblet as he drank from it deeply.

"Aside from killing, what else can you do?" Salamir asked me, abruptly, wiping his mouth with the back of his pudgy hand. His painted fingernails glinted in the dull yellow light of the cabin.

I thought briefly of telling him that I had learned my letters, and could both read and write, but again, that ancient warning from Shala, that I should keep this knowledge a secret from all, except my most trusted friends, came to my mind.

"I can work," I said.

"He can work," Salamir repeated. "And what kind of work can this Grae-don do?"

"I can work with my hands. I can craft things in wood. I can carry a load."

"Can you sail a ship?"

"I have never done that."

"Can you learn?"

"I have learned much, and can learn more."

Salamir suddenly tired of speaking with me—toying with me, I should say. It was evident in his whole manner. He turned away from me, and vouchsafed me not another glance, but spoke instead to Tuso and the guards who accompanied him. He had come to a decision about both Azora and me, and having come to that decision, he was swift in executing it.

"Send the girl to attend upon the empress," he said carelessly. "And the man," he added with a shrug of his shoulders, "Send him back to Burkov. Perhaps Burkov the Bloody can make a sailor of him."

And then, with a dismissive wave of his hand, he sent us away.

Tuso and his guards manhandled us out of the cabin, and as we came to the door, I was overcome with despair. Azora and I were to be forced apart. I struggled with the two guards who forced me forward. Azora, too, kicked furiously and spat. But it was all for naught.

I saw the hopelessness in her eyes, as we were forced apart—she, down a darkened flight of wooden stairs, deeper into the hold of this cursed ship, while I was dragged away and upward.

"We're still alive!" I called to her, and then a blow to the back of my head sent me instantly into oblivion.

11

BURKOV THE BLOODY

THE BLOW THAT TUSO gave me was most efficacious, and I did not waken until many hours later.

When I did awake, it was to find myself lying on a hard wooden deck under a bright and burning sun, the sound of loud laughter ringing in my ears. A foot nudged my ribs, and I roused myself painfully.

"Ha! Ha! Ha! So Tuso had his fun, did he?"

I recognized the voice of Burkov the Bloody. My bonds had been removed, and I had the freedom of my arms. With a struggle, I managed to raise myself up on an elbow to look about.

"Looks like he beat you up good," Burkov declared with a broad smile. His comment provoked a round of laughter from his brigands, who stood in a crowd watching.

I rubbed the sore spot upon my head, and shook it wearily.

"One day," I said, "I will kill Tuso."

"Sure you will," Burkov answered. "But you'll have to get to him before others do. Until then, you'll work. Salamir sent you to me, though by all rights you were mine already. You'll work for your keep. What can you do?"

With a shrug of my shoulders, I remarked, "I can fight."

"That's always good. We can always use another sword. But when you're not fighting, what else can you do? Have you ever worked on a ship before?"

"No," I answered simply.

"Hm," Burkov grunted. "I'll put you on the oars, then. You don't need to know anything there, except pull and push, and don't foul the other oars.

"Pusar!" he bellowed. A young sailor came hurrying up. "Pusar! Show this fellow the oars."

"Yessir," the boy replied. "Come on," he said to me, "Below decks."

Burkov's ship was not so large as Salamir's but it was yet a robust piece of work. The aft was built two decks above the waterline, while the waist rode low, almost to the surface of the sea itself. The ship had only two masts, each with one lateen sail, both of them set far astern. The ship, which was called the *Fury*, was swift in the water.

The fore of the ship was empty, as all the ships that sailed with Salamir were, to allow for the catapults which the brigands used in their assaults upon the cities from which they drew their plunder. These catapults were quickly assembled in preparation for battle, and then, after battle, just as quickly disassembled for stowage below decks to permit swift sailing upon the open seas. Even now, as I looked about, familiarizing myself with the ship, the brigands were taking the catapults to pieces.

Pusar led me to a close deck in the waist of the ship, the ceiling of which was so low that I had to crouch, nearly doubled over, to make my way. Then we made our way toward the stern, which is where the oars were situated. Rows of benches stretched across the deck from bulkhead to bulkhead, and the only light came from the ports through which the oars were thrust, and the wooden grill overhead.

Seated at the benches were two dozen men who pulled slowly upon the oars, all in a rhythm. They were unhurried in their work, and seemed even careless about it.

Pusar led me to a bench upon which three men sat, all plying the handle of a single oar.

He tapped the one sitting at the end of the bench, remarking, "Take a break, now. We have a new oarsman."

The oarsman, relieved, rose from the bench, and loped away without a word, stooping under the low ceiling.

"Quickly, now," Pusar said to me. "Into your bench, grab the oar and start pulling. Do what the others do. Follow them, and do not foul the oars."

I sidled under the heavy oar, which swept forward and backward, forward and backward, in a steady motion in the hands of the two men who shared the bench.

"Put your back into it. Carry your weight, now," Pusar said. "Pull when they pull. Push when they push. Stop when they stop, go when they go. Raise the oar when they raise it, lower it when they lower it."

I understood, and immediately threw myself into the task.

Pusar left us, and we worked the oars in silence. The work was heavy and exhausting. It took all our breath simply to work the heavy oar, so we did not speak. In all there were eight benches, four portside, and four starboard. Each bench held three of us.

I was tortured with heavy dread over the fate of Azora. What was happening to her? What was Salamir, or his creatures, what were they doing with her, to her, even at that very moment? I chafed at the onerous labor that kept me from seeking her succor. And rage built in my heart with every stroke of the oar, until I plied it with a silent murderous fury. I gnashed my teeth futilely as I worked the ponderous oar, and many times did I have to remind myself to cease grinding them, only to find, shortly later, that I had commenced grinding them again.

The air was heavy and moist, thick with the sweat of the oarsmen, and the brackish stench of the sea that splashed often through the ports. Every so often, we heard a command bellowed to us from the decks above, "Hie a'port!" And the oarsmen on the port side raised their oars above the water while the oarsmen on the starboard continued pushing and pulling. And the ship, propelled on her starboard side alone, began nosing portside.

Again, the command came shouted down to us, "Hie starboard!" And those of us on the starboard raised our oars, while the portside oarsmen continued plying theirs. And the ship nosed to the starboard. In this way, the *Fury* was maneuvered through the many narrow channels of the shallow sea.

The heavy labor soon forced all other thought from my mind, as I concentrated all my energy on pushing and pulling, pushing and pulling the heavy oar, the labor of which I shared with two others who sat upon the same bench as I did. They, too, worked in silence, with only but an occasional grunt as we ceased pulling upon the oar, lifting it, in response to a shouted command, above the surface of the water, so that the ship, the *Fury*, might ply her way through the twisted channels of this shallow sea.

I labored all that day upon the oars. Heavy sweat rolled down my face, stinging my eyes. Every so often, a boy walked through with a bucket of water and he splashed us down with it. We were soaked, and sodden. The water was cool and soothing, but we were not permitted to drink of it, as we were continuously at labor, and the drinking would have given us killing cramps. Only that which trickled through our tightly clenched jaws offered us any comfort.

Not could we pause, even for an instant, as we all pulled together, and should a single one of us slip, our oar would foul another, and the entire ship would have been thrown into catastrophe. We pulled in silence, only but the sound of our rhythmic inhaling and exhalation of breath filling the close deck.

At last, when I felt I would soon die of exhaustion and the huge cramps that wracked my body, my shoulders, my back, my arms and my belly, word came shouted from above, "Stow the oars! Ho! Stow the oars!"

And, in unison, we all ceased pulling upon our oars. Quickly the men at the benches lifted them up, and they pulled them in through the ports, laying them down, and then they rose from the benches. We crouched in the low and cramped galley, kneeling upon the deck, exhausted from our labors.

The close galley was filled with our groans of relief and the stench of our sweat as we all stretched our sore bodies.

"Ach! They drove us hard this day!"

"We've gone far!"

"My belly's growling. Drink, food and sleep, that's all I want!"

The thick odor of cooked meat and seafood wafted downward from above as a bell rang loudly.

"Git up here, you," came the shouted order from above decks.

As a group, we clambered up the stair. I followed the exhausted, sweating bodies. Swarthy arms, legs, muscular buttocks, as we all scrambled upwards out of the close and foul-smelling quarters for freedom, drink, food and sleep.

My body ached, shoulders, back and legs—huge cramps in my belly made it almost impossible for me to stand, but I forced myself up and out into the waning daylight where Burkov awaited me at the top of the narrow stair.

He stood there, hands on hips, and he laughed loud upon seeing me.

"Haw! Haw! Haw!" he bellowed, and all his crew laughed with him. "They worked you right hard this day, I see."

The sun was setting upon the far horizon, peach and salmon was the waning light of the dying day. The sky above was already dark, and the stars of the deep firmament were peering through the purple shades of twilight. My hands were raw and bleeding from the many broken blisters upon them. I brought my hands to my mouth and bit the tattered skin from them, spitting it upon the deck near his feet.

"But you did good, boy. Did yer work, did it good, and not a bit of complaint from y', not at all," Burkov went on to say. "That's good. I had my doubts, boy. You looked soft. Thought mebbe I was going to have to toss you over the side and git rid of ye. But you did good. Keep it up, and mebbe I'll think it worth the trouble o' feeding ye. Now git!" he finished, slapping me on my naked back with his huge calloused hand. "There's food for y'. Git eatin'. I need ye strong!"

Though my legs were weak beneath me, I strode to the mid-decks where the crew had all gathered about a large steaming pot. Each man served himself, each dipping his bowl into the stew, then sprawling wherever he found leg room, and gorging himself, and drinking liberally.

Burkov himself ate with his men, and made no formality about it. He dipped his bowl into the hot stew, and put it straight to his mouth, swallowing deeply from it.

I stood by helplessly, for I had no bowl to serve myself with. Burkov, seeing me empty-handed, gave his bowl to me, with the remark, "Take it. I've got others."

"Thank you, Burkov," I said.

"You owe me a favor, now," he replied, a wily smile behind the beard that covered his mouth. Bits of stew clung to his beard. "You don't want to be gettin' too deep in my debt, otherwise I'll end up owning you."

"You may be sure, Burkov, I shall hasten to return this favor, and every other. For I shall be owned by no man."

"Oh! He talks pretty, dudn't he!" Burkov bellowed, laughing. "This one's got learning! Haw! Haw! Haw!"

All the men on deck followed his cue, and laughed loudly with him, but I could see, from the quick sidelong glance he gave me, that I had made a not altogether ill-timed impression on him.

Though I was the object of their laughter, I found I could not take offense, for it was a good-natured hilarity that met my ears, not at all the sneering, cynical laugh that I'd heard from Tuso, or Salamir, or his creatures.

Brigands all, these men who surrounded me on Burkov's deck, and who shared their meal with me. Brutal men, but, as I could see, honest men, brutally honest, as the occasion might demand.

They were not criminals, as were the thugs who plagued the streets of Pella'mir. The thugs of Pella'mir took advantage of the limits of the law, though they held the law in contempt, sought its sanctuary, and hid behind it, cowards that they were, when it served their purpose.

No, these men who worked upon the ship of Burkov were not criminals, but outlaws, as they lived outside the reach of all law. Each man was his own law, and not one of them sought to hide himself behind the rule of law, nor subject himself to its whims. Each one stood on his own, yet all had gathered here upon Burkov's ship—but not to serve Burkov himself. No, they had come here, not to serve Burkov, or Salamir, or any man. Each, cunning enough to understand that in numbers there is strength, had come here to serve his own self-interest. And thus, they had made a community.

Every man on this ship was his own man. Rugged, brutal, and, of course, dangerous, as all men who live on their own legs must always be.

Though I had cause to be suspicious of them all, and knew, as I sat there among them, sharing their meal, that not one of them would hesitate to cut my throat, should that act serve his purpose of the moment, yet I found within myself a growing admiration for each of them. These men were their own men, each. They'd come together as a band, yet none of them, not one, had given up any of his own sovereignty.

Burkov himself, though the ship was his, made no pretense over his sovereign crew. He was but one of them. That the ship was his own property did not give him any rights over the lives of the men who worked it with him, and he knew it, and so did his crew.

Now the sun, small and distant, touched upon the horizon. Infinite night began her slow envelopment of us. Long purple shadows cast themselves upon the deck, and the crew lit oil lamps to light us as we ate.

We ate. We drank. We sated ourselves. And then we laid ourselves upon the deck where we were, and, at last, we slept.

My second day aboard the *Fury* was much as the first. The crew awoke with heavy heads at the dawning of the sun, and I found myself quickly ushered back to my seat at the oars.

All that morning we rowed without pause. We traveled far. The work exhausted my body, but my mind embraced it, for I must needs focus all of it upon my work, and I had no leisure to wallow in my anxiety over Azora's fate.

We broke when the sun was highest in the sky, to take a rude lunch, again a frothy broth of sea creatures brewed into a hot stew. It was spicy, and good, and the crew washed their meal down with generous swigs of *ellihi*. This meal was all seriousness, though, in contrast to the night before. Now the men ate and drank quickly, with naught but grunts to break the silence. Gone was the easy banter of the evening meal, the rude laughter and profane braggadocio.

In a very few moments, we were back at our tasks.

We had turned to the south, I saw, with the afternoon sun peering through the ports on my right hand side.

"Where do we go with such urgency?" I asked my seat-mate, as we sat upon our bench and pushed the raised oars through the hull, into the water.

"Boramok," was his curt answer.

And then, to work. We could not spare the breath to speak, but bent to our oars in silence.

The seas became shallower as we progressed further to the south, and on either hand, I saw narrowing shores upon the far horizons. Never before had I traveled so far from Pella'mir, and during those brief moments when we ate our meals, and before I fell upon the deck to sleep for the night, I studied the shallowing of the sea and the strange landscapes that crept upward from the horizon.

We rowed hard, through a region of torturous and circuitous channels that cut through the sands of the shallow, amber sea. Three lookouts, one at the bow of the ship, one perched high atop the main mast, seated, his legs dangling from the crossbars built there to hold him, and the last at the stern, all kept sharp eyes on the waters, directing us with shouted commands as we steered our way through the convoluted straits.

It was a tricky business. The sand shifted often with the currents, and what might be a very deep channel one day could be gone the next. Many of these channels ended abruptly, after many convoluted twists and turns, forcing us to reverse our course. That necessitated that we painstakingly threaded our way back, to the deeper sea where me might seek out another channel that would carry us closer to our destination.

Sailing with us were the two other ships that made up the flotilla of Burkov, the *Storm* and the *Lusty*. All three ships stayed within hailing distance, each of the others, but came no closer than that, for the risk of us fouling was too great. Further out were the many other ships that sailed with Salamir's fleet, all growing tiny in the distance as they also threaded their meticulous courses through the tortuous channels of this shallow sea.

One evening, the fleet halted as nightfall drew near, as we always did, since the channels were far too treacherous for us to navigate after dark, and we took our evening meal. Filling my bowl with the crew, I looked about for a place to sit on the crowded deck. Burkov made a gesture, and I moved toward him, sitting on a low bench near his feet.

"You work good, boy," he said. "I've heard nay complaint against ye, and that is pleasing. I needn't toss you overboard!" And he guffawed loudly at his joke.

I glanced around, past the bulwarks, into the shallow sea beyond. We were in a narrow channel, it seemed. The channel was deep enough for our ship, but just beyond it, the many sand bars broke the surface of the water.

"If you need toss me overboard," I remarked, "It seems it'd be no sore matter to me, as I could surely walk from here, though how far, or to where, I cannot say. But I would not drown, it seems to me."

And Burkov replied with loud and, to me, a most inexplicable laughter.

"Did you hear that, boys? Our precious Grae-don thinks he can walk across the Sinking Sands! Haw! Haw! Haw!"

And all those within earshot laughed loud, too.

"Those sands will suck you down in a moment," Burkov said. "As soon as you set foot on them."

"Oh?"

"Aye, boy. You are not a man of the sea, or you'd know't! Those sands will suck down a ship, if we ground on `em!"

"What makes them that way?" I asked.

Burkov shrugged his shoulders, and spread his hands out, with a quizzical look upon his face. He seemed surprised that anyone should ask why such a thing should be so. The men around us laughed at my innocence.

"That's just the way they are," Burkov said with a chuckle. "Always have been that way, always will be. I don't see no reason for sayin' anything else. So you're stuck here with me, on my ship. Get those thoughts about hoppin' off and runnin' away outta yer head."

I gave Burkov a quick glance at that remark, revealing more to him than I'd intended.

And Burkov laughed.

"Of course you're hinin' on gettin' away," he said. "Of course you are. But don't make no worry about it. You hain't goin' nowhere. It's all the way back to Boramok with us. I'll think on what to do with ye' when we get there. Maybe sell you to some rich lady, if you're good. Would you like that?"

"No, not much," I said, shaking my head.

"Some old widow, maybe with her old man's money, looking for someone to keep her warm when the wind blows... ha! Haw! Haw! A plush and easy life, that would be for ye," Burkov continued, laughing heartily at his joke. The man, for all his brutality, had a sense of humor, and he liked to laugh, often and loud.

"Not without Azora," I replied.

"Ah! That purty young ripe thing with the gold hair, huh? Well, Salamir's got her, and he don't let loose of his gold, once he's got his fingers innit. So you can say goodbye to her."

"No. I will get her back. I don't know when or how, but I will."

"Go ahead, boy," Burkov said. "Dream all you want. So long as you work, I don't care what you do inside yer head."

The conversation was disheartening to me. I looked out over the bulwarks, to the vast, flat sandy fields beyond the narrow channel in which the *Fury* was slowly making its way. The channel was circuitous and labyrinthine, twisting and meandering through the fields of rusted sand under a ceaseless amber sky. The channel was transparent, and should I have stood up and looked over the bulwark, I could have seen the bottom clearly through the crystalline waters.

A strong wind blew us from the west. Our sail was furled, and the steady beat of the oars carried us along swiftly against the wind. 'Hie a'port', I heard the call, and 'Hie a'starboard', as we threaded our way through the confusing maze.

But this crew, and its captain, were old hands, and not confused. They had made their way through these tortuous and convoluted waterways countless times, so they rowed swiftly now, knowing every treacherous corner by long rehearsal.

Some of these channels grew rocky, and we passed by regions of stony cliff faces and narrow shores. Several small villages we passed, but the brigands did not molest them.

"They got naught," Burkov curtly said.

Many of these rocky cliffs were punctuated with multitudes of caverns, I saw, and I saw evidence of pathways leading among the mouths of these caverns, but never did I see the things which made those paths, whether they were humanlike, or animal. Again, I asked one of my crewmates about them, but he impatiently shrugged the question away.

"Yew annoy wit' yer damn interrogations. Shuddup," he snapped.

During this time among the many channels, the many ships of Salamir's fleet became separated by many *yurlma*. This was the custom, I learned, when they made their way through the treacherous channels of the Malwa Initia, as I finally learned this region was called.

After we had made our way through the narrow and treacherous channels of the Malwa Initia, the ships that sailed with Salamir would regroup, in the deeper waters of the narrowing and turbulent Southern Sea.

The Malwa Initia is a monstrous folding of the rock and soil that rises above the surface of the endless seas, with channels wending through it southward from the Great Northern Sea. No one knows how vast the Malwa Initia may be, according to Burkov. No one has ever explored it, he said.

But Burkov, I had found, was every bit as incurious about the larger world as any of his crew. If it did not affect him directly, or did not immediately satisfy a craving of the moment, the man had absolutely no interest in it, and he always instantly halted the discussion, whatever it was, the instant it wavered, however fleetingly, from the subject of his own appetites or opinions.

So I had no confidence in his claim that the Malwa Initia had never been explored. But, even so, had it not been explored, someone should do so, shouldn't one?

"Yew got the time?" Burkov snapped, when I raised that question to him. "Yew gonna keep my crew fed, running about the Malwa? Huh? Whatcha gonna eat? Rocks? Here," he said, striding to the bulwark, and grabbing a mop from a deck hand's fists.

"I see I haven't been keeping yew busy enough. You got time to dream, then you got time to clean! Git to work!" he bellowed at me. I took the mop, and put myself to it, swearing that I would never again show the least interest in anything while in Burkov's neighborhood.

We stopped of a morning, Burkov's flotilla, the *Fury*, the *Storm* and the *Lusty*, at a landing, upon a narrow strand of shore, beneath a towering pile of bluffs and boulders and tumbled stones.

"Up! Up! Up! You dogs!" Burkov bellowed at us, even as we were waking, and the purple dawn had barely peeked above the peaks. We stumbled ourselves awake, climbed up to our feet, and prepared ourselves for the unaccustomed chores ahead.

"What? What is this?" I asked the crewman who woke and rose next to me.

"Boulders. Burning boulders," he answered, not yet awake.

"What?" I demanded.

"Boulders. Pitch and sere. We're here to gather them up. Against the Karzi."

"The what?" I insisted.

"Shuddup!" he retorted. He'd had enough of my questions.

We ate a hurried breakfast that morning, and then Burkov and his commanders sent us crewmen out into the stumbled shore to gather boulders, but only of a peculiar type. These, I learned, were against the battle we would surely fight against the people called the 'Karzi'. Like men, of us, but not. For we could not return to Boramok, except that we passed through their channels, and their choppy sea.

Salamir, they told me, later, had it in his mind eventually to destroy the empire of the Karzi, as they taxed him too much, in their ceaseless attacks upon his fleet, as he sailed from Boramok each season, and then, again, upon his return.

And who were these Karzi? I asked.

"You'll see, good enough. You'll see in time," was the answer that came back to me.

So, after our too-short meal, we went out upon that narrow stone-strewn shore to find these 'burning boulders' as my comrades, and Burkov, called them. Three dozen of us, a dozen from each ship of Burkov's flotilla, made the expedition, all of us armed—but I, since my sword was taken away from me, carried nothing but a knife good for splicing line and jabbing at fleshmeat in our evening stew.

We marched along without discipline, up a narrow valley, away from the twisting channel where the *Fury*, the *Storm* and the *Lusty* awaited our return. This was the first time that my feet trod upon solid ground in many *yurlma*, and, I must say, savored the experience.

The narrow valley up which we climbed turned quickly into a steep and twisting canyon. Soon it was so steep that we could not walk upon it, but could only clamber upward on hands and knees.

"How much further?" I asked, generally of those around me.

"Shut up!" came the answer, and we climbed on.

At last, we came to a ridge beneath a towering escarpment, and all along it were countless heaps of stones and boulders of all sizes, which, apparently, had tumbled down from the bluffs towering overhead. These boulders ranged in size from those small enough that we could pick them up in our hands and easily carry, to those which were twice as tall as a man.

It was those, the largest among them, in which we were most interested. These, which had the curious property of catching fire and burning long and hard when a torch was put to them, were to be used in our catapults, replenishing the ammunition that had been depleted when the brigands had made their assault upon Pella'mir. I was puzzled, though, at how it was that we few dozen men were to move them down back to the ships awaiting us.

But my companions made no trouble about the job. They moved with the easy carelessness of long routine, I saw as they deployed themselves against the many stones, three or four men to each boulder. They put their shoulders to the task, and pushed them, rolling each one toward the steep and spiraling canyon up which we had climbed.

And then, with an inexpressibly simple expedient, they shoved the boulders into the canyon, and the boulders went rolling down.

"Get to work, dammit!" one of my fellow crewmen shouted at me, as he saw me standing at the ledge of the canyon, watching one of the boulders tumbling downward.

And, finally understanding what was being done, I threw myself into the task, pushing myself between two men as they grunted heavily, rolling a large boulder toward the mouth of the canyon. The stone was black, and umber, and tacky to the touch, and it had an acrid stench to it as well, that cut through my sinuses and filled my belly with nausea. Though hard as rocks, these were not stones like others, but something else, I could tell. But what that something else was, I could not say.

All that morning we worked, shoving the burning boulders down into the canyon, where they tumbled down, until they came at last to the opening at the base of the canyon, where our other crewmates below gathered them up, and by dint of sheer labor, pushed them up into the holds of the *Fury*, the *Storm* and the *Lusty*.

The other ships of Salamir's fleet also paused here for a day or two, as they came by, to harvest the 'burning boulders' in anticipation of our coming battle against the Karzi.

At last, we had harvested sufficient of the stones to fill our hold, and in the late afternoon we returned to the *Fury* and rowed on to make room for the ships behind us that waited to fill their own holds with these burning boulders.

Once we came upon a city, deep in the shadows of a shadowy channel, and then, again, another time. But we did not attack these cities, built of stone among the stone walls, and dug deep into the cliff faces. Instead, Burkov went into these cities to trade, and to gather news, and gossip, of the waterways ahead.

Some of his men he allowed ashore, for pleasure and food and gaming, permitting them a relief from work, that they may put their backs to it that much better upon their return.

I was not among them, except upon an undertaking or two, in Burkov's company, when he needed a man of a muscular stature to stand in silent intimidation of those with whom he'd entered into a delicate negotiation. My daily work at the oars had caused the muscles of my arms and chest to swell to proportions Burkov claimed were most useful for his diplomacies.

"How long to Boramok?" I asked Burkov, as we sat once at our evening meal. My patience was wearing thin. These days with Burkov and his crew chafed me, and every passing day that kept me from Azora filled me with a growing rage that threatened soon to boil over.

"We have many *yurlma* afore us yet. Days and nights, nights and days. So rest yer mind easy on it."

A shadow crossed his face, and his eyes searched out the horizon with a grim light burning from beneath his heavy brows.

"We have the Karzi yet to pass. They never let us by without a fight. Only way out of these channels is through their waters."

"These Karzi. You speak of them. I hear your crew speak of them." I demanded, impatiently, "What are they?"

"Hungry critters. They like to fight and they's always hungry."

"Hungry?"

"Cannibals, boy. They's cannibals. We try to give them wide berth because they're insane for fighting. But they're cunning, too. They live among the few islands of rocks that you'll see starting up out of the sands. Only way to Boramok is through their waters. Meat eaters, all them, always looking for new flesh to capture and breed in their cages."

"To... breed?"

"Yup," Burkov said, a wide grin spreading under his thick and bushy beard. "Men and women from different tribes, all kept together in cages. Put there to make young 'uns for their grills."

The look on my face must have been more expressive than I realized, for seeing it, Burkov and those around him burst out in huge peals of raucous laughter. "S'true, boy! S'true! They do it. Put a man in a cage with a dozen young lovelies, just so's he's puttin' them in the family way."

"And then...?" I started. And then I stopped, unable to complete the question, my mind refusing to frame the words.

"Yup! Grills the little darlin's up, or let's 'em grow for a year or two or three, if they look promising."

"That's repulsive!" I declared. "That's absolutely..."

"Aye, that it is, boy!" Burkov replied, still laughing loudly at my disgust.

"How can such things... how can such evil...?"

"The world is full of horrors. Now doncha be sweatin' yourself all over it, boy, or you'll never get to sleep. And I need you strong. Because there are good times to be had in the world, too."

The glance I gave Burkov must have been vile, but he was not put off by it. He only laughed louder, and harder, than before.

"You take yourself too seriously, boy. But be of good cheer. If the Karzi fill you with such a rage against them, you'll get yer chance to put a hurtin' on 'em. Just be sure you're not captured by them first, or you might wind up bein' one of their breeders."

"What do you mean?"

"We'll be coming up on them soon. They never let us pass, except they try to capture somewhat of us. But, even if they don't, I toldja they's insane for fightin'. Vicious. Vicious. So you can expect they'll come lopin' up on us, sometime in the night, in their boats."

"I see. So they are sailors, too?"

Burkov spat upon the deck.

"Sailors? Them? Stinking *koraphs*, all of them, every last one! No, they learned a trick or two, muddling about their little canals, but sailors on the seas?"

Burkov spat again.

"Not a bit of it... That's it!" he suddenly shouted. "Night's on! Put on the watch, and all ye not on watch, I want ye all to sleep! We're coming up on the Karzi soon, whut! I need ye all good! To sleep! We got hard fightin' comin up!"

The conversation suddenly over, Burkov stood up and turned abruptly on his heel.

He strode to the stern of the ship, and disappeared into his cabin.

12

— • —

The Karzi

F OR MY PART, I spent the remainder of my time on the *Fury* at the oars, and in the evenings, I had a new task, being sent aloft to sit upon the cross bars high upon the main mast as a look out.

I had never done this before, and so had a companion as a teacher, a keen-eyed youth by the name of Mandar. A boy, really, but he'd spent his entire life at sea and was a quick and an engaging instructor. He pointed out to me the nearly invisible nuances of color that indicated a coming change in current, or in the winds. He showed me how to scan the horizon for the tiniest specks which would be ships, or islands, or mountains rising from the sand bars. He showed me the significance of the smallest things, things which otherwise would have escaped my notice, which, had anyone asked me before what I saw, I should have described as 'nothing'.

It was from him, too, that I learned to tell direction by the stars, and how to read their precessions and declinations through the sky, and how to make my way to the north, or the south by judging their position.

He had much to teach me, and I absorbed it all as quickly as I could, but he had little time to do it. One night as we sat watch together, talking, staring up into the stars, he pointing to a particularly bluish one, which moved through the sky errantly ("It wanders," he said), his attention was suddenly attracted by a subtle motion in a nearby channel running parallel with the one in which we were at anchor.

"Ssst!" he whispered, holding his hand up in front of my face.

I turned to look in the direction of his intent gaze, and saw nothing but shallow water, sand dunes and narrow channels radiating outward in all directions toward the infinite horizon.

Ahead of us, and behind us, and off in the far distance in other channels, were the many ships that sailed among Salamir's fleet, all of them, like our own ship, anchored for the night, for moving among the narrow and circuitous channels was too dangerous a thing to attempt after darkness fell.

Silently, Mandar pointed to the spot that had caught his attention. I peered hard into the shadows, but still saw nothing.

Mandar laid his lips close to my ear, and whispered a single word, "Karzi".

Again, I stared hard into the darkness of the channel he indicated, and then my eyes darted quickly across the waters, nearer to our own ship.

There, at last, I saw them. Tiny dark boats, each of which was so small it would carry no more than two or three people. Yes. I was certain of it now. Mandar was right. The boats were of very shallow draft, and in each of them, one or two shadowy figures lay down, paddling, it appeared, with their hands.

They moved swiftly and silently across the waters, toward our ships, surrounding them. Seeing that they had approached so closely to the *Fury* and to our sister ships, Mandar grabbed up the large straight horn affixed to the mast for this purpose, and put it to his lips.

"OOOOWAH! OOOOWAH!" came the loud warning call from Mandar's horn. "OOOOWAH! OOOOWAAAAAA-A-A-A-AH!"

All of an instant, the deck of the *Fury* and her sister ships were alive with shouting crews. I heard from the many distances between us, Mandar's warning call picked up and repeated by the other ships. Each warning call was unique, with its own notes, cadence and intonations to identify the ship from which the call came, as well as the danger being warned against.

"WAHoooAH! WAHoooAH! WAHoooAH!" came the responding clarion calls through the night, and "HAWAWAooo! HAWAWAooo! HAWAWAooo!" and many, many more. The night sky rang loud with shrill blaring warning calls.

But Mandar's horn roused not only the slumbering crews of Salamir's fleet. With that same call to arms, Mandar told the Karzi fighters that they had been discovered.

Instantly and simultaneously, abandoning stealth, they gave voice through a thousand throats to their weird battle cry. The chilling sound of their shrill ululations cut through the calling of the horns and froze my blood with terrible tremors I'd never felt before Even Mandar paused for a moment, as he cast his haunted eyes upon me, though he'd seen the Karzi fighters, and had even fought them, many times before. Casting about for courage, he managed at last to say, "We fight! Come!"

And with those words, he scrambled down the lines to the deck below, even as the Karzi fighters massed over the bulwarks, spilling onto the ship.

Not to be left cowering behind, I slipped over the side of the cross-bars upon which we sat on our watch, and, just behind Mandar, I clambered quickly down to the deck.

The ship was already thick with the Karzi. And except for the amber glow from the lamps hanging from the ships' lines, all was dark, making it difficult for me to make them out.

The Karzi were men, like us—or perhaps I should say they were manlike creatures—but they did not fight like us, on their feet. They scuttled about quickly on the deck on all fours, clambering over each other, and upon those they fought, much the same way I had seen nests of insects all crawling in a mass.

They had four fingers on each hand and four long toes on each foot, which terminated in long, sharp and curved claws. Later, when was to see them in daylight, I would see that the pupils of their eyes were vertical slits, and instead of hair, their heads were covered with feathers that bristled outwardly when they were enraged.

But the one feature that made them most unlike any man I had seen was the long, whiplike tail that sprang from their hindquarters. As long as a full grown man's leg or arm in most cases, these tails terminated in a bony, flat, disc-shaped growth with edges that were razor sharp, and which, as a weapon, they used with appalling, and deadly, skill.

No sooner had I put my feet on the deck of the *Fury*, standing next to Mandar, who had already unsheathed his sword, but I saw two Karzi warriors attack a single brigand from both sides. Darting at him quickly on all fours, and keeping their bodies flat and close to the deck, they presented an almost impossible target for the brigand's sword.

As he swung downward at the fellow on his left side, the Karzi at his right instantly swung himself about, lashing his tail like a whip. The bony disc at the end of his tail cut right through the brigand's ankles, and the man fell, both his amputated feet skittering across a deck that was already slick with blood.

The brigand grunted in pain, but there was no cry from him, no plea for mercy. A brutal man, even as death was upon him, he faced it with a grim courage that was impossible for me not to admire. Even as he lay upon his back, blood gushing from the two ankles the Karzi had rendered into fountains—even as the Karzi both rushed upon him to disembowel him with claws hard as metal—the brigand, whose name I never learned, slashed at them with his sword, and in one cut was able to decapitate the fellow who had removed his feet from him. The second Karzi was upon him that same instant, and shredded the man's abdomen with a ferocity that left me sickened and aghast.

And I looked about and saw that the deck of the *Fury* was crowded with men fighting. And these brigands were no strangers, I observed, to the way these Karzi fought, aiming almost all their blows at the tails of these strange men.

Burkov himself was in the thick of things, gripping his sword with both hands and swinging it in huge, unceasing circles about him. With each vast circle he cut through the air, I saw hands and claws, tails and heads popping up and bouncing, skittering across the increasingly bloodied deck.

And how he bellowed through the night, cursing and raging against the Karzi. And he laughed! He laughed gloriously in the slaughter, both the slaughter wrought upon the Karzi by the brigands, and, I saw, the slaughter of the brigands themselves, wrought upon them by the Karzi.

All this I describe, long in the telling, took only instants in the doing. Mandar still stood beside me, his eyes gleaming, his sword unsheathed.

And then he shouted, "Death to the Karzi!" And he leaped into the bloody battle, his sword swinging, cutting through the air, and through the bodies of the Karzi who massed upon him.

I had no sword. My one sword had been long ago taken from me by the brigands, and never returned. All I had to use as a weapon, aside from my fists, and feet, was a knife that Burkov had handed me to cut lines, or fulfil any other such tasks as might arise. It was a good knife, and a strong one, with an edge I kept sharp, but it was a poor weapon against such strange men as the Karzi.

They moved in a mass, scrambling and scuttering across the deck with shocking speed. And they lashed constantly at their enemies with their tails which, I saw, sliced hands, feet, even heads away from bodies as easily as if they were cutting through water.

I was at a loss, not knowing how I could join the fight with only a carving knife. But the fight was quickly forced upon me, as two of the Karzi caught sight of me, and came quickly crawling in my direction. Casting about, I saw the sword of the brigand whose feet had been removed from his ankles still clenched in his dying hand.

I gingerly made the short way across the deck, now slick and treacherously slippery with the blood of brigand and Karzi. But even as I approached the disemboweled and dying body of the brigand, I slipped in the thick blood, landing full upon my face with my arms outstretched. I scrambled on my hands and knees, slipping in the boundless pools of blood, seeking to reach the sword before the two Karzi fell upon me.

Attracted by my frantic motions, the dying brigand turned his head in my direction. His eyes were opaque, and the light of life was leaving them. And, with its face buried deep in the bloody abdomen of the dying brigand, the Karzi warrior who had brought him down was feasting upon his bowels.

In a supreme last gesture, the dying brigand roused himself to a gasping consciousness. He swung his blade down in a mighty sweep upon the Karzi warrior with his head buried deep in his flesh, slicing its head neatly off its neck. The body jerked backward, a fountain of blood pouring from his neck, as his hands grasped futilely, and dumbly in the air, before he collapsed in a heap upon the bloody brigand.

And then, his eyes upon me, the brigand heaved his sword toward me, sending it sliding, slick with blood, across the deck until it was in my grasp. And then I saw when his spirit fled the flesh. His eyes went dead, his body slack.

I wasted not an instant, but spun upon my attackers, swinging the blade furiously, and catching the nearer fellow directly on the side of his head.

However fierce these Karzi are, their bones, I found, are thin. My blade went right through the fellow's skull, lopping the top of it off, just below his eyes. The piece landed on the bloodied deck upside down, lying there as if it were a bowl filled with steaming stew. The upside-down dying eyes blinked stupidly, in dumb surprise, and then they shut for the last time.

The fellow's mouth, in the lower part of its head, still attached to its neck, opened once or twice, as if in shocked protest, but no sound came out. And then his corpse dropped, sprawling, legs and arms splayed out upon the deck.

I had no time to gloat over my fallen opponent, for even as the top of his head landed upon the deck, his companion was upon me. Claws sharp as knives came slashing at my face, and his murderous eyes loomed large.

It slashed my chest first with one set of claws, and then with the other. The sharp pain of it provoked me to an instant response. I leaped to my feet, sword in one hand flailing at his head, meaning to lop it off his shoulders. But he ducked beneath my blade and hurled himself at me, throwing his arms about my waist and slashing the air about us with his deadly tail.

I could only beat the back of his head with the pommel of the sword, a useless gesture. His arms were powerful, and they held me in a deathly grip. He squeezed hard upon me, and I felt the breath being pushed out of my lungs. Should he keep at this, I knew, he would kill me by suffocation. Frantic, I kicked at him futilely, while still bashing him with the grip of the sword.

He eluded all my sword thrusts, and the beating I gave him about the head and shoulders was ineffectual. I felt myself growing dizzy, and knew that should I lose consciousness, that would be the end. Without thinking, I pushed against the slickened deck with my feet. We moved forward a bit. I pushed again, and then harder, and in a moment, I was running across the slippery deck with the Karzi man still hugging me in a death grip. We passed many others as they fought, but in the clamor they paid us no attention.

Faster and faster I ran, not thinking, only running as the Karzi warrior gripped me, pushing him backwards until we came to the very edge of the deck. And then my foot slipped in a pool of blood, and we both fell, together. We slipped under the railing, over the edge, and straight down into the channel below.

We hit the water with a huge splash. Our impact upon the surface caused the Karzi warrior to lose his grip on me, and we broke apart from each other. We plunged deep into the shadowy water, and as I made my way back to the surface, I banged my head against the hull of the *Fury*. The pain of that shock roused me from the dimming consciousness into which I had been slipping. It cleared my head, and my wits were keen again.

I kept my grip upon the sword and when our heads broke the surface of the channel, the Karzi warrior some feet away from me, I paddled quickly toward him. He seemed dazed by the fall, for when he heard my splashing and turned toward me, he stared at me stupidly. Only for an instant, though. He was quickly gathering his senses, but that instant was all I needed.

Recalling the many sword-throwing contests with which Brekkex, Koax and I had passed many happy hours among the guard of Jor-Taq's, I grasped the blade of the sword in my right hand, and in a single swift motion, brought it up to my shoulder, and then hurled it directly at the bobbing Karzi's head.

The sword made one circle in the air, just barely skimming above the water's surface, and it plunged deep into his face, precisely between his eyes, penetrating at the bridge of the nose, between his wiry eyebrows.

He died without a sound. His head lolled backward upon his shoulders, and he began to sink into the water, but before he did so, I swam to him and grasped the handle of my sword in both hands. I expected difficulty in pulling the sword out, not being able to push against his body with foot or knee. But the task was less difficult than I expected, for I had only to hold onto the handle as his body sank, and it slid right off the blade.

But now what? I was in the water, alone, the dark hull of the *Fury* looming high over my head. The din of battle, the curses, the shouting, the death cries all came to my ears, but there was no way I could find to climb to the deck. And the crew of the *Fury* was far too pressed to offer me any assistance, even assuming that anyone had noted my fall into the water.

I am not a swimmer. Though I had some opportunity to learn my way in the water in the deep pools of Pella'mir and in the lakes of Taakbar, when Azora and I had gone there, my experiences with swimming have been few. Left in deep water for any appreciable period, I could only do what any intelligent man of my skill would do, and that is float until I was exhausted, then sink and drown.

But I had no reason for despair. Near at hand were the shadowy bulks of the many small boats the Karzi had used to attack us. Now empty, they lay low in the water, waiting silently for the return of the Karzi with whatever captives they managed to take.

I struck out for the boat nearest to me, reaching it quickly. Tossing my sword into it, I gripped the gunwale with both hands, and pulled myself over.

The boat was a kind of thing I had not seen before. Made of long reed-like vegetation woven together as I had seen some baskets made, it was long and narrow, with but enough room to seat three people, or four, should they crowd together, the entire interior length of it was caulked with a blackish tarlike substance. It barely crested the surface of the water. Indeed, it lay so low upon it, that it must have been almost impossible to see from any appreciable distance.

"Cunning," I thought to myself, as I examined it. "Very cunning."

Paddles lay along the bottom of it, short things with wide blades, and I also found a bag with provisions, jars with fresh water, foodstuffs of various kind, including dried flesh meat. I knew not what that was, but did not touch it. Instead, I tossed it over the side.

And then I looked up again at the *Fury*. The battle still raged on there, high above my head. The hull of the ship was cascading with streams of blood from the wounded and the dying, and the shouts and clashing of swords rang loud in my ears.

How to get back on board? I was puzzled by that, for there was no ladder, no gangway, no ropes for me to climb.

But I was puzzled only for a moment.

"Why?" I asked myself.

"Why do I want to get back on board? These brigands are not my friends. This is not my battle. For the moment, I am free. I have a boat, and somewhere ahead, is Salamir's ship, and Azora."

My decision was made in an instant. Taking one of the paddles in my hands, I began paddling my boat away from the *Fury*. Swiftly, and silently, through the cold night, I slipped past the other ships of Burkov's flotilla, where other battles raged, and deeper into the widening channels.

Long through that furious night I plied my boat, first past one ship, and then another.

On every ship I passed, a pitched battle raged. The waters of the channels were thick with blood and mutilated corpses.

Quietly, stealthily I plied my tiny boat, for many long and countless hours threading my way through the dark hulls of the many crowded ships, and the men fighting upon them. I knew only that Salamir's ship was at the head of the fleet, only that I should continue making my way past these ships until I found Salamir's.

At last the darkness began to lighten in the eastern sky as the night grew long and wan, and amber dawn touched down upon the shadowy battles. Yet still I had not found Salamir's ship.

Now I faced a new hazard. Throughout the long night, I'd hidden in the shadows. Though I was surrounded on every side by multitudes of murderous brigands and Karzi, none, not one, had taken notice of me.

But now, with the coming of the dawn, I risked their notice. Morning twilight and the mists that lay upon the waters gave me some camouflage for some moments, but for how long? I did not know. I must move quickly.

Hugging close to the hulls of the fighting ships, and fleeting swiftly from one to the next, I hurried through the quickening dawn though my arms ached, and still, peering ahead through the dusk I could not make out the shape of Salamir's ship.

I came at last to a widening of the channels. Here, they emptied out into a wide ocean, something deeper and more turgid than the shallow Great Northern Sea from which we had sailed. I saw in these choppy waters, for the first time, movements among them I later learned are called 'waves'. Instead of a placid surface, as I saw upon the Great Northern Sea, the waters of this ocean moved, and piled high, rolling across the surface, piling higher and higher, until they at last collapsed down upon themselves. The sight was most daunting to me. I had no idea how I was to navigate these waves.

Off to the left, the shore gave way to an open ocean, and then again, to the right. The shoreline pulled back away from my eye, all the way to the horizon, and before me was the wide expanse of deep and foaming waters rolling with these waves and deep and dangerous currents.St rung out in vast lines upon this sea were many ships of Salamir's vast armada. And surrounding all those ships were multitudes of boats, all like the one I had stolen, and plied now in my quest to find Azora. Under the golden light of the dawning sun, I saw countless battles on all the ships, while more and more boats launched in ceaseless streams from the low, rocky shore.

And there, off to my right, in the middle distance behind the place from which the hordes of boats were launching, I saw a huge pile of rock catacombed with the mouths of numberless tunnels. That mountainous pile of rock was enormous, and built into it, I saw, were towers, balconies, plazas, stairways, temples and twisting streets.

"That," I determined, "must be the city of the Karzi."

And, I saw, the ships of Salamir's mighty armada were making war upon the city of the Karzi. All of them besieged by the hordes of the Karzi, yet still their catapults were active. Every ship was launching fiery explosive charges against the city.

I saw the heavy charges from each of the countless ships sailing high through the air in vast arcs, and leaving trails of smoke behind them, and then come crashing down upon the pile of rock that was the city of the Karzi, all with massive explosions, and fire spilling out onto the narrow streets. Towers and temples tumbled, whole balconies collapsed and spilled down the sides of the pile of rock where they'd been built, into the sand dunes below.

And yet, still the Karzi came on. They poured out from the shore endlessly, piling into their boats and attacking the ships of Salamir's fleet with a boundless fury.

I paused there, at the opening of this channel into this raging ocean, to take in all before me. Though I stared, it was almost impossible for my eyes to comprehend. As I studied I saw, at last, the lines of Salamir's ship, off beyond the waves. It was surrounded, like every other of his fleet, on every side by the boats of the Karzi, with more and more crowding near at every moment.

There was my goal. There I would find Azora at last. There, past the waves and the swarms of the murderous Karzi, and the brigands themselves—that was where I must go.

I did not hesitate. Instantly I saw the lines of Salamir's own ship midway to the horizon on this strange and dangerous ocean, I bent to my paddle, and sent my tiny craft toward it. As I came closer to the waves that piled high and pounded the water, I watched the Karzi as they approached them, to see how they would navigate them.

I saw that they pushed their boats directly into the waves, nose first and straight on, and building great speed with their paddles. I saw that the Karzi caught the waves early in their building, riding them up and over, before each wave peaked and collapsed. I also noted that the most dangerous looking waves rushed directly at the shore. From the channel where I was making my way, the waves rose, and then dwindled again, without collapsing, and there was before me a narrow route where I might avoid them altogether.

My heart rising with hope, I paddled hard along that narrow route between the waves, only to discover that the hope was false. I had progressed some way into the ocean, thinking, indeed, that I had put the worst of the waves behind me, when I saw that the way before me was blocked by a mass of barely submerged rocks. As shallow as the draft of my boat was, still, it would have wrecked itself upon those rocks that only revealed themselves to my eye at the last possible instant.

Quickly I back paddled, away from those deadly rocks, and I paused a moment upon the surface of the surging ocean. I was nearer now to Salamir's ship, but to make any further progress, I must plunge directly into the waves that swelled so high. Here, at this distance from the shore, they grew higher at their peak than I was tall, nor could I see beyond them when they rose.

There was nothing for it but to push on, and so I did. As I had seen the Karzi do in their boats, so I aimed the nose of my boat directly at the next oncoming wave. I felt it swelling beneath me, raising me upon its back, and its current carrying me back toward the shore.

I threw myself into paddling, then, seeking to build up my speed, that I could send my boat over the wave before it broke. Harder and harder I paddled, pushing my boat, though my back and arms were aching and my belly was wracked with cramps.

At last, I broke through and pushed out past that wave, into the deeper waters beyond. And there, I found myself almost completely surrounded by Karzi, all of them in their boats, hurrying toward Salamir's ship and the others, all of them intent upon their prey.

The morning was still young, and the distant sun was just breaking the horizon. Profound purple shadows in the lurid orange twilight, a sky of amber overhead. The Karzi who surrounded me were still some distance away, all of them intent on attacking Salamir's ships.

I leaned forward, low in my tiny boat, keeping my head down, and steering my boat into the shadows of the troughs between the mounting waves, hoping that in the yet dim morning light I might not bring their attention to myself. I paddled hard, keeping pace with the Karzi, hanging to the hope that my ruse might work long enough to get me, at least, to Salamir's ship, which was growing tantalizingly near.

The battle surrounding the ship was furious. The Karzi had completely surrounded it, and were hurling stones at it with long slings. The stones rained hard upon the ship, slashing its sails, and battering the brigands.

And while many Karzi bombarded the ship with their onslaught of stones, others were climbing on board, attacking the crews. They crawled up the sides of the hull, digging deep into the wood with their long metal-hard claws, and then bounding upon the deck.

The brigands fought back viciously with sword and slings of their own, aiming their missiles with a deadly accuracy. One after another, I saw the Karzi struck by the stones hurled at them by the brigands, stones that crushed their skulls, and sent them over the side of their tiny boats, into the churning waters.

It was in the confusion of that vast melee that I made my way to Salamir's ship. As much as I could do it, I steered my tiny boat into the troughs between the heavy waves, keeping my body hunched and my head down. At times I came close to one of the Karzi boats—close enough that I could have reached out and touched the gunwale—but so furious was the battle, and so intent were the Karzi warriors on attacking the ship, they did not even notice that I was not one of them.

Salamir's ship carried two large catapults in the forecastle, side by side before the sails, and they were working ceaselessly. As one was launching its fiery missile against the city of the Karzi, the second beside it was being reloaded, even as the Karzi were scrambling up the hull and attacking in their wild frenzy. I drew closer and closer to the ship, and saw that the brigands fought back with a rage that more than matched that of the Karzi.

And, at last, I came to the ship itself, my tiny boat banging hard against the dark hull as I tried to hold it off with my inadequate paddle. Now I was truly puzzled. There was no ladder, no line, not so much as a toehold—there was nothing, nothing at all for me to grasp or to climb up on. I had not the talons of the Karzi, with which they crawled straight up the vertical sides of the hull.

What to do? Around me the Karzi were launching themselves against the hull of the ship, and climbing upward to the deck above. And at the same time, a continual fall of bodies came tumbling down, headless, armless corpses of the Karzi slaughtered by the brigands.

I pushed away from the hull of the ship, and paddled toward the stern looking for something, anything that might give me even the least bit of handhold. The stern was much higher than the waist of the ship, but above the rudder were a series of windowed galleries. The rudder towered far above my head, and I examined the bolts that bound it. They were just barely large enough to afford me a tentative grip, and spaced far enough apart that I might be able to use them to climb to the galleries.

But the ship was rocking in the choppy ocean, and the bolts were wet and slick. I reached forward and put my hand around one of the bolts. It was treacherously slippery, and I was not sure I could trust my balance on it, in these rough waters.

I was just on the point of pushing away again, and seeking some other place, when my attention was drawn toward a huge cracking sound high overhead. I looked up just in time to see the mizzen mast teetering wildly over the edge of the hull far above me. The sail upon it flapped crazily, with great 'fwoop, fwap, fwoop' sounds, and the lines that held it were alternately taut to nearly the snapping point, then suddenly slack as the mast swayed in the opposite direction.

Dimly, as I watched, I began to comprehend the danger to myself. Once again I pushed away from the hull of Salamir's ship, and then paddled hard to put some distance between us.

And just in time, for I had only made a few boat lengths' distance when I heard a huge sound of wood cracking and breaking from above my head. Glancing over my shoulder, I saw the mast come tumbling over the side of Salamir's ship, directly at me.

I had no time to do anything, but grab my sword and leap from my boat, narrowly escaping the mast as it came down with a vast concussion on the water. It crushed my boat beneath it.

But I had no time to curse my bad fortune, for I saw that my bad luck had turned instantly to good. The fallen mast was still bound to the ship by many lines, and I saw at a glance that it would provide me an excellent means for climbing to the deck.

I grabbed hold of a line and quickly mounted the mast. Looking upward to see where it was I was climbing to, my eyes were confronted by two entirely dispiriting sights. The first was the faces of a dozen Karzi warriors jutting suddenly outward and looking over the bulwark, spying me as I climbed upward. The second was the flames I saw dancing behind them, as they licked the stump of the broken mast and began to grow taller and wilder.

The Karzi had set fire to the ship. And, the moment they laid their eyes upon me, they let loose with a loud, shrill howl that pierced my ears. They leaped over the bulwark and clambered toward me with shocking speed, nor did I allow myself any illusions about their intent. But as it happened, I had come just to the level of the windowed galleries I'd seen before, just above the rudder. The windows were large enough for me to pass through, so wasting not an instant, I smashed the glass of one with the pommel of my sword, and swung myself into it. I landed on the floor in a bruised and bloody heap, the shards from the shattered window cutting me as I passed through it.

I landed hard upon a carpeted floor, but without time to take stock of my surroundings, for I quickly pulled myself up and turned to face the windows I had just broken through. The Karzi pursuing me had already climbed down to the windows and were smashing through them. Shattering glass skittered across the floor at my feet, and I slashed at the clawed hands that snatched at me through the broken windows.

With a backward cut, I managed to slice off one of the hands, and it bounded from its owner, spattering circlets of blood with a small bounce upon the carpet. Then another thrust of my blade into the face of a second Karzi, which caught him in the mouth, and skewering him, rather neatly, I thought.

But there were many more, and they came streaming in through the shattered windows. I leaped at them with my sword, swinging viciously at my enemies. Two more went down to my blade, and the others paused, just beyond my reach.

I gave them no time, but pressed on them hard, cutting one through the throat while the remaining four scrambled out of my way. A commotion behind me caught my ear, but my attention was wholly focused on the four Karzi who opposed me.

They resorted to the tactic I first saw when we fought on the deck of the *Fury*, crawling upon the floor and slashing at me with their long tails. I leaped to avoid their deadly cuts, and watched, appalled, when two of them, using their deadly talons, quickly scrambled up the walls and across the low ceiling at me.

Four of them at once, two on the floor, two on the ceiling. That was too much. I was sure now that death was upon me. I would make as good an account for myself as I could—certainly, I would kill the two on the ceiling, but with my attention engaged upon them, the two on the floor would surely cut me to ribbons. Or, I could kill the two on the floor while the two coming at me from above launched themselves upon me, rending me and disemboweling me with their deadly talons.

I had no time to think this through, they came at me so quickly. It is only afterwards, as I recall myself to that instant that I am able to put words to the many wordless impulses that passed through my unthinking mind at that instant.

I made my decision—I would kill those two who came at me from the ceiling, and I drew my sword up for a backhanded slash at the nearest fellow when I was astonished to hear a huge clash coming from behind me. On my left and on my right, two swords suddenly lashed out, chopping at the Karzi warriors crawling upon the floor with their tails whipping furiously.

One tail I saw neatly severed from its owner, with a torrent of blood spewing out upon the carpet. The tail jerked and twitched spasmodically for several long instants, and then it ceased its motion. The owner of the tail turned and launched itself directly at the warrior who, I saw with a quick sidelong glance, stood beside me. One of Salamir's men. A second glance to my left revealed to me another of Salamir's men.

The man to my right, wearing one of the ceremonial golden helmets that proved him to be a low-ranking officer of Salamir's own guard (as I was later to learn), raised a short shield he wore bound on his left forearm to deflect the attack of the tailless Karzi warrior, and then, with a neat cutting motion through the Karzi's thin neck, he removed the fellow's head, which bounced off a wall and landed on the carpet with a bloodied 'thud'.

I did not pause in my attacks, but lunged at the one Karzi crawling on the ceiling nearest me. He ducked my lunge, and threw himself at me, landing bodily upon me and throwing me backward upon the carpet. At such close quarters, I could not use the blade of my sword effectively, but could only beat him in the face with the pommel of it as he attempted to gut me with his claws. We wrestled upon the floor among the ever-increasing pools of blood. He raked my chest and my arms with his talons, gouging out troughs of flesh from me, while I smashed into his face repeatedly.

The fellow fought viciously, even after I had shattered his nose and jaw, which hung loose and broken, slapping against his neck as he fought. At last I dropped my sword, grasped his throat with both my hands, ignoring the huge gouges of flesh he was raking from my body. Forcing myself upward on to my knees, I dragged him up with me, and then I swung his body around, smashing it hard upon the floor, once! Twice! Three times!

It was only after I had smashed his still wriggling body on the floor that third time that it ceased its motion. Panting heavily to catch my breath—I was quite winded—and feeling a fleeting gratitude to Burkov for putting me to the oars for so long, for clearly the daily regimen of it had given me the strength that made it possible for me to endure thus far, I picked up my sword from the carpeted floor, and turned to join the fight again.

Salamir's guards had made good work of the other three Karzi, but they were not resting upon their laurels. A huge battle was underway behind me. Six of Salamir's guards, of whom those who had come to my succor were two, were fighting against a crowd of Karzi at the far end of this gallery.

Now I had an instant to take in my surroundings—but only an instant. The gallery was lush, and the furniture within it was rich and plush. Golden appointments decorated the walls, ornate lamps, elaborate couches and desks.

The opening of a spiraling staircase led into this room from below, and another, leading upwardly. The staircases were monumental in scale and styling, with extravagant balustrades and decorative carved and gilded nymphs cavorting themselves along the way.

And pouring down from above were monstrous numbers of Karzi. The six guards were hard put to it to keep them at bay. But they fought valiantly, and, my bloodlust up and burning wildly, I hurried forward to fight with them.

Even as I approached, I saw one of them felled by a Karzi fighter's vicious tail—it cut through his neck, and lopped his head off. It bounced on the carpet, mouth gaping and spitting, and it rolled down the staircase leading down from the gallery. The man's body stood yet for a moment, its arms waving wildly with its sword slashing the air and a geyser of blood erupting from the pit of his neck. And then it paused, fell to its knees, and then dropped backwards into the spiral staircase, sliding downward into the darkness below.

I leaped into the gap vacated by the dead guard, cutting furiously into the crowded Karzi.

"For Azora!" I shouted, my call carrying above the din of fighting.

And, out of the corner of my eye, I caught the shocked glance of a warrior as he turned toward me in seeming recognition. Only for an instant I glanced back his way, and I was shocked myself to discover, through the wounds and the blood that disfigured him, that it was Tuso himself who was fighting so pitilessly with his comrades against the brutal Karzi.

I must say the man fought with a valor I would never have expected from him. He was quick, calculating, and ruthless, but he was cautious, as well. Though he fought with valor, he took no chances and was never slow to allow others to wade into the glory of battle. Several times I saw him step back as others took up his fight for him, but

I could not call the man a coward, as much as I would say that he was afflicted, perhaps with a surplus of cunning in allowing others to exhaust themselves with the fight while he carefully measured out his own resources, keeping some strength in reverse.

The fight was silent for the most part, except for the clashing of our swords, the grunts of the fighting men as the blows landed, or the dying cries of the fallen. We fought endlessly, it seemed, and hopelessly, but after a timeless time, the Karzi fell back, and we mounted the spiral stair in pursuit.

Now the enemy was in flight, I reminded myself again that these brigands were not my allies. This was not my fight. I was here, only for Azora, and now that the instant threat of the Karzi overwhelming us there in the gallery was ended, so also was my brief alliance with the brigands.

I spun on my heel to confront Tuso, only to find that he was gone. It was only the five of us on that spiral stair, the four brigands running up into the darkness, pursuing the retreating Karzi, and myself. Where had Tuso gone?

I looked quickly around the sumptuous gallery. As far as I could see in the dim light, there were but two means of ingress and exit, and that was through the two spiral staircases, one leading up, the other down into the bowels of Salamir's great ship. Instantly, without any hesitation, I plunged down the staircase into the darkness below in pursuit, I hoped, of Tuso and in search of my Azora.

13

THE EMPRESS OF MARS

I CAME TO THE bottom of the stairs to find a narrow landing that opened to a long darkened corridor of paneled walls and a wooden floor covered by a threadbare carpet. The hallway was but faintly illumined with a yellow glow that came from a series of lamps that hung from the ceiling. Wooden columns against the walls mounted from ceiling to floor, and on either hand, between the columns, I saw doorways of dark wood.

The hallway was long, and the further end of it disappeared into an unutterable darkness. But as I came to the landing and looked down the hallway, I saw the form of Tuso, now tiny in the distance, just as it vanished into the darkness.

After the ceaseless noises of battle that had confounded my ears since early that morning, the sudden stillness of that close hallway was confounding to me. It felt as if my head had been instantly swathed in bolts of cloth.

But I did not pause to savor that silence. Instantly upon seeing his form, I set out at a run to catch up with Tuso, and to force him to lead me to where it was that Azora was held captive. And so I ran recklessly into the darkness.

The further I ran into the darkening hallway, the fewer were the lanterns hanging from the ceiling, which accounted for the growing gloom. But I did not slow my pace. Knowing that Tuso had passed that way before me only instants before, I was confident that wherever my feet were taking me, the floor would hold me too. Nor was I about to allow Tuso to slip away. At that instant, he was my only tenuous link to Azora, and if I lost him it was very possible I would lose Azora, too.

And so I ran directly into a wall. My head hit the paneling, and the thud of it echoed loudly. I staggered back a pace or two, and then I thrust my hand out. With an aching head and tentative steps, I felt for the wall in front of me. The hall had come to an end, and by feeling around in the dim light, I found that two narrow passageways led away from it on either side.

Chafing at the wasted moments, and cursing myself for my idiocy, I retraced my steps until I came to one of the lanterns hanging from the ceiling, and pulled it down, which I should have done before. I returned to the two passageways and listened intently, first at one, and then the other. But not a sound came to my ears, not the slightest echo of a single tread of a sandal upon the floor, nor the sound of a breath, nor even the faint scrape of sword against paneling.

Nothing indicated to me the direction Tuso had taken.

I could have stood there forever, puzzling over my situation, but I knew that every moment spent thus was a moment squandered, so throwing all caution away from me, I turned to the right hand corridor, and strode down it. It was narrow and stifling, and with barely enough room for me to move forward between the two walls.

I knew that the lamp I carried would reveal me to whomever might be ahead, but there was no help for that. The sallow, yellow light was absolutely necessary to me. Tuso, perhaps, knowing Salamir's ship as intimately as he must, could make his way through the darkened hallways with only but the sense of touch. But I was a stranger here, and must see my way forward.

And well it was that I carried the lamp with me, for I had not gone far into the dark and suffocating hall when I came upon a steep stairway that led deeper down into the hull. It was a dangerous business for me, climbing down those steep steps. With the lamp in one hand, and my sword in the other, I had no way to hold on to the walls as I descended. I could only balance myself with great care, with a very tenuous balance, as each step was but large enough for the heels of my feet.

Down into that darkness I descended. Intently I listened to the silence, hearing no clue, nothing to indicate that I was pursuing the correct trail in my pursuit of Tuso and my search for Azora.

Step by tentative step I went, until at last, in the dim glow of my sputtering lamp, I saw open before me the floor of yet another hallway, this one wider than the stair, and wider, thankfully, than the narrow hallways I had quitted at the top of that dangerous stair.

Another thing touched me, which gave me hope, a soft current of fresh air, from somewhere near. And then, ahead, I saw more lamps mounted in the walls, giving a distant and warm amber glow to the widening hallway. Archways pierced the halls on either side, and as I moved forward into the hall, I saw that they opened into large storage rooms filled with amphorae, crates, cages, chests and cabinets.

But I only glanced at them, and moved on. Another stairway, this one carpeted with plush carpeting, and it spiraled upward. And coming from the stairway, somewhere above, I heard the clash of sword against sword, and the curses of men fighting.

Was this the way Tuso had gone? I did not know. But ahead were men, men I could speak to, men I could interrogate, at the point of my own sword, if necessary. And that thought was all that it took me to drop the lamp and hurry up the steps.

There, at the top of the steps, I discovered six of Salamir's guard in heated battle against as many Karzi. And there, among them, I spied Tuso! He fought with Salamir's guard, edging behind them, and allowing them all the greater share of glory.

The men were defending a locked entryway, large and ornate, with absurdly elaborate paneling and gold edging. The lavish carpets before the door were all thick with the blood of the fighters. Not one of them was without several gashes from which the blood was flowing profusely, and the dozen or so corpses I saw on the carpet, of both Salamir's guard and the Karzi, plainly indicated to me that the battle had been of long duration already.

I had no interest in that battle, though. All men here were my enemies, Salamir's guard and Karzi alike. My only interest was in finding Azora. Ignoring the battle, I threw myself at Tuso and before he knew I was upon him, I had the point of my sword at his throat.

"Where is Azora?" I demanded, allowing the tip of my sword to prick the skin. A tiny trickle of blood pooled at the pit of his throat.

I saw the recognition grow slowly in his eyes as he stared at me. I must have presented quite a visage, as my face, and my body, was covered with open wounds, many of which were still bleeding. But at last he did recognize me again through all my cuts, and when he did, he sneered at me, openly.

"How should I know?" he smirked.

And then he spat upon the blade of my sword.

I gave him two quick cuts with my sword, to the left and the right. The left cut sliced through the flesh of his throat, just under his chin. The right cut went through his lip. I pointed the tip of my sword at his left eye.

"Where is Azora?" I demanded again.

He spat a mouthful of blood, this time at the carpet upon the floor. Then he jerked his head backward to indicate the door behind me.

"There. Behind this entryway. She waits upon the Empress."

The Empress. I had heard that title before, this 'Empress'. It came to me dimly, a faint recollection through the mists of vague memories. 'Empress'. Salamir had used it that terrible day when he separated us and sent me back to work on Burkov's ship. Burkov himself had made some oblique references to this 'Empress' as well.

But the title had meant nothing to me, and in the rush of all the crowded events that had overtaken me, I'd had no leisure to ponder its meaning. Even now, with the clamor of battle behind me, and surrounding me, I gave myself to time to worry over the nuances of it. Whatever this 'Empress' was, I did not care. My only concern was Azora.

"Open this door!" I demanded of Tuso.

"Idiot!" he answered, bleeding from cheek and chin. "Do you think I have the keys to open it? Or the authority?"

"How, then?"

"What? To open it? Batter it down with your head for all I care."

I saw his eyes wander, looking past my shoulder. The clamor of the battle behind me had grown more frenzied. I glanced quickly behind me. Two of Salamir's guard had fallen, and three of the Karzi. That left only three of the Karzi yet, and four guards. But the Karzi were pressing hard upon the guard, and even as I turned my head, I saw one of the Karzi drop from the ceiling onto the shoulders of one of the guard.

With profound annoyance, I spun quickly, and slashed the Karzi warrior through the neck, even as he was champing down on the guard with his needlelike teeth. The Karzi fell to the floor, dying, and whipping his tail about spastically.

This was unfortunate for his two comrades, for his thrashing tail happened to open one up at the belly, causing his interior parts to come cascading out. The other fellow, in leaping back to avoid the deadly, dying tail, stumbled over himself, giving the remaining four guards all the time they needed to gut him properly, which they did with whoops of triumph.

And the battle was done. The anteroom was bloodied, but silent in that strange silence that descends upon a battlefield after the slaughter has finished.

We all looked at each other, Salamir's guards and I, rather dumbly.

"Thank you, slave. We are grateful to you," one of them said to me at last. "Who are you?"

"I am no slave," I answered. "I am Grae-don. I come for Azora."

"Azora?" asked another of Salamir's guards. "Who is Azora?"

"My friend. My companion."

"Then we shall not hold you, Grae-don. You may seek your companion."

"Tuso tells me that she is behind this door, that she waits upon this 'Empress'..."

I turned at that moment to have Tuso confirm what I said, only to find the man was gone! Once again, he had taken advantage of the moment to slip away.

"Tuso?" asked one of the guard. "That was Tuso?"

"Yes. Of course," I answered.

"You know Tuso?" the guard asked me.

"Yes, indeed. He and I are old friends."

Though I intended that remark ironically, the tone was lost on Salamir's guards. They took me quite literally.

"And where do you know him from?"

"On Burkov's ship, the *Fury*. We served together there."

I saw the eyes of the guards grow wide. They evidently were beginning to consider me a person of great importance, due to my old friendship with Tuso.

"Pardon me," said the one, "for calling you `slave'. It was your attire. I had no way to know you were incognito."

"Think nothing upon it," I answered him. "I intend my disguise to fool the eyes even of the wisest. But now, I have an immediate concern. My Azora lies behind that locked entryway, and I will have those doors opened!"

Rather impertinent of me, I know, to impose upon the credulity of these guards, and to begin ordering them about so. But considering the many sins I had already committed that morning, this impudence was a trifling thing, and the least among them.

The guards cast dubious looks among themselves.

Finally one of them spoke up.

"It grieves me to deny you anything," he said. "You have rendered us valiant assistance against the Karzi, and for that alone, we are in your debt, but that you be also a friend to the exalted Tuso, he the confidante of Salamir himself, we should be only at your service. But..." and here, his voice trailed off.

"But what?" I demanded. It had been a long morning, and my patience was growing short.

"We are charged with guarding this door against all comers, aye, we must even challenge Salamir himself, should he confront us. We protect the Empress. Salamir holds her hostage against a great ransom, and the Empire has been slow to acknowledge Salamir's demands. Besides this, I cannot open this door. It is locked from within. She who serves the Empress opens it, only upon the occasion of Salamir's signal, or of that of his special servants, to bring food to those within."

I glared at the man for a moment. Words did not come to me. Abruptly I turned away from him, and with the pommel of my sword, I pounded loudly on the ornate doorway.

"Azora!" I shouted, "Azora! Open this door! It is I, Grae-don!"

The guards were stunned at my brazen act, and stood frozen in their spots, eyes wide and staring at me.

"Azora! If you can, open this door! Give me a sign that you are there!"

And to the astonishment of us all, the door opened, but only a crack. I saw an eye peer out through the crack, and I recognized it instantly. It was hers. I was looking upon Azora once again. Though fate and brutal hands had separated us, though it had been immeasurably long since I had seen her last, I knew her eye the very moment I saw it.

"Azora," I said again, more softly now. "It is I."

The door opened more widely, and now I saw her face, both eyes wide and tremulous in wonderment.

"Ah... ah..." she said, her breasts heaving with a choked emotion. Then she flung the door wide open, and threw herself upon me. The blood of my many wounds mingled with the blood of those I'd killed, and it smeared upon her own flesh as she embraced me, but we did not care. In that moment, all the burning and bloodied world around us vanished away, and though surrounded on every side by our enemies, we were, at last alone together.

"Oh... Grae-don," she uttered, looking up into my face as I looked down into hers. "I... I... was sure you were dead... even now, I did not recognize you through the open wounds that..." Emotion overcame her, and she could speak no more.

It was at that moment that I recalled myself to the presence of Salamir's guards. I glanced over my shoulder at them to see how they were appointing themselves to our situation, and what I saw gave me no comfort.

The guard who had last spoken had his hand on the pommel of his sword, and was even at that instant unsheathing the weapon. A glance at his face showed me that he had come to a decision, and another quick glance at the others made clear to me that they were in agreement with the first. They, too, were unsheathing their swords, and spreading themselves out in a semicircle to surround Azora and me.

But, their attention wholly upon me, they did not see what I glimpsed behind them. A group of Karzi were slinking down the stairs, and the ceiling over their heads, preparing to ambush the guard from behind.

I wasted not an instant, but pushed Azora bodily into the room she had just quitted and, following her, I quickly pushed the heavy ornate door shut. Instantly the clash of battle came from beyond.

Azora threw the locks upon the doors. And then I turned to look upon the chamber where we had found our hurried shelter. My eyes were astonished at the opulence of it. Even knowing that I was upon Salamir's own ship, and having already seen somewhat of his personal appointments, still I was not prepared for the luxury and the lavishness before me.

The chambers were great in size, and the ornate ceiling was supported by a dozen columns, all of polished bone. The columns were dyed many colors, with rich patterns that pleased the eye, and myriad gemstones embedded in spiraling patterns upon them. The ceiling itself was a vast network of intricate carved wood, of interlocking geometric designs studded with precious metals and stones.

All was carpeted with fabrics that shone and gleamed in the dim light of the shaded lamps that depended from the ceiling and from between the columns, on long ropes and chains of polished gems. Cushions and embroidered pillows lay in piles upon the floors, with silks and furs.

Sitting among those cushions were a dozen women, all in the functional garments worn by servants, thongs and sandals, and that was all. They stared at Azora and me with huge apprehension in their eyes.

And amidst it all, languishing in the center of the chamber, against a far wall upon a divan of plush crimson and gold, there, leaning upon an elbow, with her head cushioned by the palm of one hand while she studied me silently with an unhurried eye, was a woman of most astonishing beauty.

Her eyes, large and shapely, and which took in all that they saw with a measured gaze, were what first caught my attention. They were beautiful eyes, to be sure, but there was about them something I had never seen in a human eye before and which at that rushed and anxious moment I could not precisely describe. The pupils of her eyes were large, and deep—somewhat larger, I think than in others, but that was not what caught my attention.

Her eyes, in that shaded chamber, and at that moment appeared lilac in color, but I was not sure. So forgetful of my manners had I become in the time I had spent among the brigands of Boromok that I stared hard at the woman's face, attempting to discern the color of her eyes.

"Azora," she said at last, turning her gaze to my dear companion, "What is this rude creature, and why does it stare so impudently upon our person?"

She spoke with a low and measured and almost musical cadence, with the confident tone that took the instant obedience of any who heard to be an obvious thing.

"My Empress," Azora responded, and I started with a shock to hear my Azora speak to any person with the deference I heard now in her voice.

"What..?" I asked her, abruptly, half turning to her.

"Hsst!" Azora whispered to me harshly under her breath. "I'll tell you later," she said impatiently in a low voice. "No time now. Just humor her."

"Humor...?" I began to protest, but she shut me up with the eloquent expedient of a sharp elbow in my ribs. I stifled the expression of pain, but kept looking upon the empress.

"My Empress," Azora began again, "Please forgive the trespass. The man is ignorant, and unaware of the grave insult he commits upon her person."

"Ignorant?" I whispered to Azora. "What?"

"Shuddup!" she hissed. "And stop looking at the Empress. It's rude."

"I, what?"

"Shuddup and look at the floor."

"And upon what grounds would I vouchsafe this creature the forgiveness sought on his behalf?" the empress demanded, in low and measured tones, once I had properly lowered my impudent eyes.

"This is he, of whom I have spoken, my Empress. He who shall succor me, and your personage, as well, should my Empress wish it."

"Indeed?" the Empress replied, with a tone of immeasurable, and, it seemed to me, carefully calculated indifference. "He seems rather a poor specimen, we cannot avoid observing. The appearance does not instill confidence." I must have presented quite a sight, I suppose.

Between sword wounds and the raking gouges of flesh torn from my body by the talons and teeth of the Karzi, I had to admit I was not looking my best. But Azora spoke up quickly for me, as I was as short of words as I was of breath.

"And rightly does his appearance comport and bear evidence of his courage, Oh, Empress, for he has fought long and hard against our shared enemies, the brigands of Boramok and the loathsome Karzi who attack this ship, even now. Many are the dead he has left in his wake."

"Is this so?" the Empress asked, but of Azora yet, not of me.

"Yup," I said, but the Empress ignored me. "Yes," Azora assured her. "It is so."

"As your companion has proved himself a warrior, we shall grant him the honor of offering us succor from this unwholesome place. Ladies!" the Empress said, turning her attention to the servants. "We grant you your dismissal. You may return to Salamir, and please, if you will, carry to him our compliments, and our gratitude for your assistance, which he so graciously lent us. But we shall quit of his company."

And with that, the empress rose from her divan, and dismounted the dais. Her movements were monumental. Her hips and her limbs swayed with the natural majesty of ocean currents.

"You may assist," she said, inclining her head to Azora, and speaking as if she were conferring upon her a favor of unutterable magnitude.

"My empress is too gracious," Azora said, and she moved toward the Empress and took up a position on her left.

I watched all this completely befuddled by it, and with growing impatience. The Empress, however, would not be rushed. She moved at her own deliberation, and events, it seemed, would all have to wait upon her will.

Now she was standing, I saw that she was tall, as tall as me, almost. Her skin was pale, the palest I had ever seen, but with, it seemed to me a tint to it, just the lightest touch of lavender, which caused me much wonder. I was used to the reddish skin, and the golden skin of those I had met, but never before had I seen a woman of lavender skin.

This coloration, I was yet to learn, was but the least of the wondrous things about her, for the tint of her skin was temporary. As I was to later see, the color of her flesh changed with her mood. Blues, lavender tints, amethyst, lilac and others reflected moments when she was in peace of her own mind. When she entertained moments of disquiet, her coloration moved toward pinks and yellows. Anger caused her to flush deep crimson, and rust, and orange.

And so on, it seemed—the variations of her colors were nearly infinite, it seemed, and reading her moods through her colors was the study of the learned of her land.

She was shapely, and except for her polychrome skin and her mysterious eyes, she was, in every other aspect, a woman. Her hair was the color of platinum, and it shined of its own with highlights that pierced the soft light of this chamber. It was straight as any blade I have ever seen, and fell from her head, framing her face and touching lightly upon her ears and neck.

She wore diaphanous gowns and robes of emerald green and other pastel colors that hid nothing of her form, but only accentuated the lines of her body.

I'd never seen gowns before, as the people of Pella'mir wore seldom more than thongs and short skirts, or sometimes capes as marks of rank among the great houses there. The gown was most mysterious to me, and I was dazzled at the way it both clung to her body and undulated in the air with her motions. The gowns draped loosely from her shoulders, depending from pins of gold, and around her waist was a belt of precious metals and translucent stones woven with threads of platinum and other such metals. At her hip and hanging from her belt was a short scabbard, in which nestled a cunning knife with a blade of transparent ruby.

Her arms and wrists were covered with bracelets and bangles, and a dozen of more complicated necklaces of various lengths depended her throat. Complicated rings, decorated each of her fingers, and her toes. On her feet were sandals of gold, more ornamental than functional, and the straps of them wound in complicated arabesques around her legs to well above her knees, disappearing at last among the shadows of the many sinuous folds of her gowns.

All this I describe of her was long in observing. I certainly did not take this all in during those feverish moments with Salamir's guard and the Karzi battling loud outside the door, especially as I was yet striving to comprehend the great honor the Empress had vouchsafed me. She had... 'granted me leave to offer her succor from this unwholesome place'?

Directing my question to Azora, who accompanied the Empress those few steps from her couch and down the dais, and who stood at the left hand side of the haughty woman—obviously I was not of exalted enough a state of privilege to speak to her directly—I asked, rather rudely, I suppose, "What?"

Azora glared back at me, and demanded, "What, what?"

"Your precious Empress has granted me leave to offer her succor?"

"Get us out of here," Azora almost shouted, stamping her foot upon the carpet. "Or show us the way out, or get out of the way, or whatever..."

"I came for you..." I started.

"And here I am. Now let's go!"

"But, this... Empress...?"

Her haughty manner annoyed me, and I was of no mind to burden myself with the succor of a stranger. Difficult enough, I knew, for just Azora and me to escape Salamir and the Karzi. But to add a third, and especially this person, who seemed to me hardly able to fend for herself added greatly to our hazard.

The clamor outside grew louder. We had no time to bicker, so I stopped talking and looked quickly throughout the sumptuous apartment for any avenue of escape. I saw no widows piercing the thick walls, nor doors. The only way out was through the same portal through which we had entered.

I gestured toward the ornately carved door and said to Azora, "Is there no other way?"

She nodded her head and set her lips in a tight line. I had seen that expression before. She was ready to fight. But I saw she had no weapon. I plucked my knife from its scabbard and handed to her.

"Take this," I said.

She took it with a smile and a hurried 'Thanks', but turned away and dashed quickly past the servant girls who cowered on their cushions, to a pile of pillows in a corner. From the pile, she hurriedly pulled a few articles, one of them a small bag which she strapped to her waist. From it she extracted a knife of most curious aspect. It was shaped in a semicircle, with four finger-sized holes arranged in a row on the side opposite the curved edge.

Azora came quickly back to me, slipping the fingers of her left hand through the holes of the knife, and holding it so that the curved edge was aimed outward from her fist. In her right hand, she held the short knife that I had given her.

"All ready!" she said.

"Very pretty, that," I said, looking at her blade.

"I stole it!" she said, proudly beaming at me. "One of the idiot guards..."

"Very good," I said.

"So... now what do we do?" Azora asked.

"If there is but the one way out of here, then we should take it," I told her. "And the sooner we leave, the sooner we will be gone. Open the locks."

Azora did so, and I pulled the door wide. Beyond, the orgy of blood was just come to an end. The Karzi were victorious over Salamir's guard, for the last one fell at my feet just as I forced the door open. But the guards had made a good account of themselves, I saw. The bodies of a dozen or more dead Karzi lay strewn upon the stairway and the carpet before the door.

Azora and I found ourselves confronted by six Karzi, all of them bleeding from various wounds. Once their eyes fell upon me, they gave vent to a shrill howl that filled the passageway and chilled my blood.

The Empress stood behind us, and the servant girls cowered upon their plush pillows. I cast one quick glance at them over my shoulder, and then faced the rush of the Karzi. Standing as we did, just behind the frame of the door, the Karzi could not crowd upon us all at once. No more than one or two of them could attack us, which was, of course, much to our advantage.

Nor did they appreciate the deadly threat that Azora in fact was. Seeing her small feminine form, they ignored her and directed their attention to me. Which was a mistake.Before I had a chance to engage the first fellow who scrabbled through the door, on the floor, I saw the strange semi-circular blade that Azora wielded flash quickly, first to the right, and then the left. The Karzi warrior's head fell forward, the neck cut almost nearly through.

And as soon as that fellow had fallen, two more pushed through the doorway—another crawling upon the floor, over the body of the first, and the other climbing along the doorframe, midway between the floor and the top.

Azora dispatched the second warrior as easily as she had done the first, and I had no trouble with the other fellow, lopping his head smartly off as soon as he had poked it through the door.

That left three others who, seeing their numbers cut neatly in half in a single moment, made what I thought was the very intelligent decision to turn and flee. Up the spiraling staircase they fled, and in an instant they were gone.

"Come!" I said, grasping Azora by the arm. "Up the stair."

I did not wait to see if the Empress followed us, but simply hurried Azora along and she, wasting not a word, raced forward. Indeed, she was already mounting the steps before I got to them. She turned to me with a wild smile lighting up her features.

"Hurry up!" she said.

And so I did. We rushed up those stairs which started, at the base, in a wide and leisurely spiral. But they narrowed and grew tight and tighter as we rose higher. The wood was dark and heavy, with streaks of crimson through it. The steps were carpeted, and over our heads every few paces were lamps mounted high in the central column that dimly lit our way.

Azora was just ahead of me now, and the stair had grown too close to permit me to pass her to take up the lead. I chafed at that, especially as we mounted, and the sounds of battle overhead on deck grew louder in our ears. But there was nothing I could do about that, except keep close behind her, ready to leap out past her the moment such opportunity presented itself.

And it soon did. Before I scarce realized it, we burst out of the spiraling stairway on to the deck of Salamir's ship.

After so long within the dimly lit regions of the under decks of the ship, we were almost blinded by the fury of the sunlight. It dazzled us, and Azora and I stood helplessly there at the top of those stairs as our eyes slowly adjusted.

The din of battle was huge all around us, and dizzying, and fortunate it was for us in those moments that all those around us were too focused on their fights to pay us any attention. But our eyes adjusted to the light, and none too soon, and we looked about, seeking some avenue of escape from this ship. The brigands, I saw, were getting the better of the Karzi. Though the Karzi still streamed across the decks, and climbed among the rigging and the masts, swinging their deadly tails like clubs and swords, the brigands of Boramok were the more disciplined fighters.

The brigands, I saw, assisted each other in their fighting, where the Karzi simply threw themselves at the enemy haphazardly. Every time a brigand was attacked by one of the Karzi warriors, one or two others came quickly and they fought shoulder to shoulder and back to back, so it was that even though the Karzi outnumbered the brigands, the brigands were able to cut them quickly down as they came.

A glance overhead showed me that the battle had carried even to the heights over our heads. Brigands, crewmen, guards and Karzi fought among the superstructures, the shattered masts and the rigging of the ship. Several fires raged on the decks, and thick smoke rolled across the ship with the breezes from the deep ocean.

At the fore of the ship I saw the two catapults busy. These were many times larger than the catapults on the *Fury* and many times more devastating. While several dozen of Salamir's guard surrounded them, fighting off the Karzi with sword and knife, the catapults worked in concert. As one was launching, the second catapult beside it was being reloaded, the crew setting torches to the burning stones just before it was launched. In this way, a ceaseless and continuous barrage was launched from the ship all throughout the battle.

And Salamir's ship was only one of many ships, all of them sending death raining down upon the Karzi city on shore. The sky over our heads was darkened by the smoking trails of the barrage remorseless barrage. I glanced back to shore to see more and more ships of Salamir's fleet emerge from the channel I had come from some time before.

Just long enough I paused to look and, yes, indeed, there came the *Fury*, and with it, the *Storm* and the *Lusty* of Burkov's flotilla. They were badly damaged from the battle—the *Fury* had lost a mast, as had the *Lusty*, but even from this distance I could see the brigands were yet fighting and in command of their ships.

I could not help a smile of recognition, and in my mind's eye, I saw Burkov the Bloody at that moment in furious battle, glorying in the slaughter he wrought upon his enemies. I've had both bad friends and good enemies. Burkov was a good enemy, and I could only wish him well, and farewell.

For we could not dawdle upon that dangerous deck. We had come this far to escape Salamir and his minions, not to take in the sights. So, leading Azora, I threaded our way through a series of duels and batteries of bloody swordplay, making toward the railing of the ship. I had it in my mind that I might find one of the Karzi boats, and take it, as I had this morning.

Now I saw that the Empress had, indeed, followed us. Her complexion, still profoundly pale, was now tinged with amber. I was too concerned with our escape to truly notice it at the moment, but as I was to learn later, that tint of color reflected a rare and uncharacteristic agitation on her part. But, though her complexion may have indicated some agitation, or excitement, her features were perfectly well composed, even almost uninterested in the events surrounding us.

If she were uninterested in the events around us, those events were certainly not uninterested in her. We had barely made it to the railing, with two groups of fighters on either side of us, when I heard a shout, clear and clarion across the deck.

"The Empress! They have the Empress! Stop them!"

The fighters on either side of us, brigand and guard and Karzi all alike, and they turned their attentions to us. Swords, knives, talons, teeth and deadly slashing tails flashed at us from every side.

It was only by rare good fortune that they all crowded us so hard that they all got in each other's way, leaving us scant instants to act. We ran the few steps to the railing, which Azora quickly mounted.

"Go!" I shouted to her. Wasting not an instant in futile argument, she leaped.

I watched her lithe form as she bounded high into the air, and then, precisely at the peak of her jump, she turned in mid-flight, and expertly brought the palms of her hands together over her head. For an instant, she seemed to float in the sky. And then she made her body straight as a knife blade, and dove downward, slicing through the air. At last, she plunged perfectly into the water, leaving only the tiniest impression on the surface.

I stepped up to the railing myself, preparing to do the same, and gesturing to this Empress to follow. She gave me a look of haughty unbelief, and said, as if she were an adult explaining to a rude child, that one simply does not engage in such vulgarities, "The Empress does not 'dive'."

Several dozen swords, knives, talons and teeth were coming at us with a furious howls of rage, greed and bloodlust. I had no time to persuade her of the efficacy, or argue the decorum, of the method.

Having no scabbard, I thrust my sword into my loincloth for safe-keeping, and gave myself a nice long slice along the thigh. Angered at myself for that clumsiness, I rudely threw my arm around the Empress's waist and forced her forward with me. I heard a shocked gasp from her, "Huh!" I suppose at my effrontery in placing my hands upon her august person, but otherwise she made no protest, and did not resist, for which I was grateful. We had no time for bickering.

Just as I was about to hurl ourselves both over the side, my eye caught a bit of line hanging from a burning mast. Grasping it in my hand and wrapping my leg around it, I held the Empress tightly against my body and threw ourselves overboard. We slid down the rope into the raging sea below.

The rope burned. Oh! How it burned! My hand, my arm, my leg and all the left side of my body were chafed by the rope that burned through my flesh as I slid down it, with my weight and the weight of the Empress pulling us downward.

We came at last to the end of the rope, still some distance above the water. Glancing down, I saw Azora coming to the surface after her dive, and she made several long strokes toward one of the small wicker boats of the Karzi, abandoned by them during their attack, but yet surrounding the huge hull of Salamir's vast ship.

Glancing upward, I saw several of the Karzi quickly scrambling head first down the side of the hull after us. If that were not sufficiently annoying, I observed several of Salamir's guard grabbing the rope from which the Empress and I were hanging, and begin to drag us back to the deck of the ship.

"My apologies," I said to the Empress. "We must hurry."

And with that, I filled my lungs with air, bidding the Empress to do the same, and let go my grip on the rope. We plummeted downward in a flurry of the Empress's gowns that whipped about my ears. Still, the

Empress was collected. I heard not a whimper from her as we dropped, but I did feel her arm clench briefly about my waist.

We hit the water hard. Deep into the churning depths we plunged, the Empress's gowns flowing in the water, entangling my head and neck. I feared now that we might be drowned, but the Empress surprised me once again. She did not struggle, by which ineffectual flailing she might have caused us to sink further into the water, for now we were bound tightly by the confounding fabric of her gown.

No, she maintained her preternatural composure, even under water, and remained quite calm, and still. And with our lungs filled with air, our natural buoyancy brought us back to the choppy surface of the sea.

Still, her gowns were wrapped around my head, and I found great difficulty in pulling the sodden cloth away. My lungs were starving for air, and the choppy waves persisted in slapping me in the face through the fabric.

And while I was so occupied in treading water, while trying to pluck the clinging wet material from with one hand, and yet keeping my arm around the Empress in an attempt to keep her head above water, I was also mindful of the Karzi I had seen climbing down the hull of Salamir's ship after us. Any instant I expected to feel their sharp talons digging into my flesh. I grew frantic in my efforts.

Suddenly, I felt a hand pulling the robes Empress's away from my head. I gulped down huge mouthfuls of air, filling my lungs, and looking up into the beautiful face of Azora. She was in one of the Karzi boats, leaning over, and working with cool efficiency in freeing me from the entangling fabric.

"Thank you," I said.

"Quickly," she answered, looking past my head. "They come!"

I glanced behind me and saw a half dozen Karzi warriors swimming rapidly toward us.

"The Empress," I said, pushing her toward Azora. The Empress grasped the gunwales of the boat in both hands, and Azora quickly bent to assist her into the boat. She had some difficulty at it, unused as she was to such boisterous activity as climbing into a small boat from a choppy sea. I gave her a bit of assistance myself, pushing her from behind, perhaps more rudely than she was accustomed to. But between the three of us, the Empress climbing clumsily, Azora pulling urgently, and me pushing rather coarsely, we managed to get her aboard the boat.

And then the Karzi were upon us.

The first intimation I had that they had come was the icy hot raking of the claws of one across my back. The shock of it made me fairly leap, and when I turned, I saw that fully six of the fellows had swum up behind us and were slathering and slashing at me.

I put one hand on the gunwale of the boat, holding it tightly, while I dropped my other hand into the water, and whipped my sword out from where I had stowed it, jammed between my leather thong and my thigh. Once again I gave myself a cut in whipping the thing out, but I was too hurried at the moment to curse myself for my clumsiness.

The Karzi warrior upon me—the one who had slashed me from behind—was unaware of the motion of my hand. The first intimation he had that I grasped a sword within it was when the blade sliced through his abdomen under the surface of the water. His eyes, only inches from mine, went wide with shock. Another thrust from my blade, and the light of life left them completely. The corpse bobbed among the choppy waves for but a moment, as they reddened from the blood that gushed from it. And then it sank.

Azora had been busy with her two knives. The Karzi had quickly surrounded the boat, and were attempting to carry off Azora and the Empress, but in the time I had turned upon the Karzi warrior who attacked me, and split him, Azora had cut the throats of two of her attackers.

Astonishing to me to see, the Empress made a good accounting for herself, for she, too, was armed with a knife I had not seen before, a beautiful piece I had thought was a bit of jewelry upon her belt. A thrust into the eye of an impudent fellow who annoyed her sent him back into the water, blinded and bleeding profusely from his wound.

Which left only two Karzi warriors opposing us. Seeing how the numbers had changed so quickly, I was preparing myself for a moment to gloat, and to allow myself to savor the dissolution of the remaining two.

But, idiot that I was, I let my moment of gloating come too soon. Suddenly, and from nowhere, it seemed, I felt something coil itself about my ankle. Whiplike and painfully, it wrapped itself tightly from foot to knee and then jerked me instantly downward.

Down, down, into the water I was dragged. The water stung my eyes, and I could barely see. All was murky and shapeless, but I realized what had happened. One of the Karzi had caught me with his tail. Using it like a whip, he had looped it around my leg, and was dragging me downward to drown me. The instant I understood this, I felt another whiplike thing catch me and coil itself around me, this time at my waste.

I struggled manfully, and uselessly, against my bounds as the two Karzi dragged me deeper into the water, with a speed that was truly shocking. I had no air in my lungs, and felt an irresistible dizziness overcoming me. All was growing dark.

All this had happened so quickly, that I was some instants in re-calling the sword I still grasped in my nearly unconscious hand. Now frantic, and with a life-saving rage swelling suddenly in my heart, I slashed through the water with the last bit of strength I had in me. With my first slash, cutting at a bad angle, the water caused my sword to drag, and when it landed upon the tail of the Karzi, it did little damage.

But I paid attention to the tension of the water, and with my second cut, I aimed my blade more nicely, and it came down exactly right, slashing the Karzi's tail, and removing it neatly from its owner. Another cut, and then another, and the second tail was severed, and it unwound itself, limply, from my body.

What happened to the Karzi warriors after that I do not know, for I did not stay to parley with them any further. Released from their hold, I instantly shot to the surface of the water, or what I thought should have been the surface.

In that brief fight I had become completely disoriented. I swam hard, my lungs heaving. Completely out of air, they reflexively were fighting to make me inhale. But of course, if I inhaled, I inhaled not air, but water. Now I must fight my own body. I must keep my body from forcing itself to inhale, even as I was suffocating for lack of air. It should be only an instant or two, before I broke the surface of the water and could breathe to my heart's content. Only an instant.

And then the top of my head hit hard packed sand.

For a moment I was confused. What? Had the world gone insane? And then the truth came to me. Disoriented in the fight with the two Karzi, I had swum not straight, but downward. I was at the bottom of a dark sea, with no idea how far above me the surface was.

Never before had I felt such instant despair, or despair of such immeasurable depth. My lungs were already convulsing in my chest as I was swimming downward. Not I had to swim that distance and more in the opposite direction. I knew I could not do it. I knew that before I broke the surface of the sea, my lungs would spasmodically inhale huge swallows or sea water, and I would drown.

So close I had been to Azora. So briefly had I held her. And now, I was to be pulled away from her by absurd death, when we were so close to our freedom.

But, though I was despairing, I could not give myself up to it. As certainly as death was about to overtake me, I would not go down easily. I would die fighting to the very last, as I had lived.

So, though it takes long to say all this, it took me only instants to feel it, and to act. Once I'd comprehended that I had hit the bottom of the sea, I turned myself in the opposite direction, and forced myself upward through the dark and murky waters.

Upward I swam, though my chest was convulsing and my throat constricting, I forced my body upward. There is no need to detail the tortures of body and of mind I went through in that interminable journey to the surface. That I am telling this tale is sufficient evidence of itself that I lived to do so.

I scarcely believed it, when at last my head broke above the water. Air! I could breathe! A world of air and breath, one it seemed only an instant before was an impossibly far away. I breathed, inhaled the sweet air and sucked it down, my ears ringing so loudly I could not hear anything except the ringing inside my head.

That instant was an eternity to me. Some part of me still dwells there in that place, that instant of release from my watery death. But eternity though it may have been it was but an instant, and through the din of loud ringing in my ears, I faintly heard a call, somehow familiar, that recalled me to the world.

It was Azora's voice I heard. She called to me from the boat, only a few short strokes away. I swam quickly for it, and, exhausted, I grasped the gunwale, still pulling huge breaths of air into my panting lungs.

"Oh, Grae-don!" Azora said to me, leaning over and nuzzling my head with hers.

"Hah... Hah... Hah..." was what I said in reply, only taking in huge swaths of air, and too drained to speak.

"Come, Grae-don! Into the boat! They come after us, yet!"

I glanced behind me and saw that we had drifted away from the hull of Salamir's ship, but dozens of Salamir's guard stood upon it, looking after us. Apparently the battle with the Karzi was over. The Karzi were driven from his ship. The catapults at the fore were still at work, though, hurling their charges at the city of the Karzi, so I surmised that the Karzi, though driven from the ships, were yet undefeated.

That was good, as far as I was concerned. It meant that Salamir's forces would yet be occupied with their war against the Karzi, and would not have the leisure to turn their full attention on us. But again, it was too soon for me to gloat, for even as I looked, I saw a form stride to the edge of the deck of Salamir's ship.

It was a familiar form. It was my old friend, Tuso.

As I watched him, he cupped his hands together and called across the waves, "Stop! Bring the Empress back to us, Grae-don, or I will hunt you down myself, and I gut you with my own hands! I'll make you watch me, as I roast your flesh and eat it!"

That fearsome challenge gave me great motivation. Exhausted though I was, I crowded aboard the boat with Azora and the Empress. I searched out the boat's oars, which I quickly found. And then, giving myself no more time to catch my breath, I worked on the oars, and began to pull away from Salamir's ship and Tuso, into the deep and churning sea ahead.

14

—·—

FLIGHT INTO THE SEA

T HE BOAT, LADEN WITH the three of us, was heavy and I was
exhausted. But the Karzi were hard upon us in their boats, and
they hurled stones at us with a stunning ferocity and velocity, and in
numbers that were appalling.

Azora picked up those stones that landed in our boat and hurled
them back, and to some effect, for she managed to strike several of
the Karzi, bashing a number of skulls in. The empress, too, I saw,
attempted to hurl a few stones at our pursuers, but hers fell short. She
did, however assist in keeping our small boat from being overloaded
with the stones.

But the Karzi were coming at us in great numbers. Were that not
enough, I saw that several of Salamir's small ships had turned about
and joined in the pursuit. I saw Tuso himself climb down from
Salamir's great flagship, and into a swift smack with broad triangular
sails. The hull was a loud cerulean, which contrasted sharply with
the turgid orange and crimson of this wallowing sea. Its sails, a sharp
yellow that stood out against a tangerine sky. The smack pulled away
from the ship and quickly cut through the ranks of pursuers to take
the lead among them.

We were many *yurlma* ahead of our pursuers, in raging waters that were deeper than any I had ever seen. One small advantage to us was that the currents here were strong, and we were being carried swiftly out into the open sea. With my work at the oars, we were fairly skimming across the water. But the current carried our pursuers as well, and though I managed to stay ahead of them, I was not able to pull away. The Karzi harassed us with stones, until they finally ran out of them.

And the swift smack that Tuso commanded, and the other small ships of Salamir's fleet, were moving much faster than any of us in our boats. That, of course, was due to their sails. With men at their oars, and their sails swelling before the stiff ocean winds, it was inevitable that they should catch us, and rather soon at that, I saw.

Another small matter was working to our advantage. The Karzi had not given up their fight against the brigands, and whenever any of the Karzi boats came close to one of Salamir's ships, they left off their pursuit of us, and attacked their ancient enemies instead. Soon the waters behind us were chaotic with running battles. The brigands managed to pick off many of the Karzi boats, and it was with some satisfaction that I saw the Karzi overwhelm and board one of Salamir's fleet ships.

But still they came on. Tuso's smack was particularly persistent and would not be thrown off our trail. Though the Karzi boats teased and attempted to attack them continuously, Tuso clearly commanded his crew to ignore the Karzi assaults, and to bear down on us with a single-minded determination. Tuso's smack, alone of all the boats and ships pursuing us, was gaining upon us. It was but a matter of time, I knew, that they would overtake us. I must elude Tuso, but how?

Looking about our boat, I saw that a number of oars lay lengthwise along the bottom, with coils of line strewn about, as well. Seeing them, I bethought me an idea.

"Azora," I called to her, above the noise of the rough waters slapping our bows, and the cries of the Karzi. "Lash those two oars together, so they cross one another! Build a mast."

Wasting not a moment with futile questions, Azora threw herself instantly to the task. In a very few moments, she had built a fine mast, and as each oar was twice as tall as I, I was confident the mast she had shipped together would be more than sufficient.

"But what shall we use for a sail?" Azora asked.

"The empress's gowns," I answered, simply.

Azora and the Empress both gave me a stare, but I only looked pointedly back toward the ships that pursued us.

I saw the Empress's chin rise slightly, and she drew in a long breath, but she quickly saw the point. Our pursuers were gaining on us rapidly. With only our oars to move us, they would quickly overtake us. But, should we make sails for our boat, we might have the slenderest chance to outpace them.

Making not a single unneeded word of protest, the Empress rose from her seat, and standing in the aft of our tiny boat as it bounded among the swells, she began to disrobe herself of her many sweeping gowns.

The stones of the Karzi occasionally flew past, barely missing her and smacking hard into the water. Yet, with an untroubled and completely unhurried aplomb she carefully removed the brooch that pinned one great sweep of cloth to her right shoulder, and she dropped the brooch into the boat.

The single swath of viridian silk that hung from her shoulder and swaddled her breasts from right to left came loose, and she lightly flung it over my head to Azora at the bow of our tiny boat. Azora quickly fastened that bit of gleaming silk to our rude mast, while the Empress, her manner regally untroubled, was detaching another layer of fabric pinned to her left shoulder.

Removing each piece of her satin and silken robes in turn, she handed them, one by one, over my head as I worked the oars, to Azora at the bow of our tiny boat, who nimbly fixed them to the yardarms of the makeshift mast.

Facing the stern of our boat as I rowed, and with the Empress standing close above me, her long and elegant legs balancing her and straddling our struggling boat in these dangerous waves not far before me, I kept my eyes intent upon the vicious Karzi in their boats following us, and the brigands pursuing in their fleet ships.

The Empress's manner, most regal, her motions so stately, as she removed each layer of fabric from her noble self, I found myself unable to do aught but admire the dignity with which she carried herself, even under our fraught and dangerous circumstances. We were all, every one of us poised, dangerously balanced on the wild, and delicate knife-edge between life and death, and yet she comported herself here with all the quiet dignity of a lady of state, preparing herself in utter privacy for but a casual bath.

It was all as if I did not exist, and I admired her for that.

There was nothing in her manner to betray the least discomfort, nothing to suggest she was in any way disquieted by anything that had happened to her, or in what she was doing. Every least gesture, every least glance of her eyes, gave forth the impression that it was she, not circumstance, who was in command of all—even when she most clearly was in command of nothing.

At last, the Empress had divested herself of all her multitudinous robes and gowns, and she kept to herself only her thong, her gilded belt and a thin halter. All the rest she had passed over my head to Azora, and our mast was most colorful, the multitudes of sails upon it swelling wildly in the growing winds.

Now, in spite of myself, I glanced at the woman's body, feeling ashamed of my indelicacy, yet also delighting in it. Oh, Beauty, your name is Woman! And the Empress was she. Her flesh as pale as a distant star in the gleaming night sky, yet the lines of her form, her legs, her stately thighs, were lines of a poet's pen. No woman could ever take my eyes from Azora, she who fought and played and worked and danced with me, but the beauty of this Empress was dazzling.

Now, though I did not sense the significance of it, the tone of her skin was a most translucent crimson. She looked down upon me with haughty eyes, as I sweated at the oars, and then she handed over the last remaining piece of her silken robes to Azora, who quickly and adroitly fastened it to our small and makeshift mast.

The Empress's sacrifice of her gowns was not without effect. The sails we constructed from them brought about the very results I had hoped. With them, our tiny boat picked up even more speed, and we were soon able to leave the Karzi far behind us. The many silken and silvery colors of our sails swelled and danced before the shouting winds. Scarlet and cerulean, cinnamon and gold, all beneath a sky of swaddling pink, and an ocean of raging crimson highlights and the infinite purple shadows of the depths below us.

But Salamir's fleet ships were still in pursuit. We had a slight advantage in that our boat was light, and small, and could move far more quickly across the water than the heavier ships that pursued us. But those ships had more oarsmen, and more, and larger sails. It was a terrible balance—as we fled before them, our pursuers remained in hot pursuit behind us.

We were in deep waters now, deeper waters than I had ever seen before, and the sea swelled constantly under us, carrying us to great heights, and then dropping us low again, into deep and shadowed purple troughs between the ruby swells.

Now the sky was bright at midday. The battle and our flight had been long already, and the pink and amber sky cast sharp shadows in the golden troughs of the waters.

Each time the swelling sea brought us on high, we could see behind us the pursuing ships of Salamir. Now, after our long flight, there were but six of them remaining, of the dozen or so that had cast off after us. The others had given up, and returned, I guessed, to the battle with the Karzi off the shore of their mountain city.

Foremost among our pursuers was Tuso's swift smack. Its gleaming yellow, triangular sails shone bright under the noontime sun. His smack was close enough to us that I could easily distinguish among the men I saw upon its deck. They waved and gesticulated at us, and I heard their shouts and curses carried to us by the winds.

I studied the other ships pursuing us to see if any of the three of Burkov's flotilla were among them, but they were not. That made me glad. I felt no loyalty, or friendship, to Burkov, or to his men. But I wished no evil upon them, either. Though I had learned to navigate the sea through his brutal schooling, an education for which I was wholly grateful now, it was also strictly because of him that I found it needful to learn these new skills.

Azora and I had been perfectly happy in Pella'mir before he and his men captured us and carried us away. We could have lived contentedly in Pella'mir for all our lives. But Burkov and his crew tore us away from the home we had made for ourselves there.

So, between that, on the one hand, and the useful education I had learned because of him on the other, I was willing to call it even between us. He was not my friend. He was not my enemy. I had no wish to see him again.

The other small ships, five of them, struggled in the increasingly choppy waters. Again, this was another small advantage to us. Our tiny and light boat easily crested the many waves and buoyantly sailed over them. Indeed, sometimes, with the winds so strong, we were lifted into the air when we crested the swelling of the sea and carried many feet forward before we landed lightly into the trough between the waves again.

The ships pursuing us, however, had not our buoyancy, and they wallowed often in the valleys between the growing mountains of water. I began to hold out some slim hope that perhaps, after all, we might outpace our pursuers in this deepening sea.

But, even as two of the ships finally gave it up, leaving only four in pursuit, Tuso stayed persistent. Indeed, his smack was slowly closing the gap between us.

Azora and I did not speak throughout all this time. I was too intent upon my work with the oars, using them not only to propel our boat, but also to steer it through the rising seas. And, since we had no way to mount our makeshift mast to our tiny boat, Azora's whole mind and effort were put to the task of holding the mast upright against the winds and sea by her own sheer force. She had wrapped her arms and body about the base of the mast, and held it close to her, though it pitched and lurched brutally with the winds.

At last the Empress herself, sitting behind me in the aft of the boat and seeing Azora's labors, roused herself and in silence she crawled half past, and half over me to join Azora at the fore of the boat. The color of her skin, I scarcely, noticed was now tinted a pale azure. So preoccupied was I in maintaining the balance of our tiny boat among the waves and ahead of our pursuers that I was hardly conscious of the change in her skin tone. Earlier, when she sacrificed her gowns and robes to make our sails, her flesh had been tinged with translucent crimson and transparent shades of pink. But now, her skin was flushed with a pale azure tone in the highlights, fading into an indigo in her shadows.

She crawled silently past me, as I say, to the fore of our boat, to assist Azora in holding our pitiful mast upright against the winds. There, with Azora, the Empress wrapped her own long, pale arms and legs tightly about the mast, and the two women held it erect together through that long and nerve-wracking day.

After an interminable time, I saw two more ships at last turn away, though Tuso's smack was closer to us than ever before, and I was congratulating myself on having exhausted their pursuit. Now it was but Tuso's swift smack, which was but three or four ship lengths behind us, and two others, both of them far behind.

Tuso himself had taken to taunting us, hurling his shouted curses and imprecations across the waves. As we rose with the seas, his voice carried to us with its obscenities across the wind. When we plunged deep into the troughs of the waves, his voice carried over our heads, and we plummeted into a world of heavy silence.

And then we rode the sea up into the air again, and there was Tuso's ship, closing the gap between us. The oars were working furiously, the lateen sails were swollen in the wind, and Tuso, at the bow, leaned forward and shouted at me to turn to, and give up to him. I recognized him easily. His sweating, sallow, yellow face, contorted with rage, shone through the sea air.

"Grae-do-o-o-o-n!" he shouted. "Cease this useless flight! Stop and die with honor, coward!"

I made no reply to him, nor did Azora, nor the Empress. We were sodden with the brackish water of the oily sea. My muscles screamed in agony, my belly cramped with my exertions, my wounds, untreated and open, stung with every splash of water that slapped against me.

Yet we pulled on.

The two ships that sailed behind Tuso dropped back, and away. I watched as they, too, disappeared beyond the waves. Hope suddenly grew in my heart. Now, it was only Tuso. Freedom was nearer than I dared hope. I felt new strength surging through me, and I pushed upon the oars, guiding our tiny boat through the churning sea with an optimism I had not felt since, I suddenly realized, those long ago days at Pella'mir.

It was with that renewed hope and that new strength pulsing through my body that we mounted to the summit of yet another wave, and I heard Azora behind me, in the bow of the boat, give sudden voice to unmistakable and unutterable despair.

"Oh, no. Oh... oh... no."

I turned in my seat, just in time to miss the sight that sent Azora into such an instant abyss of hopelessness as our boat slid down into the shadowed valley between two mountainous waves. I must wait until we had climbed the summit again to see what it was she had seen.

I looked upon Azora, and the Empress, as they held our makeshift mast upright, their bare arms glistening with the wet of the sea, their hair sopping and flat upon their heads. Azora's eyes were large with despondency. The Empress, too, her regal and imperturbable comportment suddenly withered even before my eyes.

The wave brought us on high once again. I craned my neck to see what this new disaster was that confronted us, and half rose from my seat. There before me, as we mounted the peak of the wave, I saw spread out in a wide semicircle the five ships of Salamir's fleet that I thought before had abandoned their pursuit of us.

No. Somehow, they had flanked us and sped on ahead of us. And now, we were trapped between those five ships and Tuso's smack behind us. Now I understood the cleverness with which Tuso had herded us into his trap. Salamir's ships were clearly faster than I'd credited, and now that we were in sight of them once again, I saw them moving on either hand to completely encircle us.

They drew close, even among those rough waves, but these were experienced seamen. What a fool I had been, thinking that with my poor and amateurish skills I could outwit them on the sea! I cursed myself a thousand times over as I saw all six ships drawing the circle of their noose tighter around our small boat.

Tuso's smack loomed upon us from the rear, and now I saw Tuso himself standing in the fore. Only a few boat length's away, he cupped his hands around his mouth and shouted to me.

"Cease this silly flight, Grae-don! Give us the Empress, and I promise you, your death will be swift."

In reply, I put my back to the oars once again, and pushed hard on them. Our little boat moved forward against the waves.

"Oh, Grae-don, it is hopeless," Azora said from behind me. I turned once again to look, and saw that we were indeed surrounded by Salamir's ships. They crowded hard upon us now, looming high over our heads from every direction. Before me and all around, I saw only ceaseless walls of bounding ships' hulls.

"Bring your boat about!" a crewman from the ship nearest to us called to us. "And come on board." A rope ladder came over the side of the ship, and hung next to the hull, meeting the sea at the water line.

I put down the oars, and looked helplessly at Azora. She met my eyes but said not a word. The massive hulls of the ships that surrounded us blocked our view. It was as if we had stumbled into a canyon of surging wooden planks.

"Put about, I said!" came the command from the ship. "Do it now!"

Once again I picked up the oars. "As hopeless as it is for us, Azora," I said, "We're still alive."

"Yes," she answered. "We are. We're still alive."

I pushed on the oars again to bring our boat in line with the ladder.

But at that very instant, just as I began to move our boat toward our captors, the waters surged behind me.

Quickly turning, I was astonished at what I saw.

Bursting from the sea, in the gap between our boat and the ship toward which I was rowing, so close to us we were almost upon it, an enormous tentacle shot upward into the sky. The thing was monstrous. It soared upward until it towered over the masts of all the ships surrounding us. Wider at the base than the bodies of a dozen men standing together, the thing glistened with moisture and slime. The tentacle tapered at the top, to a narrow tip that lashed through the air like a whip. It was a rusted color, a brackish brown with irregular spots of putrid yellow.

Countless eyes grew from the tentacle on all sides, and all along its length. The eyes were of many sizes, those at the base of the tentacle being even larger than my head, while those nearer the tapering tip were smaller than my thumb. The eyes all grew on flexible stalks that thrust outwardly from the tentacle itself and that moved independently about when the eyes encountered a thing this monstrous creature wished to examine more closely.

I was shocked to speechlessness at the sight of this monstrous thing, and sat, stunned at my oars, unable to move. The monstrous tentacle thrashed in the air and in the water, only but a single arm's length from the bow of our boat. Azora and the Empress put down the mast they held between them and edged away from the repulsive thing, squeezing past me until they both had found a pitiful shelter behind me.

Azora buried her face into my back. I felt her breasts trembling against me, and her nails digging into my flesh. The Empress heroically maintained her composure, yet unconsciously did she huddle against me, too, the side of her head touching mine, as she stared upward into the horror that was unwinding in the sky above us.

"The *wahe-el*!" Azora whispered, her voice husky with terror.

I was stunned. The *wahe-el*? This thing? This monstrosity? This was a *wahe-el*? This horror was nothing like the tepid, transparent things I found floating unconsciously in the shallow Great Northern Sea so long ago, and which I had nearly forgotten in the mists of ever-flowing time. This thing was huge, agitated, thrashing and, as I was about to see, very horribly carnivorous.

The thing stank. It stank of rotted meat and putrefaction. The air was suddenly thick with an overwhelming miasma of dead, moldering flesh and other filth, and it set Azora, the Empress and me to fits of gagging. Each breath I took in seemed to me obscene in ways I'd never dreamed possible before.

The brigands aboard the ships surrounding us instantly let loose with huge distress calls from the horns mounted among their masts for that purpose, "Ooowah! Ooowah! Ooowah!" and "Awooo! Awooo! Awooo!" Upon all the ships, I saw the men rushing about the decks and rigging, arming themselves for battle.

"Hawooowaahh! Hawooowaahh! Hawooowaahh!" went the horns from ship to ship.

The tentacle coiled in the air over the ships, casting a shadow that danced mockingly against their hulls, and then it uncoiled, its tip slashing the air. Suddenly, it plunged down across the ship closest to us. The tip of that tentacle cut through the rigging that held the masts, snapping the lines and sending many crewmen falling to their deaths.

They were the lucky ones, for they died quickly. The tentacle moved with shocking remorselessness. Having cut through the rigging, it encircled the ship, plunging into the water on the port side of the ship, and then emerging on the starboard side, to loop itself about the ship in ceaseless coils. In this manner, the seemingly endless tentacle wrapped itself about the hull of the ship, even as the hapless crewmen hacked futilely at it with their puny swords. In this manner, the massive tentacle of the *wahe-el* dragged the ships down into the water, nearly swamping it.

Now, with the deck of the ship barely breaking the surface of the sea, Azora, the Empress and I could only look on in silent horror as the doomed crew battled against their inevitable end. A dozen more tentacles lunged up from the churning sea, and they quickly enmeshed the ship in a living web of death. They slid and slithered and glided across the deck, and sent probing fingers through its ports and doorways, probing deep into its hull. With the aid of their countless eyes, they sought out the unfortunate crewmen wherever they were, even as the men hacked at the tentacles with their swords.

And then I saw that the sickening slime that oozed from the tentacles was of deadly purpose. It was sticky. Deadly sticky. Any man who came into contact with the slime was instantly stuck to it, and quickly bound up against the tentacle. Likewise, the tentacles, as they glided across the deck, left thick trails of this slime upon it, and every man who stepped or fell upon it was trapped within it.

Though they fought bravely, the brigands fought hopelessly, and the battle was over in even less time than it has taken me to describe it. Within instants, every man on that ship was stuck fast to the tentacles, or torn into pieces, having been glued to the deck by the dripping slime, and then ripped apart as the sticky tentacles slithered over him.

Having harvested all they could from that ship, the tentacles left it, and turned to the next ship in the line. The first ruined ship wallowed in the waves, breaking up into pieces which floated past us.

And then I heard, from across the waves, the orders called out from the second ship in the line, to 'Man the oars!'

The captain of that ship, having seen the instant destruction wrought upon the first, attempted to turn and flee. But the command came too late. In short, hellish moments, the second ship was rendered wreckage floating upon the water, just as had the first.

Now the tentacles were obscenely crowded with multitudes of the bodies of their prey, and I observed with horror that the bodies of crewmen—not all of them dead—captured upon the sticky tentacles were dissolving against them, the fluids of their bodies running freely down the length of the stalks and then to be absorbed into the flesh of those tentacles.

The brigands, I saw, were being digested before our eyes.

Having dispensed with the second ship, the tentacles were turning their attention to the third which, along with the fourth and fifth ships that had surrounded us—and Tuso's smack, as well, making the sixth of those who pursued us—was already putting about and in hot flight away from this hellish place.

As I watched, a motion under the surface of the water caught my eye. It was the body of the vast *wahe-el* itself, following its countless tentacles as it hunted the fleeing ships. Our tiny boat, floating like a stray piece of flotsam, was barely an arm's length above it, as it flowed under us.

I could not make out the shape of the thing, as it was huge. I could make out only the top surface of it, rugged and thick, like a shell. It was covered with growths that clung to it, and trailed behind as it surged forward. Like the *wahe-el* of the Great Northern Sea, the tentacles of the thing grew from underneath its main body, and extended beyond its peripheries. Now, as this *wahe-el* hunted bigger game than us, all its tentacles were stretched out in the direction of its prey, thankfully. For that reason, though it passed so close beneath us, and would have destroyed us in an instant, should it have discovered us, we escaped its attention.

I felt a touch on my forearm and, startled, I jerked away. But it was only Azora. Her eyes huge with shock, she said to me, haltingly, "Grae-don... we... this place... we should go... before it comes for us..."

I had some trouble forming the words, or even making a sound, but at last I managed to find the coordination to nod my head and answer her.

"Yes," I said. "Pick up the mast again, and let us flee while we can."

Azora crawled back to her place at the fore of the boat, and the Empress too, squeezed past me again to assist Azora. Between them they raised the mast, and, again, they wrapped their arms and legs about it to hold it upright again.

I put myself to the oars, and worked them silently. We pushed away from the deadly *wahe-el* and the ships, once our pursuers, now pursued by the monstrous thing.

"Put the mast down, now," I told them, after we had put some distance between ourselves and our enemies. The sails of the ships were tiny upon the horizon, and the monstrous tentacles appeared like the hairs that grow upon my arm.

"Rest your sore bodies, and let us see where the currents carry us," I told Azora and the Empress. For some time I watched carefully, to see if the currents would carry us in the direction I'd hoped.

And they did. Without the wind to push us along, we were drifting now a more southerly direction, while the *wahe-el* continued pursuing its prey to the north and the east.

"See..." I said. "We are moving away from the *wahe-el* and its prey.

"And hopefully," I added, "We are too small a thing for it ever to take notice of us." Hearing the words coming out of my mouth gave me courage.

"Ye-es," Azora answered, haltingly. "I hope we aren't worth its attention."

"... there is a useful virtue, to be found, at times," the Empress said, after a moment's silence, "In the appreciation of one's own insignificance."

Those were the first words we had heard from her, since the moment before I dragged her from Salamir's ship, when she haughtily informed us that `the Empress does not... dive'.

Perhaps it was the wording of it, perhaps it was the imperturbable tone in which she gave it utterance, perhaps it was that she had said anything at all, but whatever the reason, hearing those words from her at that moment, in that way, I was suddenly washed with waves of incomprehensible relief. My spirit lightened, as if I'd suddenly dropped an impossibly heavy load.

I could not help but smile. And Azora, seeing me, smiled, too. And the Empress, seeing us smiling so, vouchsafed a smile upon us. And, all three of us looking at the others, we each began to snicker, and then to giggle.

And then we all broke into laughter. Happy laughter. Happy laughter of profound, unutterable and inexhaustible oceans of relief. We laughed wordlessly, and happily, for a very long time.

We watched, still laughing, as the distant *wahe-el* pursued the ships that had hunted us, all past the horizon. One by one, the masts of the ships dwindled and disappeared, whether by sailing beyond our sight, or crushed by the mighty *wahe-el*, we did not know.

But it made no difference. They were gone, and we were free. Free, upon the open sea.

I searched the horizon in every direction. There was not the smallest hint of land anywhere to be seen. No island, no peak, no gathering of clouds to suggest a distant landfall.

Azora and I were in a tiny boat, in an open sea, one which neither of us had ever seen before. With us, a strange and impenetrable Empress, about whom I still knew nothing.

Which way was land? How far distant? We had only barely escaped the horrific *wahe-el*. What other monstrosities lurked beneath us within the depths of this unknown sea? Now what?

15

— · —

LOST AT SEA—AZORA'S TALE

W E HAD NOTHING. THE three of us had escaped with nothing but the few weapons we had managed to carry with us. Azora still held her strange curved blade, and the knife that I had given her. I still carried the sword the dying brigand had tossed to me as we battled the Karzi. The Empress? I did not know if she hid among her rings and bracelets any more weapons, such as the knife so cleverly disguised as a belt buckle.

But aside from those small things, we were adrift upon the open sea and nearly naked. The empress's many gowns could still serve us as a makeshift sail, and by now they were far too worn and tattered by the wind ever to be useful as garments again.

Two oars, in addition to the two that Azora had lashed together for our hastily-built mast, and that was all. I searched through the bottom of our tiny boat for any possible provision. But it was a quick search. Only a tiny area, and there was nothing to be found. No water, no food.

As that realization sank in, my mood took a sudden downturn. With no water and no food, with nothing to provide us shelter against wind and sun, and with no knowledge of where we were, or how far we must go before we found landfall, our prospects were not good, not good at all.

Perhaps, I thought fleetingly, we'd have been better off to stay on Salamir's ship. At least there, even as slaves, we'd have food. But I put that thought out of my mind soon as it shaped itself in my head. Better to be free. It is always better to be free, even to die free, than to live as a slave.

Giving Azora a look, I remarked, "Well, at least we're alive."

She smiled. "Yes," she replied. "We're still alive. But for how long, I wonder?"

I could only shrug helplessly.

"I don't know," I answered. "With no provisions, and no way to know how far we are from a friendly shore..."

"And I'm hungry," Azora said.

"And thirsty, too," I added. "I am thirsty. But we have not even a drop of drinkable water."

Hopelessness overtook us, and we fell silent. The waves were still piling high, and the current was strong. Each time the waves carried us up, we searched the sea, hopelessly, for any sign of land. But nothing relieved the unbroken horizon line all about us.

"What's that?" Azora asked, her voice rising, after many long and fruitless moments of hunting the horizon. She pointed in the direction from which we had come. With the next rise of the wave, I searched in the direction she had indicated, and observed a strange clutter bobbing in the water.

It took me several moments, but at last I understood what I was seeing.

"It's the wreckage of the ships," I said. "The ships destroyed by the *wahe-el*."

"Oh?" Azora said, hope swelling in her voice. "Of course! Perhaps we can find something in it that we can use!"

"What I'm most interested in is water," I replied, picking up the oars. I set myself to paddling against the current that carried us forward, along with the flotsam that was some distance behind us.

"I'm glad we put our sail down," I remarked to Azora and the Empress, who maintained a regal silence. "It carried us ahead of the flotsam. Had we sailed any longer, we might have left it far behind and missed it. As it is, I think I might be able to hold ourselves steady here long enough for the current to bring the wreckage to us."

It was not long, in fact, before the swift current carried the debris of the wrecked ships to us, and we found ourselves in the midst of it. Boards, planks from the decks, pieces of ladders, masts, and yardarms all floated by. Several crates came near, and as I held our boat steady with our oars, Azora and the Empress broke them open and explored them.

Luck was with us. Several of the crates that came our way were laden with provisions, and soon we had sufficient food to keep us well fed for weeks. We found numerous caskets filled with fresh water as well as *ellihi* and so we had all we needed.

With ropes hanging from the ruined yardarms that floated past, I managed to lash the caskets and crates to our boat. As we were carried along by the currents with the mass of wreckage, we had leisure to examine it, and we scavenged a great deal from it.

Our first concern, having provided for our nourishment, was to make use of it. There, among the waves, Azora, the Empress and I ate a meal together of some dried *fuma*, and *h'rafa*. It was a rude meal. We had no utensils to eat with, and only the small knife I had given Azora to cut the food with.

Though we found numerous amphorae of *ellihi* among the wreckage, we deferred drinking it, for as exhausted as we were, and as dangerous as the rolling sea was, we had to keep our wits keen and sharp. We drank only water, but that water was sufficiently sweet, especially to our sore bodies. I found it, at that moment, the most delicious thing I had ever drunk. Azora and the Empress both expressed themselves in agreement with me, when I said so.

After eating, we were all overcome with a powerful drowsiness. I let Azora and the Empress both slip into sleep while I stayed on watch. A deadly dangerous thing it would have been, had all three of us gone to sleep, of course. One of us must keep watch.

The Empress laid herself down in the bottom of the boat, while Azora crawled near me where I sat and laid her head upon my lap. Both were instantly asleep.

All the remainder of that day did they slumber, nor did I have the heart to rouse them. Now with silence falling upon us, and the instant immediacy of one danger following ceaselessly upon the heels of another, giving way at last to peace and some solitude, the pains from my many wounds awoke with a clamor.

The gouges in my back and chest from the Karzi warriors screamed at me. The long rope burn down the side of my body and leg, from that moment when I carried the Empress off Salamir's ship, was scalding me. Myriad cuts from sword and knife, scraped flesh and blackened bruises, in those places where I had fallen, all in concert created in my body a veritable chorus of pain. And water from the sea kept the wounds moist, so they all oozed with slow-flowing blood. I was not languishing in comfort.

But the pain was a good thing, for it kept me awake, and alert, especially in the long and silent monotony of riding the waves under the flat and featureless sky.

Day at last turned to twilight. The glorious pink and amber skies above us turned first to lavender, then purple, then black, and the countless stars burst forth again, shining upon the deep and mysterious sea.

I was reminded of my first moments in this world, when I found myself floating, all unknowing, all unconscious and unaware in the shallow, tepid water of the Great Northern Sea. Nights like this one filled my uncomprehending gaze, when I could not distinguish myself from that I saw, when what I saw and what I was were, in my mind, the same thing.

That was long ago, and much had happened since. Though I had some dim recollection of the person I was, in those first days, I was that person no longer. Now I had a name. I had made enemies, and friends. I had lived and fought and killed. And now, with Azora asleep, and our immediate dangers past, I had some moments of quiet to contemplate the world, and what I had come to be within it. Looking up at the stars as they cascaded across the silent firmament, I let my mind wander over what I had seen and where I had been, all for a long and unbounded time.

Somewhere in the middle of the night, Azora finally awoke, and, seeing that I was sitting up, she demanded, "Haven't you slept?"

"Someone should stay on watch," I simply said.

"When did you sleep last?"

"It will have been two nights ago," I answered.

"You should sleep now, then," she said.

"I would gladly sleep, if I could. But can you stay awake through the night?"

"Yes, of course," she replied, running her hand through my hair. My scalp was scarred with scabs and open wounds, and I winced a bit.

"Oh..." Azora whispered. "I'm sorry. Sleep. Stop thinking. Sleep now."

I needed no more prompting. Azora gently urged me down into the bottom of the boat, where I stretched my long frame out, and instantly I was asleep myself.

I slept a dreamless sleep throughout the night, and long into the day again. Afternoon stretched out into early evening, and the sun was westering upon the horizon before I woke again. Azora was sitting on the low bench in the middle of the boat, her legs just above my head. As I rose up on one elbow, I saw that the Empress sat at the bow of the boat, knees tucked under her, while my large feet were crammed up next to her in the tight confines.

Hastily pulling my feet away from her, I stuttered my embarrassment.

"I beg your pardon, Empress. I am..."

"It's nothing," she interrupted with a small smile.

"You are too gracious," I said. Then, sitting up, I turned to Azora.

"Anything interesting happen while I was gone?"

"Just riding the waves," she said. "We've simply been drifting all day."

"We have found it soothing to the senses," the Empress said, still with a distant smile upon her lips. "Especially after the crowded events that brought us here."

"Indeed, so," I replied. "I am grateful for the opportunity to rest and to let my cuts heal. And to fill my belly, for I am hungry again."

"There's plenty in the crates," Azora said. "We've nibbled. So eat your fill."

"Thanks, I will," I said. And rooting through the crates, I found food and water and settled down to make my supper.

Azora peppered me with questions as I ate. Now we had had time to recover from our travails of the previous day. She wanted to know everything that had happened to me since the time we were pulled apart by Salamir's men.

I told her of my time on the *Fury*, of Burkov and his crew, the tedious routine of daily rowing at the oars, and finally, of the battle with the Karzi, and my escape from the brigands.

"... and I made my way to Salamir's ship, hoping that you were still upon it," I said, finishing my story, and taking a long swig of water from a drinking bladder. "And by luck, at last I found you."

"And we are together again!" Azora said, triumphantly. She threw her arms around me and nuzzled her face against my chest.

"And you, Azora?" I asked. "What of you? What happened to you while we were parted?"

"Not much," she answered, looking up at me. "When they tore you away from me, Salamir's guards dragged me away. Salamir had said something about the 'Empress', but I did not know what he meant."

I glanced at the Empress. She looked at me coolly from under her half-closed eyelashes, and a distant half-smile upon her face, but she said nothing. I noted that her exceedingly pale flesh was tinted now with a faintly emerald tone, and this was the first time I was conscious of her changing polychrome hues. I was surprised by it, and the hosts of questions clamoring in my head about this strange Empress crowded to the fore, but I raised none of them at the moment. For now, I was hearing Azora's tale, and was confident that all would be made plain to me, if only I listened.

"They dragged me down a long hallway, and I can assure you I did not make it easy for them. I kicked them and spat and bit for all I was worth, and did everything I could to make sure that they earned their keep that day. Finally they had to pick me up and carry me, four of them. Two men, each one holding one of my ankles, and another two men, each holding one of my wrists, and even then I squirmed and fought with them. At last, one of them said to me, 'Have mercy on us, would you, woman? Your complaint is with Salamir, not us. We are just four poor fellows doing a job.'

"Well," Azora said, "That made me laugh, so I settled down a little bit, swearing that I was going to make this Empress pay, whatever or whoever she was. They took me at last to her apartments..."

"The chamber where I finally found you?" I asked.

"Oh, no. A different suite. It was much nicer. But I spoiled that for us, so... well, let me just tell you how it all happened."

"The guards finally brought me to a gilded doorway where there were more guards standing. My guards explained to the standing guards why they brought me there, and one fellow stepped up and gave me a whole slew of orders.

"'You have been given a great honor,' he said to me." (I was amused to see Azora imitate the guard's pompous speech as she told her story. She threw her chest out, gave her shoulders a swagger, and lowered her voice, giving a quite comical rendition.)

"'... and you shall conduct yourself in your very best manner in the presence of the Empress. You shall obey her every command, and render to her every service she may require...' Well, he went on like that for a few minutes, and then he finally knocked on the doorway with his fist. The doorway opened, and a woman looked out.

"'What do you want?' she demanded.

"'Compliments of Salamir,'" said the pompous man who had lectured me and given me that long-winded mouthful of orders I'd already forgotten. 'He brings you a new servant to attend to the Empress.'

"Well, that woman gave the man such a look. She couldn't have shown more contempt for him than if she had spit right in his face, and I snickered to myself. Then the woman looked at me, and she said, after a moment, 'Come in, then.' And I did. She closed the door behind me, and she led me to a small antechamber where she gave me my instructions.

"This time I did pay attention. This woman didn't seem too bad, not like the idiot guards of Salamir. I found out later that she had been captured by the brigands herself, long before, and hated them all.

"'The Empress,' she told me, 'Is presently a 'guest' of the Great Salamir'. Oh, and she said those words, 'guest' and 'great' with such sarcasm that I knew the Empress was not a guest, and Salamir was not, in her opinion, great.

"'A guest?' I asked her. "'Like us?'

"She sneered, and said, 'Yes. Quite. Like us. She is a most honored guest, and we are to attend to her. Salamir is most solicitous on her behalf, and wishes to ensure that, upon payment of the 'trifling surety' he requests, that she returns to her people with no complaint against his hospitality.'

"'What is a 'trifling surety?' I asked.

"'Ransom,' she said. 'Salamir demands a ransom for her safe return to her people. Once that has been paid, he will set her free.'

"Well, that woman explained to me all my responsibilities. I was one of six women who waited on the Empress, including this woman, my instructor. Aside from us, there were four others. My training took several days in all, and I slept in a tiny chamber with the others. We slept, and took our meals in shifts, so that always there were at least four women attending the Empress at any time."

"I see," I remarked to Azora, glancing toward the Empress, who watched us both with her always languorous eyes.

"And on the fourth day, my instructor took me into the Empress's chamber. This wasn't the chamber you found us in. This was much larger, and everything was covered in gold. The lounges and settees were covered with gold fabric, and the ceilings and walls were covered with gold leaf. Even the windows were framed in gold, and the glass had gold veining through it. Goblets and plates and dinnerware were all gold. Everything."

"I guess that must have been hard on the eyes," I remarked.

"At first it was, but I got used to it," Azora answered. "It might have been easier for us to escape Salamir's ship, if the chamber I found you in had windows to it."

"Yes, it might have been," Azora replied. "And if I hadn't been so anxious to get away, that might have been the chamber you would have found us in, at last."

"What do you mean?" I asked.

"Well," Azora started, settling herself in for telling a story. "The other girls who waited on the Empress were pretty dull creatures. They didn't speak much, and when they did, it was, well, not much to speak about. But you know me," she said with a smile.

Indeed, I did know her. Never one to be awed by pomp or personality, Azora made no trouble speaking to anyone, and everyone, exactly in the same way. And that way was always, from the first instant they might have met, as if they were the oldest of friends, or the oldest of enemies, depending upon the terms of that first meeting. Azora had decided to speak to the Empress as if they were old friends.

"The others were shocked at my presumption, of course," Azora explained. "And they tried to shush me. But I ignored them."

"And well it was she did so," the Empress said, entering into the conversation at last. "Her charming familiarity has, in the unfolding of events, redounded great good upon us all, at least to this point."

I half turned to the Empress, and acknowledged her remark with a bow of my head.

"Empress," I said.

"Jamarra[1]," she replied.

"I beg your pardon?"

"Please, given our circumstances, it is absurd to insist upon formal titles. My name is Jamarra. You may address me with that name."

"I am honored."

"And you are Grae-don. Azora has told me of you."

"I pray the man I in fact am is not too bitter a disappointment to you," I said. Jamarra smiled. And Azora gave my shoulder a playful slap.

"See what I mean?" she said to Jamarra, apparently affirming something she had said of me in an earlier conversation.

"Indeed," Jamarra replied, with that amused smile lingering upon her stately lips. "But please, continue with your tale. I am sure Grae-don wishes to know all."

"Yes, I do," I said.

"However beautiful it was in that suite, it was pretty boring, just waiting, then eating a meal, and then waiting some more," Azora said.

---

1. I have used the letter 'J' in the spelling of Jamarra's name as the closest equivalent to the sound my patient, Paul Morgan uttered when speaking it. A poor substitute, as the sound has no analogue to the opening sound of her name in our alphabet. When spoken it is, in fact, somewhere between a soft 'J' and a 'Z'. I gave some thought to attempting to incorporate both letters in my transcriptions of Paul Morgan's narratives, but come settle upon nothing that was not unduly awkward (both Zjamarra, and Jzamarra are both too blunt to render the simple elegance of the delicate name which I have rendered here as 'Jamarra'). A.G.

"We had nothing to do all long day, day after day, except talk. And so we talked. And we got to know each other. In time, we became friends.

"And we decided that we would try to escape, somehow. I knew you'd been taken back to the ship that we were captured on…"

"The *Fury*," I remarked. "Burkov's ship."

"And I knew what it looked like, and I knew that if we could find a boat, I could find a way to it, somehow, and then we could free you, and set sail for…" Azora paused and shrugged her shoulders. "Well, wherever…"

"Oh?" I replied. "All that? A pretty ambitious plan, if you ask me."

"We were going to take it one step at a time. The first thing was to get out of the Empress's apartments and find a boat."

"Even that must have been challenging…"

"Except that it wasn't as challenging as you may have thought. The apartments were expansive and luxurious, and they had wide windows and a balcony outside."

"A balcony?" I asked.

"So the Empress could get some fresh air, when she felt the need."

"I insisted upon it," Jamarra said, simply.

"And we were out on that balcony often, away from the others and hatching our schemes," Azora said.

"And the others simply let you conspire together? They did not suspect anything?" I asked.

"They were in terror of her vast ladyship, the Empress," Azora explained, giving her hand a 'la-dee-dah' toss in the air. "And they were not Salamir's people, anyway. They were all slaves, like us. So they weren't about to do any more than they absolutely had to."

"And the guards…?" I asked.

"Were all outside the doors," Azora said. "Salamir didn't trust them with Jamarra, and they didn't trust each other. So they all stood guard outside the Empress's golden apartments. Only those servants who brought Jamarra's meals, and ours, or who carried messages from Salamir to Jamarra, or vice versa, were allowed through those doors. Otherwise, we were left alone.

"Well, hanging from the stern of Salamir's ship was a lifeboat. It was far above our little balcony, but there was so much ornamental work on the hull of the ship that I was sure it would give me more than the handholds I needed to climb up to the lifeboat.

"So we made our plans. We waited for a particularly dark night. When one finally came I climbed up to the railing at the top of the stern. It was still and cloudy that night, the stars were dim and the light was diffuse, but the climbing was easy. There were no breezes to speak of, and this was before we left the Great Northern Sea, when the waters were still shallow and calm. The ornamental work gave me plenty to hold on to, and I found it easier to climb than the rocks at Taakbar.

"And I came to the top and looked over, and there I saw a man standing watch, but he was looking to the fore of the ship. His back was to me, so I climbed under the lifeboat and over the railing without making a sound.

"Then I looked at the davit for lowering the lifeboat. I could see at a glance that it would make noise. So I looked around for something to lay the guard out with. I found a stack of deadeyes lying on the deck, waiting to be rigged, I guess. Well, I picked one up, and it was a pretty heavy fellow. It would do the job, I saw. So, slinking up quietly behind the guard, who really shouldn't have been so careless in his duties, I swung the deadeye hard, and banged him good on the back of the head. Even though he was wearing a helmet, he dropped to the deck without a sound.

Azora's eyes gleamed with a bright flame as she told the story.

"I'm glad you enjoyed yourself," I quipped.

"It would have been more fun if you'd been with me," she answered.

"Next time," I replied.

"Well, with the guard out," Azora continued, "I checked the lifeboat and saw that it had oars, and water bottles stowed in it, and everything else we might need. I began lowering the lifeboat, as Jamarra and I had planned. And it all went perfectly well, too. When the boat was level with the balcony where she was waiting, Jamarra climbed into it, and I lowered it the rest of the way into the water.

"And then I climbed down as far as the ornamentation let me. When I got to the bare planking of the hull, I simply let myself drop and landed with a splash into the sea, next to the lifeboat with Jamarra waiting.

"After that, we thought, it was just a simply matter of rowing away, as silently as we could, and finding you. But, of course, things are always easy, until you actually have to do them. Then they get as hard as can be."

I laughed at that. "Yes," I remarked to Azora and Jamarra. "I heard it put once, the definition of `easy'. It's anything I don't have to do."

Azora and Jamarra both laughed at that, and Azora went on with her story.

"Well, the first thing we found out was that the oars were a lot heavier and a lot harder to handle than we realized before. Jamarra had never worked an oar, and though I'd paddled a few small canoes in the lakes at Taakbar, it was nothing at all like rowing with these heavy oars. They're taller than we are, and it took both of us just to pull one of them through the water.

"So it wasn't going to be as simple as we had imagined. We wasted a long time just trying to understand how to work the oars, and getting nothing done except rowing in circles. We couldn't understand how to get the boat to go in a straight line.

"And, maybe I didn't hit the sentry hard enough, or maybe I hit him in the wrong spot, but whatever happened, he came to much sooner than I had expected. Just as Jamarra and I figured out how to keep the boat moving straight through the water, we heard the warning trumpet calling loud from the stern of Salamir's ship. And then that was answered by the horns on the other ships of the fleet. Soon, all the ships were crowded with their crews climbing the rigging, looking out for the escaped prisoners.

"That threw all our plans in a heap. At first, we didn't know what to do, since we were still not far from Salamir's ship, and still surrounded on all sides by the ships that sail with him.

"But the sky was dim that night, and the water was dark. And if we were cunning, we hoped, we might yet slip away. So with great trouble, we managed to row ourselves close to the hull of a very tall ship, hiding ourselves in the shadows it cast at the stern, just by the heavy rudder.

"From our hiding place, we could see all the frantic activity of the ships surrounding us. Lamps were lit, and we saw the silhouettes of the lookouts high in the rigging.

"Soon we saw dozens of boats lowered into the sea. Before long, the sea was crowded with these boats, all searching near and far, probing the night with their torches.

"We waited there in the shadow of that tall ship for a very long time, not daring to move from the darkness that sheltered us, all the while dreading the coming of the day. All that night, the search boats came and went, with the crewmen all calling out to each other. Sometimes they passed us by so closely that we could almost have stretched our hands out and touched them. But so impenetrable was the shadow under that ship, so close to the rudder, so murky was the night, and so still did we keep ourselves, that they all passed by us without noticing us.

"But, at last, after what seemed like forever, we finally saw the hesitant purpling of the sky come creeping all along the far horizon, which meant that the sun would soon be rising.

"I whispered to Jamarra, 'We cannot stay here. They will find us.' And she nodded to signal to me that she understood.

"So, taking up the oar again, we strove to row away into the dwindling darkness of the night. We were within eyesight of a shore, a line of bluffs breaking the horizon. I thought, vainly, that if we could make it to that coast, we might find a place to secrete ourselves until Salamir gave up the search for us, and we could find a way to seek you out.

"But that shore was far, and the boats still searching us were numerous. But we put a bold face on it, and our backs into it, and rowed out into the sea as if we had every business to be there, thinking, of course, that if we strove to be sly and stealthy, we would only draw the attention of so many eyes. But, if we acted as if we were not hiding at all, then we just might pass unnoticed.

"Our ruse worked, for a long while. We kept our distance from the searching boats, and, as well as we could, we rowed directly toward that beckoning shore. Oh! It came tantalizingly close. Now we were coming up on the breakers, and if we could just get past those, we might yet make it to the rocky shore beyond them. We couldn't see them clearly from where we were, but even with our imperfect view, the waves were daunting things. They rose huge and high and then crashed down on the rugged, rocky shore with a constant, monstrous roaring that grew louder as we drew near.

"But the sun rose swiftly, and the purple sky turned to peach, and soon we were exposed, not as two shadows upon a shadowy sea, but two women on a boat, who were awkward at the oars.

"And suddenly the pursuit was upon us. We heard the horns calling across the water, alerting all those searching for us that we had been discovered. From all directions they came, in boats light and swift, much lighter, and swifter, than our bulky lifeboat.

"We just managed to ride up on one of the swells that rose and began its long journey to the shoreline ahead, and carrying us with it, when two swift boats came alongside us, one on either side. In each boat were three men, two at the oars, and one with a torch to light the sea. They were shouting at us, and we could hear them just above the roaring of the waves. The men with the torches put them out and then unsheathed long swords, menacing us with them.

"'Come with us, ladies!' they said, sneering. 'We gotcha now.'"

Azora's eyes snapped as she mocked their tone. She contemptuously imitated the ugly sneers they wore by wrinkling her lip and thrusting her chin forward. The effect on her lovely face was most comical. I could not help but smile.

"Well," Azora continued, "I didn't like their tone, so I stood up, just as the water carried us high, and I took our oar in both hands and swung it straight at the fellow's head on our starboard side. He ducked the oar, but the one seated in front of him, who was working on the oars in their boat, wasn't so lucky. I clipped him right in the back of the head and laid him straight out.

"That made the others mad as anything at me. Two of them tried to climb on to our lifeboat, one from each of the boats on either side of us. But by now, the wave we were riding had grown huge and was just beginning to crest. The nose of our boat tipped down, just as the two men tried to step onto it. They lost their footing, and disappeared right into the water. If they ever got out again, I don't know, because I never saw them after that.

"So now there were just three of them, two in the boat on our port side, and two on the starboard side, minus the one who got my oar to the back of his head. He was still quite unconscious.

"And then the wave broke. The water simply collapsed out from under us. All three boats dropped, nose down, and we all came falling out, right into the huge wave.

"For a long minute there, I didn't know what was happening, or where I was, or even which way was up. And the roaring in my ears! Even under water, the waves were loud. The wave tossed and rolled us all around like we were wee tiny little bobbins.

"Finally, I came sputtering out of the water, on to the rocks, but not without plenty of scrapes and cuts. I looked around, and there was Jamarra, wading hip deep in the surf, with another huge wave bounding up behind her. I called to warn her, but my voice was too weak, and the surf was too loud. She didn't hear me, and the wave knocked her down and dragged her into the rocks, just as I had been done.

"We watched for a moment to see if the brigands in the boats were going to come scrambling out of the waves, but then thought better of that. No point in waiting for them, as we'd come this far. If we could get up among the rocks, we might find a good place to hide from them.

"So we made off, as well as well could. Those waves had knocked the wind out of us, and the boulders were pretty hard climbing, too. We scraped our knuckles and our knees, but managed at last to find our way past the rocks to the base of the bluffs when the brigands chasing us finally climbed ashore.

"There were just three of them now. The fourth one must have drowned for we saw his body floating face down in the surf. Jamarra and I ducked behind a boulder when we saw the three survivors crawling up from the froth, and we managed to elude them. Watching them carefully, we crawled away as fast as we could, rounding the cliffs until at last we left behind, still gasping for breath as the waves rolled in around them.

"But if we thought we'd escaped, that hope was quickly dashed. The shoreline we had found turned out to be but a group of islands. And, the one we landed on was, as we found, a very small one. The black, volcanic bluffs that lined the shore were sheer and steep, and impossible to climb. Though we searched, there was not a single handhold, foothold or even a toehold to be found.

"By early that afternoon we had crawled almost all the way around the tiny island, and except for the boulders that were strewn all along the shoreline, there was no place to which we could retreat or find a hideaway.

"And all around the island, on every side, we saw the ships of Salamir's fleet surrounding us. While we searched for shelter among the boulders, the three brigands who had survived landfall managed to signal the others at sea. They sent many more who swarmed the island. All that day they searched for us, and then, just as night was falling, they caught up with Jamarra and me where we had secreted ourselves within a tight and narrow crevasse in the rock.

"And that was the end or our adventure. They bound me, since I was but a slave, but Salamir had given the strictest orders that Jamarra was not to be molested in any way. I think the brigands who captured us were a little afraid of Jamarra. At least, they certainly seemed to hold her in great awe, for they were painfully polite to her.

"But I suppose their solicitude for her may have been based on the fact that Salamir had been very explicit in his orders that she was not to be harmed in any way, and when he is displeased, Salamir can be very unpleasant."

"As I saw myself," I replied, "Both times I set foot on his ship, I observed the prisoners he had hanging from the masts in cages. Even during the battle with the Karzi, when his prisoners could have been put to much better use, he had a dozen starved men hanging in those cages only but big enough to keep them cramped and tortured. Nor do I include the corpses he had hanging from the masts, half rotted and moldering."

"Those were largely for his amusement, I believe," Jamarra said. "Though one cannot overlook the very salubrious effect such lessons may have upon the more poorly mannered among his crew."

"Yes," Azora added, with a laugh. "I'm sure the thought of hanging in one of Salamir's cages was not far from the minds of the very rude fellows who finally captured us. Well, they took us back to Salamir's ship, and straightaway to the gross man's own presence. He was most unhappy with us. Most unhappy."

Azora paused and a grimace crossed her face as she remembered the moment.

"The evening was already late, and the sun had left the sky. All was dark, except for the stars and the yellow lamps of the ships before us. The shadows of the hanging men, both living and dead, were stretched out against the still canvas of the sails, and the shadows danced in the light of the flickering lamps. Once we were carried back to Salamir's ship by the crewmen who captured us they turned us over to Salamir's guard.

"Six of them in those silly golden helmets they wear ushered us back to Salamir himself. He was no different than you remember him, Grae-don. Greasy and fat and oily and smug, with painted eyes and fingernails and a bloated belly that rolled upon his knees. He covered himself with scent, and his chambers were thick with it. I almost gagged upon it as his guard pushed us through the portal to his presence. His chambers were decorated as before, with a dozen naked women lounging about on piles of purple satin pillows, and lavender, and pink. They all seemed but half-awake, and the ones who even troubled to notice us looked at us with lazy, half-closed eyes.

"Salamir looked poison and darts at Jamarra, and ignored me at first. He just stared at her for a long time, and all was silent, except for the whispered mewing of his sleepy feminine creatures. Finally, he said, 'I am crushed that you have spurned my hospitality. Had you slapped me in my face, I'd have felt the insult no less keenly.'

"Then Salamir looked at me, and pointed a lazy, careless finger.

"'Remove that creature's head and bring it here to me. We'll have no more of her nasty, nasty inducements upon our guest,' he said.

"The guards on either side of me forced me down to my knees. One of them grabbed my arms and pushed, while the other placed his hand on the back of my head, pushing it forward so I was looking at the floor. From the corner of my eye, I saw a monster of a man lurch out of the shadows brandishing a large flat sword and an evil grin.

"'Not a bit of it!' Jamarra said, her voice rising.

And she stepped between me and the monstrous man with the sword. Still watching from the corner of my eye, I saw her place her hand on the handle of the sword and draw the blade of it up to her own throat.

"'You'll have my head first, Salamir, or none at all this day. Is this what you have come to? Murdering women? Women who are bound and helpless before you? Has all honor at last fled your shallow soul?'

"Oh! The hush that came over that chamber!" Azora said.

"Even the naked, half-sleeping women awoke, and they were horrified to hear anyone speak so insolently to the great Salamir. The guard behind me released his grip upon my head, so shocked was he at the Empress's audacity. I looked up. Everyone in that yellow chamber, thick with incense and perfume, looked at Salamir to see what he would do. Perhaps, I suppose, nothing but a wholesale slaughter of all his prisoners, and perhaps even some of his own crew, would be sufficient to sate his rage.

"Salamir was silent, and one could not read the expression on his heavy-lidded face. He regarded the Empress Jamarra through his lowered, purple-painted eyelids for a long and tortured moment, without making even the slightest hair's-breadth of a motion. The man could have been carved from rock, so still was he.

"And then, we heard a low scarcely hearable laughter filling the chamber. 'Hu-u-u-uh, hu-u-u-uh, hu-u-u-uh,' and then slightly louder, a 'Haa... haa... haa...'. Salamir's face broke into a broad and toothy smile, as scary a thing as I've ever seen. And then he laughed louder, 'HA! HA! HA!' and louder yet, and then he threw his face back, with his mouth wide and distended and open to the ceiling, 'HAW! HAW! HAW!'

"Oh, how he laughed. He laughed and laughed, and then all the guards and all the naked women, and even the monstrous man with the sword—they all began to laugh with Salamir, and the chamber was shaking with their raucous laughter.

"Many long minutes passed like this, it seemed, with everyone in the room, except Jamarra and me, laughing with Salamir. Tears were rolling down his bloated cheeks, and his jewelry shook and jangled upon his rolling waves of flesh.

"At last, Salamir managed to reclaim his composure and, wiping the tears from his cheeks with puffy fingers heavy with rings of gold and jewels, he spoke.

"'Ah... Empress... you do amuse... you do amuse...' he said. 'How can I deny you? I thought only to unburden you of the ceaseless insinuations of this creature who so clearly cajoled you into this treachery, the insult you have dealt me by spurning my hospitality... it was merely my wish save you the temptation... well..."And then he laughed some more, and spoke with a tone of supreme condescension, as if Jamarra were a misbehaving child, and he was patting her upon the head.

"'The Empress will not be denied,' he said. 'She has her new companion, and this companion amuses her, as she has herself afforded me much amusement herself.

"'Oh, Empress, again, I ask, how can I deny you? You may keep your companion.'

"And then, speaking over her head, to the guards who brought us there, 'Take her to the Reserved Chambers. And bring her friend with her.'

"And that was that. The guards picked me up by my elbows and ushered me out of Salamir's presence, along with Jamarra.

"This time they brought us deep into the bowels of the ship, through narrow passageways and dark and dangerous stairs, to the chambers where you finally found us. These had no windows. We didn't know where on the ship we were, whether in the stern of the bow or amidships. All we knew was that we were deep inside the hull of the ship, and there was no escape for us now.

"After a time, the guards brought in the serving girls to attend Jamarra, and that was when I took the opportunity to steal the decorative knife one of them carried, hanging from his belt."

Azora held up the curious knife with its semicircular blade and the finger holes on the opposite side. She gave me a wide smile, and cocked her eyebrows at me. She was very pleased with herself.

"Very nice," I said.

"The guard was so stupid. He was so busy watching the serving girls he didn't even notice me standing right next to him. I slipped the knife right off his belt and straight into my harness. He didn't even notice it was missing."

"It's a beautiful knife," I remarked.

"And it's mine now!" Azora replied with a happy laugh. She slashed it through the air left and right and left again in a little show.

"I practiced with it a lot while we were scheming to find some other way to escape. But it wasn't until you came along that I finally had a chance to really try it out."

"I saw," I said. "It is very effective. Keep it sharp."

"Oh, I will," Azora said with a happy grin.

Now, having shared our tales, Azora and I, and Jamarra, too, were minded to attend to our immediate comfort. The tiny boat we rode in was already cramped, but we saw that the wreckage of the ships that were destroyed by the vast *wahe-el* floating so near to us provided us with opportunities of which we were not slow to take advantage.

With some ingenuity, and effort, and over the course of the next several days, Azora and I were able to use some of the multitudes of broken boards and planks from the wreckage to add further to our boat. Tying the planks to our tiny boat, and the caskets that floated by us, too, we were able to extend our tiny reach. Bit by bit we added to our assemblage until we had put together a rather crude and ramshackle raft.

It wasn't much to look at, and it rolled up and down with the waves, so it did not provide us anything like a sturdy foothold. Nor were we ever able to build high enough above the surface to escape the ceaselessly rolling waves, so, of course, we were constantly wet. But the raft did give us some space to move about it, and that was a comfort to our cramped bodies.

We hauled several casks filled with drinkable water on board our raft, as well as an odd crate of foodstuffs or two. And with portions of the torn and sodden sails that were still attached to the drifting ruins of yardarms, we were able to fashion a serviceable tent to keep off the sun's rays, and to protect our nearly naked bodies from the constant battering of the winds. That was a huge relief to us, and we came to spend a great deal of time huddling in the tent against the winds.

We could do nothing but drift with the currents and the winds, however. Having no idea where upon this mysterious sea we might be, all directions were the same to us. Though I had learned to navigate by the stars with Burkov's crew aboard the *Fury*, that knowledge was of little use.

We came from the north, and here, in this sea, of which we knew nothing, we were drifting toward the east. That much I knew. But how far from the north, and how far to the east we had drifted, I had no idea.

Returning to Pella'mir... indeed, even finding the Great Northern Sea itself, was a task far beyond us. All we could do at this moment was but to survive this turgid southern sea until, somewhere, we made landfall at last.

All our hopes, all our ambitions, everything we ever dreamed of and aspired to, it all came down to that one thin hope, at last—that somehow we should survive, day by torturous day, upon that ceaselessly roiling sea, until, finally, one day, we might find a footfall, a tiny foothold of any sort, upon this boundless, measureless world of constantly churning water.

And it was for that hopeless hope that we ceaselessly scanned the horizon, day after endless day.

16

JAMARRA'S TALE

WITH SOME INGENUITY, AND over the course of the next several days, Azora and I were able to use some of the multitudes of broken boards and planks from the wreckage of the brigands' ships that still floated with us to add further to our tiny boat. Bit by bit we added to our assemblage until we had put together a rather crude and ramshackle raft.

It wasn't much to look at, and it rolled up and down with the waves, so it did not provide us anything like a sturdy foothold. But it did give us some space to move about in, and that was a comfort to our cramped bodies, cooped up as we had been, upon that tiny Karzi boat.

We also managed to haul on board several casks filled with drinkable water, as well as several crates loaded with dried *fuma*, a good quantity of *stala*, *ga'la*, and *h'rafa*. We were also most delighted to find several casks of *ellihi*[1], which, aside from its other well-known inducements

---

1. Varieties of foodstuffs: Fuma, a type of fruit; Stala, a food composed of grain, somewhat similar to bread; Ga'la, a substance similar to honey; H'rafa, a food similar, perhaps to cheese. Ellihi is a fermented fruit drink, mixed with ga'la which is notoriously intoxicating. A.G.

to hilarity and conviviality, is also a most efficacious medicine, when applied to superficial wounds.

I spent the good part of many days applying a tincture Azora concocted from the *ellihi* and several other ingredients we found to my many cuts and scrapes. But we were careful in drinking of it, for the brigands of Boramok prefer their drink very strong, as, indeed, this batch we recovered from the sea proved to be.

Though she maintained a general air of aloofness, Jamarra was not unfriendly to Azora and me. And, as far as she was able, she tried to be helpful to us in putting our piecemeal raft together. But it was quickly obvious to us that the woman had no experience in labor of any sort, and we soon decided it was best if she simply stayed out of our way while Azora and I worked to bind the broken planks together into our growing raft. We set Jamarra instead to the task of gathering up the flotsam that drifted near, which might be usable to us, and dragging it aboard, a task that she took up with great spirit.

But, though not unfriendly, and in her own way helpful, yet she conducted herself always with a reserve and an aloofness of a kind and a degree that I had never seen in any other individual. When Azora and I conversed, Jamarra attended to the conversation, but rarely took part in it. Instead, she gazed at Azora and me through lowered eyelashes, as if watching us from some vast distance. Indeed, it seemed often to me that the gulf between us was unbridgeable, that, though we spoke a similar language, we came from different worlds.

We continued working on our growing raft from sunrise to sunset, and at last, after many days of labor, we had built it to a size to ensure our immediate safety, as well as providing us some comfort.

Additionally, we had provisioned ourselves with the many casks filled with supplies from the ruined ships that drifted near us.

So we were doing well, or at least as well as any three souls lost upon an uncharted sea could do.

And so we drifted for many days, slowly adding to our raft each day, and keeping watch day and night for any evidence of landfall. None did come, for many long days.

One day as we finally found time to spare a few moments of leisure from our endless labors on the raft, I asked, "How was it, Azora, that your friend, Jamarra, got herself into her predicament with Salamir?"

"That is a tale," Azora said. "Perhaps Jamarra should tell it to you herself."

Azora glanced in Jamarra's direction.

The woman was sitting inside the shade of our trifling tent, her eyes closed in some strange meditation. Hearing her name, her eyes fluttered open. I saw that at the moment they happened to be a very pale green while the skin of her body was a placid emerald. She said nothing for a time, but only looked at Azora, and then me, and then back to Azora again.

"It is a tale of sore provocation," she said at last. "A rudeness imposed upon our person... that this Empress should be bandied about, bargained over like some bit of merchandise in a marketplace..."

She fell silent, and I saw that the faded emerald of her tone deepened to a darker viridian.

"Empress?" I asked, perhaps impatiently. I had been hearing this word 'Empress' for some time now, but had no idea what it meant, and at last it occurred to me to demand to know what this strange title, always uttered with such strange reverence, meant.

"What exactly is this 'Empress'? I've been hearing 'Empress, Empress, Empress', but no one yet has told me what it means."

"She is the Empress," Azora simply said, indicating the woman with a gesture of her open hand.

"Yes, so I have been made to understand. But what is an Empress?"

"She is... um, she..." Azora fell silent, unable to explain.

"She is the Queen of queens," Jamarra explained, with supreme self-assurance. "She is the ruler of empires, of kings and all peoples within those kingdoms."

"Queens? Empires? Kings? What are all these things?" I demanded. A smile flowered upon her pale face, now a deepening lavender. With great indulgence, she answered me.

"These are they who rule over the people. As parents are to a child, so the rulers are to those they rule. And the Empress is to the rulers what the rulers are to the people."

I looked helplessly to Azora, but she shrugged her shoulders in silent reply. I heard the words this Empress spoke, but they conveyed no meaning to me. We had no such things, these `rulers', in Pella'mir.

"'As parents are to a child'?" I asked, barely able to frame the question.

"It is we who set the laws by which the people live," the Empress explained.

And, dimly, the light of comprehension began slowly to find its way into my mind.

"Somewhat like the great houses of Pella'mir?" I hazarded.

The Empress silently cocked a querying eyebrow, waiting for me to make my meaning clear.

"We have the great houses in Pella'mir. The house of Jor-Taq was one," I explained.

"It was there, in the house of Jor-Taq that I received my own education—how to read, to write, the use of the sword, a knife, and my fist. There were other houses. The house of Dak-Mar, the house of Ran-Tok, and others. These were wealthy men who surrounded themselves with armed servants to protect their property. I was one of those servants. Some of us were slaves. Some were free people. I was a slave first, and then I was a free man.

"These wealthy men, and women, too, they paid some of us to protect them, and some to look after their properties, and others to teach and train their children. And all these people joined the service of the wealthy, not only for the pay, but also for the security we found in lodging with their houses. These wealthy men used some among us to keep the neighborhoods in which they lived free of crime and the criminals who create crime.

"And so those neighbors benefited from their near association with the great houses, and they aligned their interests with those of the great houses.

"Is this what you mean, then, when you tell me you are Empress, that you are the sovereign of a great house?" I asked.

The Empress allowed her indulgent smile to broaden. Brilliant teeth shone in the deep ocher shades of the tent.

"Yes, in a manner of speaking," she answered. "All those houses and all those who preside over them, and all who are in the service of those great houses, and all peoples... these are my subjects. As upon your island of Pella'mir, of which Azora has told me much, so also with our Empire. For the sake of their mutual protection, houses banded together to create cities. Cities joined together to create nations, and nations, at last, seek unification, and become an Empire.

"I, Jamarra, am ruler of that Empire, and that Empire rules over all the world."

The expression on my face must have revealed the growing skepticism I felt. Annoyance grew in my heart as I listened to her speak, and it must have shown. Even among the brigands of Boramok, I called no one my master. And this strange, haughty woman claimed me as her subject?

I glanced out at the open sea surrounding us, and back to Jamarra. Her serene composure was untroubled.

"For one who rules an entire world…" I started.

Azora glared at me.

"Grae-don…" she warned.

But I ignored her.

"… your sphere of influence seems very tightly circumscribed." I waved my hand in an arc to indicate the extent of our raft. "…nor do I ever recall having sworn an oath of allegiance to this empire of yours."

Jamarra merely smiled at me. Her amusement at my remarks seemed entirely sincere, for there was nothing forced about her smile, nothing tight-lipped about her. Indeed, her lips parted slightly, showing a glimpse of her teeth, as they rose at either end with open amusement.

"And I don't believe, either, that I am your child, Empress. In fact, though I am no judge of such matters, your appearance seems to me quite youthful. You appear not much more than a maid yourself to my jaded eyes, and if anything, I could be your elder brother."

Despite my mounting impertinence, Jamarra's eyes sparked with mirth. Her pupils shone with sparkling ultramarine.

"… and, it seems to me that Salamir, though he feigned a mocking deference to you, was most unimpressed with your, uh… empress-ness…"

Now Jamarra laughed brightly. She threw her chin up and inclined her body backward, leaning on her elbows. Her breasts, now a delicate lilac, danced freely and her tight stomach rippled with hilarity.

"Oh, please, call me Jamarra," she said, through her laughter. "That is sufficient for us, for now."

Her laughter was light and unaffected, and Azora, who knew the woman much better than I, joined her laughter with an easy familiarity. The two of them enjoyed their moment of merriment, and their happy mirth deflated my growing annoyance. I looked from one to the other with a half-smile, waiting for either to continue.

"But we shall have to enjoin you to again give proper regard to the courtesies required of the station of Empress, when once we find our way back among our kindred creatures. We must, of course, maintain proper decorum. The happiness of the people demands that we all understand our proper places, beggars and empresses alike."

"Of course," I replied, dubiously.

"It is true, as you suggest," Jamarra continued, with a smile that looked down upon me as if from a thousand *yurlma* above, "That our authority rests entirely upon the sufferance of those over whom we rule, though many knew it not. But all governance ultimately depends, does it not, solely upon the acquiescence of the governed?"

"Except that it is forced," I remarked, though with not much interest. Philosophy tired me.

"One always has choices," Jamarra replied, quite offhandedly. "If even the choices are no more than those between death and slavery, yet still one always has a choice. Always, there will be those who choose death over slavery. And others will choose life, even as a slave, over death. And every king, every queen, and every empress is outnumbered, every moment of every day, by those who command those choices, on the order of many millions to one."

"As you say," I replied with a shrug, not having the spirit to argue the point. "But how is it, if I might impose with a possibly impudent question, that a woman of such magnitude has found herself in these straits, that her empire has dwindled to so little—a poor raft and two orphans, all adrift upon an unmapped sea?"

"Ah, yes," Jamarra replied with a wan and pallid smile. A tint of blue came upon her lips as they curled slightly with a touch of sadness about them.

"I did not seek to become Empress," Jamarra said. "It was not my ambition. I had no ambition, had no experience of the cravings that motivate such things. The title of Empress was thrust first upon me, before I was even aware. Then it was stripped from me, before I knew it."

Turning abruptly to Azora and me, with a sudden familiarity that was altogether new and astonishing to me, though not, it seemed, to Azora, Jamarra said, "If ever I had parents as the common people do, I did not know them. From my earliest memories, I was revered by strangers, attendants who waited upon me, teachers who taught me, and advisors who trained me to my station.

"But they were all strangers to me. All of them spoke to me with unceasing deference. Aged men, and ancient women, all bowed before me when I was but a child. They prostrated themselves upon the marble floors when they entered my presence. They awaited my pleasure before speaking, asked my permission first before they gave utterance to any other sound.

"Ministers, chamberlains and nobles all attended to me, all served me, even those who taught me. My teachers first sought out my permission, before they administered my daily lessons. Through them I learned my letters, and of politics, of logic, of diplomacy, mediation, justice, the law and jurisprudence—everything required to maintain the peace, stability and tranquility of the Empire.

"But of all who attended to me, who taught me, who advised me, none of them were my friends. I knew nothing of friendship, of amity, of familiarity, or comity between family, or between comrades.

"Nor did I crave it. I felt no curiosity in my heart, no need for the companionship of others, for the mere sake of companionship. For never was I alone. Always attendants waited on me. They prepared my meals, they bathed me, they cut my hair, trimmed and polished and painted my nails. When I slept, I was guarded. When I woke, it was at the appeal of my chamberlains. Never once did I have solitude, nor did I know that such a thing was possible, and, as consequence, never did I feel the need or the craving for companionship of any kind.

"It was only Azora here, my dear Azora, and yours, too, from whom I learnt the ways and meaning of friendship. Your Azora, Grae-don, is, indeed, the first person of all my acquaintance, of whom I have made a friend. She is my friend, oh, Grae-don, my first friend, in all this world. And I count myself happy that I had the opportunity to learn the way of friendship, through your beloved Azora. As she is my friend, oh, Grae-don, my sister, so then, you are my friend, and, as you have said, my brother."

I was most astonished to hear this almost fulsome speech from Jamarra, and could do no more than to give my head a slight bow in acknowledgement.

"I hope, Jamarra," I said, "That I shall never dishonor the friendship you have vouchsafed me."

"As well do I so hope," she replied.

"But I continue my story," she said, "That you may know of whom it is you have granted your friendship.

"I was," she went on, "And for the most part, a kind of a figurehead, a focal point as it were, for the good citizens of D'ar to direct their attention upon those grand occasions of state they loved so well."

"D'ar?" I asked. Jamarra gave her head a regal nod.

"D'ar," she repeated. "The Golden City of D'ar. The City of Jewels. The Precious City. The city of D'ar is the hub of the Empire, the seat of all government. All that is the Empire flows from D'ar itself, and all that is D'ar flows from me."

"I see," I said.

Jamarra smiled and continued.

"My stewards, my councilors, my teachers—they who appointed me Empress when I was only but an infant—were themselves the stewards of the empire. They selected me from... I do not know where. On the one occasion that I asked them of my origins, they told me only that I had appeared among them as an infant, without a name, a family or a home, wandering as if lost, in the streets of D'ar.

"With no family, no name, no human ties of any kind, nothing about me should raise any conflict with my first duty to the empire. My presence among them, they told me, was in fulfillment of some divination among them. Or so they told me.

"I have always felt myself a stranger among those people, never did I entertain any amity with them. Yet, curiously, they claimed great reverence for me, and it was through these strange phantasms who came and went through the course of my day, these `people', as they called themselves, that the creature needs of this body I inhabit were met.

"Through them, I ate when I hungered. Through them, I found warmth in the clothing they provided, when I was cold. A place to sleep, when my mind grew weary. So I made no trouble, but to humor them. If it pleased them to call me this `Empress', and to attend to my whims, I should happily grace their lessons with my attention, and to make the pronouncements they sought from me.

"And so I grew through the years.

"I had been taught from those earliest days to rule, and I learned early on the necessity to delegate the multitudes of tasks that demanded my attention. Impossible is it for any one person to attend to all the countless details of ruling over a people.

"And among those, my stewards, my councilors, and my teachers, they appointed themselves members and masters of what they pleased to call, the `Privy Council'. This `Privy Council' numbered some one hundred members, each one specializing in different matters of governance.

"Those matters arising from the people, seeking the attendance of the Empress, were first challenged through this Privy Council. Should the members of the Privy Council determine that the matter was of sufficient weight to trouble the serenity of the Empress, they did bring the matter to her for her judgment. Were that not the case, they attended to the matter of themselves.

"So it was for many years.

"I matured into my duties as I grew older, and with the advice and guidance of the Privy Council, I sought to rule with an even hand. The City of D'ar and the Empire knew peace and stability. Such peace as you experienced in Pella'mir was due, in no small part, to the efforts, and the sufferance, of your Empress."

I pursed my lips at that remark, and was about to make a comment to the effect that `The Empress pleases herself to take credit for the work of my sword.' But Azora, seeing the expression on my face, and anticipating the thrust of my remark, punched my upper arm.

"Ssst!" she said. "Let Jamarra speak!"

Jamarra gave Azora a long and languid look, and then turned her azure eyes to me for but a moment. I sensed, somehow, that she understood the comment Azora stopped me from making, and allowed herself to be amused by it. When at last she began speaking again, it was as if the rude interruption I did not make had never happened.

"As will of course happen," she said, "Among such diverse individuals of varying motives, there arose among the members of this Privy Council differing factions of differing loyalties. Some were loyal to the Empress. Some, to the Empire itself. Some, to the city of D'ar alone. And there were some among them who were loyal only to themselves.

"Perhaps, had I learned the ways of friendship, heart and family, and such other matters, I should not have been so unaware of the intrigues unspooling about me. But, though I was empress, I was yet young, and a naïf. My power was absolute, but my understanding…"

Jamarra opened her hands, and spread them, palms outward, in a gesture of futility.

"Absolute and unquestioned power came to me, freely as the air we breathe. I craved it not, nor did I comprehend the cravings, or the envy, of those who did long so for it."

Jamarra half-closed her eyes, with that distant smile playing lightly upon her lips. Her mind traveled far away, and for some moments she allowed her attention to wander the long corridors of remote memory. Azora and I remained silent, waiting for her to begin speaking again.

Around us, the swells of the sea had settled, somewhat, from the days before. A gentle rolling of the waves carried us rhythmically along with the current. A soft breeze touched us lightly, and we were swathed in a boundless silence. The day was warm upon the rusted sea, under a sky of peach and salmon, and the depths were cool and transparent beneath us.

"The first I knew it," Jamarra finally began again, "That any plot against me was planned was of a darkened morning, when three men wearing black hoods upon their heads roused me from my sleep. I only glimpsed the bodies of my handmaid and servant maids upon my marbled floor—six of them dead, the blood from their young bodies pooling on the polished stones.

"One of the men spoke to me, 'With us, if you please, my Empress'.

"'I do not know your voice. Who are you?' I demanded of the stranger. But he made no sound and gave no reply, except to signal to the two hooded men who accompanied him. They stepped up to my bed, each of a side, and threw the coverlets from it, making clear their intention that I should rise.

"I did so, and the one who had spoken made a gesture with his hand toward my closet. I understood him to mean that I should dress myself, which I did.

"This was the first time ever I had dressed myself. On every other occasion, that duty fell to my handmaid whose bloodied body laid upon the floor with my servant maids. But I had attended to their work over the years they had dressed me, and, save for a clumsiness in getting my fingers to work the buttons and loops, I managed at last to put my clothing on.

"With further silent gestures, the hooded man who apparently commanded this little expedition of theirs, indicated to me that I should further pack a trunk, which they had brought with them for that purpose.

"'What do you mean?' I asked.

"'Prepare for a long voyage, my Empress,' was all he said.

"I had been on many journeys of state, and knew from those experiences what articles I ought to bring on this, 'a long voyage', but wished yet that my handmaid were not dead, that she may supervise the task. That was a matter falling under her expertise, and not the expertise of the Empress. Yet, like the task of dressing myself, to which I had been hitherto unaccustomed, so did I manage to put together the articles I thought needful for this long voyage—clothing, diadems, scents, toiletries and the like—and filled the trunk with them.

"The trunk filled, the two silent, hooded men lifted it, and carried it from my chambers. He who had spoken twice to me then unfolded a silken slipcase which he then swathed swiftly about my head. The slipcase must have been steeped in some soporific medium, for with it about my head, I fell instantly into oblivion. And what happened after that, how they spirited me from the palace, and brought me to where they did, I did not know. Indeed, it was not until much time later that I again awoke.

"Why they did not simply extinguish my life, if my living was an inconvenience to them, I do not know. Why they should abduct me, indeed, even who these people were, and why they should lay such insult, not only upon the person of the Empress, but also upon the body of the Empire itself... all these things, I do not know. And a most strange thing it is.

"The person of the empress is a sacred thing to the people of D'ar, and she is worshipped by many millions of people in that city and elsewhere. And any insult upon the person of the empress would bring down the great and irrevocable revenge of the people upon he who committed such insult.

"Or, at least that is what my councilors taught me, and the cheering of the multitudes, when I appeared before them in the public concourse on those many occasions of state, gave me no reason to doubt them."

Jamarra paused, and sank her head in thought. Her complexion, I noted with wonder, deepened from a pale emerald to a darkening lavender bordering on purple. Her eyes, a liquid blue, grew murky and grey.

"But, however that may have been," she said, after several moments of silence, "I was, to be sure, not the first Empress, nor the only Empress. There had been others before me, as I learned from my instructors. They had lived, and died, in long succession. My death, too, could have been but one among others if, as I say, my living were an inconvenience to my abductors.

"When I awoke, at the last, I found myself a prisoner in the cabin of a ship upon a golden sea, under an amber sky. That much time had passed was evidenced to me by the extreme cravings of the body. I thirsted, and I hungered, as if I had not eaten in many days.

"My abductors constantly wore their hoods in my presence, and uttered scarcely a word. They brought me food, and it was only then that they entered the cabin in which they imprisoned me. Never once did they tell me why they had abducted me, or for what purpose. The cabin permitted me a view of the sea through a tiny port, a cushion upon which to sleep, and the trunk I had filled upon my departure from the city D'ar, which provided me changes of clothing each day.

"But that was all. Day after weary day they kept me in that cabin. Clearly, my abductors had some destination in mind, for we sailed with purpose. I saw the setting of the sun each evening that we moved along on a single course, never wavering from it.

"What that destination may have been, I do not know, for we never reached it. On the fourth day out, after I had awoken, I heard through the decks above me a huge clamor arise. Sudden shouts and cries, and hurried orders barked loudly. I heard a vast panic in those voices, and felt the oars of our ship working hard to propel us forward with great speed.

"That we were being pursued by something made itself evident to me, first by the shouting I could make out through the timbers of the ship, and secondly, by the many abrupt changes in our course. Now we pursued a zigzagging route, with many quick corrections. Having no knowledge of these things, I did not know that this meant that our pursuers were hard upon us.

"Finally, our ship halted its forward movement, and by the pounding of many footsteps from above, I surmised that the ship had been boarded. The sounds of fighting came to my ears, and then the death screams of dying men.

"At last, the door to my cabin was thrust open. Two men in bonds stood in the doorway, and behind them as fearsome and loathsome a crowd of human things as ever I had laid eyes upon.

"'This is she,' one of the bound men said. His face was blackened, bloodied and swollen with bruises.

"'She, whut?' one of the brigands behind him rudely demanded.

"'She, the Empress herself,' the man bound in ropes said. I recognized his voice. It was the voice of the hooded man who had spoken to me, one of my three abductors. 'Let me free,' he said, 'And I shall give her to you.'

"That prompted huge peals of laughter from the rude brigands who had captured him. 'Haw! Haw! She's ours already!' they declared. 'We don't need your permission!'

"'But she is worth much,' my abductor, now prisoner of these rude men, retorted. 'She will fetch a ransom greater than any of you can count or measure. The city of D'ar will raise more gold, more jewels and more platinum for her than you can carry in all your ships for her safe return.'

"I looked hard upon this man, now," Jamarra said, but still did not know who he was. Even through his wounds, I knew that I had never seen him before. Did he, and his conspirators, act on his own agency, or was he but the agent of another? Oh, how I wished to interrogate him, but the moment was fraught. He was, just then, parlaying for his own life, using mine as barter. If he lived, perhaps later I might find the opportunity to question him. But, should he be murdered by these brigands, then I would have no way ever to learn why it was I should have been abducted. I kept my own counsel, and permitted events to unfold around me.

"'Why do we need you, then?'" demanded one of the brigands. A huge and brutal man who stood taller than his comrades, with a beard I can only describe as outrageous."

Hearing Jamarra describe a man with an 'outrageous beard' I could not help but laugh.

"'Outrageous'? An outrageous beard?" I said through my laughter. "You may be describing my old friend, Burkov... 'Burkov the Bloody', they called him"

"Burkov...?" the Empress replied, her brow knit with a growing remembrance. "I recall those syllables..." she said.

"Yes. Burkov the Bloody. Captain of the Fury. It was his crew that captured Azora and me. And he was the one who taught me how to row."

"It may indeed have been this friend of yours, this Burkov the Bloody," Jamarra answered. "That, I think, if I recall correctly, was how he was addressed.

"My bruised and bloodied abductor, bound and shackled, he, who I did not recognize, he replied to this Burkov person, 'Do you know the way to D'ar? How will you apprise those of that city that it is you who hold the Empress? Will you negotiate the terms of her return? Do you even know with whom it is you should establish these delicate negotiations?'

"This man with the absurd beard, this 'Burkov', responded, most brutally, and succinctly, to his brethren brigands, 'Take them to Salamir!' he shouted. And that was all he said.

"And the brutal men, they all surged forward through the door. They carried off my abductor, and they swelled as a crowd, all surrounding me. A mass of surging, grimy hands and eyes coming at me... that was what I saw.

"But this Burkov fellow, as you say he may have been called, the one with the outrageous beard, the hair, and the swagger to him, he shouted out to the crowd, 'Enough! Enough, you all, you shameless *kra*! Take them all to Salamir! Let him sort them out!'

"Those shouted words from that absurdly bearded man were sufficient to make all the surging crowd cease its forward surging, and stop, and cower before him. They halted, all of them and all of an instant, and they turned to hear his next command. But I spoke up first, before this Burkov fellow could speak a single word.

"'You!' I said, to three men before me, pointing at them with my finger, 'Take up my case, and carry it! We shall address this 'Salamir' as he so pleases to call himself.'

"And the three brigands I so commanded, they obeyed me, my direct command, as only they ought. And this Burkov fellow, I saw, he laughed a loud and sarcastic laugh, to see me command his own men.

"'Haw! Haw-haw, haw, haw...' ah, haw...' he laughed, his mouth wide, and his massive belly quaking... 'Yew are the wench, are ye not? To command me own men afore me own eyes?'

"'You'd not have me carry my own parcels," I said to him, 'As if I were but a common courier?' I said to him.

"'No, ma'am,' he replied, laughing in huge good humor. His naked belly quaked under his unbuttoned, embroidered vest, I recall, and his huge beard shook hard upon it. 'I'd naught to impose upon such a grand one as yew!' he declared loudly. 'You heard the lady!' he shouted at the mass of men who surrounded us.

"'Pick up the lady's case, and carry it where she wants it!' he shouted. 'Off to Salamir with all of them! The whole lot of them! Let Salamir sort them out! Haw! Haw! Haw!' he laughed.

"And so we quit that tiny chamber, the brigands who escorted me out, those who carried my case for me, and my abductors, now unmasked, but even yet unknown to me. It seems that I moved with insufficient alacrity to satisfy the patience of one rude fellow. He made to reach for my arm as I approached the doorway, with a rude remark leaving his mouth.

"I terminated the rude fellow's remark, and his gesture, with a gesture of my own. Though the impudent move against me was without precedent, I was certainly not unprepared, and my teachers had long rehearsed me in the proper response to every possible insult upon the person of the Empress.

"You have seen my blade?" she said to me, with a smile.

"I have indeed," I answered. "I saw how you put down the Karzi warrior who likewise sought to insult your person."

"That fellow lost an eye," Jamarra replied, her smile widening. "The rude brigand, likewise surprised, suffered a most indelicate opening of the upper thigh. That was a cut most convenient to me, and requiring the smallest effort, to the greatest effect."

"'One does not lay hands upon the person of the Empress,' I told him. But he was of no mind to pay attention to the lesson in courtesy with which I honored him, as he was more preoccupied with staunching the torrents of blood that flowed copiously from him.

"The man with the heavy beard, the one of whom you claimed acquaintance, this Burkov fellow, you called him?"

"Yes?" I prompted.

"He laughed loud to see the rude fellow discomfited. 'Haw! Haw!' he laughed."

(I was amused to see Jamarra attempting, with her feminine and regal voice, and its almost musical cadences, to imitate Burkov's deep voice and huge laughter, which resonate through his huge chest, and fill all the air surrounding him).

"'Haw! Haw! Now that's a lady we got, here'," Jamarra continued, still imitating Burkov's stentorian laugh.

"'Be gentlemen, if yew know how, and mind your manners. Haw! Haw! Or she'll gut ye where yew stand! Haw! Haw! Haw!'"

"Yes, that was Burkov, all right," I told Jamarra, laughing. "I doubt any captain of Salamir's fleet would have been nearly so sanguine to see his own crew cut down like that."

"He seemed to think I'd taught the man something useful," Jamarra replied.

"If only to keep his wits about him..." I said.

"And not to be so grabby," Azora added.

"Our lesson over," Jamarra continued, "This Burkov fellow escorted me and the men who abducted me from the tiny cabin, to the deck of the ship. I saw, as we came to the deck, that Burkov's men were very busy in relieving the ship of everything of any value, and carrying it all over the side, to several boats. Not far away, I saw three ships surrounding ours, and boats traveling back and forth from ours, all laden with goods, to those three ships.

"This Burkov led me to one of these boats, with the three men who had abducted me, all still tightly bound. Together with a crew to row the boat, we made our way between the many ships of that armada to a vast and very tall ship that lay in the deep water midway to the horizon. We had gone not far, several other boats pulling with us, all of them heavy laden with plunder from our small ship, when I saw flames leap up from the deck of that ship that we had just quit. Quickly the flames engulfed the masts and sails, and very soon did the ship burn to the sea, with naught but smoldering bits of flotsam to mark, for a few fleeting moments, that it ever once existed.

"Burkov sent the others boats loaded with plunder off to the three ships that surrounded the burning hulk, and he directed the crew who rowed the boat we were on to move forward, toward the one huge ship, midway to the horizon.

"We continued on and made our way to that vast and very tall ship. It was many times larger than any other ship of this fleet, and though the hull was dark, it glinted with gold highlights in the sunlight. But even at a distance from it, I caught the stench of death and dying things about it. Hanging from the rigging were the corpses of dozens of men..."

"Yes," I said. "I've seen them, too."

"This was the ship of the one they called Salamir, a pirate king, of sorts, who rules over all these brigands..."

"Only when they are at sea, from what I understand," I explained. "I learned from Burkov that they sail with Salamir for the sake of strength and mutual protection. But when they are not at sea, or out pillaging, each is his own man."

The Empress gave a delicate shrug to her shoulders, indicating a complete unconcern.

"I see," she said, bored.

"The great Salamir himself," she went on, "Sat in a great chair carried by four stalwart men under a golden canopy on the deck high in the stern of the ship as he awaited my coming. Oh... what a creature..."

For an instant, upon recalling her first meeting with the man, the Empress permitted a look of disgust to overcome her features. But only for an instant did she let the mask slip. Quickly recovering herself, her look of disgust vanished away, and her face became, once again, an impassive veneer.

"I've met him," I said.

"Then I need not describe the man," Jamarra answered.

"Not on my account, please."

"'Very pretty', this Salamir said, when I stepped into his presence," Jamarra continued. "He was surrounded by his crew and his simpering sycophants. 'But why is she here? I have many mouths to feed already. Why should I take an interest in this creature's welfare?'

"The Burkov fellow stepped up. He gave one of my three abductors a slap to the back of the head, which nearly sent the man sprawling on the deck, and he said to Salamir, 'This 'un here say she's worth money. Lots of it.'

"Salamir cocked an eyebrow at the man Burkov had indicated, then looked back to Burkov.

"'And how is this one worth money, 'lots of it'?' Salamir asked, mocking Burkov's blunt words.

"'This 'un says she's an Empress," Burkov replied, cuffing the man again.

"'An Empress?' Salamir asked, oh, so blandly. His tone was bland, but I saw that he eyed me with a sudden, and surreptitious, sharpness under his painted eyelids. "'And an Empress is worth a great deal of money to me... how?'

"My abductor, bruised, bloodied and bound, ducked the third slap Burkov aimed at his head, and he spoke to Salamir directly.

"'The City of D'ar will pay a vast treasure for her safe return,' he said.

"'Indeed?' said Salamir. Though he affected a bored manner, his eyebrows shot up upon hearing the name of D'ar.

"'And who is this person who so presumes to inform me of these matters?' Salamir said with a profound affectation of uninterest.

"'I am...' he started to say, but Salamir cut him off with a gesture. Burkov understood Salamir's gesture, and shoved the man down upon his knees. Salamir smiled.

"'That's much better. Now you may speak. Who are you to negotiate for this Empress's return to... D'ar did you say? The city of D'ar?'

"Oh, but the man was coy," Jamarra said. "And cunning, too, after his own fashion. Cunning enough, I suppose, for the rude fellows who surrounded him. A crew such as his is quite unused to the subtleties of diplomacy, the nuance of expressions. And so, perhaps, Salamir was master of the many blunt and brutal men of his command. But to me, he was obvious as any guileless babe. By mere brute force alone did he hold me in his power, and certainly it was not by any subtlety of wit. I saw by his face that his protestations of ignorance notwithstanding, the man had certainly heard of D'ar, and well he ought to have.

"The riches of D'ar are legend, and legendary. The floors of the palace in which I dwell... or, I should say, once dwelt, are tiled with gold, emerald and ruby. For it is only right that the feet of the Empress should never be degraded by the touch of anything that is not precious. My sandals were woven only of gold thread, and when I appeared in public, a hundred slaves laid carpets of platinum, silver and... they...

Jamarra's voice drifted to silence, and her mind wandered away into the warm bosom of distant memories. Azora and I did not interrupt her reverie, but let her stroll the corridors of her mind as she would.

After several moments of musing, Jamarra roused herself to the present, and began speaking once again, picking up the thread of her tale.

"'It may be that we have heard of D'ar,' Salamir said, so cunningly," Jamarra continued. "'But why would we wish to return its precious Empress for any amount of money? It seems to me very careless of the people of D'ar to misplace their Empress so...'

"And with that remark, Salamir's sycophants and the lieutenants standing near laughed loud.

"Their laughter pushed my patience, already sorely taxed, beyond its last limits.

"'This man does not speak for the Empress of D'ar,' I said to Salamir, ignoring all the rest. 'We do not know who he is, nor why he has brought us to this place. Your Empress shall speak for herself, nor shall we tolerate the presumption of these base criminals, murderers and kidnappers, to barter our person for their lives. The person of the Empress is not a bauble to be traded by these traitors.'

"Now the sycophants surrounding Salamir had a new person to shower with their laughter, and so they directed their mockery at me. I was not moved by their scorn, but merely glared at Salamir, awaiting his response.

"Salamir opened his painted eyes wide in mock astonishment, then turned to my abductors, all three of them, bound and kneeling upon the deck of his ship.

"'Is this true?' he demanded of them. 'Have you been imposing upon me?'

"'Who would you have negotiate the terms of her freedom?'" said he who seemed to be the leader of the three. 'The Empress herself? And how could you expect her to act in good faith? I can be the emissary you require. I can lead you to the city of D'ar. I can speak to those loyal nobles who can purchase her ransom.'

"Salamir's eyes narrowed to a thin line as he studied the man kneeling below him.

"'A conundrum... hmm? Yes? This Empress... this very well-dressed Empress, I might say... may be worth much to me... but you... what are you worth to me?'

"'As I have told you,' said he.

"'And these other two with you... are they of value to me as well?'"

"'We have worked together for...'

"Salamir cut him off.

"'I have no doubt they are of value to you,' Salamir said. 'But are they of value to me? I require only but one to negotiate for the Empress. That one is you. These others. How are they useful to me?'

"Salamir studied the man carefully as he began to reply. But the man hesitated for but a moment as he gave thought to his answer. That hesitation was sufficient to prompt Salamir to his decision. Glancing at them as if he had just noticed something with a very unpleasant odor, he said, 'Get rid of those other two. Shackle this man, and we will make use of him when the time comes.'

"And then, to me, he turned and with a profoundly sarcastic smile and a bow of his head, he said, 'Oh, Empress of D'ar, I do hope you will accept my courtesies and my hospitality.'

"Speaking to two guards wearing golden helmets and their lieutenant, Salamir said, 'Do show the Empress every consideration, and prepare her suite. Make it comfortable for her, and you two, carry her case with you."

"Salamir signaled the four men who carried his golden chair with a snap of his fingers. They lifted the chair to their shoulders, and transported Salamir to an ornate doorway at the stern of the ship, disappearing into the cabin within.

"The lieutenant and the two guards stepped up to me, the lieutenant saluting and saying, 'If you please, Oh Empress'. I followed him without issue, for there seemed no point to raising one.

"And of the two fellows who had joined in abducting me from my palace, and of whom Salamir asked, 'of what value are they?'..."

Jamarra gave her shoulders a slight shrug. "Their execution was most efficiently carried out by the simple expedient of tossing them both, still bound, over the side of the ship. I heard the two splashes in the water as they struck it.

"And their ringleader, he who had accosted me in my bed, who had bidden me to prepare myself for this long journey, he who had placed the slipcase over my head... I saw him as he was led past me into the hull of the ship. Still I did not recognize his face, nor the sound of his voice. But as he passed, I said to him, 'Your friends were most fortunate. Now you must pray that this brigand will be the one to relieve you of the burden of life, for if he does not do it, then your Empress most assuredly shall'.

"Only briefly did he have the chance to return my gaze before the brigands carried him off, and upon that face I saw an expression of utter despair such as I had never before or since seen writ upon any human countenance.

"And from behind me there came huge laughter. It was Burkov.

"'Ha! Ha! Ha!' he laughed. 'You put yerself in bad, m'boy!' he shouted at the man as he was dragged down a gangway into the hull of the ship. 'Don't ever be crossin' a woman!' Burkov bellowed. 'They'll be the death of ye!'

"And that was the last I saw of the man who abducted me. Why he abducted me, if he is yet alive, who else was part of the conspiracy, what the purpose of that foul conspiracy was—these things I do not know."

"It seems likely, too," I said, "To remain forever a mystery to you."

"Unless..." Azora interjected.

I turned to her, and she returned my gaze with one of calculated guilelessness.

"Unless what?" I asked.

"We had much to talk about," Azora replied, "Jamarra and I, there in Salamir's ship, awaiting you to come and save us."

Now I looked toward the Empress. Her face, at the moment a pretty pink, was impassive. Hers may have been a face sculpted from marble, so completely without expression it was.

"It seems to me," I said to both, sensing where Azora was hoping to lead the conversation, "That Jamarra is quite capable of hatching her own plots. What have you two been scheming up?"

"Oh, nothing," Azora replied. "I only told Jamarra how helpful you were to me, and how you helped me to get away from Jor-Taq..." Azora paused and smiled into my face.

"What of it?" I said.

"Oh, just that you were so quick-witted and resourceful then, and that you might be able to..." Azora let her voice trail off.

"Yes?" I asked, my impatience growing. "Just tell me, won't you?"

"Azora is a dear, and as I have already indicated to you, she has truly offered me the first friendship I have ever enjoyed," Jamarra put in. "Perhaps, in her enthusiasm, she made assurances to me of a sort that were an unwitting imposition... You have already done much..."

Having said that much, Jamarra artfully let her voice trail off, the question yet unasked by both of them left hanging in the air.

"Clearly, Azora, you and Jamarra have had a conversation or two," I said.

"Grae-don," Azora began with sudden determination. "We will never find our way back to Pella'mir. You must know that. We have no place in this world. None. "

"Yes. That has been on my mind," I said.

"Let us assist Jamarra in finding her way back to D'ar," with a calculated, yet still impulsive unburdening. "There, we might find a place to live in peace. There, we might find a home."

I glanced away from Azora to Jamarra. Jamarra returned my glance with a steady gaze. Astonishing to me, I found her lilac eyes to be both deep and opaque. Unplumbed and unfathomable depths did I see in those eyes, measureless and countless worlds suggested in them. Yet her lusterless eyes shone also with that peculiar flatness, the dull unresponsiveness I had seen in the eyes of killers, eyes that looked out at the world, but permitted none to look in.

"That may all be so, but it seems, Jamarra, that you have enemies in D'ar."

"That is indisputably the case," she answered.

"Enemies of whom you know nothing."

"That is also true."

"This time, they merely abducted you..."

"I shall learn who these people were, they who imposed this insult upon the Empress. They shall be punished. I shall once again take my throne."

She spoke these words in a simple flat monotone, without emphasis. And the deadly simplicity of her utterance was more convincing to me than any possible emotional outpouring could have been. I knew, too, that she would do this, return to D'ar, whatever the dangers may be. Whatever the hazards that lay between her and her goal, she would do it. She would go alone if none would go with her.

Now I looked back to Azora.

"I'm going with her," she said.

The look on her face showed me the futility of argument.

"Where is D'ar?" I asked.

Jamarra, still reclining within our crude tent, stretched her arm to the east, pointing out from the shade of the tent with a single shapely finger heavy with rings.

"That way," she said.

As that happened to be the selfsame direction the currents of the sea were carrying us, there seemed nothing further to say.

"To D'ar, then," I said.

THE SAGA CONTINUES IN
THE CAVES OF MARS
PART TWO:
ROAD TO THE HIDDEN CITY

APPENDIX: JOURNEY TO TAAKBAR

Editor's note: The following story is the tale of one of Grae-don and Azora's adventures alluded to in Chapter Eight. It was originally published in the Rogue Planet Press anthology Barbarians of the Red Planet *(2014) ed. Gavin Chappell.*

"Let's go to Taakbar," Azora said.

"Taakbar? I thought you hated Taakbar."

"I do, but I need *joyu* juice for my darts," she insisted.

"*Joyu* juice?" I asked.

"Juice from the *joyu* bush. It only grows in Taakbar, so we have to go there to get it."

"Doesn't anybody ever bring it here?"

"No. It's not... well..." She hesitated.

"Uh, people don't like to have it around here. It's... a little bit dangerous," she finally explained.

"Dangerous?"

"Yes... it can... um...put people to sleep. And too much of it can make them puff up, and..." she gave me a mischievous smile, "Turn blue and die. Sometimes their bellies explode, if they get too much of it."

"That all sounds very amusing. And why do you need this stuff?" I asked.

"For my darts. I told you that."

"I see," I said.

"No, you don't," Azora laughed. "You have your sword, and that's fine for you. You're a big fellow. But I'm just a little girl."

Azora flashed me one of her sweet, wide-eyed smiles.

"Oh, my knife is fine," she said. "But I don't like to have to get so close in a fight. Sometimes I'd like to be able to hit first, before anyone gets near enough to grab me."

"I can see the point of that," I answered. "But we haven't been in a fight in..."

"... a long time, sure," Azora finished for me. "But there are still muggers in the streets. And sometimes we like to stay out late. I should be ready. I used my darts on Taakbar. And I was good. You'll see."

With these and similar arguments, some of them involving kisses and caresses, Azora finally persuaded me to go to Taakbar. We did have some savings between us. Azora's dancing on the street corners always brought in a few coins from appreciative passers-by, and a man who was ready with his sword could always find employment in Pella'mir. I'm not given to bragging, but I've made a good living.

Between us, Azora and I had managed to cobble together quite enough to buy passage on one of the rare ships that made the trip between Pella'mir and Taakbar. These ships sailed irregularly, on no set course or schedule.

So we left early one morning, before the sun had risen, and made our way through the steep and winding streets of Pella'mir to the gates that opened to the harbor at the northern edge of our island city.

I'd never been this way before. All my time in Pella'mir had been taken up, first, in the house of Jor-Taq, where I had been virtually his slave, and then, after his death, with Torq-aa and his family at the southwest quadrant of the city. Torq-aa's home was midway between the summit of the island, where the richest people lived, and the base of the island, where the walls surround the city.

Fewer people lived here at the northern end of the island. These streets were given over to the trades, mostly. Warehouses received the goods that came to Pell'amir from Taakbar, and islands further away. Some there were who made their livelihoods by dredging the sea for sea life which they sold in markets for food.

The gates at the harbor were almost always open, unlike those at other places in the walls, which were closed at night against any surprise assaults by the Brigands of Boramok, who attacked the city with a dismal regularity.

But trading ships came from Taakbar day and night, and the wharfs receiving them were always busy.

It was to these wharfs that Azora and I were making our way, to find passage upon one of these vessels. I wore the plain harness of a warrior, with the crest of Torq-aa's house emblazoned upon a medal I wore upon the leather straps that crossed my chest. My short sword, long sword and knife were strapped to my belt.

That crest gave me passage through the streets of the city, where one could not travel far without being challenged by the guard of one of the several great houses sharing power over the city, or by the many bands of thugs who prowled the alleys and unprotected neighborhoods.

Azora, forswearing the silken finery pressed upon her by Shala and Haia, wore the short leather skirt common to the working women of Pella'mir. Sandals with straps wrapped around her legs to a point slightly above her knees, and a simple cloak wrapped about her shoulders against the chill of the morning was sufficient for her. She wore the crest of Torq-aa's house on her belt, in front, along with the two knifes, one for cutting and one for throwing, which she wore in their scabbards upon her hip. And slung from her shoulder was the bag she used to carry her darts, the reason for which we were now traveling to Taakbar.

Unlike the gates at the other reaches of the island, west, south and east, which were all richly ornamented with stones of many colors, the gates to the north were plain and functional.

We walked unchallenged through the gate out into the quays from the city. Getting back in, of course, would not be so easy. The guards at the gate would certainly interrogate us closely.

The sun was low and bright, and oily sunshine glittered upon the rippling surface of the sea as we stepped out of the shadow of the walls. Here, the quays were built far outward, where the bottom was rocky and the water shallow. Hundreds of masts made a forest of umber poles all silhouetted against the pink and golden dawn.

Urgent carts and wagons crammed with goods crowded past us, their drivers hurrying down the quays to and from their ships.

Wanting not for money, we eyed the ships as we walked by them, looking for one that would offer us a comfortable passage. Almost no one travels between the wealthy city of Pella'mir and the rocky archipelago of Taakbar so there is no regular passenger service to be had. On those rare instances that people do have reason to travel from one to the other, passage must be purchased from the ships carrying cargo.

Which we did. We came upon a large, broad ship with three banks of oars, and a tall sail at the rear. All this spoke to a wealthy owner. One who, perhaps, could be trusted not to cut our throats in our sleep, take our purse and dump our corpses over the railing.

That was not an idle fear. When we put out to sea, we put ourselves in the hands of the captains of these ships, who are beholden to no law other than their own, and no man, other than their own selves. Many have been the careless travelers who woke up dead at the bottom of the sea.

"Yah, I can take you to Taakbar," the captain said, when we sought him out. He eyed us as keenly as we did him, as we all sized each other up that shining morning. He was a robust man, with the yellow complexion that revealed him to have come from those islands.

"But you are not from Pell'amir," he said, staring at us. "I have seen you pink-skinned peoples, but not much. Yellow hair. Not like the black hair normal people have."

"I am Grae-don," I answered. "And this is Azora..."

"Blue eyes..." the captain said, looking at Azora and pursing his lips.

"Well, it is not my business. Your gold is good, and that is all I need to know."

He took the two gold coins I pushed into his hand, and he signaled to a mate standing nearby.

"They sleep in the stock room behind me," he said. "Show them."

The mate led us to the stern of the ship, up a ladder, and at last to a narrow stock room with but a tiny window that looked out from the very stern of the ship.

We took the room gratefully, for the door had a lock on it. And with the few sleeping silks we had packed into the bag we carried, we made ourselves quite comfortable for the trip.

"Much nicer," Azora remarked, "Than the last time I was on one of these ships."

"This time you can afford a cabin, even if it is just a stock room," I laughed. "No need to stow away in the bilge."

"It wasn't the bilge," Azora said. "But it may as well have been."

Our trip to Taakbar was swift across the golden waters of the Great Northern Sea. For most of the journey, Azora and I stayed in the stock room, but we did step outside once or twice to catch some air and stretch our legs.

The ship was quite beautiful, and the captain, a man named Tan-Kar, quite affable. He sailed a zigzagging course to avoid any possibility of crossing paths with the brigands who constantly scoured the sea for prey. But when he was not minding his ship, the crew, or the horizon, her could be drawn into a conversation on occasion.

"We could make Taakbar in a week," he remarked to us one afternoon, "If it weren't for the brigands. But we keep an eye out, and sail the most inconvenient course possible, or they'll hunt us down in a day. As it is, we'll make good time to do it in three weeks.

"Right good thing, too, you shipped with us to Taakbar. We'll be too loaded to take any passengers on the way back from there."

The ship, as I say, bragged three banks of oars, and a crew of nearly eighty men. It lay low in the water at the fore, and had but the single mast at the high rear. The mast held only a single lateen sail, which swelled mightily with the breezes, and at top, above the sail, was a spacious enclosed cabin where the watch was stationed day and night.

"Two men to a shift," Tan-Kar explained. "Two shifts every day. We build our masts higher to see farther. And this one, you see, sways in the wind."

Indeed, it did. I glanced upward, and saw that the cabin was almost always swinging back and forth and to and fro in the wild winds that ceaselessly skirted across the sea. I imagined that it would take some doing to get used to spending even a few minutes inside, much less an entire morning and afternoon.

We at last arrived at Taakbar. The trip had been pleasant, the sea, calm, the winds, strong and constant.

I was most interested to see the many islands of Taakbar peeking up from the horizon as we approached, growing larger as we neared them.

The islands of Taakbar are many and rugged, and as different from the islands of Pella'mir as they could be. Where Pella'mir is a group of no more than a half dozen rather large islands clustered closely together, the archipelago of Taakbar is made up of many hundreds of islands, all of them ranging in a sprawling chain that spreads out beyond the horizon.

Many of them are grouped so closely together that bridges have been built between them, and there is much traffic from one island to the next. But many other islands in the chain are too distant for bridges, and commerce takes place only by means of many small ships and boats that daily ply the waters.

Also unlike the islands of Pella'mir, which are completely built up with the cities that cover every part of them, the islands of Taakbar are mostly uninhabitable regions of rocky hills and between them, heavy wilderness. The few cities that have made a toehold upon the islands dot the southern shores, and between those shores and the rocky hills are some scant regions of farmland.

It was upon one of those farms that Azora spent her childhood, as a slave, until the day she stabbed the farmer's son who got too familiar with her. She then ran off and lived in the hills, before she finally tired of living in the wild. She stowed away aboard a vessel, made her way to Pella'mir, where we met.

Our ship brought us to a city called Huiz, on the selfsame island that Azora spent her childhood. As we stepped ashore, I asked Azora, "Aren't you worried you might run into your old owners?"

She patted the knife in its scabbard on her hip and smiled at me.

"No," she said. "I'm not that lucky."

I laughed, and we walked into Huiz, arm in arm.

The buildings before us were low and built of stone, heavy blocks dragged down from the hills, all cunningly cut and laid together without grouting. The tallest of them was three stories, but most of them were structures of but one or two stories. These buildings were somewhat rudely fashioned, compared to the extravagant architectures of Pella'mir, but there was much craftsmanship going into them, and I was most impressed.

Huiz is not a wealthy city like Pella'mir, nor so large. It lies close to the coastline, and inland for some distance, along the course of a river that empties into the sea.

The people of Huiz dress much differently than those of Pella'mir, as well. Men and women both wear long skirts they call `*surpaa*' depending from just above their waists to their ankles. These *surpaa* are usually dyed with parallel stripes of varying widths and colors. About their chests, they wear loose vests embroidered with beads.

They all tie their long straight black hair into knots at the tops of their heads, letting their hair loose only when they bathe, or during their many feast days, when all work is stopped and people dance in the streets for days at a time without stopping.

Their complexions are the color of amber, unlike the people of Pella'mir, who have red skin. Azora and I, with our pinkish skin and blonde hair were unusual here, as we were everywhere.

Naturally we stood out, dressed as we were, and more particularly for the weapons we carried. The people of Taakbar are not naturally aggressive. Fights among them are very rare. And, except for the occasional knife used for cutting rope, meat or fabric, weapons are almost unheard of among them.

But the people of Taakbar are familiar with the people of Pella'mir, who do sometimes travel to these islands. And the people of Pella'mir are constantly armed. So though we drew stares, we were not completely alien to these people.

As we made our way among the crowds, which easily parted for us upon sight of our weapons, my eye fell upon some strange structures just beyond the city, and towering high in the air. They swayed in the breezes, and were by far the tallest things I had seen here in Huiz.

"What are those?" I asked Azora, pointing at them with my chin (she had taught me that gesturing with one's fingers here in Taakbar is considered very rude, and one should not indicate a thing by pointing at it, unless one wished to insult those who saw the gesture).

"Ah. I'd forgotten about them," Azora said. "Those are the kite towers."

"Kite towers?"

"Yes. It's the wind that keeps them up. It always blows here. During the day it blows from east to west. At night, it blows from west to east. And the people here have learned to use silk and parchment and light ropes to sail these things they call kites in the wind. Some days they have huge kite festivals, and they fill the sky with them. At night during these festivals, they'll hang lamps from their kites, and it's almost like a ceiling of stars just above our heads. It's really beautiful.

"They've learned to use the kites to make music, too. They stretch strings or ribbons across them, and they thrum and hum in the wind. Or whistles, or streamers or discs that spin and make a buzz. The music gets so loud you can hear it from the hills. Someday, Grae-don, we should maybe come back to see one of their kite festivals. They go on for days. People dance in the street, all the food is free, and the *ellihi* flows like river water."

Azora smiled into my face as she looked up at me.

"But as you see,' she continued, "They also learned how to use these kites to build high towers of ropes and twine and parchment.

"Starting with a small kite, they use it to raise a long line of twine, which they attach more and more kites to. Eventually, they can build something strong enough to carry a person or two. I heard that some of those towers are really elaborate inside. Since the wind always blows in one direction or another, they can keep these towers sailing day and night. Some of them have been up for years.

"There's always a ground crew at the bottom, watching the ropes and keeping them taut and always headed into the wind so the kites will keep sailing."

"But what are they for?" I asked.

"Look up at the top. See them? Those are sentries. They stay there day and night watching out for the brigands. Since the towers are so high, they can see their ships long before they even break the horizon. The brigands have never caught the people of Huiz by surprise."

"Hm. Seems to me that Pella'mir might learn a trick from that."

"Can't," Azora replied. "The winds change too much down there. Sometimes they don't blow at all. But here, the wind is always blowing, especially higher, where the tops of the towers are."

"I see." I stared at the kite towers for some time. They were most interesting.

Afterwards, we spent the day looking about the streets of Huiz. We saw much, but by that afternoon we'd had enough of taking in the sights, so we looked for a place where we could sleep for the night.

Huiz did offer some rough accommodations for the traders who came there by ship, and we managed to find a room. After taking the room, we made our way to an eating place nearby. People sat cross-legged eating outside on a patio under a latticework covered with vines heavy with fruits.

We picked our way through the people squatting on the patio floor to the interior of the eating place. There we found many more people crowding around several tables and vats, ladling food for themselves into bowls that they took from stacks on the shelves lining the walls.

Azora picked up a bowl for herself, then handed one to me, and we walked up to the nearest table where we pushed ourselves forward until we could reach into the piles of food that were stacked there. As we picked through it among many other hands, servers came to the table and loaded it down again with more.

Having filled our bowls, we moved away, back into the patio, where Azora instantly found a place to settle in. Because of my long legs, I have never been comfortable sitting cross-legged on the floor, so I found a bench nearby and dragged it to where Azora sat.

And there we ate, making our plans.

"We'll have to leave very early," Azora explained. "We'll be days marching to get to where I'm thinking about. Ready to camp under the stars?"

I shrugged. "I suppose so," I said, thoughtlessly. I'd not slept outside often, except for those hot evenings at Torq-aa's home when Azora and I sought the relief of the evening breezes by sleeping on the balcony.

"It won't be like that at all," Azora said. "There are beasts in those wild lands, and they like their meat juicy, and sleepy."

As we talked, I noted out of the corner of my eye a group sitting near to us who seemed to be taking an interest in us.

I did not care for that, so I studied them rather closely. There were six of them, young men, sitting in a circle, eating quietly from their bowls. They were garbed in the *surpaa* and the beaded vests that the folk of Taakbar wear, and in every way, they were but typical of the people of Huiz.

But they had ceased speaking among themselves, and seemed intent upon listening to the conversation between Azora and me. As time passed and Azora described in greater details the lands and the dangers through which we were passing, it became more obvious that the six men sitting next to us were indeed listening.

My patience wore thin, and I felt my anger rising. Though I was a stranger in this land, I did not brook their rude attention well.

I was at the very point of rising from my bench and unsheathing my long sword – indeed, I had already laid my hand upon its pommel – when one of the six men spoke.

"I am so sorry to offend," he said, most apologetically. "But we could not help but to hear you say you wish to go into the hills tomorrow?"

Azora stopped speaking and half turned toward the man.

"Yes," she said. "We're looking for the *joyu* bush."

"A most dangerous venture."

Azora shrugged.

"And you two go alone?"

"Why are you so interested?" I demanded.

"Ah. My apologies. We do not mean to offend."

I grunted my reply.

"Yes," Azora said. "We're going alone. I lived in those hills."

"Ah, I see," said our curious acquaintance. "I only speak because we also plan to go to the hills, ourselves, in the morning."

"Oh?" I grunted, incuriously.

"We hunt the *tumat*."

"Really?" Azora replied, perking up with interest.

"We seek its *gala*. We know where there is a colony of the *tumat*, and if we are successful, we shall return very wealthy men!" He smiled at us. His companions nodded their heads.

Gala is a secretion exuded by the *tumat*. It is sweet, thick and rich, the color of amber. The *tumaa* secrete it to feed their young. Among people, is used as a flavoring for some foods, or for making many kinds of confections popular with children. When fermented, however, it is used in making *ellihi*, and for that reason it is very highly sought after.

However, the *tumat* is a most dangerous creature. Azora had described it to me, once, but I had never seen one. She told me is can grow to be twice as large as a full grown man, and that it lives in large colonies in the northernmost islands of Taakbar. The *tumat* hunters of Taakbar are paid well for their dangerous work.

"I had not heard that *tumaa* lived on this island," Azora said.

"They did not, until just some years ago," our acquaintance explained. "Maybe they drifted here, or the young, they hid on the ships that sail from the northern islands. But they come, and they hide in the hills until they are big.

"Then on a night, they come to the town called Yuptl, on the north shore. My friend Y'ar comes from Yuptl." Our companion indicated one of his friends with his chin.

I gravely nodded in acknowledgement, and Azora did too. A youngish man with gray eyes. His vest was worn and dirty, with a pattern of beadwork different from the others.

"They kill all my family, all my people," Y'ar said. Rage smoldering behind his eyes. "They eat them in the night. Bite them to pieces. I only get away after I see my sister bit in two. I will kill them. I will kill them all."

His five companions solemnly nodded their heads in agreement.

"We kill them all. Take their *gala*," said the first one who had spoken to us. "Then we will be rich and they will be dead."

"Six of you?" Azora asked.

They all nodded.

"How many *tumaa* are there?"

"There were many," Y'ar said. "Very many. But we will kill them all. Maybe not right away. We go see how many they are, and kill some. Then we'll bring back their gala, and sell it. That makes us rich. Then we go back to kill more, and then again, until they are all dead."

"And then Yuptl will be a town again, and I will go to live," Y'ar finished.

"Sounds like a good plan," I said. But they missed the sarcasm in my voice.

"We think so," said he who started the conversation. He raised a querying eyebrow. "Maybe you would come, too? Then we would be eight, and you would not travel through the wild hills alone."

I glanced at Azora, and she glanced back at me. With a silent discussion between us, expressed wholly with our eyes, we came to a quick and mutual conclusion.

"All right," I said. "We'll come."

Arranging the time and the place where we would meet upon the morrow, Azora and I took our leave of Umir – for that was the name of the one who started talking to us – Y'ar, and their four companions. We returned to the room we had hired for the night, and made ready to sleep.

"They're brash," Azora remarked.

"Yes, they are," I said. "I doubt they've ever hunted a *tumat* in their lives."

"I'm sure they haven't," Azora replied.

"Well, perhaps their enthusiasm will make up for their lack of experience. At least we'll have an escort through the wilderness."

We lay down then and went to sleep upon our silks.

The next morning when the world was yet dark and the stars still bright over our heads, we met the six young men just outside the eating place as we had arranged. They were all dressed as before, but they wore long cloaks over their shoulders against the cold. Each of them carried a bag with his supplies, and a long quiver made of woven fabric and strapped diagonally across the back. Each quiver was filled with about twenty short javelins, each one as long as my arm.

Umir, the apparent leader of the group, took a moment to introduce the others by name.

"Y'ar, you already know," he said. "This is my friend Hakk," indicating a stout fellow with eyebrows that met in the center.

"And this," he continued, pointing with his chin, "Is Quzat. He is the strongest and the tallest one among us. Next to him, his brother, Quon, who is nearly as strong, and almost as tall."

The group laughed.

"And this good fellow," Umir said, laying his hand on a young man with bright and fiery eyes, "Is my good friend, Tumar. He will die for you, if you are his friend."

"Let us hope it does not come to that," I answered. "But I will be glad for the friendship of any good man. Let us hope your expedition meets with all the success you seek.

"This is Azora," I said, laying my hand upon her back. She leaned into me and smiled. "And I am called Grae-don."

"'Grae-don'?" Umir asked. "Have you no parents?[1]

"None that I have ever known," I answered.

"I am sorry, my friend," Umir said.

"Why?" I asked, truly puzzled by the remark.

"That you have no family."

The others of Umir's company nodded sympathetically.

"We have our friends in Pella'mir, Torq-aa and his wife, Shala," I explained. "And Haia, their daughter. They are as much a family to us," and I leaned my head toward Azora to include her, "As we have ever wanted."

"That gives me comfort, friend," Umir replied. "It should give me much sadness to know that any of my friends should be alone in this world."

"That is very kind of you," I answered. "But," I touched the pommel of my sword with one hand, and cast my arm about Azora's shoulders, "With my friends here, I am never alone in this world, and neither shall they be."

"And we shall be glad of your friendship, and your friends, especially the sharp ones you carry with you, for the way is dangerous and long."

We all laughed at that, and then began our journey.

The day had not yet broken in the eastern sky, and the stars were yet incandescent above us. The lamps of Huiz had grown dim and were burning low, and the streets were deeply shadowed. But with Umir

---

1. Note: The name 'Grae-don' (literally 'without parents') means 'orphan'. It was given him by those who took him in and gave him training, when he was discovered wandering naked and with no memory, in the streets of Pella'mir.

and his five companions to lead us, we made good time out of the city and into the fields beyond.

We passed under several of the kite towers as we made our way. An endless and complicated complex array of ropes and lines towered over our heads, silhouetted against the purple sky.

Now we were out of the city, we had no walls to buffer the constant winds. The cloaks that Umir and his companions wore flapped loudly about their ankles, and we all hunched our shoulders against the ceaseless gusts of chill air. As we walked beneath the kite towers, the winds made the ropes taut, and they hummed in the wind.

I thought we were in for an uncomfortable march, but Umir knew the way well. He led us into a depression of the ground that protected us from the worst of the chilling winds. As we marched, the depression grew into a wide gully with steep walls.

We followed this for many *yurlma*, past numerous farms and a few poor villas. By midday, we had put most of them past us, and we came upon the tumbled stones and boulders of the foothills of Taakbar.

Here, the farms were tinier things, that took advantage of the small pockets of soil huddled between the outcroppings of rock of the stony hills. As we marched further, we put even those poor small farms behind us. By the end of the second day of our march, we said goodbye to even those.

"Now we leave civilization behind," Umir said. "From here on, I no longer know the way. And here, our dangers truly start."

"I know these hills," Azora said. "I know them very well. I lived here."

Y'ar, too, had passed this way once before, when he fled Yuptl and came to Huiz. So Azora and Y'ar took over leading us. And we were able to make very good time through the hills and the gullies between them. We did not want for either food or water, for the gullies were fed by many cold streams, and where the streams flowed, vegetation flourished.

The only difficulty for us was that where the vegetation flourished, so did many animals that fed upon the vegetation. And where those animals flourished, so did their predators. And they were fierce and fearsome things, indeed.

But it was in the gullies that the *joyu* bush Azora sought grew. So we spent many days here searching for it among the dangerous animals and the plants that grew in such wild profusion.

At night, we climbed out of the gullies, and sought a place upon the hillsides to make camp. There we could often find a hollow among the bluffs where we could build a fire, and sleep in shifts. In the evenings, as we ate our supper, the stout Hakk amused us with his many witty tales. The boy was a good storyteller, and he always had us laughing.

Tumar, who would think nothing of laying down his life for a friend, was also a young man with a strong voice. He was a most able singer, and after our supper each night, he finished our meal with a song. Quon and Quzat accompanied him with their sticks. These were sticks they carried with them to make music, painted, polished and cut with notches to make different sounds, either by beating them together, or rubbing them. They beat their sticks together in a well practiced rhythm, and showed me how to do it, though I never caught on.

And sometimes, after supper and Hakk's jokes and witty stories, in the golden light of the camp fire, when Tumar was singing a particularly rapid song with a staccato tempo, and Quon and Quzat were beating a furious beat on their 'singing sticks' as they called them, Azora let the music sing through her and she leaped up and danced. Her hips and thighs were wild in the lurid light of the flames, crazy currents of pink flesh – a most exotic thing to these young men of amber skin, they were dazzled, and I was proud – and her smile. Open, wide, her perfect teeth shining white and bright under the purple star-studded skies.

Those were some happy moments, with our newfound friends. I shall remember them ever.

We had few adventures in those days. Once or twice we were attacked by a few of the strange beasts that inhabit Taakbar, but we easily fought them off. Once Tumar stopped the wild charge of a maddened *basq* as it leaped upon me from behind, with a thrust of his javelin into its belly. I thanked him for that, but the next day I cut the arms from a hanging *qylch*, just as it reached down from its perch high upon a *xuxu* tree to snatch him up, so I count us as even.

Several of the many carnivorous plants that flourish here also gave us some tense moments, but we quickly overcame those troubles, as well.

And at last, after much searching, we came upon one of the *joyu* bushes that Azora sought.

"Shhh!" Azora hushed us, seeing it in the distance through the thick and writhing vines ahead. "Don't let it hear you!"

We all stopped dead in our tracks, and dropped to our knees.

"It can sense vibrations in the air," she whispered, covering her mouth with her hand. "And it is always hungry."

We nodded to her to show her we understood.

"Stay here," she instructed us. And then she began crawling forward on her hands and knees, feeling carefully of the soil with her fingers before she made each move forward.

The *joyu* bush was a thing most strange to my eyes.

It grew in a cluster of brilliant yellow vertical stumps, each stump several times taller than the tallest man.

From each stump there grew a series of orange-colored branches, all laid out in spirals that started at the bottom of the stump, and working their way to the very top. Each branch was bifurcated into many fingerlike projections. All of it, the stumps, the branches, waved slowly and sinuously in the air.

Each fingerlike projection was covered with innumerable spikes – the spikes were hairlike and transparent, so that they appeared to be fuzz on the branch. But Azora had assured us that this fuzz was composed of countless poisonous glass-like needles that the joyu bush shot out at its prey upon the least vibration of the ground.

When the prey was paralyzed, or killed, by its glassy darts, the *joyu* bush's root-like appendages crawled out from under the ground, coiled about the victim, and dragged it toward the center of its stumps. There, at the base of its stumps, the joyu bush had a mouth-like opening into which it forced its paralyzed prey, where it digested its victim at leisure.

Azora was seeking the sac that carried the venom of the *joyu* bush, which is located at the root of the stumps. A most dangerous and delicate venture, as she had to crawl forward without triggering the splaying bombardment of glassy needles that would kill her, or worse, only paralyze her, as she waited to be digested by the thing.

I felt Azora's danger tingling through my spine. She'd thrown off her vest, lest it brush against the thick undergrowth and trigger a spray of death from the bush. Now, wearing naught but her tight loin-cloth, every muscle taut, she crawled painstakingly forward through the thick grasses.

Halfway to the base of the *joyu* bush, she looked back at us, and with a fleeting and silent flick of her arm, she waved us back.

I looked to our companions, and with a jerk of my head, I signaled to Umir and the others to back away. Silently, and cautiously, they did, and moments later, they were gone, hidden in the thick underbrush.

But I would not leave my Azora. However practiced she may have been, I was not about to leave her alone with this *joyu* bush. Clumsy as I am, though – for I am but a fighter, blunt and brutal – I could not assist her in this dangerously delicate task.

All I could do, and would do, should she make but even a single misstep, would be to charge wildly against this *joyu* bush, and to provoke from it the most furious response possible, the discharge of all its death-dealing needles, to ensure that Azora – and I – both of us would both be quite dead, and not conscious, as it slowly sucked the life from our corpses.

I looked again to Azora, watched her keenly as she crawled slowly forward. Carefully she edged one elbow forward, and then the other. Her knees, splayed wide across the grass, moved imperceptibly forward, first her left knee, then her right. And then her elbows again.

Finally, she came to the base of the *joyu* bush. A full hour had passed, I think, from the moment she espied it before us, to the moment she came upon it with her knife, though the distance was but little more than a dozen paces.

But she had made the distance. Azora carefully clambered to the base of the monstrous thing, and now she gingerly pulled her knife from its sheath. She moved swiftly. The deadly needles of the *joyu* bush were poised to shoot their death at a distance. At this moment, where she lay, she was quite safe, for even with a discharge of the needles, they would miss her completely.

Azora plunged her blade deep into the *joyu* bush's root.

A thin, airy squeal filled the jungle. It cut though my ears, and Azora's too, for I saw her wince. But, though I clapped my hands over my own, Azora did not. She only cut deeper into the base of the wounded *joyu* bush with her knife until at last she revealed a purplish bladder.

Triumphantly, and with both hands, she jerked the bladder out of the ground.

Azora leaped up, threw her head back and with a wild cheer, she howled.

"Awoooo! Awooooo!" she shouted triumphantly, her exultant breasts dancing in the viridian light of the jungle

The *joyu* bush trembled. It withered before our wondering eyes. Its fingerlike projections coiled upon themselves, and shrank, dying, even as we watched. This bladder of toxin was the very heart of the thing. Cutting it off killed it as surely as cutting the heart out of a man kills him. Azora's first cut was as grievous a wound to the *joyu* bush as a knife thrust through the chest.

Azora leaped riotously toward me through the rank grasses. She swung her trophy, the bloated purple bladder of poison, in wide and wild circles over her head. Her eyes were mad with joy, her naked breasts bounding free.

And as she ran so raucously at me, howling `Awoooo! Woooo! Awooooh!' the *joyu* bush behind her died, finger by finger, branch by branch, and, finally stump by stump.

The thing turned first gray, then it congealed upon itself, and died.

"I got it!" Azora proudly yelled loud into my ears. She threw her arms around my shoulders, leaped up and wrapped her naked legs about my waist, thrusting hard against me. She squirmed hard and squeezed me in tight sweaty circles.

"Awooo! Awooooo!" she howled.

Hearing her triumphant ululations, our companions quickly re-joined us.

"I did it," Azora proudly shouted. She unwrapped her legs from about me, stepped away and lifted the swollen purple bladder of the dead *joyu* bush over her head with both hands. She shook it vigorously.

"I got it!"

Our friends congratulated her, and swarmed around us. Each wanted to see for himself this almost mythical bladder of the *joyu* bush.

Afterwards, we climbed out of the gully and made camp in the hills.

There, Azora carefully drained the bladder of the *joyu* bush into several smaller and more easily portable bags she had brought for that purpose. Then she showed us all how she tipped her darts with the deadly toxin.

Azora poured a quantity of it into a small ceramic bowl. The poison was clear, but yellowish, and it poured out thickly, like a syrup. One at a time, she dipped the points of her darts into the toxin, turning them about for a moment, and then pulling them out again.

The toxin lay thick upon the point of her dart. She held the dart gingerly between her fingers to allow it to dry, and then carefully placed it on a cloth near her knee.

"Don't touch it when it's wet," she remarked to us. "It's all right when it's dry. Then it can't harm you, until it's got under your skin. But while it's wet it can still sink in through your pores."

Having shown our new friends how to do it, Azora said to them, "Maybe you ought to tip your javelins with this. It might help when we catch a *tumat*."

Umir and Y'ar and the others saw the wisdom of that, and so we spent the rest of the afternoon applying the *joyu* juice to all their javelins.

While we did this, we naturally fell to talking about these *tumaa* we were about to hunt.

"What exactly do they look like?" I asked.

"Um... well, Y'ar tells us they have many hands," Umir said.

"Yes. Many hands," Hakk agreed.

"And they swing from trees," Quzat added.

"I've heard that, too," Tumar said.

The conversation faltered. Everyone turned to Y'ar.

"You've seen them, Y'ar. Tell Azora and Grae-don what you've told us," Umir suggested.

Y'ar paused. He looked into himself before he spoke. And when he did speak, what he said was this:

"The night was dark, as night always is. There were many of them, and I saw them... they rushed upon us when we were asleep. Yes, they have many hands. With talons. And teeth. Many teeth. I saw the teeth cut my sister in half. And then they swallowed her, not yet dead. Her body. It bled. In parts. They fought over her. And the teeth, they seek you out. They chase you through the night... when you sleep... you cannot sleep... they..."

Y'ar dropped his head and stopped speaking.

It was clear to Azora and me that none of them here had ever clearly laid eyes upon a tumat. Even Y'ar himself, the only one ever to see them, had seen them only imperfectly, half awake, and in shock.

"Are you sure you know what you're getting yourselves into?" I asked them.

Umir gave me a defiant glare.

"We are not cowards," he said.

"I'm not saying you are, my friend. I..."

Abruptly, Y'ar raised his head and looked into my face.

"I do," he said. "I know what I am getting into." Then, after a pause, he added. "You do not have to come."

Y'ar scowled at me. His face was so fierce it only filled my heart with delight.

I laughed and shook my head.

"I am coming with you," I said. "I will not deny myself the chance to fight alongside such warriors! Now let's eat, and let us hear another of Hakk's stories."

So we made our evening meal, and deliberately spoke of happier things. Soon our mood lightened. Hakk told us several of his amusing stories, and Tumar sang for us a drinking song that soon had us all laughing.

And the following morning we rose early and made quick time northward to Y'ar's town, Yuptl. We finally came upon it after another few days' journey.

It was late in the morning, all eight of us marching in a line across the bald top of a high and rounded stony mount when Y'ar, who was in the lead, turned to us to say, "We are coming on Yuptl now. It is in the canyon between this mesa and that one ahead."

He elevated his chin to point out to us the direction of the canyon, then raised his hand to his mouth to signal us to silence.

"Do not make a sound," he whispered.

We all gathered into a knot, and marched carefully forward. Y'ar, still at the head of our group, dropped to his hands and knees and began crawling gingerly forward to the brink of the mesa. We all followed his example.

We came to the edge, and cautiously peered over it.

The canyon below us was deep, and the walls steep, almost sheer. Many deep gullies cut through the mesas into the canyon, all of them twisting and circuitous. They cut back upon themselves in endless sinuosities.

Mounds, peaks and buttes jutted up from the impenetrable forests growing at the base of the winding canyon and the gullies. Foliage of lavender, crimson and deep cerulean filled them as far as we could see.

Upon the many mounds of rock that thrust up from the depths of the forests below were many buildings built of stone. Between these stone structures were many walkways. Stone stairways wound down the sides of these piles of stone, all leading from the buildings balanced on top of them and into the forest, and to the river at the bottom of the canyon that flowed from here to the Great Northern Sea.

Many rectangular shaped windows had been gouged into the walls of the steep canyon. It was there, behind those windows, and in the courts and enclosures cut from the living stone itself, that the greatest numbers of the people of Yuptl lived, Y'ar explained to us.

"When they lived," he finished, bitterly.

Peering over the ledge of the bluff, we studied the town closely. It was a dead town, for all we could see. Patios and walled gardens upon the mounds of rock were rank and overrun. Many were the areas where brickwork in walls and ceilings had collapsed, lying in tumbled piles upon the pavements. All was silent.

None of us had ever seen a colony of *tumaa* before, so we were not sure what exactly to look for. But from our vantage, we could make out no evidence of the creatures. Y'ar made a gesture with his head, and led us, crawling, to a point down along the ledge. There, around a bend in the gully, and away from Yuptl, he showed us a stone stairway that wound down the sheer face of the cliff.

It was both narrow and steep, the steps in it treacherously uneven. Without a pause, he immediately began descending, disappearing behind another bend in the canyon wall. His companions instantly fell in behind him, and then Azora and I followed at the last.

Rounding the bend, we found our companions clustered upon a narrow stone balcony cut into the stone wall. An entryway and two windows made it obvious that this was one of the several entrances to Yuptl.

"The guardhouse," Y'ar explained in a whisper. "No one can enter Yuptl, except through the guardhouses."

The guardhouse cut into the cliff face was abandoned. It was lit only by the light that poured in through the open entryway and two windows. Otherwise, all was dim and gloomy inside.

Y'ar was the first to step into the guardhouse from outside. He turned to the left, moving swiftly and confidently. We followed him behind.

He turned into a dark and narrow passageway that was lit from somewhere ahead. The light of daylight shined past the silhouettes of our companions who walked before Azora and me. We followed the narrow hall as it wended downward in a gentle sloping curve which followed, I presumed, the curve of the gully wall.

As we moved along, we passed several rectangular windows cut into the wall on the left. They let in daylight, and glimpses of Yuptl as well. Shortly, we came to another opening that led outside once again. Here Y'ar gathered us in a group just within the entranceway.

"I have walked this path many times," he said. "And I could walk it with my eyes closed, I know it so well. But you do not. Take care. The way ahead is dangerous to unpracticed feet. Take one bad step, and you will fall. And you will die."

He thrust his chin outward, directing our gaze. His explanation was sufficient. Here, the walls of the canyon were sheer. They offered no handhold or foothold whatever. Should we lose our balance we would plunge to our deaths in the jungle far below.

Just outside the entrance was an absurdly precarious walkway. It was but a series of planks, each no wider than my foot, laid upon nails that had been hammered into the stone face of the cliff. Running along this line of planks, about waist-high, was a rope that also had been nailed to the wall.

"Like this," Y'ar said, stepping out onto the planks, facing the cliff, and grasping the rope in his hands. He then shuffled sideways along the planks, with an easy familiarity that bespoke years of experience.

Once he had demonstrated to us how to move, he let go with his hands, then turned away from us, and simply walked along the plank as easily as if he were strolling along on an open plain.

The rest of us were not so practiced, though. Following the example he had demonstrated, we each grabbed hold of the rope and shuffled carefully along, our faces fast against the sheer wall of the cliff.

It curved outwardly, and then back upon itself. Y'ar walked quickly to the point where the wall curved inward again, and he waited there for us to catch up.

As we did, he peered around the corner of the cliff. My eye happened to be upon him when he did. His reaction caused my heart to leap into my throat.

He threw himself suddenly backward, leaning flat against the wall of the cliff, and then he turned to us, his eyes wide, and shaking his head slowly. His complexion, normally an amber hue, blanched, and his face went positively white. I saw his knees weaken, and for a moment I feared that he might collapse and fall from the walkway.

Umir, who was in the lead, shuffled quickly forward, and managed to catch Y'ar by the elbow before he did, indeed, fall. The rest of us hurried forward, and we clustered on that flimsy walkway, urgently whispering and demanding to know what he had seen.

"Tumat?' Quzat asked. "Did you see one?"

Y'ar simply shook his head, staring wide-eyed at us, unspeaking.

Slowly, his color came back, and finally he managed to say, "I am sorry. No, no *tumaa*. Only their pods. And their webs. I have not seen Yuptl since I fled. When last I was here, before these things slaughtered us in the night, the city was alive. Ten thousands of us lived here. Five hundred families. Mothers and fathers and brothers and sisters. Uncles, nieces, aunts and nephews. We all lived here. And now..."

Y'ar ceased speaking. He laid his chin upon his chest. Silently, tears fell from his eyes and rolled down his cheeks.

We waited until he stopped weeping.

"Let us go," he said, finally. "Beware. The *tumaa* are deadly."

And so with Y'ar leading us, we made our way around the bend of the gully wall. Now we were at a level with a great part of the town, and could get a much better look at Yuptl than from above. Every pillar of stone thrusting up from the jungles below was cut with dozens of windows. Many broken walkways and stairways climbed the sides of the mounds, revealing what were once hidden gardens and patios. Balconies and terraces led from one level to the next. Tiny foot bridges connected the tall piles of stone, each with others.

It must, indeed, have been a beautiful town, when it was vibrant and alive.

But now it was dead. And most horrifically, it had become a colony to the *tumaa*. Long strands of webbing stretched from each of the mounds of rock, and to the canyon walls as well. The webs glistened in the sunlight. Below us was a perfect labyrinth of webs, all crisscrossing each other and creating strange patterns with the jungle below them.

They were transparent and crimson in color, which made their gleaming in the sunshine seem that much more deadly. As we looked through them, the further we looked, the deeper was the crimson hue.

All throughout the webs there hung many cocoon-like things, all irregularly shaped and all wrapped tightly in the crimson webbing. Some were small, but others were quite large, even larger than the bodies of several men standing together. Occasionally, one of them shook with violent spasms.

"Their young," Y'ar said. His face was the very picture of disgust.

Elsewhere, and hanging from the walls of the canyons, and the walls of the piles of stone, were countless huge amber sacs.

These amber sacs were translucent and their shapes struck me as something almost obscene. Pinched at each end, they were all grotesquely distended in the center. Some of them looked as if they were ready to burst.

"*Gala*?" I asked.

"Yes," Umir answered. "*Gala*. Just one of those sacs will make all of us rich."

"I think it might take all of us to carry just one of those back," I remarked.

"Just two, I think," Umir replied. "One at each end. We can maybe carry four back with us."

"That's assuming the *tumaa* will let us walk away with them," I said.

Now that I got a good look at the lay of the situation, I wasn't so sure these young fellows had planned out their campaign as well as they might have done.

Almost as if he had heard my thoughts, Y'ar spoke up.

"I come to kill *tumaa*. If we get *gala*, that is good. But I don't care. If I kill *tumaa*, then I have done what I came to do."

"We're not in any place to be killing *tumaa*, standing on this plank," I said, reminding us all of the precariousness of our position.

"Come," Y'ar answered. "We go. The footing is better in Yuptl. These planks are to keep enemies away. When they come, we hit them with our javelins. They cannot hurt us."

"Unless they're *tumaa*," I thought. But I kept that thought to myself.

Just around the corner of the cliff, we came to a stone path with a wall on one side. That was a great relief to me. The path led us to a short stairway, and that, to a walkway across the gully into one of the stone piles that rose up from below.

Here we waited, to look more closely at the town before us. Delicate crimson webs stretched across the walkway. It would be impossible to cross without walking into them. Several of the cocoons hung upon the webbing before us.

The walkway was crumbling. Stones had fallen from it, leaving gaping holes in the pavement. At the far end, the walkway came to a large terrace that was crowded with *gala* sacs hanging from an overhead trellis, and beyond that, was an empty doorway leading into a room so dark we could see nothing within.

Oh! How it stank here! The *gala* was thick in the air and we could feel the sickly-sweet stench of it sticking to us. I tasted it at the back of my tongue, felt it clinging to my sinuses. But mingled with that sickly-sweet stench was the putrid stench of rotting death. The *tumaa* were voracious things, but also quite sloppy. They hunted in the jungles below for their food. When they found it, they carried it back here, to their colony at Yuptl, to feast upon it. They left many dead things, or parts of things, to lie moldering in the walkways and patios.

The walkways were littered with the body parts of countless animals. Strange insects crawled from the jungle depths to feed off those wasted parts. Other dead things were tangled in the webs, flapping dismally in the errant breezes that came wafting through the canyon.

Azora's beautiful face puckered into a grimace.

"So that's where *gala* comes from, eh? I'll never drink another sip of *ellihi* again."

"Just think of every drink you do have as your way of getting revenge on these things for being so hideous," I said.

"Very funny," Azora replied. "I'll let you do the revenge for both of us."

We had not started across the walkway. Behind us was yet another open entranceway leading into a darkened chamber.

"Where does this lead?" I asked Y'ar.

"A stairway to the base of the canyon," he said. "And apartments here. Many families lived on this side of the canyon. My own family," he gestured with his chin, "Lived across the way there. But here, my friends lived."

"We will need a base we can defend," I said. "If we're going to provoke the *tumaa*, we want a position to fall back to, but not one they can corner us in. Will this place do?"

"Yes, maybe," Y'ar answered. "If the *tumaa* have not overrun the passages."

Umir and Y'ar lit torches and we cautiously explored the abandoned apartments, with Y'ar leading us. He carried his torch above his head before us. The rooms nearest the cliff face were lit many windows, and those next to them were always in a dim twilight of light reflected through the portals cut between the walls. Everywhere we came upon evidence of that night of slaughter.

Scrambled piles of bones - ribs, femurs, tibia, and shattered skulls, on every floor. Knuckle and toe bones crunched loudly under our sandals. Furniture overturned and smashed. Walls brown with dried blood.

Broken javelins, spears, knives and swords – grim evidence of the futile efforts of the people who had been roused from their slumbers by the shrieks of their dying neighbors, awakening only in time to fumble for their weapons before they were cut down by the vicious *tumaa*.

"We haven't come across any of these *tumaa* yet," I remarked after we had explored nearly twenty of these chambers.

"I believe they are nocturnal creatures," Umir said. "That's what I have been told."

"Then perhaps now would be the time to harvest a few *gala* sacs. We have seen enough of these chambers here. If we must retreat, we can come here. The halls and portals are narrow enough for us to defend. If we must, we can use these broken tables, stands, benches and chairs to create a barricade."

We returned to the walkway outside. We were cautious, but not overly concerned, as the morning was bright, and midday was yet some hours ahead. The nocturnal *tumaa* should be dormant, and the fact that we had neither seen nor heard any evidence of them gave us confidence.

It was Y'ar who first strode across the walkway, straight toward the taut crimson webs that stretched in such profusion across it. He said nothing, gave us no indication of his intent. When he came upon the webs that blocked his further progress he stopped. Hanging near at hand was one of the cocoons we had remarked upon earlier. It was almost as large as Y'ar himself, and it hung from the web, within his reach, just beyond the edge of the walkway. The thing squirmed as he studied it.

We all moved forward to catch up with him, and as we approached, I thought I saw within the cocoon the writhing bodies of many things. Drawing closer to it, the cocoon seemed more repulsive, a strangely beautiful obscenity.

Just as we caught up to Y'ar, he reached suddenly out to the cocoon, his knife in his hand. With a quick flash, he severed the cocoon from the web from which it hung. It plummeted, crashing into the rank foliage of the jungle many *yurlma* below. It smashed through the branches and vines, with a huge noise that echoed up and down the canyon.

"I hope that doesn't rouse the *tumaa*," Umir said.

"I don't care," Y'ar said. "I come here to kill them. And I have. With that one cut, I have killed a hundred of their young, maybe."

"Well, now we've got started," I said, "Let's do what we came here to do."

I unsheathed my short sword and made a huge cut at the webs that blocked our way. They snapped like taut wires, cutting the air with a loud 'Tzing!'

"Tzing! Tzing! Tzing!" they snapped angrily. Y'ar joined me with his knife, and together we cut a path through the webs. A dozen more cocoons fell as we sliced through the webbing, each crashing down into the jungle below with loud echoes careening through the canyon.

I glanced at Y'ar. A cold smile was tight upon his lips. His eyes were hard and flat. He worked with the cold and deadly efficiency of a machine.

The webs were treacherous. They were profoundly sticky. Once I cut it, one long strand of web wrapped itself tightly about my free arm. It coiled so quickly and so tightly about my arm that it cut off all circulation. In moments, my arm turned a vivid purple. Azora moved swiftly and cut me free.

Quon and Tumar got themselves similarly entangled. When the blood flow in their veins was blocked, their color turned a deep green, rather than red or purple, due to the normally amber hue of the skin. We cut them free also, and finally learned to step back when we cut the strands of webs, to avoid them coiling about us.

We had cut our way through the webs, nearly reaching the terrace where the sacs of *gala* hung. I was near to congratulating us all when my eyes were met with a spectacle of horror that stopped the words, even as they were upon my tongue.

Before us, not a dozen paces ahead, and just across the terrace, was the dark entranceway we had remarked upon before.

From outside we could see nothing within. The blackness inside was utter and impenetrable. We had but a few more strands of web to cut through, and we would be upon the many sacs of *gala* that hug from the trellises above the terrace.

My sword upraised for a final cut, a sound met my ears that caused me to pause, and look to the doorway. And from it, an arm came out.

The arm was monstrously long. It was twice as thick and twice as long as my own, and it was sheathed within a transparent exoskeleton. Within the exoskeleton was a viscous, throbbing yellowish ooze that pulsated with a brackish, greenish blood throbbing through visible veins.

The arm ended in a hand that was almost humanlike, in that it had a palm that ended in a cluster of fingers. The fingers moved and worked as human fingers do, opening and clenching into a fist as it grasped the walls of the portal and pulled itself through. And the almost human appearance of the hand mounted at the end of an arm that looked like something that belonged to some huge insect made it that much more appalling.

The hand gasped one of the many strands of web that emerged from the darkened entrance, and pulled itself along it. Instantly, a dozen more such hands emerged from the darkness, each at the end of an insect-like arm which was longer than the one before it.

We watched in stunned horror as the thing slowly emerged from the entranceway. Now almost two dozen of these arms had pulled themselves out, all of them clinging to the network of webs still filling the terrace.

And then the bloated body of the thing came to the doorway from the darkness within. It squeezed itself obscenely through it, its swollen body too wide for the portal. The body was also covered with a transparent exoskeleton, but it was flexible, not rigid. It was made of many supple plates that compressed together through the tight doorway, then immediately expanded again, once outside. I had the instant impression that this thing could force itself into areas smaller than its huge size would suggest.

For it was large. Once out of the doorway, we could see the thing for what it was. The longest of the two or so dozen arms that came out from the dark doorway were twice as long as I am tall. And the sloppy, bloated body they bore was again several times larger than me, both laterally and from top to bottom. The arms all came together at a central point, and they were jointed so they reached upwardly.

Hanging from that central cluster was the body of the thing, with its nearly transparent and flexible exoskeleton only partly obscuring its internal organs. We saw the beating hearts – it seemed to have two of them – pulsating lungs, its esophagus and its swollen stomach. Apparently it had just eaten a meal, for we saw that its stomach was distended and full, some of the contents within still twitching.

The esophagus extended from the stomach, between the two beating hearts, downward, and came to the base of the creature's body. There the esophagus extruded outward like a massive trunk, one nearly as long as I can reach with both my arms outspread. At the end of that trunk was the *tumat*'s mouth. It was larger than my head, and armed with many circles of glistening, transparent and needle-sharp teeth. That gaping wide mouth waved wildly in the air toward us, opening and closing rapidly, champing teeth its teeth together.

The body hung like a distended organ, and it swung with the *tu-mat*'s motions as the arms of the thing clutched onto the many strands of webbing that filled the terrace like the masts of a ship rigged by madmen.

From the top of the swollen body two large protrusions jutted upward. Mounted within those protrusions were bulbous and multifaceted insect-like eyes. The protrusions constantly swiveled about, independently of each other, in jerking motions as the eyes took in everything in the environment surrounding us. Once one of the eyes caught sight of us, the two protrusions, both of them, grew tall, and they became thin stalks, the two eyes mounted atop them, and looking down upon us from above.

And the thing stank. Oh! How it stank. The stench it raised was like the odor that had sickened us before, of cloying sweet *gala* in vast proliferation, and the rotting reek of dead and decaying things. But now, that stink was multiplied many times over.

We all retched with the stench.

"So much for `nocturnal'," I managed to choke out amidst my retching. No one else was in any shape to reply.

Gagging, we fell back upon the walkway, making a measured retreat from the thing.

But it had seen us, and it was not about to let us escape. Clambering from one strand of web to the next, it rushed us, its mouth gaping wide.

Y'ar let loose with a javelin. He hurled it with a force that would have sent it completely through the body of the *tumat*, had it hit its target. But it did not. More swiftly than the eye could follow, one of the thing's hands reached out and grabbed the javelin, snapping it between its fingers.

Never once did the *tumat* touch the pavement. It seemed as if the thing could not move, except by swinging upon the mad network of crimson webs. I later learned that that guess was correct. Though young *tumaa* can crawl about on the ground, once they reach adulthood they can only travel by the networks of webs they create.

After Y'ar's throw, Hakk, Quzat, Quon, Tumar and Umir all hurled their javelins in a single barrage. I expected that one of those javelins should have hit its target, but not a one of them did. With a flurry of motion, six of the *tumat*'s two dozen arms grabbed the javelins in mid-flight, and broke them easily.

The huge trunk of the thing snaked through the air toward us, the maw of its mouth gaping wide. Hundreds of teeth, sharp as shattered glass, champed at us. We stumbled backward along the ancient walkway, high above the jungle floor. Here, I thought, we would find some tentative safety, as we had cut away the webs that had crisscrossed across it. Surely, it would find no handholds here with which to continue its hot pursuit.

But I was wrong. I was horribly, terribly wrong.

An appendage I had not noted before, at the base of the thing's body, shot forward from behind. It was pointed, and looked something like a proboscis. Before any of us had even an instant to react to it, a long strand of webbing shot out from it, attaching itself to the canyon wall behind us. More quickly than it takes to say it, the *tumat* grasped the web from its proboscis with several of its hands, and then fixed it to the network of webs nearby.

Done with that, it aimed again with its proboscis, and shot out another strand of web. And then another. In quick order, it had created another net of webs to replace the one we had destroyed only moments before.

And through it all, it never once slowed in its pursuit.

Our companions were readying another volley with their javelins, though we all guessed it would be fruitless. I had unsheathed my long sword now, not sure what I could accomplish with it, except possibly to hack off one or two of its arms before it tore me to pieces.

Azora, standing slightly behind me and to my right, reached into her pouch, grasping a half dozen darts, now tipped with the deadly toxin of the *joyu* bush. Just as Umir, Y'ar and the others hurled their javelins, Azora, with a deft underhand move, flung them directly at the bloated body of the monster.

The *tumat*, its attention fixed wholly upon the javelins, caught them all. But it missed the tiny darts. Almost every one of them pierced through the flexible exoskeleton of the thing.

The results were instantaneous. The monster halted its charge. It shuddered through the length of its body, and its transparent amber color darkened to umber. One by one its hands let loose of their hold upon the webs, and the arms fell listless. Spasms took the thing, and it jerked about madly as it lost its grip on the crimson webs.

It fell upon the walkway, only but a pace or two from where we stood. The long trunk of its esophagus and mouth lurched wildly, slapping the pavement and the walls of the walkway with the sounds of wet meat dropped upon a hard floor.

"Splut! Splut! Splut!" the dying mouth spluttered.

The eyes sank back into its body. We saw them staring at us, saw ourselves infinitely reflected in their facets. And then they went opaque, and they reflected nothing.

We were too daunted by what we had seen to let loose with any victory cheers. Nor did any of us wish to rouse up any more of these creatures. We simply stared, first at the dead *tumat*, and then, with haunted eyes, each at the others.

I roused myself. We had no time to linger. With my sword, I cut at the webs the *tumat* had placed, and which blocked our retreat. Taking but a moment in my work, I half-turned to the cluster of *gala* sacs hanging in the shaded terrace, and pointed with my sword.

"There's your *gala*. Take what you can, and let's get out of here before the rest wake up."

Y'ar, Umir and Hakk, Quzat and the others wasted no time. Waking at my words from the fugue of horror that sight of the *tumat* had put them into, they all moved quickly toward the terrace, cutting through the crimson webbing that stood in their way. Azora, Tumar and Quon, by my side, assisted me in cutting through the webs that blocked the walkway.

We worked silently and quickly, but we had not got more than halfway across the walkway before Y'ar, Umir and the others returned. Y'ar carried but one sac of *gala* over his shoulder. It was nearly as tall as he, and he struggled manfully under the weight of it.

Without a word, Umir, Hakk, Quzat and Y'ar joined us, and set to cutting through the webs that still stood in our way.

"Just one?" I asked, quickly, between breaths. The work was hard, and we could scarcely spare the breath for more than a syllable or two.

"This one is enough to make us all rich," Umir explained. "For the rest of our lives."

"... and enough to convince others to come for more," Y'ar explained further.

"With *joyu* juice," Umir added. "Better than javelins."

"Besides..." Y'ar was beginning to say, but he stopped in mid-thought. Behind us, we heard a commotion rising.

"Cut faster," I suggested.

And we did. We hacked at the taut lines of web with fury, the sweat flying from us as we swung our blades. Webbing snapped and lashed the air. Azora stood beside me, cutting furiously at the tangle. She was breathing hard, her mouth opened as she took in air with loud panting, "Hah, hah, hah..."

And behind us, we heard ominous sounds growing. We had no time to look back, so intently were we at work, so slowly did the webs give way.

Then, without warning, a coil of web shot between Azora and me, wrapping itself around her. All in an instant, she was swathed in it, from her shoulders to her hips. Her arms pinned to her sides, she was unable to move. She looked helplessly down at the cocoon, then at me. Then a tug at the long strand that held her, and she was jerked away, back to the waiting mouth of the *tumat* that had caught her.

Its mouth gaped wide, circles of teeth poised to cut Azora into bloody pieces of dead meat. But I wasted not an instant. Turning the instant that Azora was jerked away from me, I ran quickly back to where the *tumat* hung down from its ceiling of webs.

What I saw filled me with horror. Even as Azora was whisked toward the gaping maw of the one *tumat*, a dozen more were emerging, some through the portal from where the first one had come, and others clambering up from the jungle below.

It all seemed hopeless. But I swore to myself silently as I ran to Azora that I would make these *tumaa* pay dearly for their meal. Many would die that day, before they took us down.

In the house of Jor-Taq, where I had first trained as a warrior, the guards there enjoy a sport which they practice often and on which they wager large sums. Indeed, one was never considered a warrior, truly, by Jor-Taq's guards, until one had mastered this sport, the art of sword throwing.

It takes long practice, and many swords, to learn the proper hold, balance, release and spin of the sword, and after many long weeks of daily practice, I had come to be quite good at it. I was never quite so good as my tutors, Brekkex and Koax. But yet I did still learn some proficiency at it, and several times the skill had come in very useful, indeed.

But never so useful as it was at this moment. I had never before thrown a sword while running. Always before, I had been standing still and balanced between both feet, even in the two or three times I threw my sword in a fight.

This time, though, I had no leisure to pause and take aim. The *tumat* that had captured Azora had already dragged her to its trunk, snapping at her, and she was kicking at it with her feet – a most uncooperative meal, she was!

I felt that lashes of webs snapping past me like whips, as other tumaa attempted to capture me. But I did not pause.

Pausing only long enough to grasp my sword by its tip, I brought the handle of it above my shoulder. Judging my aim in only an instant, I hurled my sword through the air. It climbed upwards, spinning as it flew. Then it came downward, picking up momentum as it fell, still spinning.

The sword came point down. It cut into the top of the thing's body, between the two protuberances of its eyes. A sickening 'splut' came through the air, as the sword plunged deep through the creature's exoskeleton. Carried by its weight and momentum, the sword sliced completely through the thing's body.

The monster's eyes collapsed, and its arms lost their grip upon the webbing overhead. Azora came rolling out of its grasp, nearly to my feet. I picked up my short sword from the stone flagging where it had fallen, and cut her free. The web that bound her was hellishly sticky, and cutting her loose from it was no easy thing. But somehow I got it done, and looked up.

We were surrounded by a dozen of the things, with even more of them coming up from the distance behind them.

Azora gave me a brave smile.

"We're still alive!" she said.

"Yes," I agreed. "For the moment, at least."

Azora did not waste that moment. She reached into her bag, and pulled out a handful of darts.

"They'll remember these, before I'm done!" she laughed. Then she positioned herself at my back. We stood that way, back to back, ready to fight.

Several of the *tumaa* moved ominously toward us. I feinted at them with my sword, and they moved back out of reach of it. Another moved quickly in, and before I could turn to lunge at it, it grabbed up the body of the *tumat* I had just killed, carrying it away several paces. Three or four other *tumaa* followed it.

Before I had a chance to wonder what they were about, the *tumaa* fell upon the body of their dead fellow and began devouring it. With loud noises of champing and sucking, they fought among themselves and pulled the dead thing to pieces, carrying away pieces of arm and body.

Some of the others moved away from us to join the feast, perhaps seeking an easier meal. But not all of them did so. We still had many to contend with, but Azora was quick with her darts. Hurling them swiftly and in a wide semicircle, she managed to kill two more. Their bloated, dying bodies hit the terrace heavily, and like the first one, they were instantly set upon by the others.

I managed to hack off the hand of one of these things, and when a champing mouth came too menacing, I cut it off, leaving but the stump of a trunk wildly spewing the creature's blood in spastic geysers. It gave off a horrid cry as it retreated from Azora and me, clambering hand over hand upon the crimson webs. But it, too, fell prey to its fellows. Its mouth hacked off, and spluttering in futile circles upon the pavement, the monster had no teeth with which to defend itself. And the other *tumaa* were swift, and ruthless, in taking advantage of that.

Step by step we fought our way away from that terrace. But with every step we took, more and more of the monstrous *tumaa* came climbing along the webs. They shot long tendrils of their webs at us, and we were kept busy dodging them.

Azora grabbed me by the arm, yanking me away, just in time as a web came swiftly shooting through the air at my neck, and then she turned again, hurling a dart against another *tumat*. And then I pushed her down, just as another web shot over her.

We were yet surrounded. For every *tumat* we wounded or killed, two more came crawling up from the depths. We were too busy fighting them off to make our retreat with any speed. I was exhausted, and Azora was too. She had used up all her deadly darts, and was left now only with her knife, which she wielded masterfully. It sung in the air as she slashed at the hands that groped at her. She sliced off fingers and talons, jabbed at monstrous eyes and hacked at the mouths that came biting at her with needle-like teeth.

But however we fought, we were surrounded. It all seemed hopeless now. Even as I plunged my sword deep into the body of another monster, I saw yet another set of hands come swinging a heavy body up and onto the webs above the narrow walkway where we stood. I am not given to despair, but I was at that moment contemplating running my sword through Azora, to spare her the agony of being torn apart while yet alive by these monstrous things.

At that moment, our companions broke through. I had not known it, so close was the fighting, but Y'ar, Umir and the others had joined the fight, armed with nothing but their knives, as soon as it had begun. The moment I hurled my sword, many other monstrous *tumaa* had climbed over the walkway behind me, and these, our friends had fought off.

Y'ar, Umir and the others, hit them first with volleys from their javelins. Now the *tumaa* were so closely crowded together that every javelin they hurled hit a target. Having taken the precaution to tip them with the *joyu* juice Azora shared with them, they killed dozens of the things.

Having exhausted all their javelins, our friends now fought with knives, and they proved very able knife workers. They fought with cunning and cool skill, waiting to allow one or the other of the *tumaa* to lunge at them with their long arms, and then with a sudden lunge, hacking off the hand that groped toward them.

These *tumaa* are very stupid creatures. However vicious they are – and they are among the most vicious creatures I have ever seen – they are simply stupid. No matter how many times they got their hands, or even whole parts of their arms, hacked off, they never once varied their attacks, but kept returning for more punishment of the same kind.

And so we managed to reunite with our friends there on the walkway. We made a measured retreat, finally returning to the stairway that led upward along the wall of the canyon, and back into the chambers we had explored there before.

Here, we found a chamber we could defend, for the *tumaa* could only come at us one at a time through the narrow doorway.

Standing there with my sword, I easily cut them down while Azora quickly whittled a new set of darts for herself from the ruined pieces of furniture we found still moldering among the ruins of these chambers. As she did that, Y'ar, Umir and the others used their knives to create more javelins. And, once they were done, they all tipped their newly made weapons with joyu juice that Azora still carried with her.

That work took all the remainder of the day, and when they were finished, the sun had already set. All the world was dark.

As the sun settled, we heard the howling of the *tumaa* grow loud. Apparently they were, indeed, more nocturnal than diurnal. Judging by the fury, what we had seen of them in the day was them at their most sluggish. Now they raged in the darkness. Hooting and howling shrieks and screeches filled the air.

"I suggest we stay here," I said to our companions. "We can defend this chamber. There is but the single doorway. If they come, they can only come at us one at a time. Between sword, javelin and poisoned dart, I am sure we can so crowd the corridor beyond that they will not be able to climb over it."

"I am all for staying here, Grae-don, my friend," Umir said.

Y'ar, Hakk, Quzat, Quon and Tumar agreed. So we stayed put.

And well it was that we did so, for the *tumaa* were not long in hunting us down. We could not possibly have escaped the canyon or their webs before they were upon us.

We were in a plain chamber of four stone walls, a floor and a ceiling, all carved from the living rock. Whatever purpose this chamber once served, we could not tell. Whatever furnishings may have been here were now long gone. The walls were once painted, but the paint was almost completely worn away.

We heard the tumaa grunting as they shot their webs into the corridor beyond the doorway to this chamber.

"Fwoot! Fwoot! Fwoot!" the webs shot past the entrance, enmeshing it almost completely in a confused thicket. I'd been standing guard at the door, and staggered back. The webs almost caught me.

I began hacking at them with my long sword. Umir and Y'ar joined me, kneeling to cut the webs that caught fast to the floor. As we worked, more webs shot past us, filling the corridor. They came so quickly that our efforts were futile, for the instant we cut one strand of web away from the door, a half dozen others took its place.

"This is no use, friend," Umir shouted above the din of the tumaa, who filled the corridor beyond with their howls of rage.

"We'll take a step back from the doorway," I said. "Do not let those webs touch you!"

My warning was an instant too late. Even as the words left my lips, I saw a strand of web shoot out from the darkness of the corridor and coil itself around Umir's wrist. I leaped for Umir, throwing my arms about his waist to hold him back. Just as swiftly, the tumat that wielded that long strand of web pulled on it. Umir was carried into the corridor, dragging me with him.

There, we saw almost nothing in the darkness, only the light from our torches within the chamber behind us reflecting though the narrow door. We were dragged swiftly into the corridor, the skin from our bodies being scraped away on the hard stone floor.

Ahead of us was but darkness, broken by points of light reflected from the eyes of the *tumaa* that hung from the webs before us. They unleashed a huge howling as they saw us being dragged toward them, a howling that echoed loud through the darkness.

Umir began to kick me.

"Let go of me, friend," he whispered loud and quick. "Do not die for my clumsiness."

"No," was all I said. I unsheathed my short sword, having dropped my long sword when I lunged for Umir. Quickly scraping my blade along the floor, and feeling about with the point of it, I found where the web had attached itself to Umir's wrist. A sharp thrust forward, a twist of the blade, and I had sliced through the flesh of his wrist, cutting the loops.

Instantly, we came to a halt, lying on the floor.

"Back, now!" I whispered.

And we began scuttling quickly backwards, lying flat against the floor, that we not brush against the forest of webs just above our heads.

Awkwardly we moved. The *tumaa* crowded against each other to rush upon us. I caught dim and frantic glimpses of monstrous hands groping along the mass of webs.

One of the things leaped, landing in the webs just above Umir and me. A dozen hands clutched at us. One grabbed Umir by the throat. He cut at it with his knife, slicing a long gash down the thing's arm. With a squeal of pain, the arm let loose of Umir. But instantly, another hand clutched at him from the darkness.

A champing, snapping mouth at the end of a long trunk came at me. Teeth slashed across my face. Acidic saliva blinded me. I slashed at it with my sword, missing it as it pulled away. Then a jab, straight upward. I felt the point of my blade cut through the exoskeleton of the monster's belly. It screeched loud in my ear. Grasping the handle of my sword tightly in both hands, then I pushed it deeper into the thing's belly.

With my sword thrust as deeply into the beast's belly as I could force it, I twisted my blade, rocking it and forth to do as much damage to the *tumat* as possible. The monster's hands clawed at me, and jets of blood splashed Umir and me.

And then the thing collapsed upon us, crushing us under its heavy body. Neither of us could move. Three more *tumaa* came rushing down upon us now. They fell upon the body of the one we had killed, and began devouring it on the spot. Bits of flesh splattered down upon us in their cannibalistic orgy.

I felt many hands grasping me.

"This is the end," I thought savagely. Angry that with my arms pinned down I could not strike even a single blow but must wait supinely for death to devour me, I plunged into a helpless, hopeless rage. Hands had grasped my ankles, and pulled. The instant my legs were loosed from under the heavy body of the dead *tumat*, hands grasped them, and pulled.

All in a huge maddened rush, the hands pulled upon me, and beside me, Umir, too. Bloodied and bleeding from his head, his chest, his arms, so much so that he was almost unrecognizable – he, too was being dragged swiftly away.

Glancing toward my feet with my sword ready to deal out death, I realized that the hands pulling me away from the cannibalistic feast did not belong to any *tumaa*, but to our friends. Azora, Y'ar, and Tumar had all crawled into the corridor after us, under the deadly crimson webs, and had fought off the *tumaa* themselves. They were dragging us away, to safety, back into the chamber where we had sought refuge before.

We were all too exhausted to speak. Azora threw herself upon me, and lay across my chest, her heart beating wildly, and panting heavily. Like mine, her body was slick with the blood of the *tumaa* she had fought. There was not one among us who was unscathed. Tearing off a long strip from his *surpaa*, Tumar wrapped it many times around his arm, which had a deep gouge taken from it, extending from his elbow to his wrist. Quon suffered a similar wound to his leg. It bled profusely.

Hakk and Quzat stationed themselves at the doorway, their poisoned javelins at the ready. And in no time, they were using them. No sooner had we stumbled through the doors than the *tumaa* were upon us again. Finishing quickly with bandaging their wounds, Tumar and Quon joined the fight at the door with their own javelins.

All that night we fought. It was endless, that battle, and some part of me is still there, I think, still fighting those things. How many dozens of them we killed, I do not know. The memories of this pitched battle are all a blur to me, now, so exhausted was I – so exhausted were we all.

But, just as we all began to give way to despair again, with the thought that these furious beasts would never cease their attacks, they fell back. We were puzzled at first by the sudden cessation of the battle, and the silence that overtook the corridor outside that chamber weighed heavily. It was ominous.

For a long time, we dared not look, but at last I crept to the portal, and peered cautiously around. From far above, where the corridor led away from Yuptl, dim and distant sunlight shone hesitantly through. The corridor was crowded with crimson webs and the mutilated and half-eaten corpses of countless *tumaa*.

But otherwise, it was empty. In the coming of the dawn outside, the *tumaa* had retreated. For now, the battle had stopped.

"They're gone," I whispered to the others.

Seeing our chance and wasting no time in futile uncertainty, we left that chamber. Y'ar picked up the huge sac of gala he had salvaged from the previous day, carrying it slung over one shoulder.

"After all we've endured, I am not leaving this behind," he said.

We all nodded our agreement.

We quickly cut through the confusion of webs and corpses that blocked the narrow corridor, and before the sun was long risen, we had made our way back to the narrow path of boards that would take us away from Yuptl. As before, Y'ar strode easily upon the planks, still carrying the sac of gala. The rest of us clung against the wall of the cliff, and weak as we were from a night of battle and lack of sleep, we were a long time in making our way.

But at last we did. We climbed back out on the bluffs that overlooked the canyon in which Yuptl was built. Y'ar cast his eyes upon his home and looked long upon it before turning away. He said, quietly, "I shall come back."

We were all thankful that we had lost none of our company, and we returned to Huiz without any further event.

There, we aroused great comment when the people of the city saw the sac of *gala* we carried with us. The people of the city crowded around us and they shouted loud questions at us. Y'ar and Umir spoke for all, and explained that we had come from Yuptl, where we had done battle with the *tumaa* for their *gala*.

We were some days marketing the sac of *gala* we had brought back with us. Many came to see it for themselves, and they wondered at the sight of it. Y'ar and Umir finally sold it to a shipmaster for a very, very pleasing sum of gold, indeed, which we all shared equally between us.

Azora and I stayed on at Huiz for some weeks after that, enjoying the company of our new friends. During that time, Y'ar and the others prepared another expedition to Yuptl. Many dozen men and several very hardy women, roused by the promise of riches, joined them.

"Once again, I shall ask. Will you come with us, my friends?" Umir asked, as they prepared to march from Huiz.

Azora and I shook our heads, but sadly.

"I am sorry, my friends. It has been a long time. We should return to Pella'mir," I said.

"I understand," Y'ar said. "You have your home. Soon, I shall have mine again."

"Take this," Azora said, pressing on him several bags of *joyu* juice. "I have more than I shall ever need, now. And you will be putting it to very good use."

"Thank you," he said, with a smile. "I shall use it well."

"I know you will," Azora said.

And with that, they left us. We watched them as they marched at the head of their procession, away from Huiz, to Yuptl.

And when they were gone, we made our way to the quays at the shore, and there found passage on a ship that took us back to Pella'mir.

Made in the USA
Columbia, SC
05 August 2023